INTO the LIGHT

INTO the LIGHT

Into the Mists Trilogy
Book Three

Serene Conneeley

Blessed Bee Books

INTO THE LIGHT: Into the Mists Trilogy Book Three

Conneeley, Serene
Into the Light by Serene Conneeley
ISBN: 978-0-9945933-5-1

Website: www.SereneConneeley.com
Email: serene@sereneconneeley.com

Published by Blessed Bee Books
PO Box 449, Newtown, NSW 2042
Australia

Cover artwork: *Dreamlike* by Selina Fenech
www.SelinaFenech.com
Illustrations: Daniella Spinetti and Justin Sayers

"Darkness cannot drive out darkness;
Only light can do that.
Hate cannot drive out hate;
Only love can do that."

Martin Luther King Jr,
American civil rights activist

Contents

Chapter 1

An Awakening

"Sweetheart, the funeral is this afternoon."

Carlie's eyes flickered to the door, where Rose was standing, gazing down at her with so much compassion and sympathy. For the first time in a week, she saw herself through her grandmother's eyes, and was mortified. She hadn't left her room in days, hadn't showered, hadn't even spoken to anyone in what felt like forever.

Forever. Suddenly her life felt way too long, stretching interminably out into the distance, too many days of torture ahead, too many months of agony to deal with, too many years of loneliness and pain to even contemplate.

Six months ago she'd lost both her parents in a car accident, and now she'd lost the love of her life too. It wasn't fair.

"I can't go," she whispered, body weak, eyes haunted. Rose wished there was something she could do, something to ease the pain etched deep into her granddaughter's face. But she knew from bitter experience that there was nothing she could say or do that would help, not really. Not yet. She could only let her know that she was there for her, ready to listen if she needed her to, or to hold her if she wanted comfort.

She understood the young girl's pain because she'd lost her family too – her daughter and her husband, more than twenty years ago –

and there were still nights when she woke up gasping for air and some semblance of sanity, plunged back into the nightmare of fresh pain, as though it was happening all over again. Catching herself as she sighed, she took a deep breath and steeled her heart. It was time for her to be there for Carlie, to be strong, and to show her there was a way forward through grief, a way to live with this searing pain and find some joy in life despite the scars that criss-crossed her heart.

Slowly she walked into the small room, expecting at any moment that Carlie would throw her out, but her granddaughter sat unmoving in her narrow bed, not exactly welcoming or inviting her in, but not forbidding it either.

Rose's eyes were drawn to the hulking hill she could see out the window, and she felt its pull, its strange hold over her. She'd never been able to leave this town, even though it was all she had wanted to do when she lost the only two people she'd ever loved.

Part of her had stayed in case her daughter ever came back to her, too scared to even go on holiday in case that was the day Violet returned home. But part of her had stayed because she felt as though she was physically connected to that blasted tor, anchored to it, weighed down by the ancient mound of earth. Sometimes she felt nurtured and protected by it, inspired even, but other times it was a weight around her heart, oppressive and dark, smothering her and any chance she ever had to escape.

"I feel it too," the girl on the bed whispered, voice cracked and broken. "I'm not even from here and it won't let me leave. It won't let me go away from this place, and it won't let me end things either." Pain seeped from her words, and was etched deeply into her face.

"Oh love, I'm so sorry."

"It's not *your* fault," Carlie retorted, and the unspoken next words hung in the air.

"It's not your fault either Sweetheart," Rose added quickly, but Carlie shook her off when she tried to hold her.

"Of course it is, don't you see? If I hadn't broken up with him, if I hadn't believed Rhiannon's story, or believed Mum's book and thought he was evil like his dad, none of this would have happened. If I'd spent the night with him, you wouldn't have even known I'd left, and he'd still be alive. Why didn't I stay with him? Why didn't I trust him?" Her chest heaved and a sob escaped, but her eyes remained dry. She had no more tears.

"Oh Carlie," Rose said, heart breaking for the granddaughter she'd only recently learned existed, but had so quickly grown to love. Finally she couldn't bear it any longer, and she scooped the girl into her arms. She felt her stiffen with resistance, then finally give in, too worn down to fight. But the close contact obviously made her uncomfortable, so Rose reluctantly let her go.

"Would you like me to come with you Sweetheart, or would it be easier to go on your own?" she finally asked.

Carlie stared up at her, expression blank. "Go?"

"The funeral," Rose said softly, gently. "We'll have to leave in an hour so we can get there in time."

Her granddaughter looked so young, so innocent, and yet so aged, curled up in the corner of her narrow bed.

"I can't go," she replied, eyes deadened and vague.

Rose took a deep breath. The last thing she wanted to do was force the girl to do something so terribly sad, but she knew that she would never forgive herself if she didn't go. Screwing up her courage, she caught Carlie's eye and held her gaze.

"I know it will be hard, and horrible, and sadder than anything you should have to face. But I also know you will regret it if you don't go. You will feel guilty and you will beat yourself up for it." Pausing briefly, she considered her words carefully, then dared to speak them. "And I know that it's not your responsibility to help her through this, but it would mean the world to Rowan's mother if you could bring yourself to go today."

Carlie glared at her grandmother, a flicker of anger dancing across her face before the vacant look returned, shutters slamming down around her heart. "You spoke to her?" she asked, aghast.

"She came into the shop yesterday, to make sure you had received her letter, and to see if you were okay," Rose sighed.

For a moment it looked like Carlie would cry, but instead she slowly inhaled, visibly steeling herself for more pain. "How is she?" she asked softly. "Does she blame me too?"

Rose stared at her granddaughter, confusion in her eyes.

"Sweetheart, no one blames you, I promise. To be honest, she's worried about you. And she wants to apologise to you."

Carlie looked at her blankly, but before she could ask what on earth Rowan's mum would have to be sorry for, they heard a knock on the door, and Rose regretfully stood up. "You'll be glad that you went," she insisted, as she headed for the stairs.

"Fine," Carlie finally blurted out, no longer caring either way. Nothing could make her feel worse than she already did.

As her grandmother went to answer the door, Carlie picked up the envelope lying on her bedside table and removed the page inside, with its curly writing and ivy leaves sketched in the margins.

Dear Carlie,

I'm so very sorry for your loss. And this is one of those rare times that a person can honestly say that they know just how bad you are feeling – all the sympathy cards I've received from friends have been full of kind words, but none of them can understand just how empty our hearts are, just how pointless our lives feel right now. And it must be even harder for you, to have lost your family so recently, and now be suffering this new blow.

I just wanted to make sure you knew how much Rowan loved you, how much he wanted to be with you. Please don't think that because you hadn't known each other for a long time that it meant any less to him – he'd never talked about anyone the way he talked about you, never cared so deeply. You made him come alive in a way I hadn't seen before, and it makes my heart a little lighter to know how happy he was before he died.

Tears streamed down Carlie's face, and she sniffed noisily as she wiped them impatiently away. She felt like a fraud, that Rowan's mother thought so highly of her, when he'd actually died miserable, thinking she hated him and never wanted to see him again. He'd died because she had made a terrible mistake, hadn't been smart enough to listen to her own heart. Hadn't believed him or trusted him.

Wouldn't it be the height of rudeness for her to turn up to the funeral of the person she'd caused to die? Wasn't it disrespectful to his grieving mother who had been through so much already? Wouldn't she be doing the poor woman a favour by *not* attending?

She turned back to the note, knowing what came next, but still not quite sure how she felt about it.

It would mean so much to me if you felt able to come to the funeral service, so we could farewell him together, let his spirit soar away on a cloud of our love and best wishes. Your presence there would give me strength, help me cope with such an awful day. Not that I want to guilt you into coming, or pressure you in any way, although you might feel that from my words.

Oh Carlie, I'm so terrified of this final farewell, but I just want to honour him and his memory properly, and I can't do that without you. The details are attached, and please let me know if you need a lift – or if you need anything at all. As strange as this may sound, I feel so close to you, because you were so close to Rowan, and knew him in a way few people ever did.

So, I really hope you are able to come, for your own sense of closure, and because I know it is what Rowan would want.
You are in my thoughts and prayers.
Much love, Louisa xx

Sighing, Carlie folded the thick paper and slid it back into the envelope, then returned it to the top drawer of her bedside table. She felt sorry for the woman, if she was pinning all her hopes on *her* to make her feel better. But she was also a little uncomfortable at how intense his mum was being, and how much importance she was placing on her to help her in her grieving – not to mention the guilt trip she was laying on her to make her come.

Still, she did feel responsible for Rowan's death, so surely the least she could do was show up to his funeral if that's what his mother wanted her to do. She felt like she owed her big time. Besides, shouldn't she want to be there anyway, to say goodbye to the person she'd loved so much? Why was she resisting it so strongly?

Crawling out of bed, she walked on unsteady feet to the ensuite and turned on the shower. The hot water was so wonderfully soothing, so she abruptly switched it to cold. She wanted to suffer in some way, do some kind of penance.

Finally though, her grandmother's words floated back to her, and she reluctantly added a little hot to the water so she could stop freezing and focus on them. She knew that her grandma was right, that she would regret it if she didn't go. Didn't they say the only things you regret are the things you didn't do? Allowing her petulance to stop her from going to say goodbye would be cutting off her nose to spite her face. Surprising herself a little, she giggled. When had she become such a lover of cliches?

Turning off the water, she stepped out onto the cold floor and wrapped a towel around herself. Gazing into the mirror, she wiped the steam off in a wide arc, and was jolted back to reality. She looked terrible. Her face was gaunt and pale, with dark smudges under her eyes, and she'd lost weight, but not in a good way. That explained the constant worry she'd been seeing on her grandma's face whenever she'd let her into her bedroom to talk. Clearly the refusing to eat thing hadn't been a great move.

Shrugging at her reflection – because what did it matter what she looked like? – she pulled on some leggings and Rowan's black jumper, one of the few links she still had to him, and gingerly walked downstairs and out to the kitchen. Her heart squeezed when she saw the fear flicker across her grandma's face as she watched her enter, still shivering from the shower.

But priestess-trained Rose recovered quickly. "I've made some vegie soup, could you try a little bowl? Or a few spoons of yoghurt? I know you don't feel like eating, but you're going to make yourself ill if you don't get any nourishment at all."

Reluctantly Carlie nodded. And suddenly she couldn't believe how selfish she'd been, again. Like her grandmother needed more things to worry about on her behalf. "Either," she sighed, and concentrated hard on trying to finish the small bowl of soup that

Rose quickly slid in front of her. She inhaled the soothing qualities of the fragrant herbs in the broth, realising immediately that this was a healing soup her witchy grandma had whipped up, filled with medicinal and no doubt magical herbs amongst the finely chopped fresh vegetables.

"I'm sorry you thought I needed a healing brew," she said, trying to sound stern, but surprising both of them when a small smile crossed her face.

"I'll take that smile, no matter how small it is," Rose beamed, and the joy and the relief in her voice made Carlie's stomach clench in guilt and fear.

"I'm so sorry Gran – again – for worrying you so much. I promise I'll start eating again. And I appreciate how much you care about me, and look after me, and that it hasn't been easy having me here. I'll make more of an effort, I swear."

Rose reached out and tucked one of Carlie's long dark curls behind her ear, her touch tender and full of love. "No one blames you for being upset and having a tough time Sweetheart, and we all have different ways of coping. It's actually normal for people to stop eating when they're grieving – and it's not a bad thing, for a few days. The numbing chemicals that the brain floods the body with so a person can cope slow the digestive system, to conserve energy just to function, just to breathe. But it can't continue – now that the shock has worn off, you need to start focusing on yourself, you need to build up your strength to help you cope with going on with your life."

"But I don't want to go on with my life. What's the point?" Carlie demanded, but her grandmother could sense in her tone that the fight was going out of her, and she would start accepting the situation, and tentatively looking forward, soon enough. It never ceased to amaze her how resilient the human spirit was. How even though you could be convinced that the grief and the pain were too much to bear, that it would be best to end it all, some part of you would eventually rally, would start to see the occasional reason to stay, the rare beam of sunlight and joy piercing the blackest moments. She knew those latter moments well, had spent her fair share of time living in that pit of despair and darkness, where it seemed there was no way out, and that life would remain an unbearable trial not worth living. But she also knew the solace that could be found in the tiniest gestures, those random acts that brought joy to the heart – the kind friend there to help shoulder the pain, or the sense of meaning and purpose that could be just enough of a thread to hang on to and move forward with.

For Rose, it had been the magical community she'd forged around her that had given her a reason to live, after her daughter had disappeared forever and her husband had taken his life. Her best friend Elsie had lit up the darkest corners of those darkest moments, had rocked her while she cried and then taken her hand to lead her out into the light. Her role as a priestess had given her purpose, and her marking of the seasonal festivals through the rituals she facilitated at her healing centre had provided her life with meaning, and allowed her to find an inner strength that she hoped had helped others.

All of which made her terrified for her granddaughter. She didn't know what she could offer to make Carlie want to go on. When her parents had died six months ago she'd lost everything – her family, her home, her friends, her future career, her country even – sent to the other side of the world to live with a stranger. Despite her pain and grief though, she'd made a friend and fallen in love, until her boyfriend had been ripped cruelly from her as well.

Her friend Rhiannon seemed to be the last thread holding her to life, although that relationship seemed strained right now. As she spooned herbs into the teapot and filled it with boiling water, she wondered if she should weave a spell to heal it, or trust that the two girls could work it out for themselves.

Chapter 2

A Friendship Unravelled

"Rhiannon's been around again, wanting to see you. And she brought some flowers, and a card," Rose said, voice tentative, as she pulled a red envelope from the kitchen drawer and gestured to the pot of purple hyacinths on the windowsill, flowers that represented apology and the asking of forgiveness. Scowling, Carlie glanced at the red envelope, but she didn't pick it up.

"For what it's worth, she's really sorry. And you have every reason to be angry at her," Rose added.

Carlie looked up at her in surprise, expression wary.

"She only told me a little, either from her own embarrassment or because she doesn't want to divulge any of your secrets, but she did say that she really regrets interfering in your relationship, and trying to make you break up with Rowan," she said.

"She didn't *try* to make me break up, she succeeded," Carlie snapped, anger shooting through her body. She flashed back to all the awful things her friend had tried to convince her were true about her boyfriend. That he would cheat on her, and hurt her, physically and emotionally. That he was just using her, and was going to destroy her.

None of that was true of course, but she'd fallen for it. And being weak, she'd done what her friend demanded. Girls were supposed to stick together, right? But what kind of friend delivers such an ultimatum? Weren't best buddies supposed to be supportive of you? Encourage you? Trust you? Believe in you, and your ability to make your own decisions?

What kind of person makes someone choose between their best friend and their boyfriend? Hot tears stung her eyes as she finally found herself back at the place where this train of thought always ended. If she hadn't broken up with Rowan, as Rhiannon had demanded she do, he would still be alive.

Rose poured out the tea and walked over to the table, placing the steaming mug in front of her granddaughter and taking her hand, yanking her back to the present. "You still have responsibility for your choices," she said cautiously. "Don't hand your power over to someone else."

"But it's not fair! How could she expect me to choose between them?" Carlie cried.

"Sweetheart, that's what she's so sorry about. She genuinely thought she was doing it for you, that it was in your best interests. It was because she cares about you so much, misguided though her actions were."

Carlie glared at her grandmother, but her face softened as Rose's black cat, Luther, leaped up onto her lap.

"I agree with you, she does seem to have been lacking any justifiable reason for her actions – and I think she's learned a lot about herself through this experience, and will be so much more compassionate in her dealings with everyone in the future," Rose added, a hopeful note in her voice.

"Well, I'm so glad someone had to die just so she could learn not to trust some old psychic who didn't know either of us," her granddaughter spat, venom in her tone.

Rose spoke as gently as she could. "You can't blame Rhiannon for his death either Sweetheart, it was just a tragic accident."

"What do you mean, *either*?" Carlie demanded, her bottom lip trembling as she pouted.

"I don't mean *that*. It's absolutely not your fault," she insisted, and at those words the young girl dissolved into tears again. Her grandma pulled her into her arms, one hand stroking her hair, trying to comfort her, the other on her back, attempting to soothe her anger away.

"There there, let it all out, you'll feel better," she crooned. "It's a horrible, horrible thing to have happened, a terrible injustice, and absolutely nothing about it is fair. But blaming someone, anyone – yourself, Rhiannon, the gods or the goddess – won't help you, or make you feel any better. It won't make it easier to cope with, it will be much harder. Believe me Sweetheart, I know."

"I just can't see her yet Gran, can you understand that? I'm just... it's just... it's all too raw," she sighed. "I don't have the energy to try to make her feel better about herself, to reassure her – I don't have it in me to forgive her yet, or forgive myself. And I can't put on a brave face right now. I don't know if I'll ever be able to, but I definitely know I can't right now."

Rose's heart clenched as she gazed at her granddaughter. She'd never seen a soul so broken, and part of her was terrified that she would lose her – that the tortured young girl would drown in her grief, unable to find a way to continue living.

But every now and then she saw a glimmer of golden light within her, strands of steeliness, strength and determination, and a passion for life that she prayed she'd be able to ignite somehow, and encourage to blossom and grow. She desperately wanted to find a way to overshadow the pain and agony that was Carlie's present reality. She could never erase all the pain – and frankly she didn't want to, because she knew it would help her eventually. But that should only be a small part of her heart, not every fibre of it, every beat it made.

Nodding sadly, she tried to infuse her smile with all the love she felt for her poor tortured granddaughter. They were each the only family they had now, the last two left standing after a trail of sadness and tragedy, but the wise priestess knew they weren't unique. At times it felt like she'd had to deal with more than she knew what to do with, more than anyone else had to shoulder, and certainly Carlie was dealing with a lot more than most teenagers had to carry.

Yet each family had its own dramas, its own loss and grief to deal with, its missed opportunities and searing pain. It was part of the rich warp and weave of human experience, the depth that gave meaning and purpose to life and made the joy so much sweeter. The important thing was to hold on to all the love and happiness you could, treasure each precious moment, every bond you had, and pray it was enough to sustain you through the harrowing days.

Rose was determined that she wouldn't lose the beautiful, fragile girl in front of her – the girl who had been such an unexpected and wonderful blessing for her, when she'd been resigned to living out the rest of her lonely days on her own, with only the magic she wove with the villagers to sustain her.

Yet she had a feeling that Carlie would be one of those people who emerged from tragedy even stronger, her character forged in the fire and steel of grief, her actions tempered by loss and the immense compassion and wisdom she would soon realise she had within her.

Shuddering, she acknowledged that it could still go either way though. Carlie could grow stronger from her journey through hell, or let it defeat her and sweep her away from the world.

"Well, when you're ready you can read her card, think about her words, and how much she cares about you and is sorry. But for now we should head off, okay?" Rose suggested gently.

Sighing as though the weight of the whole world was on her shoulders, Carlie finally nodded.

"And, um, did you want to get changed before we leave?" Rose asked hesitantly, scared that the question would anger her feisty granddaughter and change her mind about going.

Carlie's eyes flashed. "What's wrong with this?" she demanded, and Rose tried to hide her smile.

"Nothing at all Sweetheart. But we really should go now," she said, shepherding her out the door and into the car for the bleak drive to the church.

Chapter 3

Happy Never After

Carlie felt like she was sleepwalking through the funeral, her body there, responding to people's looks of sympathy, but her mind and her heart trapped somewhere dank and dark. Not the welcome blackness of oblivion, which she'd retreated into several times in the past week. This was the darkness of awareness, of suffering and horror and fear and guilt, the place where each thought brought physical agony, each word spoken rubbed salt into her already gaping wounds.

But it was the naked, raw pain etched deep into the face of Rowan's mother that almost brought her undone. Her grandmother had mentioned once that losing a child was even worse than losing a parent or a partner, because kids were supposed to bury their mum and dad. Not quite as early as Carlie had had to, she'd conceded, but it was the expected and natural order of things. When that was reversed it left an ache that nothing could ever soothe.

Seeing Louisa at the church doors, welcoming people with the ghost of a smile, a pale face and trembling hands, was a dagger in her heart. She wanted to turn and flee, to try to outrun her own pain, and the haunting pain on his mother's face, but Rose placed a hand on her back at the exact moment her body prepared for its desperate flight. There were disadvantages to having a priestess for a grandmother, she thought wryly, and heard Rose stifle a giggle at that. *Damn mind-reading witch!*

"Sorry," her grandma whispered, as she pushed her into Louisa's arms. "Sorry on both counts."

"Oh Carlie, I'm so glad you came, thank you so much. I wasn't sure you would actually turn up," Rowan's mum said.

"Nor was I," Carlie muttered, then tried to pull herself together. It wasn't just about her today. She had to consider other people too. "I'm so sorry for your loss Mrs Dunbar."

"And I'm so sorry for *your* loss," the woman replied, voice cracked with pain. "And it's Louisa, please."

Carlie nodded reluctantly. It seemed a strange time to be quibbling over names, or trying to increase their intimacy – Rowan was the only thing they'd had in common, and he was gone. There was nothing to hold them together now.

"I'm sorry I haven't been over to see you either, to spend time with you, comfort you. I feel like we're bound together forever now," his mother said, but Carlie was saved from replying to such a strange sentiment when Jay walked up and took Louisa's hand.

She hurried inside, not quite ready to face Rowan's manager. A blush stained her cheeks as she remembered her only encounter with the glamorous, beautifully dressed woman. It had been at Rowan's apartment, when he'd returned from a retreat, and when Jay had knocked on the door Carlie had hastily decided that he must have been two-timing her. God, why had she never trusted him? He'd given her no reason to doubt him, but she'd acted like a jealous kid. Which she supposed she was, or she had been. *What had he ever seen in her?*

"He saw your incredible spirit and your immense strength Sweetheart," Rose said gently from where she was seated next to her on the hard wooden pew. "Your beautiful open heart."

Frowning, Carlie turned on her grandmother, eyes flashing. "I feel like I don't have a heart," she said angrily. "It's too broken. Too many times. What's the point of caring for someone when they always let you down, when they always leave you? It would be better to never love at all, surely."

"No, of course it wouldn't," her grandma replied, shocked.

"Yet you never found love again after Grandpa died, did you?" Carlie asked accusingly. A wave of horror swept over her then, as she saw her life stretching ahead of her, lonely and filled with bitterness, and no respite in sight.

She shuddered. She'd lost her parents, she'd lost the love of her life, she'd lost her home, her school, her friends, her whole past, and everything she'd ever known – god, it seemed like she'd even lost her two closest friends, one through distance, and one through… who even knew? But whichever way she looked at it, there was no rosiness in her future.

She was saved from having to hear her grandma raving about the so-called joys of life when a woman came over to talk to Rose. Finally left in peace, Carlie gazed around the church, eyes drawn upwards to the towering ceiling – and she wondered suddenly why Rowan's mum had chosen to have a Christian ceremony. Rowan was a druid, a shaman, more spiritual than religious, and he believed in past lives and reincarnation, not some rigid notion of heaven or hell.

The thought shook her. She didn't know what she believed, or whether there was anything after death. Her parents hadn't been religious, and while she'd taken part in goddess ceremonies with her grandmother and her circle, and loved doing them, she wasn't sure whether deity was real or just a beautiful metaphor. Of course she wanted desperately to believe that there was something after death, some vague notion of a spirit realm where Rowan might be now. She wanted to feel his presence in her life, to be able to communicate with him, sense him around her – but she wasn't convinced that it was anything more than wishful thinking on her part.

And could she go on, without the knowledge that he was in a better place, or that he would always be with her in some way? With his mother? Was that the comfort people sought in religion – was it just balm for the terrifying possibility that this was all there was?

Part of her wished she could believe that his death had happened for a reason. That's the consolation people offered the grieving as comfort, but she just couldn't buy it. He'd only been twenty-three, in love with his work, so alive with the sense of purpose and passion it brought him, so happy and at peace knowing that he was helping people find their own truths, become the best versions of themselves that they could.

And as hard as it was for her to believe it, he'd been in love with her. Had wanted to marry her even, when she was ready. How could anyone suggest that there was some reason for his death, some greater purpose? And did they really believe that, or was it just a lie they told themselves to try to cope with the terrible truth – that awful things happened, all the time, and that life was terribly, terribly unfair? Was it just a platitude they uttered because they were too uncomfortable with death, with grief, with the tragedy of life?

She supposed that thinking there was a reason someone had died might make the loss easier to cope with, but would it really? The person was still gone. And what possible purpose could there be for his mother to suffer? Or for her to go through this heartbreak again? Rowan had been helping her come to terms with the death of her parents, had been helping her heal. Now she felt even worse about their loss, if that was possible.

And she wasn't sure how much more she could handle. Someone had told her once that a vase that was broken became even stronger in the places where it was mended, and that it was the same with hearts – we're strongest in the places that have been broken. But she didn't buy that. Besides, what if it wasn't just a small crack in her heart that had to be fixed, but instead it had been shattered into a million little pieces, pieces far too small to ever be able to be remade? That was how she felt. She was just broken pieces on top of broken pieces. It seemed as though her heart was just one seething mess of ever-widening wounds.

And how could scars even begin to form, and she start to heal, if she just kept being torn apart?

Chapter 4

Lightning Crashes

Back home a few hours later, Rose parked the car, turned off the engine and sat quietly, nervously, in the driver's seat.

"Will you be okay if I pop down to the shop for a little while?" she asked carefully. She wasn't sure whether Carlie wanted to be alone or needed to have someone with her, but she was prepared to spend less time at her healing centre if her granddaughter needed her. "I'm happy not to go, if you want some company," she added. "But I don't want you to feel smothered if you need some time alone…"

Carlie stared at her grandma through red-rimmed, world-weary eyes, seeing her fragility as well as her strength. Her attempt to give her space yet not leave her on her own. She didn't know what the poor woman had done to deserve a messed up seventeen-year-old landing on her doorstep, but she was grateful that her mum's friend Sandy had tracked her down.

"I really appreciate you Gran, more than you know. More than I say. And it was beyond awful today, but I'm glad that you made me go, and grateful that you came with me – I'm not sure I could have handled it otherwise. But I'll be okay. You need to go to work, and I need some time on my own," she said softly.

"I'll be fine, I promise," she continued, as she saw the reluctance on Rose's face. She couldn't blame her. She hadn't exactly been acting sane of late, or displaying the best judgement. But finally her grandma nodded, gave her a quick hug, then peeled herself out of the small car and turned and walked towards the village.

As soon as she was out of sight, Carlie opened the car door and gasped for breath. She felt the blackness descending, and shivered, wondering if she should grab a warmer coat, but she couldn't be bothered. Everything was an effort now, even the thought of unlocking the front door and climbing the stairs to her room. Shrugging, she turned and headed away from the village, her steps aimless, her mind carefully blank as she tried to avoid the painful thoughts that were attempting to land and take hold.

Being at the funeral had shattered her. Hearing people she'd never met or even heard of waxing lyrical about a man it sounded like they didn't know had disconcerted her. School friends who hadn't seen him since he'd begun walking the druid path six years ago. A now-married and pregnant ex-girlfriend who'd cheated on him when they'd dated for a few weeks in college, who said she was going to name their baby after him. Carlie had felt sorry for the husband, tied to a woman glorifying a man she'd dated briefly several years ago then forgotten about until now.

At least Jay's speech was genuine. She'd worked closely with Rowan for the last few years, had booked his events and travelled with him, been the shield between him and the rest of the world so he could concentrate on his spiritual work and not worry about logistics and other mundane details.

She'd come over and given Carlie a hug at the end of the service, and told her that she knew how much Rowan had loved her – that he'd asked her to cut back on the retreats he had to travel a long way for, so they could spend more time together.

"Don't ever doubt his love for you Carlie," she'd whispered. "No one here knew him, and he would have been horrified that all these

people were here, like ghouls in need of drama, feeding off the tragedy. Even I was intruding, really. All he wanted was more time to spend with you, to convince you of how much he loved you, and that there was no one else for him."

Carlie had broken down at her words, and Jay had patted her back kindly, if a little awkwardly, before her boyfriend led her out of the church, a supportive arm around her. Smiling as she recalled Jay's kindness and reassurance, even though it reminded her of how stupid she'd been to be jealous of her, she lifted her eyes to gaze around her.

Her heart started racing as she realised that she was walking down the oak-lined path to "their spot", the place Rowan had taken her to on their first date. The place where he'd first kissed her.

Filled with a deep sense of dread, she entered the small meadow on the edge of the stream, and felt her heart beat even louder as she gazed at the softly sloping bank shaded by two weeping willow trees that grew close together.

Back then, she'd laughed in delight at the beautiful space, had found the gentle sound of the running water so peaceful and soothing to the soul. Now, her eyes spilled over with tears as she stared at the two trees, stark in their winter guise, and saw the ghosts of her and Rowan as they'd sat on the bank together that morning, their backs to the solid, nurturing strength of the willows. She remembered the joy she'd felt in that moment, the smile that had lit up her face as his closeness had lit up her heart.

A bone-chilling wind tore through the trees, and her heart ached as she heard the whisper of her voice from back then, echoing across time. "Thank you for bringing me here," she'd said shyly, still so nervous in his presence, so unsure of herself. "It's so peaceful, like we're in our own little world."

He'd taken her hand then and kissed it gently. "I wish we could stay here always, just the two of us, away from everyone, away from friends and family and school and work," he'd said.

And he'd kissed her, her first real kiss. Raising her hand, she ran a finger along her lower lip, trying to imagine him with her still, imagine his lips on hers, his arms around her. Trying to imagine the warmth she'd felt when she was with him.

Angrily she shook off that thought. He wasn't here to hold her close, he wasn't ever going to kiss her again, or stroke her cheek. The icy fingers of wind tore at her clothes, pulling strands of hair from her messy bun and chilling her to the core – which made her happy.

She wanted to suffer, she wanted to feel her body as aching with cold as her heart ached with grief and loss.

Storm clouds gathered overhead as she stood there, and she smiled as rain started to fall. When lightning flashed, lighting up the darkness that was descending, she shivered, then started to laugh, a note of hysteria in her voice. Maybe she should just sit down on the cold earth and let the rain fall on her as the thunder crashed around her. Perhaps she'd even catch pneumonia if she stayed long enough, and not have to decide whether she wanted to live or to die – surely in her weakened state she would struggle to fight it off.

But then her restless thoughts flickered to Rose, and she knew she couldn't cause her any more pain. For a moment she felt a warmth at her shoulder, as though Rowan was standing behind her, hand guiding her to turn around, to get to shelter, to get home and to go on living. Sighing, she ran back up the hill, sloshing through puddles with grim satisfaction, shoes muddy and ruined, water seeping in and turning her toes ice cold.

Finally she made it back to their cottage, turned the key in the lock and dripped her way down the corridor. Luther took one look at her and miaowed sternly, his eyes jumping from her to the bathroom door and back again, his meaning clear. Leaning down to pat him, she laughed when he grumbled at all the water falling on his head, then stalked away from her to the warmth of the kitchen.

"I love you Luther," she called after him, giggling at the expression of indignation on his adorable fuzzy black face.

Knowing that the cat was right though, she walked into the bathroom, stripped off her wet clothes and stood under the scalding shower until the water started to run cold. Leaping out, she grabbed the towel and dried herself roughly, then raced upstairs to dress in her warmest clothes.

There was an apple on her bedside table, no doubt placed there by Rose as an unsubtle hint to eat, so she curled up in bed and crunched into it – her grandmother would have to be happy with that – then lay down and waited for the sweet oblivion of sleep to claim her.

Chapter 5

The Last Goodbye

The next morning dawned bleak and grey, but Carlie awoke with her eyes dry for the first time since Rowan had died nine days ago, shocked to feel the tiniest threads of her own strength tugging at her heart. She lay in bed, stiff and silent. It was New Year's Eve, and Rose was running a ritual at the healing centre that night, for people to let go of the pain of the current year and usher in a fulfilling and joyful new one. At least it was, quite literally, impossible for her to have a worse year than the one just gone, so she supposed she should be grateful for that at least.

She'd begged off attending though, and Rose had agreed, understanding that being with a group of people releasing pain that paled into insignificance next to her own wouldn't be good for Carlie. Not that anyone's pain was more or less important than someone else's, but she didn't think her granddaughter's presence would be uplifting for the other participants either.

Instead Carlie had decided to do her own ritual, so she spent the morning forcing herself to eat, and trying unsuccessfully to lose herself in a book. But finally it was time to prepare, so she gathered all the things she'd need, had a chamomile-scented bath, then opened her small wardrobe and reverently took out the gorgeous dress Rowan had given her for Christmas.

Her breath caught as she remembered the moment she'd lifted it from its wrappings and held it to her heart. It had been a few days after he'd died, when Mike had finally convinced her to get out of bed and eat something, for her grandma's sake, and she'd found the parcel the police officers had brought from the car wreck.

It was like a gothic bride's gown. A lump formed in her throat as she ran her fingers over the soft tulle of the skirt and gazed at the bees embroidered on the bodice, bees that had meant so much to them both. She slipped it over her head and smoothed it down. It was so soft on her skin, and somehow it made her feel closer to him. As she slid the amethyst rose-gold ring that had come with the dress onto her ring finger, she whispered the words engraved on it: *Lives entwined, souls in harmony, hearts as one.* She could sense his arms around her, feel his breath in her hair as he whispered: "Always and forever" in her ear.

Still drowning in memories, she pulled on a coat, picked up her black velvet ritual bag and slipped out the back door and through the garden to the laneway. She headed towards the tor, then turned off towards their special place. The wind whipping restlessly through the trees added to the wildness she felt, and she pulled her coat more tightly around herself as she wandered through the bleakness of the wintry late afternoon.

Although she'd been to their place by the river just the day before, the sadness she felt as she approached still overwhelmed her, and for a moment she worried that she wasn't ready for this, that she didn't have the strength to go on. The grief stabbed at her like a fresh knife wound in her heart, and she found herself crouched down and doubled over, gasping for breath. Eventually she managed to calm herself down though, imploring her shattered heart to be strong, for this afternoon at least.

Taking a deep breath, she shrugged off her coat and lay it on the ground, then sat down on it, dress whispering around her, and ritual bag in her lap. Reaching inside, she took out a tealight candle in a glass holder and carefully placed it at her feet, then pulled out the bouquet she'd carefully wound together from sprigs of rosemary and bay laurel, berries and leaves from the holly tree, and a tiny branch

 of mistletoe that she'd woven into the centre. These were herbs for remembrance, for rebirth, for the dead, for the beloved, for those left behind. Squeezing them tightly, she winced as the sharp edges of the holly leaves pricked her skin, but she kept holding them close. She needed to feel pain, needed to feel some kind of physical sensation in the hope it could balance out the anguish in her heart.

As blood trickled down her wrist from her palm, she let it slowly sprinkle over the bare earth, watching as if from a great distance as the ruby-red drops soaked into the ground. She wanted to leave a part of herself here, in their special place, wanted to feel some connection with anything that had mattered to the two of them. If she closed her eyes she could almost see the ghosts of the two of them beside her. She'd been so innocent, so full of hope then, as she gave her heart away for the first time.

"Oh Rowan," she sighed, her heart constricting in her chest. "How could you leave me? This feels like a punishment for my bad decision, like the universe didn't give me a chance to correct it, even though I had decided I was wrong, that I had to be with you, so soon after I broke both our hearts." The sky was starting to darken with the approaching night – the light faded so early here in winter – but she liked that, liked how miserable the whole world seemed, as though all of time and space was grieving with her.

"I miss you so much Rowan, and I miss what we should have had – time to get to know each other better, time to fall even more deeply in love with each other, time to grow up and grow older together. You must have thought I was so stupid, so naive, so young. And you were right. Getting spooked by the intensity of our feelings, too scared to trust you, to let myself fall, to believe that you – *you!* – could ever care about me. Yet I could feel the truth of it in my bones. My heart knew you loved me, even if my brain refused to accept it.

"I'm so sorry I wasted the precious time we had with my insecurities, so sorry I listened to Rhiannon when I should have only listened to you. How could she – how could anyone – understand what we felt for each other? Know how deep our connection was? I didn't even know myself, not consciously, even though it had become a part of me, a part of my soul. Everything seemed so hard, yet loving you was the easiest thing I've ever done. I didn't have to think about it, I just felt it, so deeply within me."

A tear trickled down her cheek and froze there, and she wished she could break it off and keep it, because it felt like a part of them, something that only they could share. But did she really want to remember him with tears? Not that she seemed to have a choice in that, she thought wryly, and laughed mirthlessly.

Growing impatient with her sadness and the endless, bottomless grief, she made her mind go blank. Carefully she laid out a black cloth, then set down the pentacle she'd been gifted by Brianna, the mysterious woman in green, just after Samhain. Then she positioned her altar tools around it – a heart-shaped rose quartz crystal in the north for earth, a chalice of spring water in the west for water, a black feather in the east for air, and a candle in the south for fire.

After that she placed the beautiful herkimer diamond ring Rowan had given her at the Yule ball in the centre of the altar, stifling a sob as she thought of the future they should have had together, the promise held in the ring. He'd told her that herkimer diamonds meant they'd be together forever, but clearly that was a lie.

Sighing, she picked up her athame and traced a circle between the worlds. It was just a small one, since it was only her now, and she felt smaller without him, diminished in size and significance. She moved widdershins, against the sun, since she was trying to release and banish what she could of her pain with this ritual.

> *Within this circle, that my intent will form,*
> *Between the worlds, a safe place born.*
> *Ancient beings of this sacred place,*
> *Smile on me with your endless grace.*
> *Please hold me close throughout this rite,*
> *And heal my heart on this year end night.*

Sensing the air shimmering around her, for a moment she felt a pang of longing for Rhiannon and the magic they'd woven together. But she pushed that thought aside as she lowered the ritual knife and focused on the sacred items on her makeshift altar. Reaching out her hand, she touched each one in turn as she invoked the energy and strength of the elements, and the power and spirits of the four directions.

> *Spirits of the east, and element of air,*
> *Please carry away my sadness and pain,*
> *and share your wisdom with me tonight.*

> *Spirits of the north, and element of earth,*
> *Please ground me with your strength,*
> *and watch over my sad yet sacred rite.*

> *Spirits of the west, and element of water,*
> *Please wash away all I can no longer bear,*
> *and soothe my heart after this lonely fight.*

> *Spirits of the south, and element of fire,*
> *Please burn away my pain and grief,*
> *and allow peace and acceptance to ignite.*

Another tear trickled down her cheek, but she took a deep breath and tried to inhale the strength and solidity of the earth beneath her, the clarity and inspiration of the air around her, the nurturing power of the water beside her, and the smouldering sensation of the fire within her. Finally she lifted the small statues of the god and the goddess and cradled them in her lap.

> *Goddess of love and compassion, magic and moonlight,*
> *Please hold Rowan safe throughout his eternal night.*

> *God of strength and sunshine, love and might,*
> *Let him know how much I love him and miss his light.*

As she felt the magic of the ritual settle around her shoulders, warming her with its growing familiarity and gentle power, she suddenly felt more lost than she ever had.

"Oh Rowan, how could you leave me? Leave me here to face life without you, face your death without you? It breaks my heart, not knowing if you knew that I'd changed my mind, that I was coming to see you the next morning, coming to tell you that I loved you with all my heart and soul. That I love you.

"Those words were for you, for always. *I love you.* I thought I would never say them to anyone else, that they were my gift to you. Now here I am, at seventeen, thinking that I'll never say them again full-stop. I just... oh god, I wasn't ready for you to leave me. Why couldn't we have had one more day, one more week, one more year? One more forever."

For a long time she sat silently, liking the sharp pain of the cold as it burrowed under her clothing and chilled her skin to match her heart.

"You healed me you know," she finally whispered, despair colouring her voice. "You helped me begin to emerge from my grief at losing Mum and Dad, begin to feel whole again, complete. But now I feel more lost than ever. I've lost my purpose, and my meaning, because my love for you was what was keeping me together. It was your strength that was holding me up, keeping my head above water. And now I'm drowning again, but this time it's even worse, because I know what I could have had, and what I never will have again."

A sob choked her, but she swallowed it impatiently back down, her words tumbling out of her, voice edged with hysteria.

"When I wrote to you that night, after I left you, and ran from you, I had finally realised how much I loved you, how important you were to me, how much I was willing to give up to be with you. And I want you to know that. God how I wish you could have known that.

It seemed like you felt my words – I sensed our souls reaching out to each other as I wrote them, felt you touch my heart and hold it close – but I will always wonder if I imagined that. Always worry that you died thinking I didn't want to be with you. Always regret that I wasn't able to tell you just how deeply I'd fallen for you. It would kill me if I discovered that you had no idea. And I'll never really know either way."

Another sob escaped, wrenched from deep within her, and she paused for a moment, trying to get her breathing under control. A viciously cold wind tore through the trees, creating tiny waves on the dark water of the stream beside her.

"Listen," a voice crooned, and she concentrated all her senses on the sound. Had it been a voice? Was it a word she'd heard?

"Listen to what?" she thought impatiently, but she closed her eyes, trying to identify the tone of the voice, or the direction it was coming from. Was it just the wind, or her feverish imagination? Or could Rowan still be with her? Did his spirit live on? In her rational mind she was sceptical of there being anything after death, but oh, she so desperately wanted to be wrong about that.

Feeling a hand in her hair, tenderly stroking it, she leaned in to the gentle touch like a kitten, almost purring. It was impossible, she knew that, but for just a moment she allowed herself to dream that he was still with her.

"Love never dies," the voice said, and she still wasn't sure if the words were in her mind or from somewhere outside, or even whether it was a male or a female speaking.

"His love will stay with you forever," it continued, a gentle sigh, but it had given itself away. It said *his* love, not *my* love. Her eyes snapped open as waves of disappointment rolled over her – and she froze when she saw there was a woman in a long red cloak sitting cross-legged before her, the tiny altar the only thing between them. She was close enough to touch – not that Carlie had any intention of touching her. Goosebumps prickled up her arms as she stared at the figure across from her.

There was something not quite right about her, something Otherworldly and strange. She had long black hair and a pale face, and her eyes were an eerie swirl of black against the stark white of her cheeks and the deep red of her lips. Her heart broke a little more to realise that it wasn't Rowan sitting with her. As cynical as she was, part of her had hoped it was him, or some spirit of him, that had been holding her so close and offering such warmth and comfort. She laughed, a bitter, slightly manic sound, and wondered if she'd lost her mind. Again.

"Oh Carlie, beloved, you have not lost your mind, you have simply lost your great love, on top of losing your parents," the strange woman breathed.

"Simply? *Simply!* This is simple to you? This has no importance to you? Because I've gotta say, there is nothing simple here. I'm a mess of contradictions – of anger and guilt and sadness and despair – and I don't know if I want to live in a world that is so cruel. How can I survive this? How can I see any value in going on when I know from bitter experience that anyone I ever meet I will lose? Love never dies, you say, but what's the point of that when the person I loved so much has died? *All* the people I've loved have died."

Her voice trembled with fury, and some part of her was distantly aware that she sounded like a petulant child, but she didn't care. And while part of her mind recognised that this strange figure must be related to the woman in blue and her green-clad friend, another part couldn't care less. What was the point of them? What had they really done? They'd given her and Rhiannon magical gifts, but those things meant nothing to her now.

All her magic had died with Rowan, so being offered a pretty wand or a silver chalice or whatever other ritual tools this apparition thought would mollify her was of no use. She wasn't even on speaking terms with Rhiannon, so she was no longer part of any enchanted circle. Besides, what good was magic? She'd created a love spell, and Rowan had appeared in answer to its casting. But then he'd been torn out of her life – torn out of his own – and killed on a lonely road in the snow, so what was the purpose of spells?

They'd only ripped her still-fragile heart out all the way. Had given her something she hadn't even known she'd wanted, then cruelly taken it away, just as she was beginning to appreciate its value. So she was done with magic, with love, with friendship. Right now she was pretty sure she was done with life.

The woman before her shifted slightly, and Carlie's eyes were drawn back to her face. There was an unearthly glow that seemed to come from within, illuminating her features in the deepening twilight.

"You still love Rose," the woman said softly. "And she loves you more than life itself. She wants to help you heal from this, to grow stronger and eventually be able to move on."

"And is that why you're here? To let me know you're taking her too?" Carlie demanded, before her body collapsed in on itself in new terror. Surely they wouldn't do that to her. That would definitely push her over the edge, way beyond recovery. Glaring across the altar at the woman, seeing her now as some kind of beautiful velvet-clad grim reaper, she shivered in the creeping cold and dawning horror that was her life.

Shaking her head, the woman handed her own cloak to her, then in the same instant had crossed the distance between them and was by her side, wrapping the soft red fabric around her trembling shoulders. Jumping in fright, heart racing, Carlie tried to shrug the cloak off, but it seemed so heavy, and made her feel so languid.

Slowly she felt herself melting into the warmth of its velvety folds, and the fight drained out of her. She turned her head to thank the strange woman, but she was suddenly back on the other side of the altar, sitting opposite her again, looking as though she'd never moved. The realisation sent a terrified shudder through her, then it too was gone, leaving her feeling empty, the fear and anger that had been consuming her somehow mellowing into acceptance. Furious, she stared across at the shadowy figure.

What spell had she cast to take away the anger that seemed to be the only strength she still possessed?

"What do you want?" she finally asked, resigned, feeling like she'd lost a battle she hadn't even known she was fighting.

"Oh Carlie, beloved, I am so very sorry for your loss. You have been through so much, and so much has been demanded of you, and I am truly sorry. You are allowed to be angry, to be hurt, to be depressed. The depth of your grief is a mark of the love that you shared, and you should never doubt how deep and powerful that love was. *Is.* Some people live their whole life without the opportunity to love like that, or to be loved like that."

Carlie scowled. "So that's it? Now I spend the rest of my life knowing what I could've had, but not allowed to feel it again?"

The woman smiled mysteriously. "Who knows? You could be blessed to experience a love like that again – it is up to you."

"What do you mean?" Carlie demanded, her voice high, panicked, verging again on desperate. "I can beg and plead and grovel, or fulfil some bizarre quest to prove myself, and you'll bring him back to me? You can do that?"

Her heart raced, and she could barely breathe. Did this woman have the ability to do that? Who was she? Was the Craft really that powerful? And what would it cost her? Didn't you have to sacrifice something really precious for such a bargain? Would she have to make a deal with the devil? She didn't mind, of course – she would give up anything to have Rowan back with her. Well, not Rose, but she'd give up anything else, even herself. What good was her shell of a life without him anyway?

A harsh slap across her face made her jump, and she crashed back into awareness of her surroundings. Riddled with anxiety and confusion, she clutched at her smarting cheek and stared across at the woman in red, her heart sinking as she saw the grim expression in her eyes. There was fire and ice there, and a steeliness underwritten with fury.

"This is what you think of the Craft?" she shrieked. "You, who have done ritual with your priestess grandmother, seriously believe that her honouring of nature and the seasons could involve ritual sacrifice, or bargains with some evil spirit?"

Blushing, Carlie reluctantly shook her head. "I'm sorry," she whispered, shoulders drooping and voice aching with desperation. "I guess that was too much to hope for. But I don't know what anything means any more, or involves. What is possible or merely dream."

The woman caressed her cheek, gently this time, cold fingers soothing where the slap had stung, and crooned to her. "Beloved, I know, and you must be out of your mind with grief. I am very sorry that I struck you, and I suppose I should be relieved that you drew the line at sacrificing Rose…"

Carlie's cheeks burned even redder, and she wanted to curl up and die of embarrassment that her thoughts had been heard, by this Otherworld being no less.

"What I *meant*," the woman continued, "was that it is your choice whether you spend the rest of your life alone, bitter and miserable, or if you can get to a point where your heart is open to the possibility of new love."

White-hot anger coursed through Carlie, but she bit her tongue before speaking, and the figure smiled approvingly.

"I know you do not want to think about that now, and nor should you. But one day you will have the choice, and I hope you will not react with such outrage and deny yourself happiness. I am not here to tell you there is a reason for his death, or some great purpose – there is not, and surely Brauna told you that – but to let you know that you can survive this. You can, if you choose, create your own meaning for this, and find something that will give your life purpose, make your life bearable. Through your suffering you will be able to help so many people, if you want to. And I know that is very little consolation for what has been taken from you, and it seems awfully unfair that you have to go through so much to benefit someone else."

Suddenly the grim-faced girl laughed. She couldn't help herself. What had happened to her? Surely she was losing her mind. Had *already* lost her mind. Here she was, sitting on the icy cold earth as night drew down around her, freezing her butt off in a beautiful but flimsy dress, talking to a figment of her imagination, and getting angry at a platitude which she'd no doubt hear plenty of times over the next few years.

A tear trickled down her cheek as she realised that she had never felt more alone in her life. She had thought things couldn't get worse than when her parents had died six months ago, but she was wrong – now she was not only mourning them, but the love of her life as well.

A flake of snow landed on her nose, and she felt hysteria build within her. Perhaps she'd catch pneumonia out here and die, and all her angst would be over, would be for nothing. Then she felt a hand on her face again, still not gentle, but not as harsh as the slap, and she jerked her head up.

"Please, do not joke about your own death. You are stronger than you know," the red-clad woman said softly, imploringly. "And surely you owe it to Rowan, and to the love you shared, and the respect he had for you, to honour his memory by making the most of your life. Becoming someone who would make him proud, who will do all the good in the world that he had planned to do."

Almost laughing in disbelief, Carlie stared across at the figure opposite, eyes mutinous. "Seriously, blackmail now?" she demanded. "You're going to guilt me into not killing myself? Does that ever work?" God, why couldn't she be spending time with Brauna, the sweet and patient woman in blue, or her green-robed friend Brianna? "Do you know them?" she asked suddenly. "Do they know you're here? Did they send you?"

But the figure of the woman was fading before her eyes, and as she left, so too did the warm red cloak she'd placed around Carlie's shoulders. Shivering in the suddenly icy air, and noticing just how dark it had become, Carlie quickly but carefully unwove her circle, farewelling the quarters and the deities, and dissolving the protective space she'd created between the worlds. Pouring the water from the chalice onto the ground, she hastily wrapped it in velvet and placed it in her bag, along with the feather and the crystal, then slid the ring back on her finger, next to the amethyst one Rowan had offered her as a wedding band.

Her heart glowed as she gazed at the rings, suffusing her with warmth, and she smiled despite her sadness. If she ever doubted that it had been real, that it had been as intense and all-consuming as she imagined, all she had to do was recall the night of the Yule Ball, when Rowan had professed his love for her outside under the oak tree.

"It's a friendship ring, if you will, a token of how I feel about you," he'd said, eyes shining with the depth of his feelings. "A symbol of my eternal love for you."

Slowly she leaned down and kissed the twinkling herkimer diamond. "This crystal binds two people together," he'd told her. "It joins their souls and makes it impossible for other people to tear them apart, no matter how hard they try. You're my equal Carlie," he'd insisted. "There is no more than or less than. I love you."

Her eyes filled as she remembered the feeling of his body against hers, the sensation of his lips on her mouth, and the vow of love he'd made to her that night. And the tears spilled over as she recalled the card that had been delivered by the police officers, with the dress and the amethyst ring, such a short time later.

"And the day that you feel ready to wear this ring, and agree to marry me, to spend your life with me – loving each other, supporting each other, helping each other dream and scheme and grow stronger and more joyful because we have each other – I will be the happiest man alive," he'd written.

God, she missed him with an ache that was physical as well as emotional, that tore at her heart. But as broken as she was, she didn't have it in her to wish she'd never met him. It was agony now, and probably always would be, but she was so grateful that she had been loved so deeply, even if it was only for a single moment of her life, one brief joyful heartbeat before a future of misery.

Picking up the candle, she slowly made her way home, forcing herself to only think of the good, to remember each precious moment they'd shared, and to let that be enough.

Her dreams that night were filled with ice-cold fear and red velvet robes that warmed her through, before turning into naked flames, smothering her and burning her to ash. She tossed and turned, crying out in the night in pain, in terror, in desperation.

Then a small paw touched her cheek, and Luther's sweet presence brought her back into the room, back into her body. Hugging her grandma's cat in relief, she stroked his head as she thanked him, and he stared at her with wise old eyes, purring and seeming to smile back at her. Settling back down in her bed, she finally drifted off again, feeling Luther's energy by her side as she slept until dawn.

Chapter 6

The Beginning of the Thaw

A few days later, Carlie was curled up on the couch, Luther purring on her lap and a fantasy novel in her hand as she tried to escape into other lands, other worlds, other lives. A tentative knock at the door brought her crashing back to reality, and her sadness crashing back into her heart. Expecting one of Rose's friends, who was dropping off some fabric for their herb bags, she dragged herself up and went to open the door – and froze when she saw that it was Rhiannon standing on the top step, shivering in the cold.

Clutching the door frame, she panicked as she tried to process how she felt. She wasn't ready to talk to her, was terrified to be alone with her. And yet that was stupid – they'd shared everything with each other, worked magic together, comforted one another in their grief, whispered their hopes and dreams to the moon as they stood hand in hand on the tor, confided their deepest secrets to each other.

Heart pounding, she cautiously faced her friend, who looked even more nervous than she was. They hadn't seen each other since the day after the ball, when Rhiannon had come over to tell her about her wonderful night with John, and that she was going to skip the Yule ritual they'd planned so she could spend the evening with him and his family. Oh, and to inform her that she couldn't be her friend any more unless she broke up with Rowan.

Anger shot through her, but she took a deep breath and tried to look welcoming. "I guess you should come in before you freeze to death," she said stiffly. Rhiannon's smile looked a little too bright, a little too forced, but she followed Carlie to the kitchen and hovered around her as she put the kettle on.

"I'm so sorry Carlie," she finally blurted. "I'm so sorry for your loss, so sorry for not being there for you – and truly so sorry for pressuring you in any way." Her smile slipped, and she reached out to her friend, trying to hug her, to connect with her, to bridge the strange awful distance between them. Carlie let herself be held for a moment, then wriggled away on the pretext of fussing with tea leaves and cups and soy milk and honey.

"I came by a few times..." Rhiannon began tentatively, and Carlie tried to remember that this was difficult for her too.

"I know," she said softly. "I just, I couldn't talk about it. I can't talk about it. And you were so great about my parents, and so kind to me, I just..."

"You just couldn't understand how I could be such a bitch?" Rhiannon asked flatly, and Carlie looked up at her, startled by her honesty and willingness to admit she was wrong.

"I've gone over this so many times, replaying each scenario, trying to work out why I reacted the way I did, what drove me to give you such a cruel ultimatum. You have no idea how sorry I am," she continued, voice dripping with sincerity.

Carlie stood frozen again, unable to respond. She'd thought her friend would gloss over what had happened between them, try to move on as though nothing had taken place. Admitting she was wrong wasn't something she'd expected to hear – it was weird. Then again, Rhiannon had apologised for her behaviour the day after the ball too – then gone right back to her "Rowan is bad" theme and demanded that Carlie choose between them, and break up with Rowan if she wanted to remain her friend.

Rhiannon winced. "I admit I could have acted better, I could have been more understanding, less selfish. I panicked. I put my own issues on you, and let my jealousy and insecurities colour how I saw Rowan. Please forgive me Carlie. I really am so sorry."

Handing her friend a mug of tea, Carlie nodded reluctantly and walked over to the table, sinking down into a seat with a heavy heart.

"I'm really sorry you had to go through all of that on your own too," Rhiannon continued. "Not that I probably would have been your first choice to grieve Rowan with," she said, trying for a flippant tone but not quite pulling it off.

"It's not like I have many options – it's basically you and Rose, whether I like it or not," Carlie replied, then blushed a little. "Sorry, that came out wrong."

Rhiannon raised one eyebrow, in that way that usually made her smile, then shrugged. "You deserve a few free shots at me," she said, but Carlie shook her head. She wasn't ready to be light-hearted, and she worried that she might accidentally blurt out too much or sound too bitter if she joked about her feelings.

"So how's Brodie, and your dad?" she asked instead, changing the subject to deflect attention away from herself. "Did you have a good Christmas? And have you seen John again?"

"Christmas was nice, just a quiet one with Brodie and Dad. I think it will always be hard for us, without Mum," she said, and Carlie nodded, understanding that. Her friend grieved too.

"I didn't know what had happened then, so I thought it was weird that I hadn't heard from you. Oh, here," she said, rifling through her bag. "I got you a little present." She handed Carlie a brightly wrapped parcel, but her friend had gone pale, eyes widening in pain as she gazed at the neatly tied ribbon, so like the one around her gift from Rowan – the one that had been delivered by two police officers informing her that he was dead.

Rhiannon stood up uncertainly, then took the gift through into the lounge room, leaving it under the pine tree that still stood in its pretty pot from Yule. "Later then," she said gently, as she sat back down and picked up her mug of tea.

Taking a sip, her face brightened. "John is still lovely. I've been over to his place a few times now, babysat his brat siblings with him one night, so we got a lot of kissing done that time, and he's come over to mine a couple of times too. Brodie has loved having something to tease me about, but it's going really well. I really like him."

Carlie tried to keep her face composed, but every word about kissing and closeness was like an arrow through her heart. Thankfully Rhiannon finally realised, and fell into silence with her, although that soon became uncomfortable too.

"So are you ready for school on Monday?" Rhiannon asked, then rolled her eyes at her own question. But Carlie was grateful for the effort she was making. She spared a thought for Emily, her best friend back home in Australia, whose head she'd snapped off after her parents died, just for not knowing what to say.

No one knew what to say to someone in the throes of grief, and she had renewed respect for Emily for trying so hard and persevering so long. What did they say? The friend who holds your hand and says the wrong thing is made of dearer stuff than the one who stays away, or something like that. She'd vowed to try harder, so she smiled at Rhiannon and did her best to reply.

"As ready as I'll ever be. On the plus side, no one even knew I was with Rowan, so no one will ask me about him or get all weird and quiet around me," she said. "But that makes me sad too, because it will seem as though he never existed." She sighed.

"Um, hon? It's a small village. Everyone knows your boyfriend died, even if they didn't know him, but they'll be respectful. And they all knew you were with someone, because they saw you lost in each other while you danced together at the ball, and being crowned Winter Queen and Sun King. Which, if it helps, means there will be lots of photos of you together."

Carlie's eyes misted with tears as she thought of Rowan kissing her on the dance floor, of melting into him and the circle of his arms, and feeling so loved. Of floating away, intoxicated by the magic of the night, the nearness of his body, and the beautiful, intense, inspiring connection she'd felt between them.

Admittedly, she'd been angry with him for a moment, because he'd surprised her by turning up, and she was worried that his presence would upset Rhiannon. But her fear had quickly passed, and she remembered every moment they'd danced together, and every precious second she'd stood outside under the oak tree with him, leaning up against it, being kissed so hard and so deeply.

"Of course they think his name is Paul, and that he went to Smithfield High," Rhiannon broke in, tone cheeky and bright with laughter. Carlie smiled too, trying to put on a brave face, but she was more relieved than she could express when Rose got home and dissolved the intensity in the room. Jumping up, she put the kettle on for another pot of tea, then busied herself in the kitchen as her grandmother and her friend made small talk.

Finally she brought the three cups over and sat down next to Rose, the tension lifting as they spoke about the next sabbat rather than the personal stuff the two girls didn't feel up to discussing. In just four weeks it would be Imbolc, the festival that marked the beginning of spring, and new light, new hope and new beginnings. Fear clutched at Carlie's heart. She didn't want a new beginning, she wanted the past to come back to life. The thought of closure and moving on filled her with dread, and she drifted off into her memories, unwilling to focus on reality and the relentless march of time and life.

Eventually Rhiannon said she had to get home, and Carlie nodded gratefully. She really needed to be alone. "So let me know if you want to do anything tomorrow or on Sunday, or I can just meet you at school on Monday?" her friend offered.

"Monday sounds good. I'm helping Rose in the shop this weekend, and getting sorted. I haven't even looked at my books since… since the last day of school," Carlie said, voice faltering.

Her friend glanced over at Rose, who stayed silent, her face devoid of expression, and Rhiannon forced a smile. Although she thought they were terrible excuses for not spending any time with her over the next two days, she didn't let on, and Rose clearly wasn't going to give away the lie.

So Carlie was finally able to escape upstairs to her room and curl up on her narrow bed with Luther. She was glad Rhiannon had come over and made the first move towards restoring their friendship, but she knew it would take a while longer before her heart fully thawed.

Chapter 7

For Whom the Bell Rings

The ringing of the bell vibrated through Carlie's body, setting her heart racing and her teeth on edge. Dread filled her, but Rhiannon took her hand, and together they climbed the steps to the front of the school. Carlie smiled at her friend gratefully as she dropped her off at her classroom, then took a deep breath, summoned up as much courage as she could and walked through the door. Avoiding eye contact as best as she was able to, she moved quickly to a desk up the back and pulled out her books. Nervously she looked up as the teacher came in. He caught her eye and smiled sadly at her, and she nodded briefly in acknowledgement then gazed down at her books, praying he wouldn't say anything.

One of the girls in her class ran in then, flustered and a minute late, and drew attention away from her. "Good morning Abby," their teacher said sternly, as the girl slid sheepishly into the seat next to Carlie. "I'm so sorry Mr Stephens," she murmured. "We were up all night with a sick cow."

He nodded, comprehension in his eyes, and Carlie marvelled at the lives of her fellow students. A lot of them lived on outlying farms, and school wasn't the only work they did. Back home in Sydney, no one would have known what to do with a sick animal, let alone how to run a working dairy, but kids here did.

"I'm so sorry for your loss," Abby whispered to her, and Carlie looked up in surprise. "Let me know if you need anything, or want to talk. Or not talk," she said simply, then turned back to the blackboard. Understanding washed over her as she remembered Rhiannon mentioning something about Abby on her first day of school, back in September. Her boyfriend had taken his own life, and Abby had struggled to cope.

"Thank you," she murmured, and Abby smiled at her sadly. "It still hurts, but it does get a bit easier," she replied quietly. "Is that what you were wondering?"

Carlie nodded, despair flooding her, but they were interrupted when their teacher started a quiz based on the homework he'd set over the Christmas holidays, and she had to concentrate to keep up. She hadn't opened her books once while they were off – Rowan had died at the beginning of their break, and she'd been in a haze of grief ever since. She'd only left the house twice, for the funeral and then her farewell ritual, and had rarely even emerged from her bedroom, so she hoped today wasn't going to rely too much on the reading she was supposed to have done. Luckily, in this class at least, she had covered the topic at hand at her old school, back home in Sydney, so she managed to fake her way through.

Back home... Was she always going to feel that way, like she was just a visitor here, and Australia was her real home? Or would she one day consider England to be home? Would she pick up an accent? Change her favourite foods and the way she dressed?

And what did home even mean? Was it where your memories lived, where your childhood roots lay, the place that felt like a physical part of you? Or was it the place you ended up, through accident or fate, or choice or chance, whether you wanted to be there or not?

Did she want to be here? She still wasn't sure, but it wasn't like she had any say in the matter. Rose was her only living family member, so that made it home, for now at least.

Her reverie was interrupted by the bell, and Mr Stephens hastily set some more homework before half the students bolted out the door. Abby smiled at her and waved as she left, and Carlie waved back. It seemed that people marked by tragedy gravitated towards each other, which made sense she supposed. Certainly she found it easier to be with Rhiannon, who'd lost her mum to cancer just over a year ago, than her old friend Emily, who hadn't experienced such loss – thank god. She hoped no one else their age had to go through that. Making a mental note to ask Rhiannon later about Abby, and whether she had close friends and some support, she pulled out her next lot of books and got ready for history.

Rhiannon hurried in just as the second bell rang and swung into the seat next to her. "You okay?" she asked, and Carlie nodded. All things considered, she supposed she was okay. Not good, not great, nowhere even *close* to happy, but she was okay.

Their teacher Laura came in – Ms Henderson, they should say, although they found it hard to slip back into student mode at school when Laura was part of Rose's magical ritual circle. Today she was followed by a tall, sporty looking guy with wavy blond hair.

Carlie blinked. He looked like half the guys she'd known back home, as though he'd just emerged from the waves after a long surf. Rhiannon elbowed her sharply in the ribs. "He's cute isn't he! He was in my biology class just then," she grinned. Carlie stared at her friend, unable to mask her shock, and a guilty look crossed her face.

"I'm sorry," Rhiannon whispered, stricken. "Way too soon for that." Carlie made her face as expressionless as she could, and turned to look at their teacher, who was trying to get the class's attention.

"I'd like you all to meet Jake," Ms Henderson said. "Jake, everyone," she added, sweeping her arm to encompass the whole class. "Jake is here from Australia for the school year, staying with his grandfather while his parents are working in Africa. So let's all make him feel welcome, shall we?"

"Hi Jake," the class replied, rote sing-song style, and he waved and flashed them a cheeky grin.

"Oh my god, he's to die for," one of the girls near Carlie said, which was followed by giggles and murmurs of agreement.

"Do you know him Carlie?" one of the guys asked from the front of the room. Rhiannon rolled her eyes. "Australia's a big country Dave," she snapped, instantly protective of Carlie and knowing she didn't want any attention on her.

"Carlie's from Sydney," their teacher said. "And Jake is from Perth, on the other side of the country. That's thousands of miles apart, right?" she asked, turning to Jake. He grinned at her and nodded, then turned and caught Carlie's eye.

His smile did strange things to her tummy, and she quickly glanced away. Rhiannon looked at her carefully, but she avoided her friend's gaze, ducking down to her bag and pretending to look for something. She was relieved when their teacher finally found Jake a seat at the front of the room and the class got underway. And she didn't give him another thought until just before the class ended, when Laura gave them their term assignments.

"You will all be examining an aspect of the British Commonwealth, formerly the British Empire, during the period from the sixteenth century until now. I want an in-depth essay that covers the history of the country you're studying before British rule, the circumstances of the colonisation from both our point of view as well as the perspective of the indigenous inhabitants, whether the place had 'belonged' to a different colonial power earlier, how the relationship has changed over the years, and what the status is now – for instance, after a century of British rule, India became an independent nation in 1947, after the struggle led by Mahatma Gandhi."

Everyone groaned – this sounded much tougher than last term's major assignment, which had actually been lots of fun.

"You'll be working in pairs for this one. Debbie and Peter, you have India. Rhiannon and Dave, Canada. Ally and Rob, Hong Kong. Karen and Mark, the colonies of North America. Jillian and Michael, the Caribbean."

She went through the whole class, until Carlie started to think she'd been forgotten, but no such luck. "And Carlie, you and Jake have Australia."

There were mutters around the room, cries of "no fair" and "that's cheating", and Carlie was aware of her friend looking at her speculatively, but their teacher stared the complainers down. "I think it will be fascinating for our two Aussie friends to study the topic from the British perspective, and I'm sure it will be illuminating for all of us to gain their point of view on British settlement of their own country. At the end we'll be making copies of all the assignments, and you'll be learning about each of the colonies – and being tested on all of them. So you had better put a lot of effort into your paper, or the whole class could fail. Don't let us all down," their teacher warned.

"I want ten thousand words by March 14," she continued. Everyone started complaining at once, and there were moans all round. "That gives you ten weeks. We'll go through the topics to cover together, and you'll have some class time to work on it. We'll also cover some aspects this term, but you'll have to organise study sessions out of school as well. The major test will be a month later, so you'll need to study hard for that one."

The whole class was speechless for once, and Laura looked around with a wide, satisfied smile. "Apparently this subject was a little too easy last term, and the assignment too much fun, so I didn't want to disappoint you again," she grinned.

"Now, you'd better hurry to your next class," she added, as the bell rang and they all started noisily packing up their books.

"Carlie, do you have a moment?" Laura asked softly as people started filing out. Rhiannon stared at her, a question in her eyes, but Carlie shrugged. She had no idea what their teacher wanted. "I'll see you at lunch, yeah?" she said to Rhiannon, and her friend nodded, obviously curious, and left the room.

Standing nervously at her teacher's desk, Carlie began to panic. Surely she couldn't be in trouble already? But Laura smiled, a comforting smile, and she was reminded of the sweet and magical woman she'd taken part in seasonal rituals with. "You haven't done anything wrong love, don't look so scared," she said. "I just wanted to see how you were doing."

Carlie shifted uncomfortably. Maybe it would have been less confronting if she *had* been in trouble. "I'm okay," she said finally, voice grim, as she tried to keep her face blank.

"I just wanted to let you know that if it gets too much, you can tell me, all right? Jake's a history wiz, so that should take some of the pressure off, and I hoped that being assigned Australia would make it a bit easier for you. But if you need a hand I'm happy to help. I can give you some input, and suggest a few shortcuts, okay?" she offered.

A wave of exhaustion washed over Carlie. It was sweet that her teacher was so caring, so concerned, but for once she wished people didn't have to worry about her or make allowances for her. She just wanted to be a normal teenager, worrying about schoolwork and friends and parties and pop music. No special consideration for grief and loss, no cloying fussing over her or asking every five minutes if she was okay. Of course she wasn't okay – how could she be? – but that wasn't what they wanted to hear.

Sighing with impatience, she thanked Laura for her concern, swore she was fine, then hurried out of the room before her tears could betray her. Her next two classes were uneventful, the teachers seemingly unaware of her drama, and her fellow students too engrossed in their own lives to pay her any attention. She was infinitely grateful for the solipsism of youth.

Finally the bell rang and she went to meet Rhiannon in the cafeteria – but one look at her friend's inquisitive face and bright smile and she started wishing she'd gone home for lunch.

"So, what did Laura want?" she asked quickly.

Carlie shrugged. "Just to see if I'm okay, although how she could think she even needed to ask when I'm so obviously turning cartwheels with joy I don't know," she snapped. Then she sighed. "Sorry, I guess I'm just tired and irritable, and depressed, but what am I supposed to say to that? 'Oh yes, I was getting a bit sick of my boyfriend, it was such a relief that he died?'" she asked, sarcasm dripping from each word. "But apparently Jake is a wiz at history, so our assignment shouldn't be too much of a struggle, but if I need some help with it I'm to let her know. Which I do appreciate, but –

"Oh no Rhiannon, what are you thinking? I know that look," she finished glumly.

Her friend tried to look innocent, but failed miserably. "So, Jake huh. Quite the hot guy, no?"

Carlie rolled her eyes. "You seriously think I'm looking at any guy right now?"

"Didn't say it had to be you looking," Rhiannon grinned.

"But what about John? I thought that all was well with your solstice beloved?"

Her friend sighed dramatically. "Carlie, please, neither of us has to date him, I'm just making an observation. Namely, that he's a good-looking guy, and seems really sweet. Can't two friends gossip about the cuteness of a hot new boy at school?"

There was a cough close to them, and they both looked up quickly, Rhiannon slightly panicked that she'd been overheard – and even more so when she saw that it was Jake standing right next to their table, a tray of food in one hand, and a cheeky smile on his face. But she recovered remarkably quickly.

"Jake, hi, welcome to Summer Hill High. I'm Rhiannon, and this is Carlie," she said, as she held out her hand to him by way of introduction. "Although you probably know that since you're partners... well, study partners," she amended quickly. Carlie was amused despite herself. She'd never seen her friend so flustered, and it made her like Jake a little more as a result.

Jake shook Rhiannon's hand, smiled in Carlie's direction, then stood above them awkwardly.

"Oh god, how rude of me!" Rhiannon said at last. "Sit down Jake, if you'd like to. Sorry, where are my manners? You're more than welcome to join us, although if you'd rather hang out with the guys that's fine too, no pressure."

Carlie stared at her friend, perplexed. Why was she so nervous around this guy? Meanwhile, Jake was smiling at them both and taking a seat.

"Thanks Rhiannon, I appreciate it. It sure does suck being the new guy, although I guess you'd know all about that Carlie? Someone said you only started here halfway through last year, is that right?"

She nodded vaguely and stared down at her plate. Sensing her distress, Rhiannon jumped in, and spent the whole lunch break engaging Jake in conversation. Her friend had quickly gotten over her awkwardness with the new guy, and Carlie was content to keep her eyes on her food and let their chatter wash over her. It was kind of soothing in a way, like she was part of the world but didn't need to actually interact within it. Maybe she could just drift through the rest of her life like that.

Panic hit though when she finally noticed that Jake and her friend had gone silent, and she blushed when she looked up and saw that they were both staring at her.

"I'm sorry, did you ask me something?" she stammered.

Rhiannon smiled at her reassuringly. "Jake was just letting you know where he lives, so you can plan your study sessions. The good news is that you're only a few streets away from each other, so yours will be easy to coordinate. My project partner Dave lives a few miles out of town, so I'm not sure how that's going to work, although I'm dreading it already," she sighed.

"But there's plenty of time to worry about that next week, once we know what we have to cover. I'm guessing we'll probably split up the topics and do some research solo, before getting together with our study buddy to write it all up?"

Pausing, she gazed at them both with a wry smile. "I'm sorry, I'm Little Miss Chatterbox today. Feel free to chime in."

But it was the bell that chimed in then, so they got to their feet, stacking up their plates to take over to the kitchen window. Carlie suddenly felt guilty that she'd ignored Jake the whole time, so she tried to summon a smile.

"It was nice to meet you," she offered softly. "I guess I'll see you again in history. I've got English now, so I'd better head off."

He looked down at his schedule. "With Mr Ferguson?"

Reluctantly she nodded. "Great, I'll walk with you," he said.

Rhiannon grinned, as though this made her happy, and was all part of her plan, and Carlie shot daggers at her. "Have fun you two! I've got PE, so I'll see you later," she called out to them, waving to them over her shoulder as she raced off.

Jake fell into step beside Carlie, and her heart clenched with the effort as she tried not to betray her impatience. Although she seemed to have failed at that. "I'm sorry, I don't want to be a bother," Jake said gently. "If you'd rather be alone?"

Carlie looked up at him, stifling a sigh. Her bad mood and lack of enthusiasm was nothing to do with him, she just didn't want to talk to anyone. But then she remembered how out of her depth she'd felt during her first week at a new school in a new country, and her heart went out to him.

"It's okay," she said, forcing a smile and deciding to make an effort. "I've just got a few things on my mind right now. How are you finding it in England? Aside from the weather change obviously – what would it be, around forty degrees in Perth right now, blue skies and sticky summer heat?"

His face lit up, and she almost felt happy herself for a moment, because his joy at life was so obvious, so contagious. Pulling his jacket a little more tightly around himself, he admitted that he was struggling a lot with the cold, and missing his friends – and that it had been quite a shock to discover that school went back in the first week of January here, rather than at the end, as it did in Australia.

Despite herself, Carlie found herself agreeing with the stranger, and actually having a conversation with him, feeling comfortable enough with him to answer his questions, and even ask a few herself. When they got to class he followed her inside and sat down next to her, and she didn't find it too unnerving. Maybe it was because he was Australian, and there was an unspoken sense of camaraderie as a result, a subconscious desire to seek out their own kind, to band together against what at times seemed so strange and foreign.

Their teacher was running late, so they continued to talk, although Carlie closed down abruptly when he asked what her parents did and why they'd moved to the UK.

"My parents died in June. And it turned out that I had a grandmother I'd never heard of, my mum's mum, who lived here," she said quietly, voice distant and cold.

"Oh god Carlie, I'm so sorry, I had no idea," he stuttered, and she smiled at him ruefully.

"It's okay," she replied softly, and realised with surprise that it was. Not that they were dead, obviously, but that people felt able to ask her about them. That she felt able to talk about them. Jake still looked uncomfortable though, so they were both relieved when Mr Ferguson finally walked in and they got to work. And when the bell rang, Carlie packed up her books to leave while Jake stayed where he was for his next class, so they said goodbye and she walked out on her own, relieved to be alone again, but glad that she'd been able to open up a little bit to him. Baby steps and all that...

As she hurried up the stairs, she tried not to think about the vivid blue of his eyes, his surfer-fit body, or the cheeky grin that lit up his whole expression – it was just nice to see a friendly face, she told herself. And she felt comfortable with him because he was from Australia, and because he reminded her of home, and the time when everything in her life had been normal, had been happy.

God, six months ago her life had been just like anyone else's – her parents were alive, she was halfway through her final year of high school, and her plans with her friend Emily were all set. They were going to rent a place together in the city while they went to uni to study law, travel together, meet nice guys, eventually have their own families. She sighed.

In a single moment, her whole life had been turned upside down. Her parents had died, and she'd been forced to leave everyone and everything she knew and move to the other side of the world to live with a stranger. She hadn't known how she would cope with the devastating loss and the emotionally crippling grief, and she was so grateful to her grandmother, and to Rhiannon and Rowan, for helping her survive the deaths of her mum and dad.

But now she was grieving the loss of the love of her life too, blow on top of blow, and she wasn't sure she could survive this new agony. Shaking her head to try to shake off the train of thought, she reminded herself that she had to count her blessings. There were people far worse off than her. And surely she could survive this too. If Rose had taught her anything, it was how much strength a person could have inside. She just had to try to find hers...

Chapter 8

Convening the Coven

In their last class at school the next day, Rhiannon passed a scrap of paper to Carlie as sneakily as she could. Carlie unfolded it carefully and squinted at the words.

"Coven meeting tonight?"

A wave of fear washed over her. Was she ready for that? Gazing out the window, she pondered how she felt about restarting their magical meetings. Their last Tuesday night magic club had been three weeks ago – before the solstice ball, before her running away to spend the night with Rowan, before his tragic death.

Last Tuesday she'd been doing her own ritual, farewelling her beloved, alone until she was interrupted by the woman in red. The Tuesday night before that she'd still been huddled in her room, lying in bed and praying for oblivion from the moment the police officers had delivered their devastating news.

God, had it only been a little over two weeks since that knock on the door? It seemed like a lifetime ago, and in some ways it was. She felt as though she'd been torn apart, and the person she had been before the accident had disappeared, never to be seen again. Yet in other ways it felt as though it was just yesterday that Rowan had been holding her in his arms, whispering his love to her, and begging her to stay with him.

Was she ready to work magic again? Ready to make herself vulnerable to Rhiannon? Creating rituals and casting spells with someone was such an intimate thing, opening your heart to your magical partner, and opening your very being to the universe. Did she want to be so naked, so exposed, to the friend she still felt resentment towards? Could she let herself?

Sighing, she stared at the note again. She knew she couldn't hide in her room for the rest of her life, but did she need more time to huddle up in bed under her mother's quilt, locked away from the world and drowning in sorrow and grief and regret? More time to snuggle up to Luther and feel his body vibrating against her cheek as she held him tight and he purred his joy at all the extra attention?

Her desk rocked a little as Rhiannon kicked its leg, and she looked up guiltily. Her teacher was staring at her expectantly, and she panicked. What had he asked her? Rhiannon cleared her throat as she hissed the answer to her, and Carlie felt a wave of relief as she replied. She was rewarded with a wintry smile from their teacher as he turned to try to catch someone else out.

Realising that had been a lucky save, she vowed to pay more attention to the world around her, not just in her classes, but in everyday life as well. She glanced back down at the note in front of her, and quickly scribbled out "yes", before she could change her mind. It was possible she would live to regret this, but she had to make some attempt to rejoin the living. Furtively she passed the note back to her friend, who smiled when she read the answer, then bent over it to write another question. Trying not to roll her eyes as she unfurled it, Carlie glanced down again.

"Your place or mine?"

Shaking her head and refusing to risk their teacher's wrath by continuing the note passing any longer, she slipped the piece of paper into her pencil case, then turned to her friend and pointed at her. Rhiannon smiled. "Great," she mouthed.

"Ms Stark, is there something you feel you'd like to share with the class?" their teacher thundered.

Blushing, her friend shook her head and said no, and that she was sorry for interrupting. And they avoided catching each other's eye for the rest of the class, in case they started giggling and couldn't stop.

Darkness was closing in and snow had started falling by the time school got out, but Carlie was now immune to its magic. The first time she'd seen snow, a few weeks before Christmas, she'd squealed like a little kid and run around playing in it for hours, building a tiny snowman and laughing with Rose as their cheeks got redder and their hands went numb from the cold. But now it just reminded her of Rowan's car sliding off the road in the snow. Of death and anger and fear and loss.

Sighing, she raced home to get a warmer jacket and the things she'd need for their ritual. Tonight was the dark moon, a time of banishing, of introspection, of going within. She shuddered. To be honest, she wasn't sure she could go much further inward before she started coming out the other side.

Continuing her honesty kick, she admitted to herself that she was nervous about tonight. She hadn't worked magic with anyone else since the solstice eve ceremony at Rowan's retreat, where she'd felt the warmth of his arms around her in the ritual circle, even as he stood across from her and spoke words for all of them, looking at each participant in turn, not just her. That night she'd felt how much he loved her, deep in her bones, in the deepest parts of her heart, and the warmth of it had settled around her, so comforting, so reassuring, so magical.

And yet somehow she'd twisted everything around in her head, had thrown off his love for her, callously, thoughtlessly. Had pushed aside the love she felt for him. That was the night she'd told him how much she loved him – then broken up with him, breaking his heart as well as her own in the process. How could she have done that? It had seemed to make sense at the time – she didn't want to keep lying to Rose about her whereabouts, and she didn't want to lose Rhiannon after her terrible ultimatum.

Oh god, she was still so angry about that. She thought that she'd let it go when her friend had come over the other day and apologised. Wasn't that what you were supposed to do? Forgive, forget, move on? But what if she couldn't?

As she unlocked the door and pushed against it until it banged open, Luther miaowed sharply, and she picked him up and held him in her arms, patting his head until he purred. "Oh Luther, what should I do? Will I always be angry with Rhiannon? It's not really fair to her if I am, but suppressing it and trying to hide it won't be fair to me either," she moaned.

The black cat looked up at her, green eyes filled with love and understanding, then licked her on the cheek, his tongue like sandpaper. "Hey, stop it Mister," she giggled. "That tickles!"

It had done the trick though – she'd stopped obsessing over their friendship and was back in the moment. "Okay, fine, thank you," she said to Luther, affection in her voice, as she raced up to her room and grabbed what she needed. "But I do have to go now. Wish me luck!"

Rushing down the stairs and out the front door, she slung her bag over her shoulder and started to walk through the softly falling snow. As the cold sent its icy fingers through her coat she shivered. Was she ready for this? Did she want to do spellworkings to achieve future goals? Did she want to acknowledge the future, let alone plan for it? And could she open her heart to her friend, which she'd have to do if they were going to work magic, or would her anger make it impossible?

Taking a deep breath, she tried to calm herself down. This was Rhiannon she was thinking about – the girl who had helped her grieve the loss of her parents, who had helped her settle in to a new school, who had helped her find her inner magic, and who had always been so kind and considerate.

Could all of that good be wiped out because she hadn't been supportive on one issue? It didn't say much about her if all she could focus on was the bad, when there had been so much good. And who was she to think everyone had to be perfect all the time, because she certainly hadn't been. She of all people knew about getting a second chance, so she had to do the same for Rhiannon, surely. She deserved that much.

Cheeks red with cold and breath puffing out in little clouds of white, she finally got to her friend's place and knocked on the door. Carefully keeping her mind blank, she smiled as Rhiannon let her in and led her upstairs.

"Dad's at a meeting, but he sends his love. He's been really concerned about you, and about Rose," her friend said.

"Thank him for me, please. He's so kind. I can see why Mum loved him so much," she replied.

"Did she though?" Rhiannon asked, perching on her bed. Carlie stared at her, puzzled, and her friend lowered her gaze. "He's been talking about her recently, and he seems to think that she hated him, and that he failed her in some way."

Carlie looked shocked. "Not at all! Mum cared about him deeply," she insisted. She always felt weird talking to her friend about her dad's long-ago relationship with her mum – it felt disloyal to Rhiannon's own mum Beth. But she couldn't let either of them think that was true. "Mum felt that *she'd* disappointed *him*, treated him badly, and that she no longer deserved his friendship. She felt so bad for hurting him, and even though she realised later that she'd been manipulated into losing touch with him, she was still so angry with herself for letting him go."

Rhiannon stared at her, curious. "How do you know that?"

"It was in Mum's diary, the one Sandy sent me. She regretted hurting Gran and your dad more than anything – she said that he'd been so kind and supportive to her, so sweet and caring, but she had been too stupid to see it. Although she did mention that she hoped he would find much-deserved happiness with a lovely girl called Beth," Carlie said, smiling as she referred to Rhiannon's mum.

"Also, I know it myself, from what I've experienced and what I've seen," she continued. "Mike has been so wonderful to Gran all these years, and he's helped me too. It was your dad who finally convinced me to get up and eat something on Boxing Day, to stop worrying Gran, so please let him know that. And let him know how much Mum, Gran and I *all* appreciate him. And I understand that it's hard for you to hear him talking about my mum, but I think it's just because he's such a kind-hearted man, and cares about everybody."

"I know, and it doesn't bother me any more, I promise," Rhiannon said, voice soft. "I'm just sorry that Dad has lost both of his great loves, and we've both lost our mums. It's not the kind of kindred spirit thing I wanted to share with you."

Carlie smiled wistfully. "It doesn't seem fair, that's for sure." Gazing around the room, she decided it was time to change the subject. The scent of sandalwood was reassuring, and the candlelight made it feel so warm and inviting. Inhaling deeply, she tried to centre herself and her thoughts, throw off the sadness that always threatened when she thought of her parents.

"Do you want to do a ritual tonight, or would you rather we continue our study, or just talk?" Rhiannon asked. "It's the dark moon, so, I don't know, is that too intense?"

Carlie shrugged, still not sure herself. "I guess I've gotta get back on the horse some time, right?" she said, then groaned at the cliche.

Her friend nodded. "Was Yule the last working you did?" she asked cautiously, as she slipped off her shoes and sank down into one of the big purple pillows in the centre of the room.

Tears threatened as Carlie did the same, but she steeled herself against them and nodded. "Yep, the last group ritual I did was with Rowan that night. And it was so beautiful. So powerful and magical. Oh, and…" she began, then trailed off. She had a sudden memory of the woman in red facing her across her altar, during the ceremony she'd done down on the banks of the stream in her and Rowan's special place, but she wasn't ready to talk about that yet.

"That was the night I met Jasmine too," she offered instead, and was surprised when Rhiannon looked confused. "Oh, you don't know any of that yet do you? Jasmine was at Rowan's retreat. I ended up sitting with her at dinner, and she looked like she'd seen a ghost when she first looked up at me. When she told me her name, I realised why – I'd been reading Mum's journal on the way there, and she'd mentioned a woman named Jasmine who'd tried to help her get away from Andre, despite being in his circle and risking his wrath by befriending her," she explained, shuddering as she remembered all that her mum had been through.

Rhiannon looked rapt, and eager to know more, so in the end the two girls didn't perform a ritual or cast a spell, they just talked. Carlie shared everything Jasmine had told her about her mum and the once-loving shaman who'd treated her so badly. Rhiannon was shocked by the awful violence and abuse, both physical and mental, that Violet had endured in that relationship, and she cried when Carlie revealed that Andre had smashed her mum into a glass table, as Rhi's psychic had seen – that it had been a past event of what had already happened to her mum, not a future vision of something Rowan was going to do to her, as her friend had believed.

"Oh god, Dad would just die if he knew. He suspected that that man had been cruel, but I can't believe just how terrible it was," Rhiannon said, voice thick with tears.

Carlie nodded grimly. That hadn't even been the worst thing he'd done, but she couldn't bring herself to reveal that he'd also held her mother down and raped her. "She thought he was going to kill her," she said instead. "She'd given up, and begun to pray that he would just get it over with, but Dad found her one day, battered and bleeding, and helped her escape." Then she smiled. "Mum really did get her happy ever after, eventually."

The door downstairs banged closed, and Carlie jumped. "It's just Dad," Rhiannon said softly. They looked over at the clock on the bedside table, and were surprised to see that it was already 10pm.

"Oh god, I'm so sorry," Carlie said. "I've taken up the whole evening! But I do actually feel a little better for having shared it all with you, so thank you," she added. "I guess I should get home though – I still have a fair bit of homework to do for the morning, and I imagine you do too."

Rhiannon rolled her eyes. "Yeah, a little bit. But thanks for tonight, it's been really nice. I've missed you."

Carlie gave her friend a hug, ran down the stairs, then lowered her head and forced her way home through the still-falling snow. She was glad they'd ended up just talking all night, because she felt closer to Rhiannon again after sharing so much with her. Although she did wonder why she hadn't felt ready to tell her about the red-robed woman yet. Still, there was all the time in the world for that...

Chapter 9

A Faerytale Curse

The next few days at school passed quickly. Laura had them sit next to their study partners in history, so Jake ended up hanging out with Carlie and Rhiannon a lot, eating lunch with them each day, and walking with them to class when their schedules coincided. And she wasn't sure why, but for some reason Carlie didn't mind. Jake was a lovely guy, unfailingly polite and sensitive to her moods, and it was nice to hear an Aussie voice, and have him understand the obscure pop culture references and jokes she made, which often flew over other people's heads.

It surprised her though, that she was happy to talk to him so much after so recently insisting that she just wanted to be left alone. Maybe it was because he'd be going back to Australia soon, so there was no pressure for a lengthy or lasting friendship, which meant she didn't need to censor herself when she spoke.

Carlie was also beginning to suspect that her friend liked him, and that the feeling was mutual, which made her happy as well as less guarded in what she said to him. It was a relief that he wasn't interested in her, because she wanted nothing to do with relationships. She kept her suspicions to herself though. Rhiannon was still dating John, and she still wanted to avoid any conversations even remotely related to romance.

Her friendship with Rhiannon was also getting back to normal, which she was glad of. She didn't have the energy to be resentful, and she really wanted to be a better person, and be able to forgive her and move on. But that was tested when she met up with a visibly nervous Rhiannon at lunchtime on Friday.

"Do you mind if I spend the day with John tomorrow?" she asked, frowning in apprehension. "We could do something together on Sunday though," she added quickly.

Carlie shrugged. "That's fine," she replied. "Rose wanted me to help in the shop anyway, so it's all good. And you don't have to ask my permission – I don't expect you to be miserable and not see your boyfriend just because I can't," she added.

Her friend looked unconvinced. "But if you'd rather we hang out tomorrow, I can cancel my plans with John," she offered. "Honestly, I want to be there for you when you need me."

Carlie struggled to dampen her annoyance. "I know that. And it's fine, really, I'm not just being a martyr," she sighed. "But don't use me as an excuse, if you'd rather be here this weekend, seeing someone closer to home," she added. Rhiannon looked puzzled, but Jake came over to join them then, and Carlie changed the subject to include him.

The next morning, Carlie waited until she knew Rhiannon would be on the bus to Smithfield, then made her way over to her house. Nervously she climbed the front steps and knocked, and before she could change her mind and flee, Mike opened the door, smiling when he saw who it was.

"Carlie, hi. I'm so sorry, but Rhi's not here," he said gently.

She smiled. "I know, she's spending the day with John. I came to see you," she explained.

Looking puzzled, Mike ushered her inside out of the cold and through to the kitchen. "Is everything okay?" he asked, voice betraying his concern. He gestured to a stool at the kitchen bench, and turned to put the kettle on.

Carlie smiled. "Yes, everything's fine, or as fine as could be expected. It's just, well, I wanted to show you something."

She broke off, suddenly anxious, as she reached into her bag and felt for her mum's diary. Would it upset him to see it? Would it be better for both of them if she left it alone, minded her own business? She gazed at him, and almost chickened out, but then she remembered what her friend had said the other night. He didn't deserve to keep torturing himself over an imagined slight.

"Rhiannon mentioned that you thought Mum had been angry at you, or disappointed. But she wasn't," Carlie finally said, and she saw hope flare in Mike's eyes before it died away, and he reached into the cupboard for tea and mugs. Hesitating for a moment, she gathered her thoughts, then dove back in.

"The biggest regret of her life was that she'd let you and Gran down, and pushed you away. She really missed you. And she considered you one of her dearest friends, even years after she left home – she called you the truest friend anyone could ever have."

Mike turned back to her, hands on the kitchen bench to hold himself up. "Oh Carlie, that's so sweet of you to say, but you can't know that. You'd never even heard of me until you got here. I've always regretted how things ended with Violet, regretted not doing more to help her. She pushed me away, yes, and that hurt, but I should have tried harder," he sighed.

"I do know," she said firmly, and pulled the diary out of her bag. "Mum wrote about you and her, and how terrible she felt at the way she'd treated you. She admitted that she'd thrown away your friendship, and that she should have trusted you instead of him. And she paid for that decision," Carlie added, voice faltering a little. "It ended very badly with Andre, let's just say that. It was more awful than anyone could imagine. But as bad as it was for her, she was just really sad that she'd let you down."

Mike stared at her, eyes assessing, trying to work out if she was telling the truth. The whistling of the kettle halted his examination, and he turned away for a moment. Dazed, he poured boiling water into the cups then handed one to her, and she whispered her thanks, unwilling to point out that he'd forgotten the tea, milk and sugar, and waiting instead to see what he'd say next.

"You know, I went to see him once," he finally admitted. "Andre. To try to reason with him, convince him to leave her alone. But he just laughed in my face and threatened me. Said he'd already started turning her against me, so it would be very simple to ensure I never saw her again…" He trailed off, gazing with unseeing eyes into the distance, before finally noticing her pale, stricken face. "What's wrong Carlie?" he demanded.

"I dreamed that," she blurted out. "Months ago. You were at his place, and argued with him, and I heard him threatening you. Then Mum arrived, and asked what you were doing there. The mean guy said you just wanted to join his next tarot class, then she went inside, and he turned back to you and laughed."

Mike's face was as pale as Carlie's. "That's exactly what happened," he whispered, fear in his voice.

Carlie had frozen, hand clutching the bench top for support. "So that was him? That was Andre? He did look just like Rowan?"

Mike glanced up at her, seeing her distress. "Yes," he said, sighing. "But they weren't alike, not at all. I know that."

Smiling, she touched his hand. This wasn't about her. But it was freaking her out that she'd had the dream about her mother aged seventeen, Mike and the strange man who looked like Rowan long before she'd met Rowan, and had only discovered that her boyfriend was the son of the man who'd tortured her mum the night before he died. She tried to shake it off though. She had to be strong for Mike.

"And then he cursed you," she choked out.

Mike gasped, shocked, then reluctantly nodded. "He told me that if I got in his way, he'd make sure every woman I ever loved would die by her fortieth birthday," he shuddered.

"But he couldn't have that kind of power, surely," Carlie said, alarmed. "No one could. Curses are from faerytales!"

"Beth died on her fortieth birthday. I obsessed over it for weeks, and it still terrifies me – does it mean Rhiannon will die at forty too? That it will all be my fault?" Then his head snapped up. "Oh god Carlie, when did your mum die?"

She stared down at the diary on the bench, unable to meet his eyes. "The accident was the night before her fortieth birthday, and she died the next morning in the hospital. But that wasn't your fault Mike, it was on the other side of the world for a start. And if anyone should be blamed, it's me. I was driving the car," she choked out.

Mike looked aghast. "Carlie, no. It wasn't your fault!"

She smiled ruefully. "I know. A drunk driver went through a red light and hit us, so technically it wasn't my fault. Gran is very insistent about that. But Andre has been dead for more than a decade, and he didn't know where Mum was, and there's no way he knew the driver. Besides, you didn't come between them, he did that himself with the awful way he treated her."

Tears welled in her eyes, and Mike felt helpless all over again. He stared at the diary on the table as he took a sip of the hot water in his cup, not even registering that there was no tea in it. His face was conflicted – half of him wanted to read the book, and half of him wanted to burn it and all the awful things that must be in it.

"Was it really so bad?" he asked, voice pleading for it not to be true. "Did she get over it, do you think? I mean, was she happy in the end?" His hands shook as he tried to lift the mug again.

"It was beyond awful," Carlie said at last, finding no reason to lie. "I don't know how she survived it – she's the bravest person I'll ever know, and I didn't even realise until I'd lost her." She saw that Mike was about to break down again.

"But she was happy," she added quickly. "And it was because of you that she eventually remembered she didn't deserve to be treated that way, and because of Dad that she healed from it. I had no idea how amazing he was either," she sighed. "But I know Mum felt truly blessed because she'd been loved by two extraordinary men."

Mike started to protest, but she cut him off. "She always loved you, don't you see? She still thought of you as her best friend, and she was so devastated that she'd hurt you, that she hadn't trusted you. She still longed to see you."

Mike was shaking his head, but she took his hand again, trying to reinforce her point, while her other hand rested on the diary. "I don't think it will help you to read all of it, it will tear you apart, but there are some entries I know she would want you to see, and a postcard she wrote to you but never sent," she explained, pulling out the pages she'd photocopied in the school library and handing them to him.

Reverently he placed them on the bench between them, and a look of wonder crossed his face as he traced over the letters. "I always loved her handwriting," he said, but Carlie saw he was talking to himself now, not her. He'd disappeared into a fog of memories and regrets.

Smiling, she stood up, carefully placed the diary back in her bag, then took her cup to the sink and poured the water down the drain.

"I'll see you later," she whispered to Mike as she walked past him, but he barely acknowledged her presence, so wrapped up in the past had he become. Letting herself out the front door, she wandered back towards the cottage, towards home.

It was still chilly, but she must have been getting used to it, because she barely noticed. Her skin started prickling though when she stepped into an apple-scented mist that was wreathing itself around the base of the tor. Feeling something soft brush against her ankles, she reached down, an automatic reflex because Luther was usually weaving around her feet wanting a pat.

Then her breath caught, and she had a moment of panic as her focus shifted, and she was suddenly disorientated from the fog that seemed to be clouding her brain as well as her vision. A hand touched her arm just as she heard her name being called, and she screamed. Laughter echoed around her, before the red-clad woman materialised in front of her.

"God!" Carlie exclaimed, heart beating wildly from fright.

The figure smiled. "Hardly! But I suppose I could be described as an aspect of the goddess," she teased, head tilted as she gazed into Carlie's eyes, and into her very soul.

"Why do you have to sneak up on people?" she snapped. Her emotions were drowning her, the image of Mike's heartbroken then hopeful face fresh in her mind, and she had no patience for the infuriating apparition, who spoke in riddles about things she had no idea about.

The woman in red laughed. "Oh Carlie, beloved, it is not like I haunt this town, making conversation with everyone who passes me in the street. You are the only person that I communicate with in this place, although I have had some wonderful conversations with your grandmother over the years."

"So couldn't you have given her some comfort then?" Carlie demanded. "Why didn't you tell her that her daughter was okay, spare her some of the torture she's lived with her whole life?"

The red-clad woman gazed at her, expression stern again. "Oh Carlie, I do not know what you think I am –"

"I have no idea!" she shouted, frustration colouring her voice and upping the volume. "Half the time I think you're a symptom of my insanity, a delusion I'm creating to give myself comfort – not that you're especially great at that, by the way," she snarled. The laughter echoed around her again.

"Rose and Rhiannon seem to think you are all spirits of the land, figures from another dimension who can come through to our world to share your wisdom with us," she sighed.

"Really? But you have not told Rhiannon about me yet," the woman said, reproach in her tone.

Carlie stared at her, horrified that this... being... knew everything she said and who she said it to. That was totally creepy, but she'd have to think about that later. She needed all her wits about her to make it through this conversation.

"Well, she's met Brauna and Brianna, and she thinks they're real," she retorted. "To be honest, I haven't been sure of what to tell her about you. I don't even know your name."

"My name is Aideen," the woman said calmly.

"Fine, great, lovely to meet you," Carlie snapped. "If you must know, Rhi and I haven't been telling each other everything of late anyway," she finally admitted. "I haven't told her about you because I'm not ready to tell her about my ritual to farewell Rowan. I want to keep that to myself for a while longer."

Aideen's face softened. "Oh Carlie, you are allowed to keep some things close to your heart. And I understand that you are struggling to trust her, but she is remorseful about what happened, and feels terrible that she let you down. Try to cut her some slack. You are no angel yourself."

Carlie glared at the woman, then started laughing. What was the point of being angry at a sprite? A wisp? Someone who may or may not even exist.

And what she'd said was true. She wasn't perfect, but she'd been very open about that to everyone – family, friends *and* phantoms.

"Will I ever get past it?" she asked at last, voice thick with longing. "I want to forgive and forget, and usually I think I have, but then Rhiannon will say one thing the wrong way, and all my resentment will come flooding back. And although she apologises, and I do know that she's genuinely sorry, deep down she still doesn't approve of Rowan. And she thinks I should be over him already and off with some new guy," she huffed.

The woman in red smiled. "Carlie, you cannot expect her to think the way you do or change her fundamental belief system just because you want her to. Everyone is entitled to their own opinions, their own morals and acceptance of things. The only thing you can expect is for her to support you, even if she does not personally agree with what you are doing. You cannot control her actions, just your reaction to them. She will always think Rowan was too old for you, lots of people will, and that is fine – it only matters how you feel about it. But despite her feeling that way, she is still there for you now."

"I know that," Carlie sighed. "Deep down I know that, but how do I stop resenting her? I can't just turn my emotions on and off, yet she and Rose are all I have, so I need to find a way to deal with it somehow. And I do care about her, so I don't want my hurt to come between us and poison our friendship."

"Oh Carlie, I am so proud of you. You have learned so much in the last six months," Aideen said, beaming at her. Puzzled, Carlie lifted her eyebrows in question, and the woman in red continued. "You are accepting your part in this, and trying to meet her halfway. You are acknowledging that you need to do something to help defuse the situation, that it is not all up to Rhiannon."

Carlie smiled. The praise was very welcome. It was nice to be credited for once, to be considered sensible, since she always felt that Rose and Rhiannon were so much wiser than her. It was a tough act to follow, having a priestess for a grandmother.

Aideen touched her cheek, gently this time. And had the grace to blush slightly when Carlie flinched, recalling the night she'd slapped her across the face. "You have your own wisdom Carlie, and you have learned a huge amount in a short time. You may have only discovered magic in the last six months, but Rhiannon sees herself as your equal in your workings, not as your teacher. You have hard-won knowledge that few people your age, or indeed any age, possess, gained through your losses as well as from the time you have spent with both Rowan and your grandmother, in addition to your own seeking of answers."

Carlie nodded uncertainly. She would happily give back any knowledge she'd gained to have her parents back, to have Rowan back, but she knew it didn't work like that.

The figure gave her a sad smile. "I am sorry I cannot help you with that Carlie, truly I am. But I have something for you," she continued, reaching within her long robes.

"This is for Rhiannon," she said, handing her a red-velvet-wrapped parcel of what felt like metal rods. "And this cauldron is for you, because you have been dancing in the fire, and have survived the burning, and now have the strength to wield its power."

Carlie was speechless, staring at the old-fashioned wrought iron pot in her hand. It was beautiful, and she could sense deep magic in it, but she knew the woman had got it wrong. She wasn't the strong one, the one who could weave magic and change fate. That was Rose. And Rhiannon. And it had been Rowan, and her mother. Pretty much everyone she knew, just not her.

Slowly she gazed back up, needing to confront the Otherworldly figure, deny her words, but there was no one there. She was standing alone at the bottom of the tor, and the mists were starting to clear. Sighing, she headed home, heart full of memories of Mike's scared face, which turned into images of Rowan's as he'd whispered to her that he loved her and believed in her. If only she could do the same.

Chapter 10

No Place Like Home

On Monday Rhiannon seemed really happy, after spending the weekend with John, and she talked about him and every moment they'd been together non-stop. At lunchtime she was a lot less flirty with Jake, although he didn't seem to have noticed she was behaving any differently towards him, or that she'd been interested in him in the first place. And Carlie was relieved to discover that she was glad for her friend, that things were going so well for her with her boyfriend. A part of her had worried that she'd be annoyed, or jealous even, that Rhi got to spend time with the guy she was dating while she was alone, while her beloved was dead, so she felt good about herself that she was nothing but happy for her.

On Tuesday Rhiannon reluctantly told Carlie she couldn't meet her that night for their magical working. Her little brother had a school play on, and their dad would be working late, so she needed to go along and support him. "I'm so sorry Carlie, I feel terrible, especially after I was with John all weekend," she said. "I'm not trying to ditch you, I promise!"

Carlie laughed. "Don't be silly, I don't think that! I understand. And it's awesome that you can be there for Brodie. Please tell him to break a leg from me," she replied. And was surprised that she felt relief, not disappointment, that they wouldn't be convening their coven that night. For a moment she wondered if she should be worried about that, then dismissed her fears – she probably just needed a bit more time before she could fully trust Rhiannon again, and let herself open up to her magically. Or maybe this was just about her? Maybe she needed more time before she could open herself up to anyone, or any thing, without being swamped in the darkness of her loss.

Smiling at her friend, she told her, truthfully, that it was a good opportunity for her to do some individual work, to try to make sense of her muddled feelings, and consult Rose's books for inspiration on how to heal her grief and move forward.

Rhiannon touched her hand, eyes wide with compassion. "You'll get there," she promised. "Time really does help, even though we don't believe it while the pain is still fresh."

Carlie bit down her angry retort. Her friend was just trying to offer comfort, and she'd suffered a terrible loss as well. She wasn't the first person – and would hardly be the last – to grieve a tragic death.

The following Tuesday, the girls both had to organise last-minute study sessions with their research partners for history, after Laura sprang on the class that they'd be discussing where they were up to with their papers the following morning. The panic in the room was palpable, as it was revealed that no one had actually started their home study sessions yet.

So that afternoon Rhiannon got the bus home with Dave so they could work on their project, and Carlie stood on the doorstep at Jake's place, palms sweaty and butterflies in her stomach. Impatiently stamping her frozen feet, she wondered why she was nervous. It was just Jake. He was her friend, so there was nothing to be afraid of. Still, they'd never really been alone together – Rhiannon was always with them at lunch, or they were in a classroom full of fellow students.

Before she could wonder any further, Jake opened the door and invited her in. Following him through to the kitchen, she felt a little less anxious when she saw that his grandfather's house was much like Rose's cottage, small and cosy, with a warm kitchen towards the back and a small table in a similarly situated breakfast nook. While Jake put the kettle on and made them tea, Carlie sat down at the table and pulled her books out.

They worked well together – Carlie had done a lot of background research, now that she didn't have Rowan to spend her afternoons with, and Jake had too. And it actually felt nice to be hanging out – they talked a bit when they paused to make more tea, reminiscing about the long hot summers of Australia, and Carlie found herself laughing far more than she'd expected to, appreciating his Aussie humour and cheeriness.

As they finished their third cup of tea, Jake paused halfway through telling a joke and stared at her, face serious. "What's wrong?" she asked, assuming she'd done something to offend him.

He smiled, that sweet smile that made her tummy flip. "Nothing, it's all good," he replied quickly, stoically, but his voice was shaking a little. "I just, um... well, I was wondering if you'd like to go for coffee sometime, or maybe see a movie or something? Pop said I could take his car."

He looked so nervous, so earnest, that Carlie felt bad that she had to say no. But she just couldn't. She was in no fit state to be dating, and he was far too lovely for her to lead him on. Reluctantly she shook her head. "I'm sorry Jake, I can't. It's not you, you're a sweetheart, but I just... I can't," she whispered, staring at the floor, and feeling miserable for hurting him.

"What about just as friends then? You know, fellow Aussies, a long way from home, keeping each other company and reminding each other how to speak, what words to use..." he trailed off.

"I'm not going back to Australia. This *is* my home," Carlie said softly, wonderingly. And as the words came out, she felt the truth of her statement, and was as surprised as Jake at the sentiment. She thought she'd pictured herself going back to Sydney in a year or two, once she'd finished school and qualified for uni, but it sounded like that plan had gone out the window, some time between landing here six months ago, a stranger in a strange land, and today, a sad but strangely content student who had come to love her grandmother deeply. How unexpected.

"Are you okay Carlie?" he asked, voice gentle, and she looked up at him and saw the concern in his eyes, the softness of his mouth as it turned down in compassion, the kindness of his expression.

"What do you mean?" she stuttered, as she felt her body preparing to flee. But was running the way to handle anything?

"You have the saddest eyes I've ever seen," Jake blurted out, then blushed. "I'm sorry, I shouldn't have said that."

She stared across at him. "You think it's weird that I feel sad?" she responded, genuinely curious about what he thought.

"I'm not sure what's going on in your life – I know your parents died, and of course that would make you grieve deeply. But when I asked Rhiannon why you were always so sad, she said to ask you myself, that it was your story to tell."

Carlie raised her eyebrows, pondering. Did Rhiannon just mean she should tell him about Rowan herself, or was she alluding to the fact that she had hurt Carlie so deeply, and that might be what was upsetting her? Or did she just think that the more she said out loud that Rowan was dead, the more she told people, the more quickly she'd face up to it and move on?

"My boyfriend died on the morning of the winter solstice," she said finally, deathly calm. "Just before Christmas. He was coming to see me, and his car went off the road in the snow. So yes, I'm pretty sad, and I imagine I will be for quite some time."

Shock flashed across Jake's face, then he stood up, moved around the table and drew her into his arms, holding her tight.

"I'm so sorry," he whispered, voice low and gentle. "Of course you have every reason to be sad. My god, after everything you've been through, that seems like the cruellest blow."

Time seemed suspended as they stood there for several long moments, Carlie in the warm cocoon of his arms, not thinking, barely breathing, just grateful for the comfort and strength she felt pouring into her. For a split second when he'd embraced her she'd frozen, her first instinct to slap his face and run out the door, but his holding her didn't feel sleazy at all, it just felt warm and supportive and like a friend should.

Gently he let her go. "Friends?" he asked, and she nodded slowly, shy all of a sudden, but touched that he'd had the courage to ask her about it, and the understanding to not press her on anything more than friendship. He really was a great guy, she thought ruefully. It was a shame she wasn't interested – he'd make someone a wonderful boyfriend.

"I don't have much experience with loss myself, but if you ever want to talk, or if I can ever do anything for you, let me know, okay?" he implored her, and she nodded and thanked him profusely.

The sound of keys rattling in the front door broke the emotion of the moment. "I should go…" Carlie whispered, and was confused when she felt relief warring with disappointment in her mind. But before she could examine her response, Jake shook his head.

"It's just Pop, and he'd love to meet you. He's Australian too," he grinned, then turned and walked out to the front door to help his grandfather in with the grocery bags.

"Pop, this is my friend Carlie, the Aussie girl from school. Carlie, this is Richard Mattherson."

Carlie held out her hand. "Hello Mr Mattherson," she smiled.

He shook his head and pulled her in for a hug. "Richard, please. Mr Mattherson makes me feel so old, although I guess to you two I am," he said, eyes twinkling. "Now, have you got the kettle on yet Jake?" he asked, turning back to his grandson, and sighing theatrically when Jake shook his head.

"Youngsters these days, I don't know," he chuckled. "Come on, it's time for tea, and I've got some lemon cake to share – Iris insisted on baking me one because I've been fixing her gutters and clearing out her back shed."

Jake smiled at Carlie as he turned to fill the kettle. "Pop lost his wife eighteen months ago, and he's got more women looking after him than he can handle. He's always done odd jobs for the women of his church – taken them grocery shopping each week, kept their cottages in working order, sorted out their gardens – all of which he'd happily do for nothing, but they all insist on baking him dinners and leaving them on the front porch, or dropping off cakes or jams or pickles or freshly baked bread. I've never eaten so well in my life – these women can really cook!" he said, then lowered his voice conspiratorially. "I think they're trying to win him over through his stomach. There are a few widows with their eye on Pop."

"I heard that Jakey," his grandfather said, mock stern, but then he laughed. "They're all lovely women, but I don't think any of them want to be tied down, so there's no need to worry. It will still just be you and me here."

Jake clasped his grandpa on the shoulder as he walked over to the pantry to get the tea, and Carlie's heart lifted to see the obvious affection between them. He motioned for her to take a seat again, while Richard sliced up the cake and handed her a piece.

"Thank you," she said, and politely took a bite. "Oh my god, this is so good! I might need to meet this Iris, and see if I can steal the recipe."

Richard grinned. "She keeps them pretty close to her chest, but I'll see what I can do. Do you like cooking?" he asked her, as he brought the milk jug, sugar pot and some delicate cups and saucers over and sat down with her at the table.

"I never used to, but since I've been living with my grandma I've been helping her out, making dinner some nights, but also baking desserts and other treats for our rituals and things…" Her voice faltered, and she suddenly worried that this man might not approve of Rose and her seasonal ceremonies. If he was a serious churchgoer, he might frown on energy healing and crystals and honouring the goddess and the forces of nature.

But he laughed as he cut her another slice of the lemon cake. "Don't you worry, no one in this village has any problem with Rose Tyler. Marcy was a churchgoer, but she told me once that she and her sister had been to a few of Rose's full moon ceremonies when they were younger. And as far as I've heard, I don't think there'd be a single person in this village that Rose hasn't brought healing or comfort to in some way, be it with her herbal remedies or her midwifery skills, or raising money for someone in need."

Carlie was grateful. That description certainly gelled with the impression she'd formed of her grandma, and she was relieved that religion hadn't caused any issues for Rose, with Richard and Marcy at least, as she'd discovered it sometimes could.

"She's certainly had her hands full dealing with me for the last six months," she admitted, and there was admiration in her voice. "And it was hard for her, because my mum – her daughter – died just before I came here. Gran had always hoped that one day she would return home, or get in touch with her at least, but unfortunately I was the bearer of bad news." Her eyes misted with tears, but she kept talking.

"And I feel sorry for her, because I was not a nice person in those first few weeks. I was so angry, so nasty, so consumed with hate and suspicion. Rose is an amazing woman to have put up with me."

Jake smiled at her, and reached over and squeezed her hand. "I can't imagine you being anything like that," he said, and she laughed.

"I was, believe me. Rhiannon helped too. She told me I was allowed to lash out at people for the first few weeks of grieving, but then I had to get over myself and stop being so selfish."

"Sounds like a sensible girl to me," Richard said, and Carlie nodded. He'd just lost his beloved wife, but could still appreciate Rhi's blunt survival comments. Yeah, her friend was pretty smart.

The three of them talked for a while, Carlie enjoying being amongst Australian voices again, and feeling relaxed and at home. But when Jake stood up and said he had to start cooking dinner, Carlie finally looked at the clock and realised she'd better get back to her grandma's to start the food prep too.

"You're welcome to stay and eat with us," Richard said, voice threaded with hope, but Carlie thanked him as she shook her head – she had to get back to Rose. She had a new appreciation for caregiver grandparents, and wanted to do her bit.

"Thank you so much for the tea, and the cake, and for making me feel so welcome. It's really nice to hear Aussie voices – it's funny how comfortable it makes me feel. But I'll see you tomorrow Jake, and Mr – I mean Richard, thank you, and I'm sure I'll see you soon, with this crazy assignment we have!"

Jake led her out to the front door and offered to walk her home, but she said she was fine, and that he'd better get back to the kitchen and get cooking. They laughed at that, then he gave her a quick hug goodbye, and Carlie headed off, smiling in delight at the few soft snowflakes that were falling, all lit up by the golden almost-full moon. As much as she'd loved talking to those sweet Australian guys, she felt amazingly at peace with her surprising realisation that England was now her home. She'd experienced tragedy here, but also so much love, and she felt as though she was more herself here than she'd ever been.

Maybe that was what loss did, strip away the things that weren't important and make you really look within and work out what was meaningful to you. For her, it was her grandmother, her last remaining family member, and her friends. Despite her current issues with her, that meant Rhiannon, her magical partner and ally in grief, and Emily, her childhood bestie who she was determined to stay in touch with even though they were now so far apart geographically as well as emotionally.

And maybe it would also include Jake, a kind, thoughtful boy who seemed to care about her. She smiled too as she realised how much she'd come to appreciate and value Rose, and how much she already liked Richard. There was wisdom in age, now that she had the patience and the opportunity to experience it.

Then she giggled. She couldn't forget the strange women she'd met in the mists either. She still wasn't entirely sure that they weren't just figments of her imagination, or a trick of the light, or something else equally bizarre, but whatever they were, they'd offered comfort when she was distressed, and a metaphorical kick in the butt when she'd needed to stop obsessing over her own misery and realise that other people were suffering too.

She was still puzzling over the Otherworldly beings when she walked up the garden path of their cottage, calling out to Rose that she was home as she wandered down the hallway and out to the kitchen. The whole house smelled delicious.

"Hi Sweetheart! The vegetable and tofu lasagne will be ready in about fifteen minutes, and the salad is almost done," her grandma said as she whirled around the kitchen, chopping up fresh herbs from the garden, grating cheese, dancing over to the fridge for another cucumber. "How was school? And I got your note, thank you. How did your study session go?"

At Carlie's silence she glanced up. "Is everything okay?" Rose asked, a touch of panic crossing her face.

But her granddaughter smiled. "Yes, it's all good. Jake and I got a lot of work done, then we had a cup of tea with his grandfather, who he's staying with while his parents are working in Africa. And we had the yummiest lemon cake – although I'll still eat dinner, I promise!" she added quickly.

Rose laughed. "There's nothing wrong with the occasional piece of cake, and you more than burn it off with all your tor climbs. I didn't know Jake was staying with his grandfather though. I'm trying to figure out who it could be – I thought I knew everyone here."

Smiling, Carlie raised her eyebrows and looked questioningly at Rose. "Guess you don't know all the eligible bachelors in town after all," she teased. "But he hasn't been here for that long. His name is Richard Mattherson, and he's from Perth originally, in Western Australia, and although he met and married Marcy in London, and lived there for a long time, they went back to Perth years ago to be close to their son, Jake's dad, and look after Jake when his parents had to travel for work. But when Marcy got sick they moved back here so she could be close to her sister and their other kids, and they bought a little cottage at the bottom of the tor," she explained.

"Marcy and her sister used to stay in Summer Hill when they were teenagers, and she and Richard spent their honeymoon here, so it meant a lot to both of them. And when Marcy died eighteen months ago, Richard couldn't bear to leave, because he feels like her spirit is still here – and her ashes are scattered on the tor and in his garden, so physically she's here too. And their daughter lives in London with her kids, and their other son is in Wales, so he wants to stay close to them, especially as Jake's parents are off working in Africa – there's nothing for him in Australia now, even though he was born there."

Rose stared at her. "And you relate to that somehow?" she asked, trying to interpret her granddaughter's tone.

Carlie laughed self-consciously. "Wow, you're good Gran. I hadn't even made that connection, but yes, I guess I do, because today I was actually thinking that this is my home now. That there's nothing holding me to Sydney, no reason to go back." She blushed a little, and her voice softened. "Despite everything that's happened here, it's started to feel like home."

Panic constricted her heart as she suddenly wondered if Rose would think that was a good thing or a bad thing, and whether she actually did have a long-term home here.

"Oh Sweetheart, of course it's a good thing! And of course you have a home here, for as long as you want it," her grandmother said, coming over and drawing her into a hug, and Carlie relaxed into her arms, feeling a weight lift from her shoulders, and a contentment settle in her heart. She felt so safe here, so secure, so at home – just the way she'd felt in Jake's arms that afternoon.

The thought shocked her, and she untangled herself from Rose and strode across the room, getting the plates and cutlery out for dinner, body moving as her panicked mind tried to compute that stray thought. How could two people feel like home? And how could a boy she barely knew make her feel so safe? Finally though she laughed at herself. How silly she was. Something about Jake or his grandfather must have reminded her of her dad. Maybe their Australian accents, or a phrase or expression they'd used that her dad had used too.

Quickly changing the subject, she asked Rose how the healing centre had been that day, and when they'd start preparing for Imbolc, and every time the thought of being in Jake's arms flitted into her mind, she shook it off and asked another question about what she needed to do for the ritual.

Chapter 11

Twisting the Knife

"So, how was your night with Jake?" Rhiannon asked Carlie, wiggling her eyebrows suggestively, when they finally caught up in their lunch break the next day.

A flash of annoyance swept over Carlie, and she stared at her friend in confusion. "What do you mean?" she asked. "We did some research, I had a cup of tea with his grandad, then I walked home and had dinner with Rose." She pushed the thought of being in Jake's arms out of her head. That had just been a strange mix-up of memories and wishful thinking, of missing her dad and the times they'd spent together.

"But he's nice, isn't he?" Rhiannon pressed, her tone teasing.

Carlie shrugged. "I guess so, why?"

"And he's cute, right?"

Impatience stabbed at Carlie. "Do you want me to ask him out for you?" she asked, barely containing her frustration.

"Don't be daft, I've got John," Rhiannon laughed. "I was thinking of you. Maybe the four of us could double date or something? He does seem to really like you, like, *like* like you. And you're both Aussies, so you have a lot in common."

"Seriously Rhi?" she snapped, and she was as sad as she was upset with her friend at her line of questioning. She'd thought that she and

Rhiannon were beginning to understand each other again, to move past their little bust-up and be supportive of one another like they were before.

"The love of my life just died, or have you forgotten about that? The funeral was only three weeks ago. I'm not sure if you remember him? His name was Rowan, and you used to think he was really amazing," she said, her voice dripping sarcasm. "He helped us with our assignments, and took us to festivals – and he respected you as my best friend perhaps more than he should have, if you can seriously ask me this."

Rhiannon blushed a little, but she didn't seem perturbed, or put off in any way. Nor did she seem to hear the warning tone in her friend's voice. "I know Carlie, and I get it. But you'd only been together for a few months, so you need to keep a bit of perspective," she replied, laying her hand on Carlie's arm when it looked like she was going to get up and flee.

"I don't mean you should be totally over him already and never think of him again, or try to forget how important he was to you, but life goes on. You can't put your whole life on hold and act like a widow at seventeen," she said.

"Surely I'm allowed to grieve for a few weeks though?" Carlie retorted, voice cold.

Rhiannon mustered a smile. "I'm sorry, I guess this is coming out wrong. I just don't want you to punish yourself for something that isn't your fault, or feel that you have to deny yourself happiness and friendship, or a new relationship, because he died. I don't mean to offend you hon, I promise."

Carlie stared at her friend, genuinely puzzled. Rhiannon had lost her mother, so she knew grief didn't pass quickly, or have rules or set start and end points. At the very least she should realise from her angry response that she obviously wasn't interested in Jake, and let it drop.

"I'm glad you're not *trying* to offend me," she said, as politely as she could muster. "But I don't know how to be any clearer – I don't want to date anyone right now, so there's no point going on with this. Why don't you tell me how Brodie's play went, or how it's going with John, and let this subject drop?" she insisted.

Finally her friend seemed to hear her. "Brodie was adorable – he was really confident, and did such a good job. I was so proud of him," she beamed. "And it's going really well with John, I really like him. Actually, we're going to see a band near his place on Saturday night, if you want to come. You could ask Jake too," she suggested.

Carlie rolled her eyes in exasperation, and Rhiannon sighed. "I meant as friends, so you'd have someone to talk to while I was with John, and so you could meet my boyfriend properly, okay? But Carlie, don't exaggerate the impact too much. I know you think you really loved Rowan, but there's a chance that you would have broken up with him a few months from now, and dealt with it all then, and then you would have moved on, met someone else. And later you would look back and think your time with Rowan was a nice teenage romance, one of many," she said, blundering onwards, oblivious to the increasingly angry expression on Carlie's face.

"Death can add more weight to a relationship than what was truly there," Rhiannon continued. "Like, for example, someone having a nasty ex-wife to deal with is one thing, the guy can move on and date again, and the new girlfriend doesn't feel threatened, but being a tragic widow with a sainted dead wife is a totally different story, and is so much harder for someone new to deal with."

Carlie glared at her friend. "I'm guessing you're not trying to upset me as much as it sounds like you are?" she asked, her eyes starting to water a little as the hurt lodged in her heart.

"Geez, you're so sensitive," Rhiannon griped.

Shocked at her friend's words, Carlie blinked in surprise, then took a deep breath to try to compose herself and respond calmly.

"Let me be clear. The guy I love just died in a tragic accident. He'd told his manager he wanted to travel less so he could spend more time with me. He was helping me heal my grief at the recent death of my parents, which, you know, is still pretty hard to deal with, and he loved me deeply. I can't just 'get over it', no matter how much I want to. And I really thought that you would understand this.

You've lost someone close to you, you know that it's hard to cope with, and that it's impossible to go on like nothing happened."

"You can't compare losing my mother to losing your boyfriend," Rhiannon said indignantly.

"I'm not Rhi, god! I'm just asking that perhaps you could be a little more understanding, and try to hear me when I say that I need some time to process my grief and loss, to get over the guy I loved so much – and that finding someone else to date is really not at the top of my list of priorities." She sighed impatiently. "I can't even look at another guy, let alone want to go out with anyone. And seriously, someone being Australian – from the other side of the country no less – is not really a reason for me to want to go out with them."

"I'm sorry Carlie, I do understand that it's hard for you," Rhiannon said, tone conciliatory. "And I'm sorry about the way my words came out – I didn't mean to be insensitive, or to upset you in any way. I guess I just hope that soon you'll be able to look at your relationship slightly more big picture, and put it all in context. You hadn't been together with Rowan that long, and... well, you know, if something happened to John now, I mean it would be awful, and I'd be sad, but I'd get over it."

"Please stop," Carlie said sharply, imploringly, her voice thick with pain and unshed tears. "I really can't talk about this any more. And Rhiannon, wow, maybe you should have a think about why you *wouldn't* be a mess if your boyfriend died. What's the point of being with someone you're not totally in love with? Who you wouldn't miss if, heaven forbid, something happened to them? And how can you even talk about him like that?" she asked.

And, face showing her horror, she picked up her bag and ran from the cafeteria.

Chapter 12

Wishing On the Moon

Avoiding Rhiannon the next day was fairly easy – they had no classes together on Thursdays, and Carlie raced home for lunch instead of getting it at the cafeteria as she usually did. She hated being upset with her friend again, so soon after they'd reconnected, but she knew if they continued their conversation from the previous day she might say something she would regret, something that would hurt Rhiannon as much as she'd just hurt her, and she didn't want to do that, no matter how satisfying it might feel in the moment.

As frustrated and annoyed with her friend as she was, she was hoping they could get past this, and she figured that some time apart, for both of them to calm down a bit, might help.

Which explained why she was climbing the sacred tor alone at three in the morning, to perform a full moon ritual on her own. Remembering back to the first full moon ceremony she'd done, just a few short weeks after she'd arrived in England, she marvelled at how far she'd come in less than six months. Her wide-eyed naivety and the scepticism she'd thought was protecting her had unravelled during her time here, as she walked through the countryside, took part in Rose's beautiful sabbat celebrations, and let down her guard at coven meetings with Rhiannon. Her heart had broken open to the magic she now saw so clearly in nature, and in people.

Finally she reached the summit of the tor, with just moments to spare before she knew the moon would become perfectly full. With growing excitement, she opened her ritual bag and took out the athame, then slowly, reverently, stepped out the protective circle.

> *Within this circle, that my intent will form,*
> *Between the worlds, a safe place born.*
> *Ancient beings of this sacred hill,*
> *I call to you with my deepest will.*
> *Please hold me close throughout this rite,*
> *Reveal the magic on this full moon night.*

Gently, solemnly, she honoured and invoked the elements and the directions.

> *Guardians of the north, and element of earth,*
> *Please ground me with your strength and nurturing,*
> *and watch over my sacred rite.*

> *Guardians of the east, and element of air,*
> *Please grant me your intuition and clarity,*
> *and share your wisdom with me this night.*

> *Guardians of the south, and element of fire,*
> *Please burn away my fears and doubts,*
> *and flood me with your power and might.*

> *Guardians of the west, and element of water,*
> *Please wash away all I no longer need,*
> *and allow me to soak in this magical moonlight.*

Confidently, joyfully, she welcomed the god and goddess to join her.

> *Goddess of love and compassion, magic and moonlight,*
> *Please bless me with your presence during my sacred rite.*
> *God of strength and sunshine, love and might,*
> *Please shine your blessings on me tonight.*

While her brain still wasn't certain that there were literal gods and goddesses, or actual beings of light or guardians of the directions, she knew there was *something* up on this hill. A sense of magic that settled around her like a cloak as she carved out a space between the worlds. A sensation of mystery where all things seemed possible. A moment frozen in time, where she felt Rowan's arms around her, his sweet breath in her hair, his warm kiss on her cheek.

Was that all magic was? A remembrance of who you were, a glimpse into the potential of what you could become? Did she even exist? Was everything an illusion? And if so, was there a way for her to slip between dimensions again, to find a parallel world where Rowan still lived?

Sinking to the cold ground to sit cross-legged in the centre of her sacred circle, she closed her eyes and slowly inhaled, feeling herself descend into a meditative state. She was hoping the full moon would illuminate a way for her to resolve her issues with Rhiannon, and let her know how hurtful she was being with her whole "get over it already" attitude to Rowan. It was only a month since she'd lost him, and she still missed him terribly, with an ache that hurt her physically as well as emotionally. Why couldn't her friend understand that?

Sighing, she pushed that dilemma to the back of her mind and tried to focus on the coming month. What did she want to manifest into the world, into her life, in the next moon cycle? Could this high tide of lunar energy enhance her healing?

Yet as she peered into the very depths of her soul, she saw the conflict within herself. Did she even want to have her grief soothed, or would she prefer to hold on to it, wear it as a badge of honour and strength? But that was crazy, surely. What benefit was there in continuing to suffer? Yet did that mean Rhiannon was right? *Should* she be over Rowan by now?

Continuing to breathe in the moon's silvery light, she tried to centre herself within her heart. There was no joy in martyrdom, she knew that, nothing to be gained by closing her heart and walling it off forever to avoid hurt. Then again, what did she gain from opening her heart? More pain? More hurt?

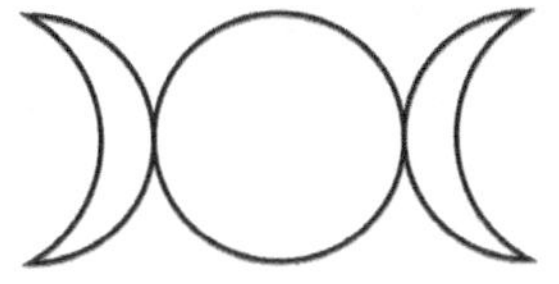

Bringing her grandma's face to mind, she tried to envision what she would suggest, going deep within, into a kind of trance state. What would a wise priestess elder say about grief, about loss, about pain? Surely she would say to honour the blessings of your time with your loved one, to hold them close always but to move on, to risk everything to love again.

And yet… Rose never had. She'd stayed in the same house all these years, a space infused with the tragedy that continued to define her, a space holding her heart captive. She encouraged Carlie to appreciate life, to make herself vulnerable, yet she was still trapped, still waiting. Her heart broke at the thought of her grandmother in pain all this time, alone all this time. How had she not seen that before?

Sensing movement, she snapped open her eyes, and was relieved to see that it was just a small rabbit creeping across the grass in front of her. She smiled, the spell breaking as she came back to the world. Her time was up – it was time to go back down the hill, back to the "real" world, and try to get some sleep. Heart surprisingly light, she farewelled the directions and the deities, and closed her sacred circle.

But as she bent over to pick up her bag, a wave of emotion slammed into her and she fell to the ground, still clutching the athame she'd used. As she tried to catch her breath and refocus her blurry eyes, she stared at the knife, which seemed to be burning in her hand. It had been a gift from Brianna, the woman in green, for her coven dedication ritual with Rhiannon five moons ago.

"It's to cast a circle, to focus and direct energy within that circle, and to remind you to focus on the positive in your life when you are away from the circle, away from your friend. Keep it – and your friend – close to you," Brianna had instructed.

Reluctantly she admitted to herself that she hadn't really done that. She was here on the hill on her own, without her magical partner, and suddenly she felt furtive, sneaky. She could have invited Rhiannon to join her, to make up for the ritual they'd missed on Tuesday night, but she'd wanted to do this on her own. And what had that achieved? Now she was sitting here alone, and feeling just as miserable as she ever had, with an extra dose of guilt to top it off. God, why was everything so hard? She'd never analysed her every thought and emotion before, never obsessed over how her actions impacted on other people. Never given such weight to one bad thing a usually perfect friend had done. What was wrong with her?

"There is nothing wrong with you beloved. You have just had your heart split open by all of your losses, so everything has more weight," said a voice, and Carlie jumped in fright. She stood up, athame still in hand, and turned towards the sound. It was Aideen, the woman in red, no doubt here to gift her with some more cryptic comments.

The mist-shrouded figure laughed. "I will try to be less cryptic this time, shall I?" she asked, and Carlie blushed. She still wasn't enamoured with the mind-reading skills of the people – or beings – here.

"You keep being disappointed that Rhiannon is not perfect, but no one is. She is seventeen, give the girl a break. She is an amazing young woman, but you expect too much from her."

Sighing, Carlie interjected. "But she was so mature, and so compassionate, when we first met – she knew the perfect things to say, and was so wonderful and supportive, so understanding of my grief and anger over the death of my parents."

"Yes, and she is still that caring and compassionate, especially on the topic of losing a parent, because she has been through that too, and worked a lot of it out as she went, realising what she needed and what would have helped her to heal in the best way. And because of that you put her on a pedestal – then when she did not have the answer you wanted, and did not understand your new grief, you decided she must be a terrible friend and that she had failed you. But it is only because of your expectations that you are so disappointed. If you had not held her up to such a high standard – one that *you* set, not her – you would not be feeling let down," Aideen admonished.

"You are not being fair to her Carlie. She is not perfect, and she would be the first to admit it, to insist on it. Certainly she does not expect you to be perfect all the time, or to always know the exact right thing to say. She is forgiving of your less-than-perfect moments. She cuts you slack because you are grieving…"

"But I'm not perfect, she knows that!" Carlie cried.

"Exactly. And nor is she. But you expect her to be perfect, and act like she has committed an unforgivable crime when she is not.

She cares about you Carlie. And yes, it was incredibly insensitive of her to try to set you up with someone so soon, but she just does not understand the depth of your loss, and she cannot. No one can," Aideen said, tone softening a little.

"Well, Rose can understand, because she loved Louis so much, and could never be with anyone else after he died," she continued. "But your connection with Rowan was much deeper than people know – and that was primarily because you were both keeping it a secret, so you cannot blame them for not realising."

The red-clad woman's voice became gentler as she continued. "Rhiannon just wants you to be happy, and she thinks that spending time with Jake, and having a boyfriend again, will make you happy."

Carlie stared at the mist-wreathed figure mutinously. "But what right do I have to be happy, when there's so much suffering, so much pain, in the world?" she demanded.

"Oh Carlie, what right do you have to be unhappy? Everyone deserves happiness," she replied, compassion and love in her voice.

"But I can't just replace Rowan with the first guy who comes along," Carlie argued. "Doesn't Rhiannon realise how hard it will be to find anyone even remotely interesting enough, amazing enough, compassionate enough, after him? He's the most incredible person I've ever met, and no schoolboy, however sweet, could come close to him. I can't imagine I'll ever love anyone as much as I loved him, or meet anyone who loves me as much as Rowan did, who sees so much potential in me, and inspires me so deeply to want to be a better person. How could she think just anyone would do?"

The woman in red gazed at Carlie serenely, and placed a soothing hand on her shoulder. "She does not know because you did not share that with her. I am not blaming you for that, beloved," she added quickly. "You knew that she did not approve of your relationship, so you tried to spare her feelings, tried not to upset her. But you have not even spoken to her about your decision to refuse her ultimatum and choose them both, or explained to her just how much you loved and valued Rowan, and why, and how much he loved and adored you. Perhaps you could show her the letters and cards he wrote to you, and the one you wrote for him that final night?" Aideen suggested.

"It might help her to understand just how deep and devastating this loss is for you. If you are able to really open your heart to her and allow her to see your vulnerabilities, see all of your grief and the full depth of your pain, she may be more sympathetic. Rhiannon cares about her boyfriend, but it is nothing like what you and Rowan shared, and she will not be heartbroken when it ends. That is why she does not comprehend the immensity of your grief."

"Wait, it will end?" Carlie interjected, forgetting for a moment all the other advice the red-clad woman had been trying to impart to her.

"Oh Carlie, she is only seventeen. They only get to see each other on weekends, and they have different goals, different values, different hopes for their lives. It is pleasant enough for now – he is a wonderful boy, and she is getting to experience a relationship that does not demand too much from her. But John is not her grand, all-consuming love, not like Rowan was for you," Aideen said softly.

"So help Rhiannon to understand, help her to see what a relationship can be. And start judging her the same way you judge yourself. She is human. She is kind and compassionate, but she is not all-knowing. And her choices and opinions and actions come from what she has been through and experienced, her worldview, her values, her self-worth. Give her a break Carlie, let her be her imperfect self, and be patient with her. Help her learn a new way of seeing things, a new way to approach things. You both care about each other dearly, so do not let your hurt and indignation, and your need to be right, come between you."

Carlie sighed, but she reluctantly nodded her agreement.

"Now go, dawn is not far away, and you need a little sleep before school," Aideen whispered.

"Thank you," Carlie began, but the red-robed woman had already faded into the mists. She laughed. She would never get used to these beings who were there then not there. Apparitions perhaps? Ghosts? Figments of her imagination? She'd given up on trying to figure them out, because whether they really existed or not didn't actually matter – they always gave her great advice, advice that she knew deep in her heart to be true, and gave her new ways to see the situation she was facing.

As she stumbled back down the tor in the pre-dawn dark, she wondered whether Rhiannon had met the woman in red too, and vowed to finally tell her friend about her encounters, and ask about hers. Yawning, she let herself into the cottage and tiptoed upstairs to bed. Luther miaowed impatiently, then walked up onto her pillow, snuggled up close to her head, and started purring.

Feeling content, she drifted off into a dream of Rowan. He was sitting on the bank of the stream at their special place, leaning up against the trunk of the willow tree and smiling at her, that smile that lit her up inside, and made her feel so safe, so loved. The sun beat down on them from a cloudless blue sky as he beckoned her to him, then stood up to enfold her in a warm hug. Leaning down, he gently kissed her, and her heart overflowed with love for him...

Until suddenly her eyes started to fill with tears as she realised this couldn't be real. It was the sunshine that had given it away, because they'd met in autumn and loved each other through the turning of the leaves and into the snowy chill of winter. Her dream self pushed that logic aside though, even as tears leaked out onto her pillow, disturbing Luther, who licked at her face in concern and compassion, grounding her back into her body.

But she'd take it, take these hours with him on the bank of the stream in their special place, take these kisses and this embrace that was melting her heart with joy. She'd take anything, for as long as she could hold on to it, even if it wasn't real. Sighing in her sleep, she turned onto her side and hugged Luther close, and the little black cat started purring again, glad that she was safe, and feeling okay again, for these hours at least.

As a wintry beam of pale sunlight crept in the window and softly caressed her face, Carlie's eyes slowly opened, and she smiled, relaxed and happy for the first time in ages. She snuggled down into the covers, into the warmth of Rowan's strong, supportive arms, and the love she'd seen shining in his eyes – until real life crashed over her, and she sat up abruptly as she realised it had only been a dream.

Tears threatened, but before she lost her cool, Luther climbed into her lap and batted her with his paw, and she gazed into his deep green eyes and felt the strength flowing from him, calming her, soothing her. She patted his soft, fuzzy head and smiled at him.

"Thank you buddy," she sighed. "I really am so grateful to have you in my life."

Shivering as she climbed out of bed, she grabbed her school uniform from the back of the chair where she'd thrown it the night before, and hurried into the ensuite to have a scalding hot shower. God it was cold here in winter!

Tiptoeing downstairs, she was surprised to find Rose already in the kitchen. "Tea?" she asked, and Carlie nodded gratefully. "Are you okay Sweetheart?"

Carlie shrugged. "Okay-ish. How about you? And how's work? Sorry, I've been so caught up in my own dramas I haven't been paying attention to anyone else's," she said guiltily.

Rose hugged her. "Everything is fine. How was your full moon ritual?" she asked, eyes twinkling.

"Oh no! Did I wake you up when I got home? I'm so sorry!"

"Don't worry, I never sleep the night of the full moon," Rose laughed. "I spend the night in bed, reading my Book of Shadows by candlelight and writing – dreams, spells, meditations, invocations, whatever comes to me. I can always have an afternoon nap if I need to, but somehow the moon seems to recharge me enough anyway," she said, then broke off.

"Are you and Rhiannon friends again yet?" she finally asked.

Carlie shrugged. "I think so... well, I don't really know. I mean, we were, but then she started harassing me about going out with Jake, and when I told her that it was too soon to even think about dating, she snapped at me to get over Rowan and move on, and said that I needed to get some perspective. That we weren't together long enough for me to be grieving. But it's only been a month since he died. Surely I'm allowed to be sad for a little while longer?"

"Oh Sweetheart, of course you are," Rose said, pulling her into a warm embrace. "Take as long as you need. Grief is different for everyone, and yours has been loss on top of loss, so don't feel any pressure to 'get over it'. There are stages and phases of grief – you might feel okay one day and soul crushingly sad the next, and that's fine. I'm shocked that Rhiannon would be so impatient with you though, I thought that she of all people would understand."

Carlie nodded, although oddly enough Rose's condemnation was making her feel a little defensive of her friend. "Well, I guess I never really told her just how much I loved Rowan, and how close we became," she said sheepishly, echoing Aideen's words. "I knew she didn't approve of us, so I played it down to her."

"Maybe it would help if you explained all of that to her," Rose agreed. "I know she really does care about you Sweetheart, and I'm sure she just wants you to be happy."

"I guess so," Carlie conceded. "But that reminds me, I need to show her something," she said. Grabbing an apple from the bench, she drained her mug of tea, kissed Rose goodbye, ran up the stairs to her room and pulled a package from her bottom drawer, then hurried out the door to school.

Chapter 13

A New Friend

Disappointment swept over Carlie when she got to school and remembered that Rhiannon wasn't going to be there that day – she and Brodie had left early to spend a long weekend with their grandparents. When she noticed Jake walking towards her, looking so happy to see her, she blushed and raced off in the other direction, suddenly paranoid that he knew Rhiannon had been trying to set them up. Keeping to herself all day, she managed to avoid him by sneaking off to the library and studying in the lunch break, and taking the seat next to Abby in their English class so they couldn't sit together as they usually did.

Giving Jake the cold shoulder made her feel bad – they were friends after all – but she saw him differently now, felt pressured by him because of what Rhiannon had suggested. It wasn't fair to him, but she felt irrational and out of sorts today, her emotions jumbled. One minute she thought Aideen was right, and it was her fault Rhiannon had no sympathy for her loss, then the next she'd be overcome with anger at everyone around her for not knowing how she felt and what she needed, with her deepest fury reserved for the friend who more than anyone *should* have known.

When the bell finally rang she breathed a sigh of relief and dragged herself home, feeling even sadder than usual. Walking numbly through the cottage gate and up the steps to the front door, she jumped in fright when she heard a loud, angry sound. It was Luther, looking ferocious and making a terrible racket.

"Hey buddy, what's wrong?" she asked, kneeling down and tentatively stretching out her hand, careful not to scare him. What could make him utter that kind of noise? He allowed her to pat him, then finally rubbed up against her leg, purring, so she figured he must be okay, although she still had no idea what he'd been so upset about. But when she rose to head inside, he led her over to the corner of the front porch, and miaowed insistently. Slowly she crouched down and peered into the shadows.

A pair of frightened green eyes stared back at her, and a tiny pink tongue peeked out as she heard a soft squeak. Carlie turned back to Luther, who pushed her outstretched hand towards the shivering ball of black fluff. He nudged her again, until she cautiously extended a finger to stroke the small cowering creature. Breath held, she waited, not wanting to alarm it, and terrified that she'd hurt the scrap of a thing if she touched it.

Luther miaowed at it once more, reassuring, and the tiny kitten lifted its head nervously to Carlie's finger. Gently and very carefully, she patted the soft fur between its tiny ears. It was shivering, but she wasn't sure if it was cold or scared, or both. Feeling totally out of her depth, she looked down at Luther, and after some pointed glances and a few nudges, she finally got the message that he wanted her to sit on the top step. Dropping her bag, she slowly lowered herself to the cold slate, and watched as Luther half shepherded, half pushed the little ball of fluff up onto her lap.

When Rose came home an hour later, Carlie had the kitten in her arms, snuggled up against her heart and gently purring, both of them oblivious to the cold, while Luther sat on her lap looking like a proud parent as he watched them both. Tears rushed to the older woman's eyes, but Luther gave her such a stern look that she took a deep breath, sniffed once, then straightened her back and got her emotions under control.

"So, we have a new addition to the household," she finally said, voice composed. "You must all be freezing though, and hungry. Come on inside and I'll fix us some dinner, and we can all warm up."

Together the motley crew traipsed inside, Carlie and the kitten shaking with cold, and the warmth of the kitchen suddenly more inviting than ever.

Rose slid a lasagne into the oven, then busied herself with saucers of milk and cat food. Carlie sat on the floor, looking dazed, the tiny kitten cradled in one hand against her chest while her other hand gently stroked it. The bundle of fur gazed around, curiously taking things in now as its fear began to dissipate. And Luther stood by their side, supervising still, like a royal guard.

"What are you going to call her?" Rose asked, her heart swelling with love and pride when she saw the compassion and concern in her granddaughter's eyes as she carefully held the precious little creature. It seemed that Luther had known what she needed to heal her heart better than anyone.

Carlie looked up, joy warring with caution in her eyes, still scared that the small, sweet creature could be snatched away from her at any moment. "Call her? Do you think we can keep her?" she asked, excitement and hope rich in her voice.

Rose laughed. "I don't think we have any say in the matter – Luther has decided for us. You're this little one's keeper, her warrior while she grows up. She'll need a lot of care though, because she looks really young. Are you up for it?"

Carlie's smile was the only answer Rose needed, and she felt some of the weight she'd been carrying lift from her shoulders. The morning the police officers had come around to inform Carlie that Rowan was dead, she'd feared for the sanity of her granddaughter, who was already so tragically bereaved and dealing with so much loss and upheaval in her life. She hadn't been sure the poor girl would survive this second loss, which had made her doubly concerned when Rhiannon had confessed that she'd hurt Carlie so badly with her actions. Who knew it would be an animal to look after that could provide just the thing she needed to have a reason to want to live, a reason to get up each day? Well, *she* should have known, Rose thought, but recriminations were pointless. Luther had got it sorted.

Sinking down on the floor opposite her granddaughter, Rose smiled as Luther came over and sat in her lap, looking up at her with so much love and trust. He'd been such a wonderful companion to her for so many years, and she was so very grateful to him. There had been days when she'd felt the same way Carlie did now – hell, she still had those days sometimes – and Luther had been there with her, knowing when she needed him to stay close to her, to curl up on her pillow with her and guide her through her dreams and nightmares, drawing her out at crucial moments with his little paw on her face, and also knowing when she'd needed space.

And it had been Luther who had gotten through to Carlie too, she reflected. When her granddaughter had arrived on her doorstep almost seven months ago, she'd been terrified for the child. Her grief and anger were writ so deep in her heart, pain was scored across her face, and bitterness was poisoning her soul. But Luther had gently led her back to herself, giving her something to love that was not human, since she'd been so deeply suspicious of people in general, and Rose in particular, back then. The sweet cat had sat with her in her darkest moods, kept her company when she needed it, and stood over her as a brave guardian during her night terrors.

Rose couldn't lie – she had felt hurt when her companion of so long had ditched her so quickly and easily, as though he no longer cared, but she'd known he was helping her granddaughter as much for the girl's sake as for her own. Carlie had hated her when she arrived, with a vitriol that had shocked Rose. It had taken several weeks to discover the reason – that Rose's daughter Violet had never mentioned her own mother to Carlie, had never told her that she had a grandmother in England.

The poor girl had been under the impression that Rose was a cruel and unforgiving woman who'd driven her own child away from her, so nasty and mean-spirited that Violet had fled to the other side of the world to escape her.

It was some time before Carlie began trusting her, and started to open her heart again. To lose both parents just after your seventeenth birthday was a bitter blow for anyone to deal with – and to then lose your boyfriend so soon after that, when you'd only just started to inch back out into the world, well, Carlie was far stronger than Rose was, to still be here, to still be standing.

She was damaged, of course, and hurting more than she was letting on, but after she'd opened the package Rowan had been bringing her, put on the beautiful dress and the gorgeous ring, and read the two heart-wrenching, love-filled cards, she had seemed to rise from the ashes of her soul, to make a decision to live. Yet Rose knew it was a knife-edge situation that could change at any moment, and Rhiannon's strange attempts to set her up with a new boyfriend had her teetering back on the brink of despair.

Gazing down into Luther's green eyes as they communicated their love and respect to each other, Rose didn't realise her granddaughter was staring at her just as intently. The look Luther and Rose were exchanging made a lump form in Carlie's throat, so touched was she by the obvious love and respect these two had for each other, cat and crone, witch and familiar.

"I'm so sorry Gran, that I took Luther away from you," Carlie whispered, heart catching as she watched them together, Luther curled up in Rose's lap, purring and rubbing against her as she stroked his sleek black head.

"Oh Sweetheart, not at all! Luther is his own very independent being, and he's known better than me this whole time about what we both needed, and what he could best do to help us heal and grow stronger. And now he's brought you this precious little scrap of a thing to care for, and love, and be responsible for. Are you up for the challenge? She'll need a lot of attention, a lot of love."

Carlie grinned, eyes on the tiny bundle of fuzzy black fur in her palm, well and truly in love with the cute creature already. "Oh yes," she breathed. "I'd be honoured to care for her."

Luther purred even harder at that, and looked up at Rose with a slightly condescending air. She laughed as she patted his head. "I know my sweet, you've always known better than me, had more magic than me. You truly kept me wanting to live when the despair was getting too much for me."

Carlie looked up in shock, and Rose sighed even as she smiled. "Oh Sweetheart, I know what it's like to lose your beloved, it's like your very heart has been torn from your chest, and you think there's no point going on, no point living without them in the world. Luckily for me I suppose, I had to stay strong, stay living, just in case Violet ever came home."

Carlie's breath caught. "You mean, you thought about…"

Rose nodded reluctantly, eyes sad. "Of course, but I could never do it, not when there were reasons to stay. And Luther was one of them, of that I am sure," she said, smiling again. "And of course if there was ever any chance of your mum coming home, well, there was no way I was going to let her down…"

"But now?" Carlie asked, fear clear in her voice.

Rose stared at her, puzzled. "What do you mean?"

"Well, Mum isn't ever going to come home," she whispered.

Understanding dawned in Rose. "Oh Sweetheart, I have you to live for now, and you have me. And this one too," she added. "What will you call her?"

Carlie gazed down at the fuzzy little midnight-black creature now snoring gently in her lap. "I've thought of a few possibilities, but the more I sit with her, the more I think she should be named Luna," she finally said, and at the name the kitten opened her eyes and peeked up at the girl she'd happily accepted as her guardian, and gave the tiniest mewling squeak.

"Sounds like she approves of that name," Rose said, laughter in her voice, and Luther, still sitting in the older woman's lap, lifted his head and miaowed his agreement too.

The delicious aroma of the lasagne eventually drifted over to them where they sat on the floor, and Rose carefully put Luther down beside Carlie, then creakily got to her feet to get their dinner out of the oven and serve it up.

"You happy down there?" she asked, and Carlie nodded. Rose handed her one of the bowls, then settled down next to her again, Luther returning to her lap. They spent the evening on the floor, the cats purring in their laps, and occasionally allowing them to get up to make another pot of tea.

Rose shared some of her memories of Luther, and what a wonderful support he'd been to her, in her magic, in her life, and in her grief. Carlie apologised again, for monopolising him since she'd arrived, but her grandmother brushed her off. Luther went where he was needed, where he needed to be, and now he'd brought Carlie a new companion, a precious little friend who required her to focus all her love and attention on her, invest herself and her presence into her, which seemed to be the perfect antidote to her sadness.

For a moment Carlie felt overwhelmed by the responsibility, and the fragility of the life that had been entrusted to her. Could she guarantee that she was prepared to stay alive? But just as she wondered that, Luna looked up at her with wide, trusting eyes, and her heart melted. Yes, she would stay alive for this small bundle of fur, and for her grandma, who had suffered enough for one lifetime.

Finally, as their eyes began to droop, cat and human alike, Rose announced that it was time for bed, so they all stood up and stretched.

"Where should Luna sleep?" Carlie asked. Rose glanced down at Luther and he seemed to nod, before gently nudging the kitten towards the back door and leading her outside. Rose and Carlie did the dishes together as they waited, and put saucers of fresh water out, then the two cats popped back in through the little cat door, and Luther led the way to the stairs.

Rose laughed. "Looks like Luther has it all worked out. He has always thought this was his house though, not mine," she said, voice thick with love and amusement.

Carlie kissed her grandma goodnight, then followed her feline friends up to her bedroom, trying not to laugh as Luna struggled so comically with the size of the stairs. Quickly she brushed her teeth, then slipped into her pyjamas and under the blankets, giggling at how adorably cute the critters were. When she was settled, Luther picked Luna up in his strong jaw and leaped up onto the bed, then prodded her until she was curled up on Carlie's pillow.

Then, job done, he retired to the end of the bed, standing guard over them both. Carlie's heart filled with love as she slid down under the covers. She patted Luther and thanked him again, then wished him sweet dreams and settled down on her side, eye to eye with the fluffy black kitten.

"Okay little one, I promise I'll do my very best not to squash you, and I have a feeling Luther will be watching over us anyway. I hope you can get some rest." Smiling sleepily, she scratched the kitten's soft head. "Thank you both for caring about me," she whispered as she drifted off to dreamland.

She woke up once in the night, to a soft, furry paw on her face, and realised that she'd been sliding into a nightmare again. Gazing at the kitten in wonder, she thanked her, murmured at her to go back to sleep, then passed out again herself. It was the best sleep she'd had in weeks, her dreams guarded by the ferocious protector cat and his sweet new charge.

When the pale sun drifted through the curtains the next morning, Carlie sat up and gazed around her. Both of the cats were sitting at the end of the bed, giving themselves a bath, and she laughed in delight at how cute they looked together.

"What are we going to do today guys?" she asked. Luther jumped gracefully down to the floor, and he and Carlie watched, breath held, as Luna stared at the distance between the bed and the ground, seeming to weigh up her options. Plaintively she miaowed at Carlie, who scooped her up in her arms for a quick cuddle, then gently placed her on the floor next to Luther.

He looked at her approvingly, and she felt ridiculously happy and accomplished for getting that job right at least. But it was a short-lived feeling, as Luther's gaze quickly became impatient. He stared at her, then turned to the door, then glared back at her again, until she finally got the message: *Hurry up and get dressed so we can eat.*

Quickly she did as she was told, and the three of them were soon downstairs again in the warm and cosy kitchen, having breakfast and drinking tea with Rose. Carlie grinned, her spirits lifting as she felt the pure, uncomplicated love of their two animal companions, and feeling so grateful that it was Saturday so that she could spend the day just chilling out with Luther and Luna.

Chapter 14

Moving In and Moving On

The weekend was filled with laughter and joy, as Carlie and Rose delighted in Luna's bouncy, pouncy cuteness. As they gathered in the kitchen at lunchtime on Sunday to make a pot of vegie and lentil soup, Luther suddenly turned serious, going into teacher mode. He shepherded Luna around the cottage, showing her all the rooms, miaowing a little at the bottom of the staircase as if giving the kitten instructions, then demonstrating how to best climb up the lounge chair to get to the window, where a cat could perch on the sill and look out to the garden and the tor.

The two of them also spent a long time at the cat door leading from the kitchen to the back garden, Luther patient yet insistent that the little ball of fluff work out how to push against it herself and get outside. It was probably a good lesson, Carlie thought, in case Luna wanted to go out in the middle of the night and Luther didn't feel like leaving the cosiness of the bed they all shared.

Once the kitten had mastered getting out, they spent almost as long on the other side, until the shivering pair finally burst back through into the warmth of the kitchen.

Carlie swooped down and sat on the floor, gathering them to her and holding them close, patting them until they'd stopped shivering with cold and were purring contentedly again.

"Crazy kitty," she said to Luther in a mock scolding tone, although the love in her voice was evident too. "Did you really have to go out while it was so chilly? I'm sure I saw snow!"

He gazed at her calmly, and it looked as though he was raising one eyebrow in scorn, to let her know the question was beneath him. She laughed. "Okay buddy, you know what you're doing. I'm just glad you both eventually worked it out – it's freezing out there!"

After bowls of hot soup and more cuddles, and a little saucer of milk for Luna, Rose went to the cupboard under the stairs and pulled out a thick woollen midnight blue blanket flecked through with golden stars. Bringing it back out to the kitchen, she made a little nest under the table, close to the heater, and offered it to the kitten, who stared at it blankly.

Finally Luther sighed dramatically and nudged the little kitten over to it, showing her how she could snuggle down into it and create a warm bed. The two of them curled up in there together and had an afternoon nap, and Carlie marvelled at how peaceful and relaxed they both looked, and how easy it was for them to fall asleep.

Rose busied herself making a new pot of tea, then sat down at the table above the snoozing cats. Handing her granddaughter a steaming mug of chai, she gazed nervously across at her.

"What's up Gran?" Carlie asked, sensing immediately that there was something on the older woman's mind.

"Ah Sweetheart, you're getting more intuitive by the day," she smiled. "But it's nothing bad, not at all..." Trailing off, she took a slow sip of tea, breathing in the warming, soothing scent of the cinnamon, ginger, nutmeg, cloves and cardamom, and seeming to draw strength from the familiarity of her herbs and spices. Then she put down her cup and spoke.

"I was wondering whether you'd like to move in to your mum's old bedroom?" she began tentatively. "Yours is so tiny, and the front room has a desk in it, and bookshelves, so you could do your homework in there if you wanted to, and there's lots of cupboard space, and room for Rhiannon next time she stays over. And of course, now that there are two royal creatures living with us, you might need a bigger bed. I'm just really sorry I wasn't ready to open it up and clear it out for you when you got here," she said with a sigh, then paused when she say the concern on Carlie's face.

"Don't worry, I've totally cleaned and dusted it since you were last in there. There's a new bed, and new sheets and things. And I promise there are no spiders, or webs, any more, and not a hint of mustiness. It's as good as new," Rose insisted, misconstruing Carlie's emotional concern for one of cleanliness.

Carlie's mind raced. She wasn't sure how she felt about it – did she want to spend her life in the shadow of her mum's memory? If she moved in to her old room, would she be committing to nights spent with ghosts? Days haunted by what-ifs and never-weres?

Her mind jumped from reason for to reason against and back again – until it hit her, just what it would have cost Rose to clear out all traces of her beloved daughter, and what a sacrifice she had made for her. Despite her hesitations, she was touched.

"I'd love to," she said firmly, trying to convince herself as much as her grandmother. She wasn't at all sure that she wanted to move in to Violet's bedroom, but she didn't think she could say no a second time. And it would be great to have bookshelves, and a proper desk for studying. Sealing the deal was the fact that she could already picture Luna and Luther racing around the room, and peeking out from the glass-walled balcony, which would be beautiful in summer.

"Thank you Gran," she said, and her smile was genuine this time. "I really appreciate you doing all this. But how on earth did you manage it without me knowing?"

Rose laughed. "Miri came over and helped me with the cleaning and sorting, the first few days you were back at school, and Mike helped with the bed – he ordered one online for me, and came over when it was being delivered to help them get it in and set it up, and they took the old one away."

Carlie's brow furrowed, and both of them realised at the same time what that would have cost Mike emotionally, having to dismantle his dead childhood sweetheart's bed.

"Damn it, I didn't even think of that," Rose sighed.

Carlie shook her head. "It would have been so much harder for you," she replied, feeling the weight of it, the pain it would have inflicted, for her grandma to have to go through all her lost daughter's things, things she'd locked away for the last twenty years so she didn't have to look at them, or remember, or hope.

"It was hard, harder than I imagined," Rose admitted. "But it was time. And it was wonderful too," she added, eyes glistening. "In hiding away and avoiding the bad memories, I also lost the good ones. I've been going up there some nights, after you went to bed, and sitting in the chair on the balcony, remembering. Going through her wardrobe, smiling as I recalled when we made a certain dress, being proud of how she'd saved up for a particularly elaborate ritual gown, laughing at one of the skirts that had taken us days to sew because we'd cut the pattern wrong. And sitting on the floor with her jewellery box, recalling the stories of every piece, where they'd come from, the times she'd worn them, the significance they each held."

Carlie refilled their cups as she tried to disguise her longing to have known that side of her mother, then handed one to her grandma. "I'm really sorry I didn't appreciate you when I first got here, and that I didn't understand the depth of your pain. But I know that this must have been really difficult for you, and I want you to know how much I appreciate you doing it for me, and how much I appreciate you full stop. But you didn't throw everything out, did you?" she asked carefully, not knowing what answer she hoped for.

Rose smiled and shook her head. "I couldn't quite bring myself to do that. Besides, as we know from the Yule Ball, you fit into most of Violet's clothes, so the offer still stands – it's all yours now. You should go through it all, if you'd like to, and see what you want to keep. We can take the rest to the homeless shelter, or we can just bag everything up right now, if you'd rather not look at any of it. But there's an empty wardrobe in there, as well as the one filled with Violet's clothes, so there's no hurry – you'll definitely be able to fit your meagre possessions into the second one, so just do what feels right for you."

Before Carlie could answer, there was a knock at the front door. She glanced over at Rose, quizzical, but her grandma shrugged and shook her head, so she stood up and went to see who was there, the two cats suddenly awake and weaving around her ankles, Luna following Luther's lead as closely as she could, with hilarious results. Still giggling, Carlie pulled open the front door, and froze. It was Rhiannon.

"Oh, it's you," she said, a little surprised, and suddenly anxious. They hadn't spoken since Wednesday, when she'd been so angry at her friend for trying to push her to date Jake, and telling her to get over Rowan. Should she do as red-robed Aideen suggested, and show her the letters in an effort to resolve the situation, or would it be easier to remain aloof, and let the distance grow between them?

Noticing that Rhiannon looked even more nervous than she felt, she softened a little, and smiled at her.

"Um, hello," her friend began. "I just got back from Nan and Pop's, and I was wondering if I could join you for a cup of tea or something?" she asked, her words so formal, her voice shaking a little with apprehension. Carlie finally took pity on her. Life was too short, surely, to hold a grudge.

"Come in, we were just about to make a fresh pot of tea," she said, and ushered her through into the warmth of the kitchen. Realising her friend had stopped, she turned around, and laughed as she saw her face, eyes wide as she stared at the kitten.

"Oh, this is Luna," she explained, just as the little ball of fluff tripped over her own feet again. "Luther brought her home for us to look after. You can pat her if you like, she's very friendly now."

Rhiannon slid down to the floor and cautiously held out her hand. Luna looked over at Luther, who inclined his head in what seemed to be approval, because the curious little kitten stepped closer to the new arrival and let herself be patted for a moment, before racing back to Carlie and hiding behind her legs, then peeking around them and regarding Rhiannon with mischievous bright green eyes.

"She's adorable," she said. "And she clearly loves you already."

Carlie's face lit up. "I think that's why Luther brought her here, to give me something to love, something to be responsible for, something to want to hang around for."

Rose tried to hide her tears by busying herself making the tea, and Rhiannon felt ashamed. She really hadn't been there for her friend when she'd needed her, but she could change that from now on. She looked around until she spotted Luther, and went over to pat him. "You're a very wise cat Luther," she said, sinking down onto the floor next to him. "Thank you for caring for my friend when I was too stupid to do it myself."

Rose poured out the tea and brought the steaming mugs over to the kitchen table, near the warmth of the heater. "Okay, enough of us sitting on the cold floor – my poor old bones don't appreciate it, and I think the cats will be okay without us being down on their level for a little while at least," she said, casting a hopeful look over at Luther.

"He really does run this house, doesn't he," Carlie laughed. "But I think you're right, I'm still a bit stiff from sitting on the floor for so long the last two nights – although it was worth it to help her settle in," she added, scooping Luna up for a cuddle then placing her gently on her lap, where she purred much more loudly than they would have thought possible from such a tiny body.

Luther, work done for now, curled up on the blanket at Rose's feet and had another nap.

Beckoning Rhiannon over to sit with them, Rose gave her a hug, then handed her a mug of tea, and the three of them talked happily about the upcoming ritual at the healing centre, the slow approach of spring, then about the assignment Laura had set them in history. When Carlie mentioned Jake, Rhiannon kept her face carefully expressionless, not saying a word that might annoy her friend. Instead it was Rose who asked a question.

"How's his grandfather doing? I remembered a bit more about his wife after we spoke the other night. Her sister asked me for a herbal remedy to lessen Marcy's pain in her final weeks, and Marcy sent a lovely card thanking me. I never met her husband though, I think he was a bit suspicious of us 'long-haired hippie women', as Marcy's sister told it." She smiled as she said it though – it had taken a while to develop the strength, but Rose had stopped taking offence at the way some people viewed her and her healing work long ago.

"He's good, I think," Carlie replied. "He said he's really happy that Jake is staying with him this year, that it gives him a reason to get up in the morning."

Rose smiled. "I can relate to that sentiment. Well, you're welcome to invite them over for a cup of tea if you'd like to. But now I'm afraid I'll have to love you and leave you for a while, because I must get back to the healing centre for a few hours. Will you be okay with the cats? And are you happy to just have soup again tonight Sweetheart? I'll pick up some fresh bread on the way home."

Carlie nodded and kissed her grandma goodbye, then turned to her friend. "I'm going to move in to Mum's old room, so do you want to give me a hand? Or just chat while I do it?"

"Sure, if that's okay," Rhiannon said hesitantly. "But I can go home if you'd rather do it on your own?"

Shaking her head, Carlie stood, holding Luna close to her heart, and led the way to the stairs. "You can help me go through Mum's clothes if you'd like to. Gran said we can keep what we want, and take the rest down to the homeless shelter, so maybe that would be a good first step. I'm sure there are some people in need of extra coats and jeans right now. And maybe we'll find something to wear to the Imbolc ritual next weekend."

Luther got up and followed them, and leaned gently against Carlie's ankle as she stood at the door to the upstairs front room, heart hammering in her chest. The last time she'd been in there had been the night of the Yule Ball, when she and Rhiannon had got dressed together, in her mum's clothes, and had so much fun doing each other's hair and make-up, laughing and feeling so happy and excited about the night to come.

God, that was only five weeks ago, yet her life had spiralled so badly off track since then. Her beloved boyfriend had died, and she'd thought she'd lost her best friend too – had *wanted* to lose her best friend. But Imbolc was all about new beginnings and fresh starts, so perhaps it was the perfect time to move in to a new bedroom, with Luther and their new little furry companion, and to forgive and forget with her friend.

Taking a deep breath, she opened the door and stepped across the threshold into the room.

"Wow!" Rhiannon exclaimed from behind her. "When did you do all this? It looks amazing!"

Carlie shook her head. "I didn't do anything. It was all Gran, and Miri helped her, and your dad too. I'm not sure about the painting and stuff though…" she trailed off, gazing around herself in wonder.

The walls had been transformed with the palest purple paint, with a contrasting deep violet shade around the windowsills and the door to the balcony. The thick dark curtains had been replaced with gauzy white ones, which brightened the room immensely and filtered the soft winter light in beautifully. The desk in the corner had been cleared, and there was a lamp with a purple shade on it in the corner. The bed was a new four-poster made from wrought iron, with ivy swirls worked into the frame, and black netting draped around it, making it look cosy and inviting.

Carefully she set Luna down on one of the four big pillows, and grinned as the kitten snuggled down into it and closed her eyes. Looking around for Luther, she saw him standing near the door, waiting. "Come on buddy, you're welcome too. Hop up with Luna if you feel like a snooze," she said, pointing to the bed, and Luther leaped up gracefully and cuddled up to the kitten.

"It looks so different to when we were in here getting ready for the ball, and even more so from the first time I saw it, when it was dark and dusty, like no one had been inside, or opened the windows, for decades. Which was the case I guess. There were cobwebs everywhere, and thick layers of dust," Carlie said.

"I just can't believe what an amazing job Gran did with it – she must have been planning this for weeks! And to have managed to keep it a secret is impressive too. I don't know how she did everything without me knowing."

Walking over to the larger of the two wardrobes, Carlie opened the door, and was met by a riot of colour and fabric. They both gasped, overwhelmed at just how many clothes there were.

"Gran said they made most of the clothes themselves, which amazes me – I can't even sew on a button," Carlie grinned.

"Me either," Rhiannon replied. "And I just love how colourful everything is too. Look at this gorgeous dress," she said, pulling out a peacock blue confection that was layered over vivid green tulle and shot through with golden thread.

"Try it on," Carlie urged, and the girls spent the next two hours pulling clothes out of the wardrobe, trying them on, swapping outfits, laughing as they swirled around in jewel-bright creations, sighing at the ones that were too tight or too loose, cooing in admiration when something fit like a glove, when the colours best suited them, when the style was totally them. Halfway through, Carlie paused, shocked to realise that she was actually having fun.

"I thought it would make me sad to be in here, to be wearing Mum's clothes, but it makes me feel closer to her," she admitted when they both collapsed on the floor for a mini break. "It's the strangest thing – all my memories of her seem to have been enhanced by my time here, by getting to know what she was like when she was younger. I think she's morphed into something between Rose's idea of her and what she was actually like when I knew her, as an adult – part truth, part ideal, part figment of my imagination made real. And I wonder if I'm somehow affecting Gran's memories of her too, since we apparently look so much alike, and share some character traits. It's such a strange thing, memory..." she sighed.

"And in a weird way my dad is more real to me now, because nothing has changed my idea of him. He's still exactly as he always was to me, and always will be, yet here I sit in Mum's childhood room, amongst all her clothes – none of which she would have been caught dead in when I knew her, by the way, she was always so elegantly dressed, so lawyerly professional, so black-grey-beige. It's like I have two mothers, and I'm not sure which one is the real one."

"I guess they both are," Rhiannon said softly, and her heart lurched when Carlie looked up at her with her sad green eyes, so much pain in them along with the hope. Then just as it was starting to get a little too intense for them, Luna woke up, so they crawled over to pat her, and dance around the room with her, giggling as she tried to pounce when the curtains stirred in the breeze, trying to maintain their composure when Luther jumped from the bed and went to the kitten's side to calm her down, his seriousness in contrast with her frivolity making them want to collapse on the floor and laugh forever.

Later Luther pushed open the little cat flap in the balcony door and took Luna outside to look around, to sniff out the corners and oversee their new territory, which the girls agreed was the sweetest thing ever. When the cats eventually tired themselves out, they curled up in the comfy reading chair next to the desk and napped, and the girls turned back to the wardrobe, determined to finish their job.

Carlie pulled out several pairs of jeans, woollen coats and jumpers, some hand-knit, from the shelf above the dresses. She kept a pair of jeans that fit her perfectly, a long violet-coloured coat and two thick jumpers, since her own clothes weren't really designed for the icy English winters. The rest they folded up for the shelter, since warm clothes would be far more useful for people in need than the beautiful but less substantial dresses, although they added them to the pile too, after they'd chosen three each. Carlie also kept a pair of warm and sturdy winter boots that would make walking outside far less gruelling, but put the rest of the boots and shoes aside, knowing there were plenty of people who needed them more than she did.

They both jumped when they heard the front door, and realised Rose was back home from work. Four hours had passed, and they hadn't moved a single thing into Carlie's new room. But she shook her head when her friend apologised – there was no hurry, and besides, the bed had been made up with gorgeous midnight blue sheets patterned with stars and two matching blankets, so she could easily grab her mum's old quilt and sleep there tonight regardless.

Rose knocked at the door then, and laughed when she saw all the neatly piled clothes. But she was impressed when the girls showed her the few things they wanted to keep, and told her everything else could go to the shelter. Glancing at her watch, Rose asked if they wanted to help her take some of it down now, since it looked like it was going to be another freezing night, so they leaped up and started squeezing

all the clothes and shoes into bags. Rose added a few blankets from the linen press on the landing, picked up the basket of food she'd brought home to add to their contribution, asked Luther to keep an eye on Luna, then led the way back outside and into the village.

Carlie was grateful for the warm boots she'd kept – and really glad that the rest of the footwear and all the clothes could help keep someone else warm through the icy nights. As the volunteer's eyes lit up at the size of their bundles, Carlie's heart swelled, and she was glad her grandmother had suggested it – it certainly put her own problems in perspective. There were people in this country, in every country, sleeping on the streets in ridiculously cold temperatures. She may have lost her parents and her beloved, but she still had people who loved her and a warm bed to sleep in.

After they'd dropped off all their bags she hugged Rose and Rhiannon, and thanked them for looking out for her. Then they headed back to the cottage to eat hot vegie soup and fresh warm bread. Later Rose made herself scarce, sensing that the two girls still needed to talk. It was awkward for a moment, but eventually Rhiannon screwed up her courage and spoke, her face contrite and her voice a little shaky.

"I'm so sorry about the other day, I really am. Everything I said came out wrong, and I wasn't being fair to you, or honouring your grief. I of all people should know there's no timetable for healing, and simply being told to snap out of it is worse than useless. Please forgive me Carlie," she implored.

Carlie reached out and hugged her. "I'm sorry too," she said. "And I can't expect you to understand how I'm feeling because I never told you just how much I loved him, or how close we had become, because I was scared of upsetting you. I played down our feelings for each other because I knew you didn't approve –"

Rhiannon tried to interject, but Carlie shook her head. "It's not a criticism of you, I'm just explaining why I didn't share everything about Rowan with you. And I've realised that I told you about my struggles with him and the one time I thought he was cruel to me, but I never told you how easily it was resolved, and that it was my own misunderstanding, not his actions, which caused the problem in the first place. He was always so kind and sweet and protective of me, and never did anything to hurt me. I just let my insecurities run away with me, which was unfortunately the bit I confided to you," she sighed.

"So I feel awful that I misrepresented him to you, because that wasn't fair to him. And it also means I can't blame you for thinking badly of him as a result, because I never told you that I'd been wrong about him that day. And I never told you how amazing he was to me, how much I loved him, how deeply he cared about me, how kind he was." She paused for a moment, trying to keep her emotions under control enough so that she could continue.

"Plus we were keeping our relationship a secret from Gran – which was my idea, not Rowan's – so that also meant I couldn't share everything with you. And I feel awful that I left you thinking that he wasn't good for me, because that wasn't fair to Rowan, and it also meant that you didn't like him, and led you to make that awful ultimatum," she said, her voice a sigh, her face creased with bitterness.

But Carlie's angst wasn't directed at her friend, it was directed inward, at herself. If only she'd shared with Rhiannon just how much she'd loved Rowan, just how amazing he'd been to her, how good he was, perhaps none of this would have happened. They'd all be friends now, and Rowan would still be alive.

"You know what's funny?" she mused. "After all my efforts at secrecy, Gran knew about us anyway. Rowan was brave enough and grown-up enough to go into the shop and talk to her. She'd met him before and really liked him, and she liked him even more when he told her how he felt about me, how much he loved me. He wanted to reassure her of how much he respected me too, and that he would never hurt me. He told her that I was the goddess to him, and shone brighter than the moon and the stars."

Taking a deep breath, Carlie willed the tears not to fall. "Anyway, I can't change the past, I can't erase my regrets or what they wrought, but maybe I can help you understand how I felt, how I feel now, and show you why I'm so devastated still." Her voice trailed off, and she almost chickened out, but then she decided to be brave for once and take Aideen's advice.

Walking over to the corner where her school bag sat, she tentatively lifted out the pile of cards and letters that were tied together with a red velvet ribbon. "Someone suggested to me that showing you these letters and cards from Rowan, and the one I wrote to him but didn't get a chance to deliver, might help you see why it's so hard for me to just get over him."

Rhiannon watched her friend, seeing the indecision and fear on her face as she held the letters close to her heart, wanting to share them, but equally not wanting to let them out of her sight.

Tentatively, she leaned in and placed her hands around them. "I'd be honoured to read them, and don't worry, I'll guard them with my life," she whispered. Carlie stared at her, trying to determine if she was being sarcastic or poking fun at her, but there was only love and compassion in her friend's eyes, so reluctantly she surrendered the package. The red-robed woman had said that showing Rhiannon would help both of them, and she had to trust in that. She needed something to happen to bring their friendship back to the way it had been, to cut through the impasse they found themselves at.

Both girls jumped when Rose came in to put the kettle on, and Rhiannon carefully slipped the letters into her bag before hugging her friend and making her farewells. Exhausted from the moving and sorting and lugging, and all the kitten activities, Carlie soon headed upstairs to bed, cuddling up with the cats in her new room and sending a silent prayer out to Rowan, wherever he was, to let him know how much she missed him still.

Chapter 15

A Friendship Restored

When Carlie got to school the next morning, Rhiannon was waiting for her out the front. As soon as she saw her approaching she ran over and pulled her into a hug, squeezing her tight. Rhiannon's eyes filled with tears as she told her friend, over and over, just how sorry she was. Carlie smiled at her. "It's okay, you didn't know," she said gently. "I should have told you sooner."

Rhiannon shook her head as she returned the letters. "I should have had more patience. I should have asked you. Can you forgive me?"

Carlie smiled and took her hand, leading her up the school steps as the bell rang for their first subject. "Of course. Life really is too short. Now come on, we can't be late for Laura's class. We don't want her telling Gran we've been slacking off."

Feeling lighter than they had since their blow up the week before, the girls headed into their room for history, and Carlie was relieved when she noticed that a lot of her resentment towards Rhiannon had dissipated. They didn't get a chance to talk about it much, since Jake sat with them at lunch, but maybe they didn't need to. Maybe they could just move forward together, back on track, with a new understanding of each other.

The next day they headed to the healing centre after school. Rose and her inner circle were preparing for the Imbolc ritual that weekend, and the girls had offered to help. It was the night of their coven meeting, but assisting their priestess and learning how a ritual was woven together was certainly a perfect way to spend the evening they'd committed to their magical studies.

They raced up the stairs to the beautiful room above Rose's shop, but stopped abruptly in the doorway, always awed by the sense of enchantment the space held, even in between rituals. Rhiannon watched Carlie greet Rose and tell her about her day, and she smiled even while she felt a wave of sadness. Her heart had broken a little when her friend had showed her the letters and cards she and Rowan had written to each other. What they'd shared together was so precious, so surprising, so huge and all-encompassing. She'd never felt anything like it with anyone, and while it made her feel terrible, she had to admit, even if just to herself, that she was desperately jealous of her friend. To have been loved so deeply by someone – especially someone as amazing as Rowan – blew her mind.

Pangs of guilt swept through her though. Guilt for being jealous of a dead man, guilt for the unfounded suspicions she'd harboured against him, guilt for the way she'd treated her best friend, guilt for not understanding the depth of Carlie's grief. So much guilt, so much anguish, so much longing.

With regret, she remembered that first night at the party in London, when she'd been so impressed by Rowan's kindness towards Carlie – and his politeness and consideration towards her, the tag-along friend. The day they'd all been together at the autumn festival, when he'd arranged tickets for them both and spent the whole time being so careful to include Rhiannon, even though she knew how much he'd wanted to spend the time alone with Carlie. And the way he'd honoured her, and her importance to Carlie, even when she'd been an angsty teenage bitch about him. God, she'd misjudged him so badly.

Not at first – she'd encouraged her friend to be with him in the beginning, pushed her to get past her shyness and get to know him. But later she'd tried to talk her out of the relationship, worked against her, been so negative. She couldn't even remember why, which was embarrassing. Had she acted like that purely out of jealousy? What was her motive for her actions? It was true that some of her concerns were valid. Carlie *had* skipped school one day to be with him, although even that had been for a very good reason, and had never been repeated. And she'd been lying to Rose, or withholding the truth at least, which wasn't good – especially as Rose would have been supportive of her dating Rowan. Oh the irony.

The more she thought about it, the more dreadful she felt. It pained her to admit that she hadn't been a good friend to Carlie, before Rowan's accident as well as after. Yet as cruel as she'd been, Carlie had always been good to her, had encouraged her when she talked about John, even though it must have been a knife through her heart to hear about it.

Goddess, she'd been feeling so superior, because she thought she was so mature, so grown-up, so supportive, so kind, and all along it had been Carlie who was the better friend, the better person, the less judgemental and petty. She'd actually agreed to her ridiculous ultimatum, out of respect for her, because she valued their friendship above her own needs, even after that friend had demanded such a terrible choice from her. She was just glad that in the end Carlie had realised she shouldn't have to make such a decision. And even then, she hadn't ditched Rhiannon – which she wouldn't have blamed her for, frankly – but had explained to her and to Rowan that she loved and valued them both, and refused to choose between them.

Not that Rowan had demanded such a choice. God, they were both better people than she was, yet here they were, Rowan dead and Carlie so devastated, while she was happily living her life with her family and her boyfriend. Carlie was more compassionate, even in her own grief, than she was, and it hurt her to realise how much pain she'd caused her friend. If she hadn't pressured her to dump Rowan – after she'd just stood Carlie up for their Yule ritual that night to spend time with her own boyfriend no less – she wouldn't have gone to see him that night, and...

Oh god, would Rowan still be alive? Was it her fault he'd skidded off the road in the snow, because he was so desperate to convince Carlie not to do as Rhiannon had demanded and break up with him? Her blood ran cold, and her face was frozen with fear. And when she felt Carlie's hand on her shoulder, she stared at her in growing horror. Did her friend blame her for Rowan's death?

But Carlie was smiling at her. "Did you want to come to the cafe for dinner with me and Rose when we're done here, or do you need to get home?" she asked.

Rhiannon stared at her, numb, incapable of speech. Carlie looked puzzled, but they were interrupted by Miri before she could ask what was wrong. "Hey girls, would one of you be able to help me with the long trestle table?" she requested.

Carlie nodded and walked out to the storeroom at the top of the stairs to wrestle the heavy furniture inside, and Rhiannon felt even worse. The girl who'd lost everything was still the first to offer to help others. Mentally shaking herself, she took a deep breath, and decided it was time to turn over a new leaf. First, heading over to join her friend and help set up the table.

But she paused when she felt eyes on her. Turning, she saw Rose approaching her, and was suddenly nervous, but the older woman took her in her arms and enfolded her in a hug.

"Lovely Rhiannon, stop torturing yourself, please. She doesn't blame you – in fact she's only just beginning to stop blaming herself. But it's in the past now. Don't beat yourself up over past actions, past words – just be the friend for her now that you wish you had been. She's still fragile, and she needs you now more than ever. So get over yourself, okay? Snap out of it, and be the young woman I know you're capable of being."

Rhiannon hugged the wise priestess, tears of gratitude in her eyes. "I will, I promise," she whispered, and Rose felt a weight lift from her own heart. "Will you tell Carlie I had to go though? There's something I need to do."

The next day at school Rhiannon couldn't stop yawning. Carlie teased her when they sat together in class, but when her friend seemed just as exhausted when they met up for lunch, she started feeling a little concerned.

"Are you okay Rhi? Are you coming down with something, or were you up all night partying? You can't be sick for Imbolc."

Rhiannon laughed. "I feel okay, I just didn't get much sleep. But I wasn't out partying, silly! I was searching for some things I thought you might like," she explained.

Carlie stared at her, puzzled. What on earth would she like? And was this why she'd left without saying goodbye last night?

"Well, um, I hope it won't upset you, but I'm not sure what you have to remember Rowan by," Rhiannon began, voice hesitant. "So I went through all my old spiritual magazines, and the newspapers Dad keeps, and searched online as well, and looked through all my photos too," she explained, then pulled out a thick purple folder from her bag and handed it over with a sad smile. "How about I get us a drink?" she asked, and stood up at her friend's vague nod and went over to join the long cafeteria line.

Carlie gazed down at the folder, curious but apprehensive. Screwing up her courage, she slowly opened it and pulled out the contents. On the top were several large photos of her and Rowan at the Yule Ball, as they were crowned Winter Queen and Sun King, and as they danced together afterwards. The joy on her face in the photos stabbed at her, but it was the love in his eyes as he gazed at her that broke her heart and made the tears fall. She traced over his face with her finger, remembering the way she'd felt in his arms, the whole world receding, as though they were the only two people on earth.

There were also a few snaps of the three of them together at the Autumn's End festival, pictures she didn't even remember being taken. She smiled through watering eyes as she saw how happy the three of them had been, how supportive her friend looked back then, how kind Rowan had been to both of them.

Under those was a series of interviews he'd done over the last couple of years, but it was the most recent one that made her breath catch in her throat. While the others talked about his work, his healings, his retreats, his oracle deck and his upcoming book about the magical and medicinal power of herbs, which she knew she would love reading later, the one on the top was a newspaper interview he'd done just before his winter solstice retreat. It had come out on the morning of the Yule sabbat – the morning he'd skidded off the road in the snow and died.

"Young healer in love" was the headline, and she quickly scanned the article, smiling sadly at the photo of him, his deep brown eyes piercing to her very soul, and his admission that he was cutting back on his travel because he'd fallen in love a balm to her wounded heart. It was tangible proof that she hadn't imagined how he'd felt, or exaggerated what she'd meant to him.

"I've never seen a love like it," Rhiannon said softly as she came back to the table with two juices. Carlie looked up in surprise, forgetting for a moment where she was, and that her friend had been sitting with her just moments before.

Rhiannon handed her one of the cups. "Do you want me to leave you alone for a while?" she asked quietly.

"No, it's fine. Thank you for these," she said, gesturing at the photos and articles strewn around her. "It means a lot to me."

Rhiannon nodded sadly. "It's the least I could do," she sighed. "I am so sorry that I was such a bitch to him, and to you. Seeing the photos of us at the festival together reminded me how wonderful he was to me, when he really didn't have to be. Which made me feel even worse for coming between you."

Carlie smiled through her tears. "It's okay," she whispered, and Rhiannon leaned in and gave her a grateful hug.

When the bell rang for their next class, Carlie considered feigning illness and going home, but then decided to tough it out. Tonight she could read everything her friend had compiled for her, and gaze at the pictures to her heart's content, but she needed to keep up with her schoolwork if she wanted to make it to university, and be able to study in order to help others who were grieving. Although for the first time she wondered if she was really going to be any use to other people suffering the death of their loved ones, when she was still so easily brought to her knees by the pain of her loss...

Chapter 16

Her Sweet Protector

School seemed even longer than usual the next day, and Carlie was filled with a sense of dread and anxiety throughout each class that she just couldn't shake. She drifted off in history, disappointing Laura when she fudged an answer, and was impatient with Rhiannon when they sat together at lunch, unwilling to confide in her about what was stressing her out, and hoping to avoid discussing it. Because this afternoon Jake was coming over to the cottage to work on their assignment with her, and she was nervous.

The last time they'd been alone together was when they were studying at his grandad's place, and he'd asked her out on a date. He'd been lovely about her turning him down, and seemed content to just be friends, but since Rhiannon's insistence that she should go out with him she'd suddenly started feeling uncomfortable around him, as well as guilty for rejecting him. She was also a bit worried that she'd freak out having him in her home, when the only guy who'd ever been there was Rowan.

Finally though the school bell rang, and it was time for her to face her fear. Telling herself that there was no need to worry wasn't helping, but she had to calm herself down somehow. Although she was mostly moved in to her new bedroom, and her desk and books were in there, she'd decided they should work in the kitchen, because she felt weird about the idea of inviting a guy into her personal space. She wasn't sure what that meant – she had no qualms letting Rhiannon in, and Jake was nothing more than a friend. But she could tie herself in knots trying to psychoanalyse herself, and she wasn't in the mood for it right now. Nor did she have the time.

They walked to the cottage together, not saying much, then she led him through to the kitchen and offered him a seat at the table. Turning the heater on, she looked around for Luna and Luther. They usually hung around downstairs, mostly in the kitchen, but she figured that if it had gotten too cold they might have looked for somewhere warmer to burrow.

"I just have to find the cats – we have a new kitten, so I want to make sure she's okay," she explained. "But how rude. I'm sorry, would you like a cup of tea?" she asked, and Jake nodded gratefully. She put the kettle on and got the teapot and tea leaves out, then walked through to the lounge room, peering into corners before racing up the stairs.

Standing in the doorway of her old room, she looked around in astonishment. Now that she'd been sleeping in her mum's room, this one looked so tiny in comparison. The narrow bed seemed as though it wouldn't fit a child, let alone her and two cats, and she wasn't sure how she'd crammed all her clothes into the small wardrobe.

Yet the view of the tor out the window still took her breath away, and she could feel its energy reaching out to her just as strongly as she had the very first time she'd stood in this room, staring at the hill, being so deeply affected by it yet having no clue as to what it all meant. Not that she had much more of a clue now, but she'd done some amazing rituals atop it, both alone and with Rhiannon, and met some... Women? Otherworldly beings? Figments of her imagination?

Jumping when she felt a hand on her shoulder, she spun around, scream in her throat, and came face to face with Jake.

"Sorry, I didn't mean to scare you, I just wasn't sure where you were. Are you okay?" he asked, concern on his face.

She blinked. God, had she just totally zoned out, and been standing there for ages, lost in a world between worlds?

"I'm fine, sorry," she said, trying to step around him, to go and check her room for the cats, and resigned to the fact that he'd follow her there too. But he'd stopped in the doorway to her old room and was staring out at the tor, just as drawn in as she'd been by its magic.

"Can you feel it too?" she asked softly.

He nodded, eyes still focused on the hulking hill. "I've never seen it from this angle," he whispered. "But I've dreamed about it, without really knowing what it was. Last night I was running through these tunnels that were inside the hill – which doesn't really make sense, I realise that – and it felt like I was being chased by something, and yet I didn't know what it was, or what it could mean..." he trailed off. "Sorry, now you probably think I'm completely nuts," he added, rolling his eyes at himself.

Shaking her head, Carlie turned back to him, and the hill. "You're not crazy," she offered, unsure of just how much she wanted to tell him, or how far to go to reassure him. But he looked really nervous, clearly wondering what she thought of his announcement, so she figured it couldn't hurt to put his mind at ease.

"I've had loads of dreams where I was running through those tunnels, sometimes chasing, sometimes being chased," she began, voice a little hesitant. "And sometimes they're more magical-slash-bizarre than reality based. But there really are tunnels under there, a whole network of them. Surveyors found them a long time ago. So you're not as weird as you imagined."

Jake smiled, that genuine, slightly cheeky smile that transformed his face. "Thank you for laying that worry to rest," he said, tone jokey and light-hearted, but his eyes revealing just how relieved he was. "Now where are these cats of yours?"

Reluctantly she led him across the landing and up the stairs to the front room, her room now, and opened the door. Luther looked up from the bed as she walked in, stretching his big cat stretch, and Luna woke up at his movement and tried to imitate him, which was adorably cute. She still had no idea how Luther got through closed doors into their rooms, but she'd given up thinking she'd ever discover his secret. Sitting down next to them, she patted them both, glad to see they were warm and happy, but when Jake poked his head around the door, Luther immediately jumped onto her lap, so that he was positioned between her and the stranger in the entranceway, fur standing on end, his eyes boring straight into Jake's.

"Wow, you really have a protector there!" he said, taking an involuntary step backwards.

"Sorry," she replied, as she placed a calming hand on Luther's head. "It's okay buddy, Jake's a friend, just a friend," she whispered soothingly. She felt a stab through her heart as she recalled Luther's reaction to Rowan, and how happy her boyfriend had been to meet him and know that she had a guardian watching out for her.

After a wary, suspicious beginning, Luther had ended up loving Rowan, and had somehow managed to communicate with him, which had puzzled Carlie no end. She recalled the day that Luther had jumped up on her bed – the old narrow bed – when she and Rowan were kissing, and somehow let her boyfriend know that Rose would be home in ten minutes. If only he could have warned him that awful solstice morning as well…

"Are you okay?" Jake asked, his voice seeming to come from a great distance, and she crashed painfully back into the present.

"I'm sorry, I'm just… remembering. Luther *is* a protector," she agreed. "And this is Luna, our new kitten. She's just a ball of fluff right now, but Luther is showing her the ropes."

As she tenderly picked her up, she noticed Jake looking around her bedroom, and all her feelings of discomfort returned.

"So, we should probably go downstairs and get to work," she said hastily. "And I really need to feed the cats, and finally make our tea." Jake blushed a little at being caught snooping, and quickly turned and led the way back down the stairs, Luther at his heels, and out to the kitchen.

The afternoon passed quickly, and by the time Rose arrived home they'd done a big chunk of work and felt happy with their progress. Jake leaped to his feet when she walked into the kitchen, and had his hand out to introduce himself before Carlie had even put down her pen and said hello.

"Gran, this is Jake," she said, trying to smother a grin at his eagerness. "Jake, this is Rose Tyler."

"It's so lovely to meet you Mrs Tyler," he said, his face lit up again as he turned his smile on her. "I've heard so much about you, and it's an honour, really."

"Rose, please," she said, smiling back, although she looked a little perplexed at his enthusiasm. "It makes me feel so old to be called Mrs Tyler. And sit down, please, just relax. There's no need to stand up on my account."

Nodding, he sat back down, but he continued to stare at her as though she was something wonderfully unusual, totally fascinated by her and hanging on every word she uttered.

Carlie stood up. "Tea for you Gran?" she asked. "And would you like another one Jake?"

"Oh, I don't want to impose," he replied, almost shy, as she filled the kettle with water and put it on the stove.

"Nonsense Jake, it's no imposition," Rose said. "And I was just about to put a spinach and ricotta pie in the oven, if you'd like to stay for dinner. There's plenty – I made it this morning, and Carlie and I certainly can't get through a whole one."

He turned to Carlie, eyebrows raised in question, and she shrugged, concentrating on scooping out fresh tea leaves into the pot and rinsing their mugs. "Well, that would be lovely, if it's no trouble to either of you. Can I help with anything?" he asked.

"If you two could make the salad, that would be great," Rose replied. "I just have to finish up some bookkeeping, but the pie should be ready in twenty minutes, if that suits everyone?"

Jake nodded eagerly, and Carlie piled up their books and cleared off some room for her grandmother at the table, then started pulling ingredients for the salad out of the fridge. She wasn't sure how she felt about this development.

She'd been ready to say goodbye to Jake, but she knew better than to challenge Rose when she'd made up her mind about something. So while they washed and chopped the lettuce, capsicum, carrots, radishes and tomatoes, she and Jake chatted about Australian summers and what he usually did in his school holidays. Pausing to make the tea and take her grandma a cup, she smiled as she realised she was actually enjoying talking to Jake. Who'd have thought?

Finally, as the enticing aroma from the oven was making their tummies rumble, Rose packed away her paperwork while Carlie set the table and Jake put his books, notepads and pens back in his school bag. Then she carefully took the pie from the oven and carried it over to the table, before grabbing the salad bowl and taking a seat opposite Jake.

"It smells amazing Mrs Tyler," he said, and Carlie smiled. He was very polite, she'd give him that.

"Thank you Jake, and it's lovely to have you here. Are you okay with me saying a blessing before we eat?"

His eyes widened, but he nodded quickly, and Carlie tried to smother another grin. Rose took Carlie's hand in her left, and Jake's in her right, so Carlie took Jake's other hand in hers, then bowed her head and closed her eyes.

> *Goddess, we thank you for the bounty we are about to eat,*
> *And for the family and friends who make us complete.*
> *In gratitude we share this simple meal,*
> *Grateful for the love and support we feel.*

After a moment of silence, Rose squeezed their hands, opened her eyes and served out a huge piece of pie for Jake. "How are you enjoying your new school?" she asked, as she handed him the salad. After thanking her for the pie and spooning out some lettuce and tomatoes, Jake told her that he was settling in well, but was always really grateful to hear a familiar accent whenever he had a class with Carlie. Then he talked about the aid work his parents were doing in Africa, which fascinated Rose and Carlie, and the various travelling they'd done over the years that had taken them away from him.

Later Rose brought a hot apple and cinnamon crumble over to the table, which she'd also whipped up that morning, and Carlie eyed her suspiciously. Had her grandmother known they'd be having a dinner guest tonight, long before she even knew that Jake would be there to study this afternoon?

Her attention was brought back to the present when Jake admitted that part of the reason that his parents had sent him to stay with his grandfather this year was that they were starting to worry a little about him living on his own.

"I could have stayed with my best mate and his family, but Dad was really concerned about Pop living on his own. He was devastated when Nan died, obviously, but he's had a few niggling health issues too, so my parents sat me down and asked if I'd be prepared to spend the year with him, help him out a bit. You can't mention any of this to him though," he insisted, suddenly looking panicked that he'd revealed too much.

"Your secret is safe with us Jake," Rose assured him. "And that's lovely that you were so happy to help him out."

"It's no trouble, and it was the least I could do. Nan and Pop moved to Australia for ten years just so they could live near us and look after me when my parents had to travel for work – they'd stay with me at home so my schooling wasn't disrupted, and they'd cook for me, and take me to school and to sport and to piano lessons and what-not. They were so wonderful. And I really miss Nan," he said, and his eyes glistened a little as he spoke.

"But you two must have had wonderful times together over the years too, right?" he asked, trying to deflect their attention away from him while he composed himself.

Carlie blushed and Rose looked uncomfortable, and they caught each other's eye, wondering what to say, and who should say it. Finally Carlie spoke. "I didn't know I had a grandma until last June, after my parents died," she said softly, simply. Jake looked shocked for a moment, then remembered a few comments Carlie had made in previous conversations that now made sense.

"Mum lost touch with Rose after she moved to Australia – it's a long story though," she muttered, before moving on quickly. "And to be honest, I was a horror when I first got here. I blamed Gran for everything, and had decided that she must be a total monster, so I was really awful to her. And so angry. It took a while for me to untangle my misconceptions and get to the truth of it, and I'm still mortified by what a bitch I was to her. I'm not sure I'll ever forgive myself," she sighed.

Rose shook her head sadly. "Sweetheart, you have to stop beating yourself up over this. You didn't know, neither of us knew. And you were grieving the worst kind of loss. We got there in the end," she said soothingly, then turned to Jake.

"Don't you listen to her. We had a little misunderstanding when she arrived, but we quickly got over that, and it's been wonderful ever since," she explained. "I lost my daughter and my husband more than twenty years ago, so it's been a dream come true for me to have Carlie here. And we've done some amazing things together, and shared so much. We've cooked, we've planted herbs, we've sewn, we've travelled, we've woven magic together..."

Carlie looked up at her grandmother, a warning in her eyes – Jake's grandfather was still a churchgoer, no matter what he'd said to her the other day about acceptance, and she wasn't sure what he really thought about Rose's more esoteric interests. But Jake jumped in eagerly as soon as she mentioned magic.

"Actually, Pop and I were wondering if any of your rituals were open to outsiders to participate in," he said, and Carlie nearly fell off her chair in surprise. "And whether it would be okay for men to come, or are they only designed for women?"

"A lot of them are open to the public, to friends of friends, and definitely to both men and women," Rose replied. Then she paused for a moment, considering her answer carefully. "Although I don't want to give you the wrong idea Jake. Certainly there are many more women than men who attend, but that's not because we discourage them. I've always just assumed it was because less men wanted to take part, but perhaps they're not sure that they're welcome either," she mused. "Hmm, maybe I need to make that clearer to people, to the community? Thank you for voicing that," she said.

"But there are a few men who take part regularly, and a couple more who come from time to time. The next ritual is this weekend in fact, if you and your grandfather would like to join us?"

Jake's eyes lit up with joy. "Thank you, that would be fantastic," he replied. "Pop will be really happy, and he's been wanting to see you again too Carlie. I've been hoping to get him more involved in things, to meet new people, open up a little – to get him out of the house, out of his comfort zone. He lived in London and Perth for most of his life, and when he came here with Nan, she was already sick, so he barely left her side, which means he hasn't met many people outside of the church group that Nan was involved with.

"And I'd love to come too, and be part of it. I think we can all use a little more magic in our lives," he said, smiling brightly. "Do we need to bring anything, or prepare in any way?"

Rose shook her head. "There's always a brief explanation before we start the ritual, outlining what will happen, and there are people you can ask questions of at any time during it. And you can choose which bits you want to participate in, and just watch other parts if you'd rather. It's always totally up to you."

Jake suddenly looked nervous, and Carlie took pity on him.

"I was apprehensive before my first ritual too – but it was really relaxed," she assured him, and his expression lightened a little. "I didn't have to speak at all, just listen, and the directions were really clear. It was really beautiful."

Smiling with pride as Carlie spoke, and marvelling at just how much she'd changed in the last six months, Rose stood up and walked through to the lounge room, returning with a book outlining all the sabbats, which she handed to Jake.

"You don't have to read this – there's no homework, I promise – but if you're interested you can skim through a bit about the festival we'll be celebrating. It's known as Imbolc, and it marks the end of winter and the start of spring, so it's all about new beginnings, the return of light to the land, an honouring of seeds starting to sprout, the fresh growth that sustains life, and also the germination of things in our own lives that we wish to grow and nurture. Fresh starts, optimism, seeing the world anew," Rose revealed.

Jake looked fascinated, and read the back of the book with great interest. "I'd love to borrow this for a few days, if that's okay?" he asked, and Rose nodded cheerfully.

"Most people bring along a few cans of beans or a packet of rice or a carton of soy milk or something, for the homeless shelter,"

Carlie added. "I remember being so impressed by that at my first ritual, when I realised that their honouring of the cycle of the seasons and the wheel of life was not just lip service – everyone in the circle really is grateful for all the blessings they feel they have, and they're all eager to give back, and to keep things balanced."

"Yeah, Pop mentioned that you had helped Nan, and refused any money, even for the cost of the herbs you had to buy. He thought it was a bit odd at the time – sorry," he said quickly to Rose, but she smiled and waved her hand, dismissing his concerns. "He said he was so used to the church expecting money from them, that he was a bit suspicious at first – no offence!"

Rose laughed. "None taken."

"But he was very grateful – he said your herbal concoctions eased Nan's pain a great deal towards the end, which gave them more quality time to be together. He said that was the best gift of all, the thing that meant the most to them. There's no present like time, isn't that what they say?" he asked.

Rose smiled sadly. "I'm so sorry you both lost her," she said simply, voice heavy with compassion.

"Thank you," he replied softly. "That means a lot to me."

Carlie sighed. He was so much more gracious than she'd been. Was she the only ungrateful, moody, angry person in this town?

"Sweetheart, give yourself a break," Rose implored her, and Jake looked puzzled, clearly unaware of this priestess's mind-reading skills. Carlie smiled at her grandmother, and nodded, then got back to the topic at hand.

"After the ritual we gather together for a while, and have a cup of tea or some juice and eat a bit of food, to ground ourselves back in our bodies, and just to catch up with people, talk about the evening, or about normal life," she explained.

"So you're welcome to bring a plate if you'd like to, but you really don't have to – there's always plenty of food," she continued. "But if you don't like going somewhere empty handed, a plate of cookies, or carrot sticks and dip, just something small, would always be gratefully accepted. And I think that if there's any food left over it goes to the homeless shelter too, so nothing is ever wasted," she added, looking at Rose with eyebrows raised in question.

Nodding, Rose stood up and cleared the plates, telling Jake to relax when he tried to help, then put the kettle on. "But you really don't have to bring anything," she insisted. "No pressure, no stress. It's meant to be a relaxing, reinvigorating occasion."

The three of them continued their conversation while they had another cup of tea together, then Jake said he had to get home, and thanked them for the wonderful dinner and their company.

"It wasn't as bad as you'd expected, was it?" Rose asked her granddaughter once he'd left.

"What do you mean?" Carlie asked, shocked at her grandmother's perceptiveness.

Rose smiled at her, a knowing smile. "He cares about you very much Carlie, but you don't have to feel nervous or threatened by that. He'll never push you to do anything you don't want to do, and he is genuinely happy to just be your friend if that's what you want. I think it's important for you to know that."

"Thanks Gran," she replied, for once more grateful than alarmed by her priestess powers. "And now I really should get to bed – we have a test tomorrow, which I'm a bit worried about."

They hugged good night, then Carlie headed upstairs to bed with the two cats, and slipped into a surprisingly peaceful, dreamless sleep.

Chapter 17

A Festival of Joy and Renewal

On Saturday Carlie and Rhiannon spent the whole day with Rose in the kitchen of the cottage, grinding herbs, sewing dream pillows and blending incense in the morning, then starting to bake for the following night's ritual in the afternoon.

Carlie made chocolate-orange poppyseed cupcakes, since seeds symbolise Imbolc's energy of growth and fertility, then whipped up mini lemon cheesecakes, as dairy foods are also a strong part of the seasonal theme. Rhiannon created individual pots of baked custard flavoured with ginger, cinnamon, nutmeg and other spring spices, then churned some cream into butter and buttermilk. And Rose kneaded several trays of Bridie's bread, small loaves made from buttermilk, flour and salt and sprinkled with sunflower and sesame seeds to capture the energy of new life and new beginnings inherent in this time of year, then blended and poured out little gauze bags filled with an Imbolc tea crafted from chamomile, nettle and violets.

As the evening drew in and the sky faded to black, the silver-haired priestess taught the girls how to weave Bridie Crosses, the traditional fire wheel symbols of the goddess, out of stalks of wheat, so they could hang them around the house and in the ritual room. Then they started making candles for the ceremony. Each participant would need one for the ritual itself, and Rose also wanted to gift each person with a set of Imbolc candles along with their tea, so they could continue to weave the magic of the season when they returned home. Half of the candles would be white and the other half pale blue, to embody the innocence and purity of the sabbat and represent the cleansing power of the element of fire.

Halfway through dipping one of her candles, Carlie paused and gazed around the room. The cats were purring at her feet, the flickering light of the pillar candle in the centre of the table gave a rosy glow to everything, and she suddenly realised, in this moment at least, that she was happy. Despite all that she'd lost, she could actually see something positive in her life. Not all the time, but in brief snatches coloured by friendship and family, or magical purpose. She knew it was a fleeting state of being, for now anyway, but if she could continue to experience these golden moments, perhaps her desire to flee, to disappear from the world, might eventually wield less and less power over her.

"Oh Sweetheart, I'm so glad," Rose whispered, eyes twinkling in the candlelight as she gazed across at her granddaughter.

Carlie laughed. She would probably never get used to her grandma reading her mind, but she was starting to be less disturbed by it.

"Please don't worry. I can't read your every thought, I promise, and even if I could, I wouldn't," Rose said. "I just pick up brief flashes of emotion, not specific thoughts, and it mostly happens when we're in a ritual head space, like now – I'm sure you could glean my mood right now too, if you wanted to. But I'd never invade your privacy like that, and you can rest assured that you never gave anything away about Rowan when you were with him, so don't be scared that I know what you're thinking or what you've done or not done, okay? It doesn't work like that."

Rhiannon looked over at her friend, nervous that the mention of Rowan would upset her and spoil her fragile peace, but Carlie smiled at her. "Don't worry so much Rhi, I'm not going to fall apart every time his name is mentioned. But thank you for your concern," she said, hugging her friend, then laughing when she realised she'd just done the same thing that Rose had.

At that moment Luna woke up, yawned, then jumped into Carlie's lap, and the focus of their attention shifted. Rose got up and popped a pot of soup on the stove to warm for their dinner, and Carlie cleared some space at the table so they could eat.

After Rose had gone to bed, the two girls tiptoed upstairs to Carlie's room, flopped down on her bed and opened their Book of Shadows. Their coven homework for the week was to write about Imbolc, so they could compare notes and add to their own entries, so they stayed up for a while, scribbling down information, whispering together and trying not to laugh too loudly, before finally changing into their pyjamas, brushing their teeth and climbing into bed.

The next morning, Rhiannon left for her place to spend time with her little brother and get some homework done, before returning to Carlie's so they could take all the food down to the healing centre for Rose. Once it was all set up, they headed back to the cottage to get ready, weaving together wreaths of snowdrops and primroses for their hair, then slipping into their long velvet ritual dresses and putting on the rings they'd received from their Otherworldly friends on the night of their coven dedication.

Carlie's was a delicate silver one with a butterfly on it, with the wings made up of aquamarines, crystals of truth and trust. And Rhiannon's ring had a silver dragonfly on it, with pink rose quartz, the crystal of compassion, love and healing, forming its wings.

A flash of memory from that night hit Carlie – the two of them taking their own path to the top of the tor as darkness descended, a candle in one hand and flowers representing their friendship clutched tight in the other. An image of Brianna, the green-clad woman she'd encountered, fluttered into her mind, and she smiled as she recalled their conversation, and the beautiful athame she'd given her.

And Rhiannon had met up with blue-robed Brauna, and been gifted a gorgeous silver chalice. They still used both of these magical tools in their private rituals, along with the wand and pentacle Brianna had given Carlie for the two of them a few months later.

Now her friend caught her eye and smiled back. "It's hard to believe that it's been six months since the Lughnasadh ritual we did with Rose, isn't it?" she asked, voice hushed even though there was no one around to hear them. "I feel like I've lived a lifetime since then, so I can't even begin to imagine how you feel," she said softly.

Carlie's mouth curved upward for a fleeting moment. Rhiannon was right. Well, half right. In some ways it did feel like a lifetime ago, yet in others it felt like only yesterday that she'd been at home in Australia with her parents and her best friend Emily, cheerfully planning their university studies in law, and the apartment they were going to move in to together. But Emily had started her uni degree last week, and was meeting new people and getting on with life without her. For the first time Carlie realised that the death of her parents in a car accident and her being sent across the world to live with a stranger had impacted on Emily's life too.

God, was it really only seven months since she'd landed on her grandma's door step, hating her before she'd even met her, acting like a selfish bitch for the first few weeks as she drowned in grief and loss and a tidal wave of anger? Although the memory mortified her, she acknowledged that she really had come a long way in a short time. Much of that had been the result of the patience and compassion of her grandma, another part had been Rowan's love for her, and his ability to make her see herself in new and better ways – to want to be new and better. And another part had been Rhiannon's friendship, and her empathy and support.

"Thank you for all you've given me," Carlie said quietly. She may have lost Rowan, but she didn't have to lose her friend too. Yes, she'd been angry with her, for good reason, but if she thought everyone had to be perfect all the time, she'd have no one in her life. And she was far from perfect herself. Rose had given her a second, and a third, chance, and excused all kinds of behaviour, so the least she could do was give Rhiannon a pass. As awful as she'd been, and as bad as the consequences of her actions had turned out, she had good intentions.

Rhiannon took her hand. "And thank *you* Carlie," she whispered, a catch in her voice. "You still don't realise all you've given me. And forgiving me now is the biggest gift of all. I'll always feel bad about how I acted, and wonder if it would have panned out differently if I'd done something, or not done something…"

Carlie forced a smile. She'd always wonder that too, of both her friend's actions and her own, but obsessing over that wouldn't bring Rowan back. And hating her friend so she could carry on blaming her was pointless and wrong. She remembered Aideen telling her to let go of always having to be right, and realised that was good advice. They were both at fault, in some ways, yet at the same time neither of them were. Her head spun.

Consequences. Fate. Destiny... Action and reaction...

Sometimes she thought life was just a big cosmic joke, one that wasn't even funny. When she'd met the blue-clad woman on a misty mountain top, she'd warned her there was no deeper meaning, no grand purpose or design. That sometimes really bad things happened to really good people, for no reason at all. At the time she'd thought that was a horribly fatalistic way to live, yet it absolved you of responsibility when something bad happened, while empowering you to make your own choices and create your own life too.

Back in the village as night began to fall, the two friends made their way to the healing centre. A feeling of reverence descended on them as they climbed the stairs, and when they stepped across the threshold into the ritual room, the rows of blazing candles took their breath away. They hugged Laura, who was transformed into a strong, beautiful priestess, a million miles from her school-teacher persona, and greeted several other women from Rose's inner circle, touched that they were invited to be part of their magic.

As Rhiannon straightened her floral headdress, Carlie spotted Jake and his grandfather standing in the doorway, looking a little lost, so they went to greet them. Richard shook Rhi's hand and beamed at her when they were introduced, then leaned forward to hug Carlie, and she felt the strength within him as well as his fragility. Jake's parents needn't worry too much on his behalf.

Rhiannon tried to hug Jake then, but it was made a little awkward by the platter of food in his hands, so he quickly presented Carlie with the plate of warm scones with fresh berry jam and cream.

"Pop loves to cook, but he just doesn't do it much because it's only the two of us, and all the church ladies leave him food anyway," he grinned. "But he found a recipe in an old cookbook of Nan's for Bridie scones, which from what we read seemed fitting for this ritual, and it made him feel useful. He's been lacking in purpose since she died, so this was really nice for him."

Carlie smiled as she carried the plate over to the end of the trestle table, where it joined a beautifully coloured spread of seasonal foods and cakes. She loved the effort everyone went to here. At parties back home, her parents would grab a packet of rice crackers and a container of dip, or something equally quick and easy, to take along. But here everyone made their contributions from scratch, blending together their own dips and baking savoury crackers to go with them, whipping up cookies or desserts, even roasting potato cakes sprinkled with rosemary, as someone had done tonight, and often using their own home-grown produce.

Everyone did that here, even her. Before, she had thought that she couldn't cook, but it seemed that she could, she'd just never really tried. And she'd discovered just how therapeutic it could be, almost a meditation. She especially enjoyed it when she was making something for a ritual, and she could immerse herself in the meaning of the sabbat and the energies of the season.

Today she'd spent the afternoon slicing up the halva they'd made a few days earlier, which was infused with vanilla and sesame seeds, and cooking buttermilk pancakes sprinkled with herbs and flowers. Soon she and Rose would make them with the added magic of ingredients fresh from their garden... *Their garden...* How funny that she now thought of this place as hers, as home.

There wasn't much still growing in it right now, as the harsh winter was only just beginning to loosen its grip, so she'd used Rose's stockpile of herbs instead, the ones her grandmother had dried from her garden at the end of the previous summer. Which was when she'd arrived in the village to live with her, yet she hadn't noticed her grandma doing that. Although she hadn't been paying attention to anything back then, she thought regretfully. Still, no point dwelling on that now.

Forcing a smile, she walked back over to where Jake and his grandfather were standing, looking awkward and ill-at-ease, yet interested in everything happening around them. She remembered that sensation so vividly from her first ritual, and it shocked her, just how at home she felt here now, in this room where magic was woven, and this village where people lived close to the earth. And how confident she felt as she greeted the people she'd started to become close to, people she never would have known back in her old life in Sydney.

When Rhiannon's dad Mike arrived, she beckoned him over and introduced him to everyone. He and Richard started chatting, while Carlie and Rhiannon told Jake about their weekend of cooking. And after complimenting the girls on their dresses and the flowers in their hair, and asking after Luna, Jake told them about the plans he'd been drawing up with his grandfather to replant their vegie patch, which was inspired by his stories of Rose's amazing herb garden.

Finally the lights dimmed, and a hush fell as Rose gracefully stood up from her position behind the central altar. Carlie's breath caught as she watched her grandmother take up the etheric cloak of the priestess, marvelling as the sense of power and strength settled around her shoulders. At a gasp beside her, she turned and caught the look of wonder on Jake's face, and the gaze of surprise and admiration on his grandfather's. Catching Rhiannon's eye as she turned back, the two girls smiled at each other, more used to Rose's transformation, yet no less awed by it.

Carlie would never tire of seeing her grandma lead a ritual. It was like something out of a movie, but there were no special effects in this room. Gazing around her, she focused again on the golden threads of light she could see vibrating between everyone in the circle. The one linking Jake and his grandfather was thicker than the others, and she felt a lump in her throat as she sensed the deep love between them. Her heart ached as she thought of all the special moments they'd shared – a lifetime of beautiful memories and rich experiences, from the grand adventures they'd no doubt had to the equally wonderful and equally precious ordinary moments.

Reluctantly she admitted that she was jealous of them, and of Jake, that he'd grown up with such amazing grandparents, and had such a close relationship with them, such a strong bond, and had spent so much time with them. It was the time she envied most. But she had Rose now, and Rose had her, and they were building a universe of golden moments together. There was no point pining for what she'd missed out on – what they'd both missed out on. She just had to make the most of their time now. And she couldn't have dreamed up a better grandmother if she'd tried.

Suddenly realising that Rose had started speaking, she crashed back into the room. Oops! Wasn't that the first lesson – be present now? She didn't want to daydream away such a magical night.

"Welcome to our Imbolc ritual," their priestess began, her voice rich and deep and powerful, as though coming from the very centre of the earth itself. "Imbolc is the festival of joy and renewal that marks the turning of the wheel from the end of winter to the start of spring. It celebrates the lengthening of the days and the return of the sun and its life-giving warmth – the return of the light as it illuminates the land as well as our hearts. We honour the fertility of the land and of our own selves, in this time of hope, fresh starts and new beginnings.

"Energetically it's a time of re-awakening and re-emergence, as all of nature fills with life force and begins to quiver with the energy to grow again, and we too start to emerge from the chill of winter to re-engage with the world. And it's a time of purification and cleansing after the long dark of the winter months, of stripping away the old so that the new can emerge," Rose continued.

Feeling someone watching her, Carlie turned to meet Jake's gaze. His face was lit up with curiosity as well as awe, and she smiled at him, at his openness to new experiences, and his joy at being alive. She was suddenly really grateful for his friendship, and admiring of his attitude, and she hoped that some of his positivity would inspire her to feel that way too.

Her attention returned to her grandmother as she picked up a beautiful crystal-tipped wand from the altar, and stepped outside of the circle of people. With the wand held high, she walked slowly around the perimeter in a clockwise direction. Carlie shivered as she felt the priestess pass behind her, and her skin prickled with a sense of magic and anticipation as Rose spoke.

By my will a circle formed,
Between the worlds where magic's born.
Contain the energy raised within,
As the veils between these worlds do thin.
Hold us safe throughout this rite,
As we create magic together on this night.
The circle is cast, so mote it be.

Returning to the starting point, Rose linked the hands of the two women at the portal to close the circle, then walked back to the central altar, and the four women calling the directions raised their wands and one at a time invoked the directions in sweet, strong voices.

Water: I call forth the guardians of the west to cleanse, consecrate and protect this space during our rite, and I ask the waters of the oceans and rivers and sacred springs to wash away anything that no longer serves us. Element of water, welcome.

Earth: I call forth the guardians of the north to cleanse, consecrate and protect this space during our rite, and I ask the stones, the crystals and the very earth that we walk upon to ground and strengthen us. Element of earth, welcome.

Air: I call forth the guardians of the east to cleanse, consecrate and protect this space during our rite, and I ask the winds of the planet, both stormy gales and gentle breezes, and the very air itself, to inspire and uplift us. Element of air, welcome.

Fire: I call forth the guardians of the south to cleanse, consecrate and protect this space during our rite, and I ask the flames of light and heat, and fire itself, to burn away anything that no longer serves us. Element of fire, welcome.

As each direction caller finished her invocation, there was a gentle murmur from the rest of the circle: "Hail and welcome." At her first ritual, Carlie had been too shy to add her voice, but tonight she spoke the words with everyone else, and felt a part of something that warmed her heart, something that rooted her in this time, in this place, in this community that she knew cared for her and her family, past and present. Then Rose raised the central altar candle high, and gazed upwards.

> *Great Mother, divine goddess of wisdom and moonlight,*
> *Please shine your love on us tonight.*
> *Lord of the woods, of nature and sunlight,*
> *Shine your blessings on our sacred rite.*
> *And Bridie, please grace us with your transformative flames,*
> *and help us to purify and burn away our doubt and pain.*

Carlie embraced the mystery of how she felt in these moments, how connected she was to everyone in the room, how engulfed in love. Catching Rhiannon's eye, she smiled, knowing her friend understood perfectly, and the sensation of sharing this magic with her made her feel close to her again. A weight lifted from her heart as she felt their connection fall back into place.

Turning back to the circle, she blushed when Rose beckoned the two girls forward to hand out the candles they'd made the previous night so that everyone in the circle had one. A flush of nerves swept over her, but she took a deep breath, willing herself to be calm, then picked up the basket at her feet and walked around her half of the circle, distributing the pretty beeswax candles, and feeling so deeply touched by the sense of camaraderie and connection as each person received their candle and whispered a blessing to her in return.

As she moved around the room she heard Rose's strong, powerful voice outlining the ritual. Their priestess would begin, by lighting her candle and making a wish or a statement of intent as the flame caught, then she would offer the candle to Laura, who would light hers from its flame as she spoke her own wish, then offer hers to the person next to her, and so on around the circle until everyone's candle was aflame and they had made a vibrant ring of fire to fuel their wishes. Then the last person would light the large pillar candle on the altar, which would absorb and hold the magic of the group, so they could light it at future rituals to reawaken and reinforce the magic they wove tonight.

Smiling at Richard and Jake, Rose added that they could speak their wish aloud or send it out as a silent prayer, whatever they felt comfortable with, because it was the intent with which they formed and focused their wish that gave it its power, not how loudly or publicly they made it.

Then she began. "Dearest Bridie, maiden goddess, at this time of new beginnings I wish for health and healing for everyone here, and inspiration to fuel their creativity," Rose said, as she lit her own candle, then glided over to Laura and offered its flame to her.

"Blessed Bridie, I ask for your healing for my mother, who couldn't be here tonight," their teacher whispered as she ignited her candle. Then she offered it to Miri, who was standing next to her, and so the flame travelled around the circle, with wishes and prayers igniting with it as it journeyed.

One person asked for insight into an issue she was facing, another for inspiration with a project he was about to begin, a third for the strength to face a challenge she felt unprepared for.

When the flame got to Richard, he closed his eyes and took a deep, silent breath, then he dipped his candle to the flame of the person next to him, and held it to his heart as he gazed at Rose in the centre of the circle. Then he turned and offered his flame to ignite Jake's candle. His grandson looked dazzled by the occasion, his eyes shining and his face lit up with purpose and passion.

"I wish for healing and comfort for a friend who is suffering and heart-sore," he said quietly, then looked directly at Carlie, compassion softening his features as he smiled at her. She was overwhelmed by his sentiment and deeply touched by his words, and started to panic a little as the flame came ever closer to her.

What should she wish for? Could she say it aloud, or would she keep it private? Should it be a personal wish, or one for Rose or the community? Could she even keep it together long enough to make hers, as she listened to all the beautiful wishes, felt the people in the circle connected, all one heart and mind?

Finally the candle reached her, and she tipped hers to the flame and whispered her wish so quietly that only Rhiannon, standing next to her, heard it. "Sweet goddess, or the universe, or whoever is listening, please help my heart to heal, and to one day open again, without walls, without fear," she mumbled, then turned to her friend and offered the flame to her.

Rhiannon spoke just as quietly, a little embarrassed because her dad was in the room, and not quite ready to reveal herself so deeply, yet swept up in the magic of the night and the power of the group's sharing. "Dearest Bridie, thank you so much for my remaining family and my friends. I am so grateful for all of your blessings. My wish tonight is to some day find a love like Carlie and Rowan's, and to feel worthy of the depth and the joy of it."

"Oh Rhi, of course you're worthy," Carlie whispered, after her friend had passed on the flame to the person to her left, since they were working deosil, with the sun, to raise energy and manifest their dreams and wishes into reality. Rhiannon blushed, and tried to shush her friend – she didn't want to break the spell of the ritual or distract anyone from their wish. Carlie mouthed: "Sorry," and brought her attention back to the circle.

Next Rose led them in a meditation to focus on the new beginnings they sought in the coming month, which she followed with a spiral dance to wake everyone up, refocus their minds and get their energy swirling again. Then, as laughter rang out, Rose brought them back to her again, mood serious, and began a healing spell that they all contributed to and then sent outwards over the land. At one point Carlie glanced over at Jake and his grandfather, and was moved almost to tears by the wonder in their eyes and the golden energy that surrounded and linked them.

Then finally Rose stood in the centre of the circle again to thank and farewell the deities.

> *Great Mother, divine goddess of wisdom and moonlight,*
> *Thank you for shining your love on us tonight.*
> *Lord of the woods, of nature and sunlight,*
> *We are so grateful for your blessings on our sacred rite.*
> *And Bridie, sweet maiden and fire goddess, thank you*
> *for inspiring us with your grace, and offering us the power*
> *of your transformative flame. Hail and farewell.*

After that, the four priestesses thanked and farewelled the elements and the directions for their assistance and support.

Fire: *Guardians of the south, and of fire, thank you for cleansing, consecrating and protecting this space during our rite, and offering to us your flames of light and heat, and fire itself, to burn away what no longer serves us. Element of fire, hail and farewell.*

Air: *Guardians of the east, and of air, thank you for cleansing, consecrating and protecting this space during our rite, and bringing to us the winds of the planet, both stormy gales and gentle breezes, and the very air itself, to inspire and uplift us. Element of air, hail and farewell.*

Earth: *Guardians of the north, and of earth, thank you for cleansing, consecrating and protecting this space during our rite, and sharing with us the strength of the stones, the crystals and the very earth that we walk upon to ground and strengthen us. Element of earth, hail and farewell.*

Water: *Guardians of the west, and of water, thank you for cleansing, consecrating and protecting this space during our rite, and giving to us the energy of the waters of the oceans and rivers and sacred springs to wash away anything that no longer serves us. Element of water, hail and farewell.*

Finally Rose walked gracefully back over to the portal where it had all begun, and the two women on either side unlinked their hands and took hers in theirs. "By my will this circle is closed. Blessed be!" their priestess announced.

Everyone raised their still-linked hands, then spoke as one. "May the circle be open but unbroken. Merry meet, merry part, and merry meet again. Blessed be!" This time Carlie was prepared for it, and spoke the words along with the rest of the participants, as everyone enthusiastically echoed the phrase. She was surprised by how confident she'd become in these rituals, and how much a part of the circle, and of this community, she felt now, especially considering how angry and confused and almost foreign she had perceived herself to be when she'd arrived. Yet it made her heart ache for her mother, who had been at the centre of this magic once, at the same age she was now, but who had, as an adult, buried it all deep within her, cutting off all of her connection to magic, and to her past.

When Jake shyly touched her arm, she came abruptly back into the room, and the present. Turning to him, she smiled and asked what he'd thought, and he couldn't get the words out fast enough to share his excitement, and let her know how much his grandfather had enjoyed it too. She glanced around, wondering where Richard was, and was happy to see that he was chatting animatedly to Rose.

After speaking to her dad, Rhiannon came back over, and she and Carlie led Jake to the table filled with luscious seasonal treats and suggested that he eat something, to ground his energy back into the real world, and his spirit back into his body. He raised his eyebrows at the girls, looking a little puzzled – until he swayed slightly, and Rhiannon grabbed his arm.

"We mean it," she said sternly, as Carlie handed him a chocolate-orange poppyseed cupcake and watched over him until he'd eaten every last crumb.

Laughing, she suggested that he tuck in to anything else he wanted to try as well, before she headed over to help Miri make cups of tea for all the guests, leaving Jake and Rhiannon alone to talk about the ritual that had left them both buzzing.

Chapter 18

Searching for Satisfaction

Jake had taken to sitting with Carlie and Rhiannon in the cafeteria every lunchtime, chatting up a storm, but the next day he was uncharacteristically quiet, eyes gazing off into the distance. The girls giggled as they tried to get his attention.

"Earth to Jake!"

"Oh, sorry!" he said, eyes focusing on them again. "I was off in another world, a magical world, still thinking about last night," he admitted shyly. "Your grandmother is amazing Carlie, it was like she became someone else, so wild and strong and powerful, yet so welcoming and nurturing too. I've never seen anything like it.

"And you'll probably think I'm crazy, but I swear I could see golden strands, like electricity almost, running between each person, connecting all of us, all different widths and different intensities of sparkle," he raved, then suddenly looked sheepish. "God, I know that really does sound insane. I'm sorry, I'll get over it soon, I promise. It's just... well, I just loved it so much."

Carlie smiled. "You're not crazy Jake, I see it too. It's like a giant web or something, all sparkling and golden, running through the room. The connection between you and your grandfather was the thickest – it was so strong, so vibrant. The love you share is so clear," she said, smiling although her heart was crushed with longing.

"Really?" he asked, voice shy but eyes shining with hope.

Nodding, Rhiannon broke in. "I don't see it so much as sense it, and my heart felt so full when I looked at you and your grandad. Your relationship is just beautiful, and he adores you. It's given him a new purpose, you being here, much like what Carlie's arrival gave to Rose."

Jake beamed at them. "You can really see and sense those things?" he asked, as incredulous as he was excited.

"It sounds like you can too," Carlie grinned, keeping her tone light-hearted, in case it was freaking him out. She tried to remember how she'd felt that first night when she'd seen the golden threads in the room, how she'd been so cynical still, yet secretly so hopeful that there really was magic in the world. And she'd been so awestruck by the immensity of what Rose wove within her and sent out to every person there too.

"Is there a way to practise it, or to develop it?" he asked hopefully. "Is there any way to get better at it?" The two girls exchanged glances. Should they include him in their coven study group? Did they want anyone else – and a guy no less – working with them?

They were saved from having to reply when Dave came over to talk to Jake about their athletics team training, and he reluctantly stood up, grabbed his bag and said goodbye to the girls, leaving them alone at the table.

"What do you think?" Rhiannon asked, excitement in her voice. "It sounds like he's really interested in learning, and you said he's been working hard on your assignment, so he wouldn't be slack. But do we want anyone joining us? Especially a guy?"

Carlie shrugged. "I'm not sure. I mean, we shouldn't feel obligated – we can lend him some books and head him in the right direction for his own study, and just invite him to the public rituals. And maybe he'd rather find someone more experienced to teach him anyway. It's not like he asked to join our coven."

"True," Rhiannon conceded. "But I don't think he knows we have one, so how could he ask that? I'm sure he'd be more than happy if we wanted to help him out. And it would be pretty awesome to have the power of three..."

Carlie stared at her. "You like him, don't you?" she asked, eyebrows raised in surprise, and her friend squirmed a little.

"No, of course not, he's just a really sweet guy..." she began, but her blush gave her away.

"Oh my god Rhi, you do!" Carlie said, a grin splitting her face. Then she frowned. "But what about John? I thought you guys were really happy?"

"We were. We are," she muttered, but she looked a little miserable.

"What's wrong?"

"Nothing's wrong, not really. It's just really hard because we don't get to see each other very often. I mean, we talk most nights on the phone, but we're kind of running out of things to say. And we see each other on weekends, but I can't help noticing that there are times he'd rather be with his mates, and to be honest, often I'd rather be with you, staying here, than travelling to see him. And if I *really* liked him, I probably wouldn't feel like that, would I?" she asked, voice trembling with uncertainty.

Carlie shook her head. "I'm not sure – Rowan's the only boyfriend I've ever had, and we know how that ended."

"But don't you see, it's partly because of Rowan that I don't feel satisfied with John," her friend wailed. Seeing the pain on Carlie's face, she quickly backpedalled. "Sorry, I don't mean that the way it sounded. It's just that ever since you showed me the letters and cards you wrote each other, I've wanted more. I've wanted someone to love me like Rowan loved you, and to be with someone that I love as much as you loved Rowan," she said.

"I really like John, he's a lovely guy, but we just don't have any of that passion. I'm not desperate to see him when the weekend comes around – I like seeing him, don't get me wrong, but I want someone to feel the way Rowan felt about you, about me. To be that smitten, to want to be with me every minute, to hurt when we're apart. Rowan was cutting his work back because it took him away from you –"

"Jay wasn't real happy about that though," Carlie sighed, but Rhiannon ignored her and kept talking, on a roll now.

"But that's so romantic. You were prepared to make sacrifices for each other, because you loved each other so much. And I guess I've just realised that I don't feel that way about John. He's a great guy, and we really like each other, and we enjoy hanging out together, but I can't imagine he'd be especially devastated if we broke up."

Carlie remembered the words of the red-clad woman from that night by the stream, that Rhiannon wouldn't be upset when her relationship with John ended. She wondered whether she should tell her about Aideen, but her friend was still speaking.

"And maybe even more importantly, I want someone to love *me* – the real me, the magical me – to understand how important this part of my life is to me. Someone who'll inspire me on my magical path, like Rowan did for you. I want a boyfriend who will come to rituals with me and share this aspect of my life, but John has no interest in anything remotely spiritual, and I have no interest in going to his football matches, which is what's important to him, and which I should care about, surely, if I was a good girlfriend? I guess that's why the idea of Jake is so appealing – he's interested in all this too."

Carlie smiled. "So what are you going to do?"

"Goddess, I don't know. I don't think I realised until this exact moment, telling you, that this is how I actually feel about being with him. I mean, I hadn't questioned my being with John – or whether I even wanted to be. But now it kind of sounds like I should break up with him, doesn't it?" she asked, her eyes pleading for answers, for reassurance. Carlie wasn't sure whether her friend wanted her to encourage her to break up with John, or to stay with him, though. She really sucked at this relationship thing.

"I'm so sorry Rhi, I don't know what to say – I'm really not the best person to ask about this kind of stuff. But is it just because you  think Jake is cute and he came to a ritual that all of a sudden you're not sure about John, or is it separate to that? Like, if Jake wasn't around, would you still be happy with John?"

Rhiannon sighed. "That's no help, that's just even more questions with even less answers," she said, pouting at her friend.

"What do you need help with?" Jake asked, suddenly reappearing and sliding back into his chair opposite Carlie. She started laughing, while her friend blushed furiously, eyes begging her not to say anything. Still, Carlie figured that she'd been no help to Rhiannon – maybe Jake had more experience in these matters and would have better advice for her.

"Well, we have a friend who's been dating someone for six weeks, and they get on really well, and have a nice time together, but it's not that desperate romantic love that people dream of, you know?" Carlie began, with a wicked grin at Rhiannon.

"So, this friend is wondering whether they should stick it out, because maybe the love will grow over time and they should just be patient? Or should they break up with the person now, even though there's really nothing wrong in their relationship, so that they're both free to find someone better for them, that mystical soul mate who'll inspire them to write poetry, and make them want to become more than they are, to fulfil all their potential, be all that the person sees in them, even if they can't see it themselves yet."

Her breath caught, and she choked on a sob. *Damn it.* She'd meant to keep her voice breezy and light, but she still wasn't able to think about Rowan and how much she'd loved him without her heart being ripped apart all over again.

"Sorry," she whispered to Rhiannon, and stood up abruptly to flee. But the bell rang right at that moment, so her friend stood up with her, since they were going to the same class, and put an arm around her shoulder as they turned away.

Jake sat for a moment, puzzled over what had just happened, and his heart heavy with sadness for Carlie. He'd had to leave behind his high school sweetheart when he moved to England, but what she'd just said made him realise that they hadn't been as in love with each other as he'd thought. It hadn't broken his heart to say goodbye to her, it hadn't even really saddened him, and now that struck him as strange. Shouldn't he be missing her like crazy? Yet he'd barely spared her a thought since he'd arrived here, and had only written to her once – and that was a brief Christmas note on a postcard. He'd felt worse having to leave his dog with his high school buddy Jeff.

He daydreamed his way through his next class, unsettled to realise just how much he was thinking about Carlie, and how many times her face drifted into his mind. She had looked so beautiful at the ritual, so radiant, so full of compassion and empathy, and when he'd opened his eyes and caught her looking at him, he'd got a queer feeling in his stomach, like butterflies.

But he couldn't like her, could he? She was gorgeous, sure, and sweet, and it was nice to hear an Aussie voice, but she was all eaten up over some dead guy, so it was pointless to think about her like that. Yet he couldn't get his mind off her. And the fact that she was so magical, that just drew him to her more.

Sighing, he tried to focus on his class, and was relieved when the bell finally rang. He wasn't sure what had come over him, but he figured that when he saw Carlie again in the next class, he'd realise how silly he was being. What on earth had made him start thinking about her like that? It must have been her talk of soul mates and poetry, mixing up with his memory of her from last night, with the magic of the ritual making her seem so mysterious, so inspiring, so free.

But when he walked in to history and took his usual seat in front of Carlie and Rhiannon, he was surprised to feel flustered. Why was he suddenly obsessing over her? He took a deep breath as he smiled at them both, trying to calm his emotions – and noticed that Rhiannon was blushing. God, what was going on today? He tried to remember their conversation from lunch, and recalled the dilemma Carlie had mentioned. Maybe it was Rhiannon who wasn't sure of her feelings for… what was his name? He vaguely remembered that she was dating someone from Smithfield High. He tried to focus on her.

"So, I was thinking about what we were talking about earlier, and I think your *friend* probably should break up with the person. Which is just my opinion of course, but if you're not in love with the guy, maybe you should end it, so he can find someone who'll love him as he should be loved, and you have the space in your life for someone you could potentially love to fit into." He was looking directly at Rhiannon as he said this, and she blushed a little, but nodded.

"In fact I've been thinking about what you were saying before Carlie, and it made me ponder my own life too. My girlfriend and I decided we'd try the long distance thing, but our chat at lunch made me realise that I don't miss her as much as I probably should. And it's the same as you Rhiannon," he said, letting the pretence they were talking about someone else drop.

"I really like her, and I'm sure if I was in Perth right now we'd still be together, but I've realised today that she's not the love of my life, so it's not fair to her to make her wait for me, and to turn down the possibility of her meeting someone who really does adore her. She's a wonderful girl, don't get me wrong, but she doesn't make my heart sing like in the movies – and she certainly doesn't make me want to be more than I am, or inspire me to be all that I could be, like you said Carlie." And he looked at her with so much love that Rhiannon felt a physical pain in her chest. A longing. Why did the good ones always fall for her friend?

Sighing, she opened her books. Still, maybe he was right – whether or not there were any other potential love interests, was she wasting her time with John, and wasting his time too? And had she just become excited at the possibility of dating someone *like* Jake, not Jake himself – someone who would make magic with her? And now she knew that nothing would ever happen with Jake, should she see if John could be that person?

She had to admit that she'd never actually asked him if he'd like to come to a ritual, she'd just assumed that he wouldn't. Maybe she just had to give him a chance. The Yule Ball had been pagan-themed, and he'd enjoyed that. Terror clutched at her as she contemplated revealing her magical self to him. Could she be brave enough? Did she have the courage to allow herself to be vulnerable enough, to show him her true heart and see what he thought of it? To be rejected after that would be awful, humiliating, but what was the alternative? To hide her real self just to keep the peace? And was it fair to him to not give him the credit for being strong enough to accept her, pointy witch's hat and all?

Chapter 19

Ritual of the Dark Moon

It was Tuesday night, coven night, and the girls had planned their own Imbolc observance, a ritual of forgiveness, new beginnings and moving on. Since it was also the night of the dark moon, they'd decided that it was the perfect time to let go of the darker emotions they'd been battling, especially the resentment and bitterness they had harboured against each other through their misunderstanding, and banish it for good.

It was their first coven meeting in Carlie's new bedroom, and as she set up for their evening she was grateful for the extra space. Soft light flickered from every corner, from tall pillar candles and spirals of tealights in small coloured-glass holders, and incense burned from a wrought iron censer on her dressing table.

At the knock on her door she gazed around and, feeling satisfied with how everything was set up, walked over and welcomed her friend in. "Wow, it's beautiful," Rhiannon said, eyes shining in the candlelight. They sat down on the floor, one on either side of the altar in the centre of the room, and Rhiannon raised her eyebrows. There was an object missing from the representations of the four directions, which wasn't like Carlie.

Her friend just smiled mysteriously. "I thought tonight we should focus on fire," Carlie said. "The fire of the Imbolc flame and new beginnings, and the fire that can burn away pain and regret, and leave only what is pure and good behind."

"That sounds really great, but you don't have fire on the altar," Rhiannon replied, feeling a little embarrassed that she had to point this out to her friend.

With a grin, Carlie placed the small wrought iron cauldron that the red-robed woman had given her in the centre of the altar space, then handed the long red-velvet-wrapped parcel to Rhiannon. "A gift for you," she said simply.

Her friend raised her eyebrows again. "Really? Another one?"

"Really," she giggled. "The woman in red this time, Aideen. Do you know what that name means?"

"Fire," Rhiannon said, gazing down at the parcel in her lap.

"Of course," Carlie laughed. Brauna, the sweet blue-clad woman of the mists, had represented water, and Brianna, in her soft green robes, had symbolised the earth. It made perfect sense that the woman dressed in the long red cloak symbolised fire.

"When did you meet her?" Rhiannon demanded, curiosity burning in her voice.

Carlie paused. Would her friend be hurt that she hadn't told her before now? "Um, two weeks ago, on the full moon," she replied.

It wasn't really a lie – she had met her then too, it was just that she'd first met Aideen five weeks ago, during her New Year's Eve farewell-to-Rowan ritual, and had seen her again and received the gifts two weeks after that, on her way home from Mike's. It was her third and most recent encounter that had happened two weeks ago.

"I'm sorry I hadn't told you about her, or the gifts, before – it's just, well... We haven't had a proper Tuesday night coven meeting, what with school plays and studying and Imbolc prepping, for so long," Carlie said, realising how lame that sounded as she spoke.

But Rhiannon shook her head. "It's okay," she whispered, knowing that it was her own fault that the woman in red had gone to Carlie when she was on her own, rather than when they were together. She'd hurt her friend badly, and as a result she didn't deserve all the magic she'd had access to before.

"That's not true," Carlie said sharply, and Rhiannon stared at her in horror. Was she reading her mind now?

"I can't read your mind Rhi, don't worry," she explained, reacting to the look on her friend's face rather than any divinatory powers, and wanting to set her mind at ease. "But I can sense your sadness, and that's why Aideen gave us these gifts I think, so we can use them to burn away the memories of past hurt between us, yet not burn the bridge that links us, because that's what we want to keep. And I reckon she's right. But please hurry up and open it! She gave me the cauldron unwrapped, but said that this one is for you, and I've been dying to know what's inside. So come on, unwrap it so we can see what it is! I have an idea, but I'm not sure I'm right," she said excitedly.

Bursting with curiosity, Rhiannon untied the ribbon and opened the parcel, then smiled. On the top was a small wrought iron tealight holder, with a vanilla-scented tealight candle nestled within it. Laughing, she lit it and placed it in the south of their altar, as the missing element she'd wondered about.

Carlie grinned too. "Lucky guess huh? Otherwise you might have thought I'd forgotten the fourth element."

Rhiannon blushed a little – she *had* assumed that – then turned back to the parcel. She gasped at the beauty of the two elaborate wrought iron candle holders, both wreathed in sculpted metal ivy leaves, one with a sun on it, and one with a moon. Two tall candles, one silver and one gold, lay beneath them, and she placed the silver one in the moon holder and the gold one in the sun holder, then positioned them on the altar too, one on either side of the cauldron.

A small folded note caught her eye, and she slowly unfurled it and read it out. "My dearest Rhiannon, here is some light to illuminate your own light, when you feel that you are drowning in darkness and cannot see what others see in you. Please trust yourself, and your worth." Tears welled in her eyes. How could a woman who'd never met her know how she would feel tonight, when she'd passed on the gift two weeks ago?

Carlie smiled at her friend as she lit the candles, then settled back in the cushions to prepare herself for the head space she required for the ritual. Breathing in the peacefulness of the dark, candlelit room, the sweet scent of the incense and the quiet exhalations of Luther and Luna as they slept on her bed, she felt her shoulders relax. She'd missed their Tuesday night magical meetings, and the sense of enchantment that they created together. And suddenly she knew that she didn't want to share it with anyone else – adding another person would throw off their carefully crafted balance, and the comfort they felt when it was just the two of them.

"I agree," Rhiannon said softly, and Carlie opened her eyes and smiled at her. "Still reading my mind, huh?" she asked, but she was amused, not angry. Her friend laughed.

"No, it's just that I was thinking the same thing. I've missed this too. Jake can join us at the sabbats and moon rituals, but there's no need for him to totally cramp our magical style."

Carlie laughed too. "Cramp our style?"

"Yes, we are very stylish – just look at us," Rhiannon said with a grin, sweeping her hand in front of them to take in their bulky woollen jumpers and the thick tights they both wore under their velvet dresses. "Now, how shall we begin things tonight?"

"I thought we could write down the things we want to let go of, then burn them in our Imbolc fire," Carlie replied, waving her hand over the cauldron in the centre of the altar, which Rhiannon saw was filled with sabbat herbs.

"We can harness the spirit of the dark moon to burn away our regrets, extinguish our bitterness, and release all the stuff we want to get rid of," she added. "Then after that we can use the energy of fire and the Imbolc flame to ignite our new passion and purpose, and make our own fresh start."

"That sounds perfect," Rhiannon said, then sighed. "I really am sorry Carlie," she whispered, sorrow colouring her voice.

"I know you are. And I'm sorry too."

"Why are *you* sorry?" her friend asked.

"I've been sad and angry, and full of the injustice of it all. I'm sure I haven't been all sweetness and light to be around."

"You've been fine," Rhiannon admitted softly. "And I'm glad that you called me out on my awful behaviour. You needed a friend and instead you got a jealous harpy, someone who wanted you to get over such a heartbreaking thing in an instant, just so I didn't feel uncomfortable. I really am so sorry. I was selfish to harp on and on about how you should just 'get over it', as though you can just flick a switch and turn off all the pain."

Carlie smiled sadly. "True."

"I mean, god, it's only six weeks today since… well, since you lost Rowan," Rhiannon said. "So you be as sad as you need to be, for as long as you need to be, and please know that I am here for you now. For what it's worth, I really regret the way I treated you, and I promise I will be more considerate in the future."

Reaching over to hug her friend, Carlie was happy to realise that their ritual of forgiveness and moving forward had already begun, even before they'd stepped out the boundary of their sacred space between the worlds and welcomed the deities and the directions. Rose was right, elaborate rituals were wonderful, but intent was the most important thing. What was in your heart meant so much more than just having the right herbs or ritual tools – although she loved all of that too.

"Okay, ready?" Rhiannon asked, and Carlie nodded, then began to slow her breathing as her friend cast the sacred circle and invoked the elements and directions. Once that was done, Carlie called on the god and the goddess to join them, aiding them on this dark moon night as they went within on their own personal journeys of introspection and reflection.

Opening her eyes, she handed Rhiannon a piece of pale green paper and a gold pen, then picked up her own and began to write what was in her heart.

Dear Bridie, maiden goddess of love and healing,
Tonight I call on you to take away our pain,
guilt and anger, to assist us in letting go of our
resentment, and to fill us both with love and
contentment.
Please guard my heart as it heals from its loss.
I know that it's better to have loved and lost
than never to have experienced such

pure joy, and I am grateful to have been loved so deeply by such a beautiful soul, and to have been able to share so many precious moments with him, but I still ache with missing him. So please help me let go of my resentment and anger that he was taken away so soon, and dampen my fiery sense of injustice...
Perhaps most importantly, help me forgive and forget with Rhiannon. I don't want to resent her, or dwell on my bitterness at her actions. I know that she's sorry, so guide me to ignite the forgiveness I feel in my head, on a conscious level, into my heart.
So mote it be xx

Glancing up, she saw that Rhiannon had finished writing her piece too, so she passed her hands over the cauldron, infusing the herbs with her wishes, then lit them up. "We're shaking off the negativity and burning it away," Carlie said, smiling as the scent of sandalwood, basil and bay infused the room. "Ready?"

Taking a deep breath, she gently fed her piece of paper into the flames, watching as it blackened and burned away. For a moment she saw an image of the red-clad woman, and she flinched as flames threatened to burn her where she sat. Aideen's eyes flashed with fire, with danger, and her smile had a cruel edge to it.

"You don't need to be afraid Carlie, I won't hurt you," she crooned, as she reached in and tore open her soul. "Fire can destroy, but it creates as well. It can be healing as well as harmful. Love is like a fire, as you've learned, and there is a cost for dancing within it, but also a reward. Let this fire inflame you with the courage to take chances and risk everything, harness it to scorch and burn away your pain, then let yourself be cleansed by it. Please Carlie, let it spark new passion, inspiration, decisiveness and intention, and get you to the heart of your fears," she whispered.

Rhiannon touched her hand. "Are you okay?"

Startled, Carlie looked around the room. There was no fire, no flames, no woman in red. "Yes, I'm good, your turn," she whispered, and watched as Rhiannon did the same. As the last of the smoke drifted skyward, they both felt a shift in the room, and a great weight lifting from their shoulders, and their hearts.

"So what will we fill ourselves with instead?" Carlie asked as the fire burned down. "What's your purpose and passion for the year ahead? What new beginning do you want to bring to life?"

Rhiannon took a deep breath, centring herself as she delved into the depths of her heart, and her eyes flickered in the light of the candles. "I wanted to burn away my impatience and my guilt," she said at last, breathing her words into the cauldron. "And I also asked for the fires of compassion to light me up, and to help me develop patience and caution when I deal with anyone. Especially with you, but with others too. With guys even…"

Carlie frowned. "But what about your open heart, the passion that's so much a part of you? Don't punish yourself because of what happened with us, or rein in your free spirit and your love of life. That's not what this is about, surely?" she asked.

"You have to dive in, take a risk, be brave – you taught me that. And it might not always work out, but you have to try. It's the only way to live, to grow, to discover. Otherwise you'll regret not finding out what could have happened, and always wonder. Because you only regret the things that you *don't* do, right? Imagine if I'd followed my plan, and not stayed in London for the party you made us go to, where I talked to Rowan all night," she said.

"I wouldn't feel so terrible, so distraught, so lost and alone, right now – but I wouldn't have had the time with him that I did either, the privilege of loving and being loved, and I wouldn't give that up for any amount of peace now, as hard as it is to cope with the loss." Her voice was sad, but there was a thread of steel in it.

"No regrets, that's our motto, right?" Carlie added. "That's what Rowan would have said too – live every moment to the full, because you never know how long you have." There were tears in her eyes as she spoke, but she felt strong.

Rhiannon crawled across the floor to her and hugged her tight. "Here's to living every moment," she said.

Carlie smiled too. She had a best friend again. A new magical ally. And the power and passion of fire.

Chapter 20

Pale Green Stars

A few mornings later, Carlie woke up shivering, and stretched out her legs, hoping to burrow her feet back under Luther's warm body. With him it was as though she had her own personal hot water bottle at the end of her bed, one that was far more soothing and long lasting than the rubbery kind. A stab of fear shot through her when she couldn't feel him, and she sat up abruptly. Luna squeaked as she tumbled from Carlie's pillow onto the bed next to her, and she scooped the little kitten up in her arms, smiling at her as she stroked her adorably fuzzy head and tiny ears.

"Sorry lovely Luna, I didn't mean to startle you. Or myself. I must have had a bad dream, because it scared me when I couldn't see Luther, which is just plain silly. No doubt he's downstairs with Gran, sharing the heater with her," she said, then glanced at the clock. "Oh, and probably eating too, because it's definitely time for breakfast. We should go down and join them, huh? Are you hungry little one?" she asked.

Luna miaowed back at her, still such a tiny sound, and Carlie laughed. She was such a cutie. Pulling her warmest coat on over her pyjamas and slipping her feet into thick woollen socks, she picked up the kitten and held her close to her heart, crooning to her as she walked down the stairs.

"Morning Gran," Carlie called out as she and the kitten waltzed into the blissful warmth of the kitchen.

Rose looked up from the book she was reading and smiled at them. "Hello Sweetheart, hello little Luna," she said, and the little black ball of fur miaowed at her happily. "I've put some milk out for the cats, and I just made a big pot of chai, if you'd like a cup. Is Luther with you guys?"

The alarm Carlie had managed to set aside earlier slammed back into her, taking her breath away. Frowning, she shook her head, trying to clear it, then all three of them, as one, looked outside into the frosty back garden. The sun was rising, casting a pale golden glow over the world, and the green of the grass seemed more vivid than usual, yesterday's snow melted away and leaving a particular lushness to the garden.

She froze, her heart thudding, then set Luna down on the floor by the saucer of milk and flew out the back door. Her feet were freezing on the cold grass, the dew seeping through her woollen socks, but she didn't notice. Panic washed over Rose as she followed her granddaughter, not sure what she'd seen, but her emotions so tightly woven with the young girl's that she knew *something* was desperately wrong, even if she didn't yet know what it actually was.

Carlie had sunk down onto her knees in the dirt under the old apple tree, next to the rosemary bush she'd planted in memory of Rowan. Tears spilled over and traced an icy path down each of her cheeks, as her nameless dread finally found its reason. She reached out her arms, distraught, then rocked back and forth on the ground, Luther's lifeless body clutched to her chest, eyes streaming with tears, mind elsewhere, unseeing, recoiling in horror as she tried to understand what the frozen body in her arms could mean.

Rose reached her arms around her devastated granddaughter, heart breaking for the young girl's pain, and aching for her own. As a priestess she knew the cycles of life began, ended and began again, but as a woman she was desperately sad to have lost the companion she had loved and lived with for so long, who had worked magic with her, healed and helped her through loss, and given her something to care for when she had nothing else. And as guardian to this fragile girl in her arms, she was terrified. She could barely begin to imagine how this would affect her after all her other losses.

It was a tiny paw on Carlie's leg that brought her back to the present, back to the pain. She stared down at the delicate ball of black fur perched on the grass beside her, gazing up at her with wise and patient green eyes. The kitten was shivering as deeply as she was, and for a moment she marvelled at the effort it must have taken her to push her way through the cat door on her own and cover the vast expanse of back garden to get to her and Rose.

And to Luther. Poor dead Luther. Her eyes misted as she took in his still body, felt the chill of his bones against her heart, felt the yawning pit of loss and despair opening up around her, ready to pull her down into it again. And this time she just didn't know if she'd have the strength to climb back out. The sides got steeper every time, and far more difficult, and the effort just seemed too much to face once more.

"Miaow." It was the tiniest of sounds, but Carlie looked back down at the kitten, at her trusting gaze and small body wracked by shudders of cold and sadness, and felt the cord linking her to this tiny creature, and to life. It seemed tenuous still, but it was there, the possibility of a way up the steep sides. Luna was even more delicate, even more needy, than she was. Her eyes lifted to her grandma's, and she saw the agony of loss there too.

"I'm so sorry Gran," she whispered. "I know you loved him more than anything, and that you shared so many years, so many experiences, together. And I'm so sorry he had to look after me these last months, that you didn't have as much time as you should have with him." Her voice cracked, and she stopped, unable to go on.

Rose leaned over and hugged Carlie again, Luther's body cold and stiff between them. "And you Sweetheart, I'm so sorry for your loss. Before you trusted me, he was there for you, and I'll be forever grateful to him for that. He was the dearest friend, the closest companion, for both of us."

Gently she took Luther's body from her granddaughter, holding him close to her, and gazing down at the kitten as she awkwardly tried to climb her way up into Carlie's lap. Without conscious thought the young girl reached down and scooped her up, holding her shivering body close, against her heart, as she had that first night they'd met the sweet little kitten.

Bravely smiling through her tears, Rose looked down at Luther's body. "He knew. Luther knew that he didn't have long here, so he brought you Luna. To give you a reason to stay," she whispered. She couldn't bring herself to finish that sentence – to not just stay here, in England, with Rose, but to stay alive. How much more pain could this poor child bear?

"And you," Carlie said gently.

"No Sweetheart, I didn't need another reason, because I have you." The truth of her words hit Rose as she spoke them, and warmth flooded through her. "Don't you know how much you mean to me yet? What you've brought to my life?" she asked.

"It doesn't seem enough," Carlie sighed, pain writ large across her face. "Luther was part of you, part of us. How could he leave us like this?"

Tenderly Rose tucked a fallen strand of Carlie's hair behind her ear, the way Rowan used to do it. "He didn't want to go, didn't want to leave us, it was just his time. And really, he had a far longer life than most cats – I think he made a bargain with someone, or some thing, to be able to stay here with us longer than is usual. He wouldn't want us to be sad, he'd want us to celebrate all that we were able to share with him, and be grateful for the time we had," she said, though tears still choked her voice.

"And you are more than enough Carlie," Rose added firmly, and the young girl looked up at her, surprise on her face. Her grandmother never called her by her name, and it seemed that she'd used it to add impact to her words. How strange that her own name could sound more loving and important to her than the endearment her grandma usually used. Yet none of that changed the pain she felt now.

"It's not fair though!" Carlie moaned. The ball of fluff in her arms squirmed, and she looked down just as she felt the little paw on her face, then saw Luna's tiny pink tongue flick out to mop up her tears, taking the pain into her own body, and trying to leave only strength for her new protector.

A warmth spread through Carlie, almost against her will, and she half-smiled down at the kitten and her earnest little face as she busied herself comforting her new friend. "Thank you little one," she breathed. "I guess Luther knew me even better than I realised. And clearly I need you just as much as you need me."

Rose felt some of the weight lift from her heart as she saw the change in Carlie's face, saw the flash of joy and gratitude hiding within the sadness. Still holding Luther's body, she closed her eyes and sent a prayer out into the universe, a prayer of thanksgiving for the years she'd had with her furry companion, a prayer expressing how grateful she was for his love of her granddaughter, and a prayer to send him peacefully from this world to the next.

She wondered whether she'd still feel him with her – or see him, the way Carlie had seen Luther's mother Shadow – and the sensation of a paw on her hand, and what felt like the brush of warm fur around her ankles, sent waves of relief through her. Perhaps her familiar hadn't abandoned her just yet. But it also made her aware of just how cold it was on the frozen earth, and how cramped her legs had become, kneeling as she was in the dirt, and she shook herself. Letting herself or Carlie catch a cold or worse was not going to help Luther. Steeling herself, she placed his body gently on the ground then got awkwardly to her feet.

"Come inside Sweetheart. You and Luna must be freezing to death," she said, then cringed at her choice of words. "I'm going to get Luther a blanket, then I thought maybe we could have a little ceremony this afternoon, and bury him under the apple tree. But you need to get out of those wet clothes, and those wet socks, and get warm, and Luna needs to get out of the cold too, and have some breakfast. She's still only small, so she needs us to look after her."

Carlie stood up reluctantly, stamping the foot that had gone to sleep on the icy ground, and finally noticing just how wet and cold her soggy woollen socks were. She should have waited to put some shoes on, she knew, but when she'd seen Luther's still body she hadn't been able to think of anything else, she'd just had to get out to him, see if he was okay. The weight of grief threatened to squash her again, and drag her back down to the ground, but Rose took her arm and gently led her back inside.

"A hot shower for you Missy, then warm clothes, and boots this time. Go on, upstairs. I'll heat Luna up and get her some food."

Too exhausted, both mentally and physically, to argue, Carlie headed up to her room to get some dry clothes, then entered the small ensuite, turned on the hot water and stood under the full blast of the shower. Some of her bone-deep weariness and tension began to ease as the scalding water fell on her shoulders, but she also flashed back to other times that she'd stood in here under the falling water, feeling totally numb after learning of Rowan's death, then just as devastated still as she psyched herself up to go to his funeral a week later. Hot tears splashed down into the bath tub, mixing with the water streaming down the plug hole.

An image of Luna's delicate little face popped into her mind though, and she took a deep breath. Yes, she had to focus on the positives. Her grandma was right, it was terribly sad that Luther had died, but he had lived a long and full existence, and been so cared for and adored. He had brought so much love and healing to Rose, and to Carlie, and his life should be celebrated. Losing him was not so much a tragedy – as her parents' untimely deaths had been, and as Rowan's accident had been – but a sad yet real part of life.

Suddenly she realised the real and deeper meaning of Rose's rituals, of her honouring of the wheel of the seasonal year as a metaphor for the wheel of life, and why the wise priestess could be sad that Luther had died, but not raging with the injustice of his passing. That was the truth of nature – things were born, and they died – and it wasn't good or bad, or happy or sad, it just was. She knew that her grandmother also believed that Luther had gone to another place now, and could perhaps communicate with her from there, which would be some comfort to a person who was grieving.

And Rose also held to the idea, or at least the hope, that as well as birth and death there was also rebirth, and she could see why that would be such a reassuring belief system.

Turning the water off, she quickly dried herself, pulled on her jeans with one of her mum's thick woollen jumpers, and warm socks and boots, then slowly made her way back downstairs. Rose was at the stove, cooking a pot of cinnamon porridge, while Luna lay curled up by the heater in Luther's old basket, her tiny ears twitching as though she was dreaming.

A flash of irritation slammed into Carlie, that the kitten could already have moved into Luther's bed, but then she felt the older cat's steadying presence around her, and closed her eyes for a moment, seeing his wise old eyes gazing at her, his face smiling as he let her know that he wanted Luna to be comfortable, to be loved – that he had brought her to the cottage so the three of them could all look after each other.

Smiling that her imagination already had her communicating with Luther, she accepted that his basket no longer mattered, his body no longer mattered. He had no need of those things now, and she had to let go of her attachment to him and focus forward, on life, and on love, and on Luna.

"Can I help you Gran?" she asked, carefully averting her eyes from the back garden as she turned away from Luna and walked over to lean against the kitchen bench.

"Thank you Sweetheart, that would be great. I have to go into the healing centre for a few hours, so if you could do any of this –" she began, her arm sweeping around to encompass the three recipe books lying open on the bench, and the containers of flour, jars of spices, bowls of nuts and collection of fruits and vegetables strewn next to them. "That would be wonderful."

When her granddaughter nodded, Rose gave her a quick hug, then picked up her bag and raced out the door. Which was kind of odd, Carlie mused – she'd thought that today was her grandma's day off, but maybe she'd got it wrong. Hastily she spooned out a bowl of porridge and brewed herself a pot of earl grey tea, then she leaned over and examined the recipes she was supposed to whip up.

Gulping at their complexity, she rolled up her sleeves and got to work, determined to do her best. The hours flew by as she sifted and stirred, fried and steamed, baked and even bottled – Rose had left the ingredients and some sketchy instructions for an apple and cinnamon jam that smelled heavenly, and was probably designed to be eaten on the chai spiced bread she had beaten and kneaded into submission, and which was now rising under a tea towel before she would pop it in the oven to bake. Which she could do as soon as the nutmeg custard tarts and the delicate vegetable and ricotta filo pockets and various savoury mini pies had cooked until golden brown, and the rosemary and baked vegie quiches had firmed up.

She did have one shaky moment, when she'd forgotten what she was avoiding and glanced out the window into the back garden, her eyes staring for long moments at Luther's body, wrapped in a dark blanket emblazoned with pale green stars, before her mind took in what she was seeing, and the tears started to flow again.

Pouring herself another mug of tea, she'd gone over towards the heater and sat on the floor next to Luna, who opened her eyes at her approach, stretched and yawned adorably, then clambered awkwardly into her lap, curling up again and starting to purr as Carlie stroked her soft head. Equilibrium at least partially restored, she'd gently placed Luna back in her basket, where she'd settled down and was soon snoring peacefully, and gone back to work.

Chapter 21

The Honouring of a Dear Friend

When Carlie heard the key in the front door she looked up at the clock and realised it was already 3pm, and she'd spent the last six hours cooking. No wonder she was hungry. Putting the kettle on, she filled the teapot with fresh leaves, and was pulling a tray of apricot scones out of the oven when Rose wandered into the kitchen with a bag over her shoulder.

"Cup of tea?" Carlie asked, and her grandma nodded gratefully and sat down at the table next to Luna. "I've cooked everything that you had marked, even the jam. Is there a ritual I've forgotten about or something?"

Rose shook her head. "No Sweetheart, I just figured that having something to do while I was out would help you keep your mind off things," she replied, and looked slightly sheepish. "And we'll get to have a really yummy dinner tonight."

For a moment Carlie glared at her grandmother, then she started laughing. She could have felt angry that she'd wasted her time, but her grandma was right – it had helped her to have something serious to focus on, and suddenly the surprising complexity of some of the recipes made sense.

"So would you like a warm apricot scone with freshly whipped butter and some apple and cinnamon jam then?" she asked wryly.

"I'm having some, because I was so wrapped up in getting these dishes made properly that I forgot to have lunch. But you were right, the baking did also distract me from being quite as sad as I would have been otherwise."

After pouring out some milk for Luna, Carlie took the mugs of tea, a platter of scones and the dishes of jam and butter over to the table. "And it was a nice touch, having to whip the butter myself in order to get the buttermilk for the scones," she said, tone a little accusatory, but mostly amused.

"Sorry about that," Rose said, trying not to grin. She lifted the bag onto the table and started rummaging through it.

"I thought we could have a ceremony for Luther this afternoon, so we can lay him to rest before nightfall," she added. "Do you feel up to it Sweetheart?"

Inhaling deeply, Carlie straightened her back and squared her shoulders, marshalling her courage, then she nodded. "Should I get changed?" she asked nervously, but Rose shook her head.

"Luther would just want us to be warm and comfortable, and it's getting really cold out there. The sun's still setting pretty early."

As they drank their tea and ate their scones, Rose outlined the ritual she'd constructed, but told Carlie to jump in with any ideas she had, and to feel free to change it as they went.

"Luther loved us, the ordinary-women us, more than he cared about the priestess role, and he wouldn't want us feeling pressure to do anything too elaborate. We just want to show him how much we love him, and thank him for all he gave us, and send him safely on his way to wherever he's going next," she said, voice warm with affection.

Still feeling apprehensive, but trying to relax, Carlie followed her grandmother into the lounge room, and watched as she set up an altar on the floor, laying out a beautiful silk scarf then reverently placing the representations of the elements in the four directions. There was a small golden candle in the south for fire, a silver chalice in the west for water, a pretty pink rose quartz in the north for earth, and a dish of incense in the east for air – she could smell lavender and mint, and smiled as Rose added catnip to the blend and lit the charcoal disc. In the centre of the altar the priestess added four pieces of sugilite, a crystal associated with crossing over, in a small golden dish she'd brought from the shop.

Then just as she was about to step out the circle and create the sacred world-within-a-world they would perform their ritual inside, Luna padded into the room and awkwardly hauled herself up onto Carlie's lap. Rose smiled over at the two of them, then raised her crystal-tipped wand.

Within this boundary a circle formed,
With this energy raised, sacred space is born.
Goddess, see that our love for Luther is true,
As we entrust our dear friend's soul to you.

The hairs on Carlie's neck rose as she felt the power shifting in the room, and Luna clumsily stood up in her lap, back arched for a moment as her fur stood on end. But the kitten calmed herself when Rose sat down opposite Carlie on the floor and took her hands, and the energy around them settled. Lighting the candle, the priestess began her invocation.

Power of the south, and energies of fire,
Please hold Luther safe as he journeys through you,
Let him know he'll remain as a flame in our souls,
And we'll hold him in our hearts as a friend so true.

Motioning to Carlie, Rose handed her the glass bottle of new-moon-charged spring water, and Carlie poured some into the chalice as she shakily, shyly, began her invocation.

Power of the west, and energies of water,
Please hold Luther close as he journeys through you,
Cleanse his spirit and soothe his fears,
As we hold him in our memories as a friend so true.

Rose smiled at her granddaughter, then lifted the rose quartz crystal and held it to her heart as she invoked the powers of earth.

Power of the north, and energies of earth,
Please hold Luther safe as he journeys through you,
Ground him with our love and lend him your strength,
As we hold him in our hearts as a friend so true.

Looking over at Carlie, she inclined her head in the direction of the incense and smiled gently, proudly. She was impressed with her granddaughter's strength, and the new confidence she'd developed to take part in their rituals, especially one as sad and deeply personal as this one. If she was honest, she'd expected that Carlie would have left it all to her, not wanting to say anything aloud, but she had drawn on her love for Luther to give her the courage to act and to speak.

Fanning the incense through the air and inhaling it deeply, the young girl invoked the last of the elements.

Power of the east, and energies of air,
Please hold Luther close as he journeys through you,
Let him know we are with him in spirit, as he is with us,
And we'll hold him in our hearts forever as a friend so true.

After that Rose raised her arms skyward, eyes closed, as she drew down the goddess and welcomed her into their circle, into their grief, and into their love for their animal companion. Carlie felt a shift in the air and sensed Luther with them for a moment, paw on her knee. Then she leaned over to comfort Luna, who was glancing frantically around the room, trying to understand the changing energies.

The priestess glamour came down over Rose, and she began to speak, voice quiet yet immensely powerful. "Thank you Luther, for your kind and loving companionship, for helping me through my losses, and for being part of my magical life for so long. Even as a tiny kitten you could sense when I needed you, could sense people's energies, and could sense the swirl of magic when it visited us. You gave so much of yourself, yet asked so little in return, and I hope you always knew how much you meant to me," she said, her voice raspy with unshed tears.

"You also had a wonderful sense of fun and cheekiness, and I am grateful that you added levity to my life too, with your lightness of being and your love of merriment. For all that you were my familiar, and walked other dimensions with me in ritual and spellcasting, it was our ordinary moments that I treasure the most, cuddling up on the couch with me while I read a book in winter, playing with me in the garden and helping me dig when I was planting flowers or herbs, sitting on the back step with me and basking in the sunshine as I drank my morning coffee. And I think it will be the cat and the companion that I miss the most, even more so than my familiar."

Rose paused for a moment, overcome with emotion, and Carlie smiled sadly as she watched the joy and celebration mix with the sadness and grief in her grandmother's face, and in the set of her body. Too choked up to continue talking, she finally motioned for her granddaughter to speak, if she wanted to.

"Sweet Luther, I will miss you so much, and I'm so grateful for everything you did for me, keeping me company when I first got here, when I felt so alone..." She hesitated, embarrassed, and looked at her grandmother with eyes full of apology, but Rose just smiled and waved her hand at her to go on.

"I'm so grateful that you journeyed with me into my dreams, protecting me from nightmares, drawing me out with your little paw on my face when there was evil lurking there."

Rose's eyebrows lifted in surprise, but she didn't interrupt.

"And I'm so grateful to you for seeing Rowan's pure heart, and helping me to know that it was okay to trust him – and for warning him when he had to leave."

Rose's eyebrows shot up even further, and Carlie blushed, then nervously admitted that the first day Rowan had visited her, Luther had come in and somehow told him that Rose was on her way home, so he could leave before they were discovered. But rather than being angry, the priestess surprised her granddaughter by laughing heartily at that story, then whispering her thanks to Luther for being Carlie's confidante when she'd so sorely needed one.

Pushing through her sadness, Carlie continued. "Mostly I'm just so grateful to you for being so kind, for accepting me as I am, and seeing the good in me when I couldn't, when I was so angry and bitter that I thought there was no hope left for me." Wiping a tear from her eye, she paused for a moment and tried to compose herself.

"And thank you so much for knowing what we needed and bringing Luna to us. I promise that I will love her and care for her, and make you proud of me. Blessed be sweet Luther. Hail and farewell."

Bowing her head, Carlie sat there in silence, feeling the sadness wash over her, but concentrating only on her love for the creature who had been so dear to her, and her gratitude for all that he had taught her and brought her.

Rose gazed over at her granddaughter, proud of her that she was holding it together so well, and focusing on the joy they'd shared with Luther rather than the emptiness they both felt now that he was gone. She was struggling herself, although she'd presided over more than her fair share of funerals, memorials and rituals of farewell. So easy it had been then, to talk of the journey to the next world, to convince the mourners that their loved one was going to a better place, or a good place at the very least. That the person or animal would still be with them in spirit, still be part of them and their life.

And yet for all that she tried to convince herself of that now, she felt the hole in her heart where her familiar had resided, and acknowledged that while he may still be with her in some way, on some plane of existence, it wasn't the same. She couldn't hold him close or hear him purring as she stroked his soft head. So were her reassurances to Carlie, to her community, nothing but a lie?

A soft paw on her leg brought Rose back from whichever dark place she'd been, and she opened her eyes and looked down to see Luna gazing up at her, as though she knew what she was thinking, and was offering herself as a gift of healing. Laughing, she picked the kitten up and held her close.

"Thank you Luther," she said, smiling and looking skyward. "You will be in my heart forever. And thank you for the reminder of the wheel of life," she added, as she kissed Luna's soft head then gently placed her in her lap.

Leaning forward over the altar, she picked up three of the four sugilite crystals that had sat in the golden dish in the centre throughout their ritual. Handing one to Carlie, she then placed another one under Luna's little paw, and squeezed the third one tightly in her hand. "One crystal to represent each of us – you, me, Luna and Luther," she explained to Carlie.

"I thought we'd keep the four of them together here in the lounge room, in their dish. They've been charged with our love and our loss, and our gratitude for every day we had together, so I thought it would be a nice reminder, the energies of all four of us intertwined and woven together, throughout time."

Carlie sighed. "That's really beautiful."

Luna miaowed, a contented little sound, and pushed her crystal towards Rose.

"Thank you little one," she said, smiling as she picked up the crystal and placed it back in the dish, alongside hers and Luther's. Carlie kissed her crystal and added it to the others, then Rose positioned the dish back in the centre of the altar and began to farewell the elements and the goddess. It was time.

Carlie felt the magic swirling around her, felt her skin tingle as she watched the power collect around her grandmother and touch each of the elements in turn. Luna stared around her again, wild eyed yet safe in Rose's lap, and seeming more curious than scared. Carlie wondered what the little kitten could see, what she was feeling. Could she still communicate with Luther?

And was Luther now with his mum Shadow, the sweet ghost cat she'd met in the cottage in the mists? That thought gave her comfort, and strength, and after the circle was closed she stood up, gently lifted Luna and placed her on the floor, then took her grandmother's hands and helped her up. It felt complete.

"So, a cup of tea and one of the many platters of cookies I baked this morning?" Carlie asked, but Rose shook her head. "No Sweetheart, we still have to bury our little friend, and let him settle peacefully for his long rest."

Carlie blushed. How could she have forgotten that part of the ritual? Guessing that it had been wishful thinking on her part, that they wouldn't have to face the harsh physical reality, or perhaps denial, she began to wonder how they would do it, and whether Rose had a shovel or they would have to dig the grave with a small gardening spade. Blanching at the thought, she pulled her coat more tightly around herself, and led the way out into the garden.

Catching sight of a neatly dug hole beneath the apple tree, she stopped, startled, and almost tripped when Luna barrelled into her ankles from behind her. "You did this Gran?" she asked. "When?"

"While you were in the shower this morning."

"But I could have helped you, or done it myself," Carlie argued.

"I know Sweetheart, and I appreciate that, but you've been through enough. And I wanted to do it. It seemed right somehow, to be preparing my familiar for the next life, when I had been with him when he came into the world too."

They stopped side by side at the edge of the tiny grave, shivering from the cold and the emotion of it all. A lump rose in Carlie's throat, but she swung down when Luna looked as though she was about to jump into the hole, and quickly scooped her up. "Come on little one, you stay with me."

Rose leaned down, looking suddenly frail again, and picked up Luther's blanket-wrapped body from where it rested against the trunk of the apple tree. She held it close to her heart one last time, and whispered something softly to him, then laid him reverently in the grave. Picking up a handful of the dirt piled along the edge, she gently placed it on top of his body, then turned to Carlie to let her do the same. Her granddaughter did, then sank to the ground, the sight of the grave and the small body wrapped within the star-emblazoned blanket bringing back so many sad memories that she could no longer bear the weight of them all. Luna bounced over to her side and curled up against her knees, lending her warmth and support, and Rose placed a comforting hand on her shoulder.

They stayed there together for a long time, the three of them, lost in thought, before Rose carefully filled in the rest of the grave then scattered handfuls of rose petals on the bare earth on top. When a misty rain began to fall, just as the sun was starting to set, Rose squeezed her granddaughter's shoulder and told her firmly that they had to go inside. So Carlie stood, eyes unseeing, and followed her grandmother back into the warmth of the kitchen.

The scent of freshly baked cookies and spices hit them as soon as they walked inside, swirling around them. Carlie's tummy rumbled, and she suddenly realised how hungry she was. It seemed insensitive to eat though, but Rose frowned and gestured sternly at her to sit down at the cosy little table near the heater. As Luna leaped up into her lap, Rose put the kettle on for tea then fussed around in the kitchen, filling a platter with a selection of the treats Carlie had baked that morning, and another with more substantial fare — spinach and feta triangles, sweet pepper tarts and corn and mushroom quiches, some of them still warm from the oven.

Forcing a smile, Carlie nibbled on a vegie filo pastry and made herself focus on the positives. By the time there was a knock on the door an hour later, she was giggling at her grandma's stories of Luther as a cheeky young kitten, digging up her newly planted herb garden and shredding the new altar cloths she'd painstakingly sewn from rare and expensive fabric someone had gifted her in exchange for healings.

Still smiling, she opened the door to see Rhiannon standing on the front step, looking forlorn and bedraggled. "Come in," she said, hugging her hello then dragging her quickly inside and shutting the door on the now icy wind. "Are you okay?"

Rhiannon shrugged. "I've been better, but I'm okay. I just had a really weird day with John," she explained as she entered the kitchen and greeted Rose. "Oh my god, all this food looks amazing! What's the occasion?" she asked, as Rose instructed her to take a seat and brought her over a plate, then went back and put the kettle on to brew another pot of tea.

"I'm afraid Luther passed away this morning," Rose said softly, and Rhiannon's face registered shock and sadness, before she turned to Carlie with fear in her eyes.

"Are you okay?" she whispered, and Carlie nodded.

"I've been better, but I'm okay," she replied, echoing her friend's words from moments earlier. Luna's little head popped up from Carlie's lap and peered over the table at Rhiannon, who couldn't control the grin that spread across her face.

"She's such a cutie!" she giggled. "But how are you really going Carlie? And what happened? Will you have a funeral? Sorry, perhaps I should leave you some time to reply."

"Gran said it was just old age, and there was nothing we could have done, so we're trying to focus on the fact that he had a great, and remarkably long, life, and be grateful for the time we did have with him. And he didn't suffer, so we're doing our best to convince ourselves not to be too sad, and that it's just part of the enchanted wheel of life – but it's really hard," she said with a sigh.

"Do you think he knew he was going to die? Is that why he brought Luna to you?" Rhiannon asked.

Rose spooned fresh tea leaves into the pot before she answered. "I think so. And he was very old, although he never seemed that way. But I think he was worried about making Carlie face another loss, and of leaving her without a companion, so he found a replacement for himself," she said, as she pulled another mug out of the cupboard and poured some soy milk into a jug, and took them over to the table.

"We had a ritual of farewell this afternoon, and buried him just as the sun was setting, out under his favourite tree," Rose said, voice faltering only a little. "I'm trying not to be sad, because the underpinning of my faith is the natural cycle of life, death and rebirth, of things happening in the right time, and of energy continuing to exist even as we change form, but of course I miss him terribly. Yet I can't be anything but grateful for all the time I had with him, and I'm determined to honour his memory and focus on all the precious moments we shared."

Picking up the teapot and a jar of honey, she carried them over to the table too and set them down in the middle, then refilled the platter of cakes, scones and cookies before sliding into a chair and picking up her cup of tea.

"Should we really be eating cookies for dinner Gran?" Carlie asked, although she didn't wait for an answer before she picked up a cinnamon scroll and took a big bite.

"Oh Sweetheart, if you can't eat what you want to at a wake, when can you?" Rose said, and they all laughed. It wasn't the happiest laughter in the world, but it held a tiny bit of joy.

After a while, sensing that Rhiannon had things to talk about and confide, Rose excused herself and left the girls to it. The moment the door to her room closed, Carlie turned to her friend. "Are you okay? What happened?"

"Oh Carlie, we don't have to talk about it now! How are you doing? I can't believe Luther's gone. I'm so sorry!" she exclaimed.

Carlie smiled sadly. "I'm all right. We had a beautiful ceremony, and Gran reminded me that we should be celebrating and focusing on his life, not his death, and that he had an uncannily long one for a cat. But tell me what happened with John."

Rhiannon toyed with her mug of tea, eyes on the last choc-chip cookie on the plate. Carlie pushed it towards her. "Chocolate helps you know," she said with a wicked grin.

Rhiannon took a deep breath, then managed to smile. "You know, death really puts things in perspective, doesn't it," she mused, as she reached for the cookie. "I was stressing about John, wondering what to do to fix it, trying to figure out how much I liked him, whether we're good together or not, or whether I just like having someone to be with, as opposed to really liking being with him specifically. I'd worked myself up into a real frenzy, like it was the most important thing on earth, when really, what's the big deal? I date him or I don't date him, it's as simple as that. It's hardly an earth-shattering dilemma, so why was I tying myself in knots about this?" she asked, shrugging in an effort to seem nonchalant.

Carlie smiled at her friend. "You know, a wise person once told me that being a teenager is all about drama. That whole 'I'll *die* if he doesn't love me,' or: 'I love you, best friend, no wait, I hate you and I'll never speak to you again!' That we feel everything much more intensely than adults."

Rhiannon started laughing, so hard that she ended up doubled over, clutching her stomach, tears of amusement running down her cheeks. "I can't believe you remember that!" she giggled. "That was at Brodie's party, the day after we met. My god, I really thought I knew everything, didn't I?"

"How could I forget? I was incredibly impressed by your maturity that day. Although it seems we forget our great advice when something crops up in our own lives," Carlie replied.

"Or it's: 'Do as I say, not as I do,'" Rhiannon added with a grin. "It's always so much simpler to see the answer to someone else's dilemma than your own. Of course I could see that your mum was being overly dramatic – no offence…"

"None taken," Carlie replied, and was surprised that she hadn't become anxious at the mention of her mother.

"Yet I couldn't see it in myself," her friend sighed. "I don't know, I'd pretty much decided I should end things with John when we were talking about it with Jake the other day, but when we met up this morning I remembered all the reasons I liked him."

Smiling ruefully, she rolled her eyes at herself. "We had a lot of fun – I helped him buy a present for his younger brother, then we drank coffee for hours, and he asked if I was going to be on the summer ball committee, and said he'd love it if I was because he'd already volunteered. And then he confided in me some problems he was having with his dad, which were really heavy, and I felt honoured that he could tell me, because he's been struggling with it for a while, and doesn't feel able to tell his guy friends. So now I'm even more confused, because today I really like him, and want to be with him."

Carlie smiled. "That's great then, isn't it? You really like him, he clearly likes you, and he feels close enough to you to share personal issues with. Isn't that what you want in a boyfriend?"

Sighing, her friend nodded. "You'd think so, wouldn't you? But now that I'm away from him again, back here with you and Luna, and eating magical ritual food, I feel like I want more from my relationship. Which I know sounds insane!"

Carlie laughed. "It's not insane at all, it makes perfect sense. Especially as the reason you seemed to suddenly like Jake the other day was that he came to the ritual with us. I'm guessing you didn't bring up the witch thing today with John?"

Her friend blushed. "I'm not sure if I forgot or just chickened out. But it was going so well, I guess I didn't want to ruin things. Which in itself says something, I'm sure."

"Well, maybe you're over-thinking it now," Carlie said. "What if you try not to think about it for the rest of the weekend, and on Tuesday night at our coven meeting we can do an exercise to go within, and connect with our inner wisdom. Maybe you'll be able to figure it out then."

Rhiannon smiled. "You really are smarter than you look."

"Hey!" Carlie protested, and her friend laughed.

"Just joking. But I guess I'd better get home and let you get some sleep. And I'm really sorry about Luther," Rhiannon added, leaning down to pat Luna on her tiny head.

"Thank you," Carlie said simply as she walked her friend out to the front door. "Now, no thinking, all right? We'll figure it out on Tuesday night."

They hugged goodbye, then Carlie quietly closed the door, sagging against it as she realised how exhausted she was after such a sad day. Quickly she tidied away the dishes in the kitchen, then scooped Luna up and took her upstairs to bed, where the kitten curled up on her pillow and sighed herself to sleep.

Chapter 22

Learning To Let Go

Carlie slept in on Sunday, too depressed at losing Luther to want to get up, but finally Luna's tentative little paw on her cheek drove her into action, and she sat up and scooped the sweet creature into her arms. The kitten looked at her with so much trust that Carlie sighed and stood up. That's what she'd promised Luther, that she would care for this tiny scrap of a thing, and so she would. There was no room in her life for grief between schoolwork, homework, helping in the shop and looking after and spending time with Luna – she just had to get on with it.

With a distinct lack of enthusiasm, she moped through the next two days at school, and when she headed to Rhiannon's on Tuesday night she thought it was perfectly fitting that the whole world was grey and miserable. Dragging her feet, she recounted all her losses – her parents, her friends, her childhood home, her school, her future in Sydney, her career as a lawyer, all topped off by the death of her beloved, and now Luther, the first friend she'd made here. Just as she was getting sick of her self-pity, it started raining, so, sighing melodramatically, she pulled her mum's old coat more tightly around herself, put her head down and started to run as fast as she could.

Then abruptly she stopped, and started laughing. It was only a bit of water. She lifted her face to the sky, loving the feel of the raindrops on her cheeks, and trying to appreciate the crisp coolness of the air and the cleansing power of water as it soothed her tortured thoughts. Silver linings and all that, she thought wryly, making an effort to change her mindset to a more positive one. But when it started bucketing down, she groaned, rolled her eyes and bolted up the road. There was only so much good humour she could keep up while feeling so much like a drowned rat.

By the time she knocked on her friend's front door she was wet and shivering, out of breath and somewhat out of sorts. Rhiannon laughed as she ushered her inside, hanging her dripping coat on the stand in the hallway as they passed.

"How come you never bring an umbrella?" she asked.

Carlie shrugged. "It seemed like it was only the tiniest of sprinkles when I set out. And isn't it spring already? Why is it still storming?" she protested, petulant and borderline whiny.

"It is, but it's still the very start of spring. And sometimes winter holds on longer than we'd like it to here," Rhiannon replied calmly, as she guided her out to the kitchen and put the kettle on. "Tea? And do you need some dry clothes to change into?"

Carlie stomped her feet to shake off some of the rain. "I'm sure I'll survive," she said, voice surly, then mentally kicked herself. It was time to drop the woe-is-me attitude. "And tea would be great, thank you."

Mugs in hand, they entered Rhiannon's room, and Carlie was surprised to see it devoid of the altar that was usually set up. Her friend smiled. "I thought we could just use oracle cards tonight, find the answers to our questions. Is that all right?"

"Of course," Carlie said. "You have a big decision to make."

Picking up the card deck from her desk, Rhiannon moved to the centre of the room, and waved Carlie over to one of the big purple cushions. Casting circle around them both, she then sat down opposite her. "Want me to do yours first?"

Carlie shook her head. "You're the one who desperately needs to figure out what to do, so ask your question as you shuffle the cards, then hand them over," she instructed, her grin belying the sternness of her voice.

Laughing, Rhiannon did as she was told, then gave the deck to Carlie, who was surprised to see how nervous her friend was.

"Hey, you know that *you* decide your destiny, right? The cards are just to inspire and uncover your own heart, your own truth and choices. If you don't like the answer, you don't have to take it on board – you can do the opposite. They'll still have served a purpose by crystallising what you want to do in your mind. They're just a tool to help you see what you already know."

Rhiannon nodded. "I know, but I just have no idea what I want. When I'm with John I really like him and want to be with him, but then when I'm away from him I think we should break up."

"Yet deep down you know what to do, you're just not ready to face it. Maybe you'll get some clarity tonight though," Carlie said. "Are you ready?" Her friend nodded reluctantly, still looking worried. Smiling reassuringly, Carlie laid out the cards.

Past: Be Gentle With Yourself
Present: Be True to Yourself
Future: Learn to Let Go

Rhiannon raised her eyebrows as she gazed intently at the cards, but kept her face blank. Carlie tried to read her expression, but for now her friend was holding her cards close to her chest, so to speak. She turned her own attention to them, looking at the images on them, the words and the symbols in the borders, as well as how they'd appeared in relation to each other. Then she closed her eyes, trying to open her mind and her heart to the meaning they held for Rhiannon. Inhaling slowly and deeply, she finally started interpreting them, talking fast so her logical mind couldn't get in the way and try to influence the reading or make herself doubt what she was saying.

Past: Be Gentle With Yourself

You've been beating yourself up over things you have done and choices you have made, but it's time to stop. The past can't be undone – you need to own your decisions and take responsibility for your actions, then let it all go so you can move forward. No one is perfect, so give yourself a break. And be as gentle and forgiving with yourself as you would be with anyone else.

In relation to your question, there is no blame to be cast, and you shouldn't have any regrets about the time you've spent together. Whether you stay with him or end it, you have both cared about each other, and enriched each other's lives, and nothing will change that. He has helped you learn more about yourself and what you want – and what you don't want – in a relationship. And he encouraged you to break through your shyness, to become more active with school committees, to communicate with people you normally wouldn't, and that is a valuable thing. He's helped you to grow and become stronger and more assured.

Don't regret your time together on his account either – you have helped him immensely too, been a confidante when he needed one, and shown him a new way to look at the world. Whether your relationship endures or not, the things you have given each other will stay with you both, and you'll look back on your time together with fondness and gratitude.

Present: Be True to Yourself

At the heart of your question is insecurity about your own deepest self, and a fear that he won't like you if he really knows you. Yet it's also a wider feeling, about the whole world accepting you for who you are, and the fear you have of revealing yourself. We show a different side of ourselves to everyone we meet – we play up some aspects of ourselves with one person, play down or even hide others, and that's fine. It's not important that everyone knows everything about you. Fellow students, workmates, potential bosses, none of them *need* to know your religious, spiritual or philosophical beliefs if you don't want them to.

But for real trust and real love to grow within a relationship, you can't pretend away the things that have the most meaning to you. You can't dim your light for acceptance, deny the beliefs that are so  central to your very being, or hide what's in your heart. Magic and ritual is vital to you, and any relationship where you feel you have to hide that will remain superficial in many ways. For a true heart connection, you have to be able to share that, not laugh it off or lock it away.

So don't deny him the chance to see you, all of you, and make up his own mind. Share your spirituality and what is important to you. Be brave enough to tell him you're a witch. If he has a problem with it, then it's not meant to be, and it would be better to find out now. But imagine how beautiful it will be if he does embrace it, and embrace you in all your complexities and depths. If he can share this precious thing with you, and come to rituals with you, it will make them even more magical.

Future: Learn to Let Go

Some people come into our lives for a long time, and that's wonderful. But others only come into our lives for a short time, and that's okay too. It doesn't mean the short-term people are less important — sometimes you can learn and grow more from someone you only spend a few precious hours or days with, than someone you've known your whole life. So look for the good in your relationship, for the things you've learned and the things you've shared, and celebrate that, without feeling that you have to remain stuck there just because it was once good, or because it isn't bad. You deserve to be with someone who makes your soul sing, who loves all of you, not just the parts you choose to show, and who inspires you to be *more* yourself, rather than diminishing what's most important to you.

Cherish the people who are in your life for the long haul, but also express your gratitude for those who only come into your life for a short time, then say goodbye with a clear heart. If John isn't the person who will share your magical life with you, that's okay. Don't be scared of letting him go so you can find someone who *will* embrace your spiritual side. It's better for John too, if that's the case, that you let him go and allow him to be with someone who shares the things that are most important to him.

Suddenly nervous, Carlie looked at Rhiannon. "Thoughts?"

Her friend laughed. "When you put the cards down, and I saw what they were, all I felt was relief. Relief that I should end it. And that last one made me really happy — I love that you said you can touch someone's life and heart, and be glad of that, but you don't necessarily need to stay with them. Because John is a lovely guy, and there's no real reason I can think of to break up with him. He hasn't been mean to me, he treats me well, it's just not... well, it's not what you and Rowan had," she admitted.

"I'd rather hold out for that than settle for something that's nice, but not amazing and magical and heart-opening. I want to love and adore someone, and feel inspired and passionate about them, about us, and I want to be loved and adored too. And I want that for John as well," she added.

Carlie hugged her. "Oh Rhi, you'll find that for sure, I know it. And you deserve that. You both do."

"It feels strange though," Rhiannon said haltingly. "I mean, what do I tell him? Shouldn't I have a good, clear reason? And I'm not sure that 'You're not Rowan' will cut it."

"You don't need any other reason than that you want more for both of you. You care about him, but it can take more than friendship for a relationship to work, especially if you can't — or won't — share the thing that's most important to you with him."

"But what if he argues with me, and I can't explain why we should break up?" Rhiannon asked.

Carlie stared at her, brow furrowed. "You don't actually need a reason to break up, and you don't even really owe him an explanation, if it comes to that. If it doesn't feel right to you, then you should end it. You don't need to convince him or win him over with your reason, and you don't need an excuse. It's not a topic open to discussion, it's not a debate where the person who has the most convincing argument 'wins'. If you don't want to be in the relationship, then you shouldn't be, no matter what he says to convince you otherwise. I mean, would you want him to stay with you even if he wanted to break up?"

"Of course not."

"Exactly," Carlie said. "And it doesn't mean that he's a bad boyfriend, or that you're a bad girlfriend. He'll be someone else's perfect boyfriend, he's just not yours, and that's okay. It totally depends on the chemistry of the two people involved. You and Rowan probably wouldn't have worked out either, but not because of any failing on either of your parts," she smiled.

"Hell, I'm sure psycho shaman guy was a great partner to someone else, but for some reason he and Mum brought out the worst in each other, not the best. There's someone out there who will love and support you in ways that will make you want to be the best *you* that you can be, who will recognise the deepest parts of your heart, and see you as the embodiment of the goddess. And you'll bring out their best too, and support them in following their heart and manifesting their dreams into reality."

Rhiannon reached over and hugged her friend. "Thank you for your wisdom, and your truth telling. If I'm brutally honest with myself, I would say that John really likes me, really likes spending time with me, but it's not like he couldn't imagine his life without me. So that makes perfect sense. He'll be an awesome boyfriend to someone else, and no doubt someone else will be the perfect girlfriend for him, but we just aren't that for each other.

"Thank you for this Carlie, really," she continued. "I know it can't be easy for you to talk about. But I really appreciate your analogy about me and Rowan, because he was perfect for you, but wouldn't have been for me, and vice versa. And I have to remember that it's not the worst thing in the world to be single, especially as it means I'll get to spend more time with you. Now, do we need more tea before I do your reading?"

"I don't need a reading, I'm fine," Carlie insisted, as they wandered downstairs to put the kettle on. She was quite happy for now to dwell in the present moment, to wallow in memories of Luther and the loved ones she'd lost. Not in a morbid way, but because she was finally beginning to see how blessed she had been to have them in her life at all. Of course she wished they were still with her, but she was going to focus on her gratitude that she'd known them at all, and appreciate every single moment they'd shared. She knew that some people lived their whole life without ever experiencing the love she'd had with her parents, or with Rowan.

Perhaps that last card meaning had also been for her – to embrace the time they'd had together and appreciate it, and let go of the anger that she couldn't have more. Appreciate that her life was half full from them being in it, not half empty now that they were gone. No one could take away the love they'd shared, or their presence and influence in her life.

"Earth to Carlie. What kind of tea would you like?" Rhiannon asked, breaking into her thoughts.

Carlie smiled. "Do you still have that grounding tea? The one with dandelion root, blackberry leaves, sage, and what was the other thing? Red clover? I'm feeling a little spaced out."

Her friend found the pretty jar of herbs that they'd blended with Rose during one of their practical coven-evening lessons with their priestess, and spooned the leaves out into the teapot.

"I've got some choc-chip cookies too, if you need more grounding. But you're not going to get out of having your reading hon, it has to be an equal energy exchange."

Carlie smiled, and tried not to feel too annoyed, but she suspected that Rhiannon wanted to somehow include a little "Jake's so sweet" message in any oracle reading she did for her. With that in mind, she was relieved when Mike arrived home early and sat down with them in the kitchen to catch up on their lives and their magical adventures. It reminded her, with a pang of guilt, that she still hadn't figured out anything more about the curse he believed in, and she was filled with a sudden fear for her friend.

"Oh my, is that the time? I should get home," Carlie said, standing up abruptly. "I need to finish that assignment for class tomorrow. It was lovely to see you Mike, and I'll catch up with you at school Rhi," she added, then picked up her bag and rushed down the hallway and out into the cool night air.

Chapter 23

Tea and Sympathy

As she wandered slowly home, Carlie started thinking about the curse Rhiannon's dad Mike believed had been laid on him by Andre the shaman all those years ago – to try to keep him away from her mum Violet – and his fear for his own daughter and how it would affect her. She'd meant to check some of Rose's books to see if she could find any answers there, but she'd been distracted by Aideen right after her conversation with Mike, and by her ongoing saga with Rhiannon ever since. But now she vowed to continue her search for answers, and wondered desperately if she'd be able to break the curse somehow, or at least figure out a way to protect her friend.

Part of her was amused by this new obsession. She didn't even know if curses were real, and not that long ago she would have laughed her head off at the very idea that someone could believe they had magical powers. But that was before she'd arrived in Summer Hill and discovered that her priestess grandmother could change the energy of a room with a flick of her hand. Before she'd patted the ghost of a cat, and spoken with beings of mist who took the shape of women and gave her real gifts before dispersing back into thin air. Before she'd wandered into a cottage in the mists and read a book there, one that she later found at home, just after she'd learned the cottage had burned down twenty years ago and didn't actually exist any more.

So she had to concede that although a curse seemed crazily far-fetched to her, she wouldn't be totally knock-me-over-with-a-feather shocked to be shown that they did exist. It wouldn't be the first time she'd had to open her mind to concede that something mysterious and highly unlikely was actually real, after seeing it with her own eyes or experiencing it with her own body. This village was weirder than anything she could have ever imagined, so who knew what was actually possible?

As she walked down the deserted High Street she shivered suddenly, feeling the cold mist curling around her neck. Seeing the lights of her favourite cafe on, she decided to go in, drawn by the cheeriness of the open fire and the twinkling candles on the few tables scattered around the room. She wanted to write down what she remembered of tonight's reading into the divination section of her Book of Shadows, while it was still vivid in her mind. And who knew, maybe as she wrote about the words she'd channelled for Rhi, her mind would lead her down possible avenues of how she could learn more about curses.

Ordering a pot of chai tea, she wandered over and collapsed down into one of the comfy armchairs by the roaring fire. She stared into the flames, losing herself in their dance, mesmerised by the swirling patterns that rose and fell then rose again, and trying to decipher the images she saw. What had Aideen said, harness the power of fire to scorch and burn away your pain?

The waitress brought her tea over and she smiled her thanks, still lost in thought. The cinnamon-drenched steam from the teapot brought her back into the room though, into the present, its warm earthy scent making her feel safe and soothed. She pulled out her Book of Shadows and opened it to a blank page, then selected one of her favourite purple pens to write with.

"Excuse me?"

Carlie jumped in surprise, dropping her pen as she looked up in confusion at the stranger standing over her.

"I'm sorry," she said automatically, as she picked up her pen and set it down on the table, before turning her eyes back to the tall woman before her. She was dressed in a long green velvet skirt with a long black velvet coat over the top, and looked vaguely familiar.

Maybe she'd come to one of Rose's rituals? She couldn't remember her name though, if that was the case, or place her. And she was pretty sure she knew all the women of Rose's inner circle at least, and would recognise the other ritual participants.

"Didn't your friend tell you to stop apologising?" the woman asked with a smile. Ignoring Carlie's confusion at that – since Rhiannon had certainly said that to her once or twice – she pressed on. "Do you mind if I sit with you?" she asked, and Carlie, embarrassed that she couldn't recall her name, nodded.

"Of course," she said, closing her book and stuffing it into her bag before the stranger asked about it, and mentally running through the list of all the names of the people she'd met recently. *Damn, she'd have to pay more attention.*

Then she paused. Why was this making her so anxious? Surely the woman wouldn't be too offended that she couldn't remember her name, since she was still relatively new in town and had met so many people. Yet she seemed to know things about her that someone she'd only met once or twice should have no way of knowing.

Elegantly the woman folded herself into the armchair next to Carlie, hands wrapped tightly around her mug of hot chocolate. She inhaled the sweet aroma and let out a deep, contented sigh.

"They really do make the best hot chocolate here," she smiled, eyes lit up with the joy of simple pleasures.

"I'll have to try it one day," Carlie replied, as she poured out a cup of chai, buying time as she tried to puzzle out who the woman was. She looked so familiar, it was driving her crazy.

"We haven't met before Carlie, so you can stop struggling, and thinking you're rude to have forgotten me."

Staring at the woman in confusion, Carlie was now worried in a different way. What did a stranger want with her? And how did she know so much about her?

"You could say that I'm a friend of Rhiannon's," the woman said, her voice cracked and aching with pain. "I can sense that you're worried about her. And I'm so glad that you've both reconnected. That you've been able to forgive her, and are such a good friend to her. She's true to you too, and she'd never knowingly hurt you."

Carlie nodded cautiously. "I know," she whispered.

"And I can sense how much you're worrying about Mike too. You have a beautiful heart Carlie. Your grandmother must be so proud of you," she continued.

Blushing a little, Carlie tilted her head in acknowledgement of the compliment, without actually agreeing with it, and took a sip of tea. She felt like she was dreaming, one of those dreams that doesn't make any sense. Perhaps she would wake up soon, safe at home in bed, with Luna cuddled up in the crook of her arm, warming her up, and anchoring her to safety, and sanity.

The stranger laughed, a high, tinkling laugh. "Well, maybe it is some kind of dream," she said. "But you're awake now. And the thing is Carlie, you really need to wake up. Not from sleep, but from the fog in your brain, from the fog of your memories. You already know why the curse isn't real, why Rhiannon is safe, but you're too scared to linger on how you know that."

"That's not true! I'd do anything to put Mike and Rhiannon's minds at ease," she protested.

"I know," the woman replied. "You're kind like your mother."

Carlie gasped. "You knew her?" she asked, voice full of pain.

"I did. Everyone here loved her, and felt her loss when she left the village. I know Mike never stopped loving her."

Brow crinkling, Carlie stared hard at the woman. "Who are you? How do you know this stuff?" she begged. "And how could you know about Mike loving my mum? Because that's not true. He was married to an amazing woman who he adored, who he adores still, and whose children miss her terribly."

Tears pricked the woman's eyes, and she smiled sadly. "I'm sure she misses them more than anything too," she whispered. "But this is too long a story for tonight, and all you need to know for now is that you already have the answer to Mike's fear of a curse, you just have to dive within and rediscover it. I have faith in you Carlie," she said, then stood up abruptly and walked out of the cafe.

The door banged shut behind her, making the candles on the tables flicker, and Carlie shivered in the cold draft that had rushed in. Trying to ground herself, she finished her tea and poured out another cup, noticing as she did so that the woman hadn't had a single sip of the hot chocolate she'd professed to love so much.

Who was she? How could she know so much about so many people? And who could know so much about *her*? She'd only just moved to the village. And most importantly, if the woman knew so much about the curse, why didn't she just tell her? Why was she being sent on a quest for find answers?

And what if she couldn't work the puzzle out? God, was the woman related to Brianna, Brauna and Aideen somehow? They happily handed out cryptic clues that made them seem helpful too, yet really weren't. But that was crazy, surely. Those three had materialised out of the mists, and this woman was flesh and blood, walking into the cafe, talking with her, ordering a drink and sitting opposite her.

She was jolted out of her thoughts by the waitress coming over to tell her they were closing up, so Carlie quickly drank down the rest of her chai, steeling herself for the chill outside, then wandered home in a daze. Rose had already gone to bed, so she tiptoed upstairs, brushing her teeth quickly then crawling under the covers.

Her heart lifted when Luna walked up from her warm nest at the end of the bed and cuddled in against Carlie's chest, her gentle purring sending her off to a sleep filled with dreams of her mother as a young woman, walking and talking with the woman she'd met in the cafe. Had they been friends?

She cried out for them to slow down, to stop and talk to her, to explain things, but when she spoke they faded into the mists and she was left alone. Sighing, she rolled over, and felt a little paw on her cheek, guiding her back to a wonderful dream of when Rowan was alive. She threw herself into his arms and let her mind drift away into a deep, comforting sleep.

Chapter 24

The Lure of the Dark Side

Carlie spent the rest of the week trying to nut out what the woman she'd met in the cafe had meant. How could she know something but at the same time not know it? Why hadn't the stranger just given her the answer, instead of making her feel like a failure for not being able to figure it out? And who was she anyway, and how did she know so much about her?

She'd tried to explain what she looked like to Rhiannon, hoping she might know who it was, but her description of a beautiful woman with long blonde hair, wearing a long velvet skirt and coat, didn't really narrow it down in this town.

Most frustrating of all, the harder she tried to concentrate on these problems, the further she felt she was getting from an answer. It was also making her a little unfocused at school, and Rhiannon had twice asked her what was going on and where her head was at. Fortunately she'd managed to convince her, for now at least, that she was just feeling anxious about her history assignment, but she didn't like lying to her.

Nor did she like having to keep Rose and Rhiannon in the dark. They were the two people who would be most able to assist her in figuring out the curse, but she didn't want to upset her grandmother by bringing it up, scare her friend at the thought of it, or break Mike's confidence. If only Rowan was still alive, he'd know what to do. He always knew what to do.

If only she could communicate with him in some way. Was there a magical way she could do that? She skimmed through Rose's magical books whenever her grandma was out, but she never found anything that looked especially useful. There were veiled references to seances and ouija boards, but only in reference to dark magics and mysterious ancient sects.

On Friday at lunchtime she asked Rhiannon if she'd ever performed a seance, but her friend shook her head vehemently.

"Don't even joke about it," she said, which Carlie thought was odd, since she'd meant it as a serious question. "I know how tempting the idea can be, but it's not real, and it can mess with your head. I do know how much you miss Rowan, believe me – I still miss my mum every day – but at some point we have to accept that they're gone. And while we can trust that they are still with us in some way, it's not in a tangible way that allows us to have a conversation with them."

Carlie nodded. "I know. And I do accept that he's gone. But isn't there some –"

"No, there isn't. Now promise me that you won't mess around with this kind of stuff," Rhiannon demanded.

"I promise, but geez, why are you so against them?" Carlie asked.

Rhiannon lowered her voice. "You know how Abby lost her boyfriend? He took his own life, and she was crushed. She felt really guilty – which was not helped by a few idiots at school who kept insisting that if she'd really cared about him she would have known what he was planning and stopped him, or that maybe he did it to get away from her."

"No!" Carlie cried. "That's dreadful!"

"I know, it was really awful. She was devastated, but Laura sorted them out. But my point is, Abby ordered a ouija board online, and used it to try to contact her boyfriend – but she ended up freaking herself out so badly, thinking she was communicating with demons, that she started going to some weird revivalist church, and now she's sworn off anything even remotely spiritual or magical or so-called new age. So don't be offended if she avoids you by the way, because she was warned to stay away from Rose and her 'demonic' crystals and things."

Carlie started to defend Abby, to tell her friend that she'd always been really nice to her, but then she realised that after that first day back at school, when Abby had offered some words of sympathy and comfort, she *had* avoided her. She hadn't chosen to sit next to her in a single class since. The only time they had been together was when Carlie sat next to her to avoid Jake that day, and now that she thought about it, Abby *had* basically ignored her, she just hadn't noticed because she was too busy being paranoid about Jake. Still, if it was helping her to heal to stay out of her way, well, that was fine. She knew exactly how devastating losing your boyfriend was.

Rhiannon smiled sadly. "She has been avoiding you, hasn't she?" she asked, and Carlie nodded reluctantly.

"It's nothing personal, don't worry. But Rose would warn you off seances and ouija boards too, if you asked her," Rhiannon added. "But *don't* ask her, she'd be really upset to know you were even entertaining the idea."

Carlie stared at her friend, puzzled by the secrecy. Surely she could give her a straight answer. She was even more intrigued when she figured out that Rhiannon hadn't actually said they didn't work, just that she shouldn't try them. But the bell rang before she could grill her any further, and they hugged goodbye. Tonight Rhiannon was looking after her brother, then tomorrow she was going to see John, to let him see her magical heart.

"Good luck and best wishes with it all," Carlie said softly, kindly. "I really hope he's open to your witchyness, but don't worry too much if he's not – there will be guys who are, and you deserve to be loved for your true self, your whole self."

Rhiannon smiled. "Thank you, for making me finally realise that, and giving me the confidence to reveal myself to him. I'll let you know what happens," she yelled, as she ran off to class.

Chapter 25

Right Here, Right Now

The next morning dawned grey and cold, and Carlie spent her morning doing chores and hanging out with Luna. Her thoughts were with Rhiannon though, and she hoped it was going well with her and John. After lunch with Rose, she went in to the healing centre with her and did some reiki for a few regulars.

The skies cleared in the afternoon, just as the last person left the shop, so she wandered up to the top of the tor, grateful for the time and space to process all she'd experienced in the last two weeks, from the Imbolc ceremony with Rose that they'd shared with Jake and his grandfather, to her lunchtime chat with Rhiannon and Jake about relationships, her dark moon ritual with her friend, and that strange late-night meeting with the mystery woman in the cafe. And she was still obsessing over Mike's worries about the supposed curse, and how that might affect her friend in the future. Life was certainly more magical here than it had been in Sydney, and in some strange ways more real and deep, but it was also more challenging, with the potential for more heartbreak. As what she loved grew – friends, magic, her bond with her grandmother – so did the fear of losing it all.

Breathing deeply, she tried to let her mind go blank, to let her fears wash over her, and see them being blown away by the cold breeze at the summit of the sacred hill. It was a struggle though – the more she tried not to think of something, the more her focus homed in on it, and she sighed in frustration. But the wide open sky and the energy pouring up from the earth and into her heart calmed her, and she stopped suddenly as an idea formed.

They were faced with a magical curse, so maybe that meant they could break it magically. For the millionth time she wished that Rowan was still with her, because she was sure he'd know what to do. But he was gone forever. And Rose might know something about curses, but she wasn't ready to share that part of her mum's past with her – she didn't want to upset her needlessly, or get her involved in Mike's issue without his permission. An image of some older books Rose had stored in the cupboard under the stairs leaped into her mind though, so she stood up and headed back towards home, intent on restarting the search.

As she meandered down the tor, she let her mind drift. The mists were rising up around her ankles, and she watched it form then dance apart, then reform, delicate wisps reaching out to her, beckoning her forward. Sometimes it made her smile, this magical-looking fog that cloaked the world in softness and mystery, but today the mists made her feel sad, and filled her with longing. She daydreamed about Rowan, picturing him walking by her side, holding her hand, talking as he used to, telling her that he loved her, that she was amazing, and that she could do anything with her life.

Her ankle twisted as she stepped into a depression in the earth, probably part of an old rabbit hole, and panic clutched her heart as she crouched down, clutching her foot in her hands. *Please goddess, don't let it be a break, I couldn't bear it!*

Bleakly she looked around, and realised that somehow she'd come down the slope much further along the laneway than she should have. Sighing that she'd have to backtrack even further to get home, and cursing her sore ankle, she started hobbling along the lane.

Then abruptly she stopped, staring in disbelief. Intellectually she knew that the cottage wasn't there, yet there it stood, as solid as any other house as it peeked out of the mists that wreathed it, defying her not to acknowledge it. The candle in the window flickered, and overhead, clouds that hadn't been there earlier rushed together, darkening ominously then opening up and pouring a deluge of rain down on her, soaking her to the skin and chilling her to the bone.

Shivering, she raced up the steps to the back verandah, and was only mildly surprised when Shadow, or the ghost of Shadow, rubbed against her wet legs. Desperately she looked around for Luther, praying she could hold him one last time, but she couldn't see him, and perhaps it was better that he wasn't there, or she might have started crying and never been able to stop.

Nervously she opened the creaky door and walked slowly inside – then she sank to her knees in shock and pain, the breath smashed out of her. Rowan was standing against the far wall, leaning up against the kitchen bench, the scent of the rosemary in the pot on the windowsill drifting through the dusty air between them, bringing her back to her senses.

Rosemary for remembrance. She closed her eyes, trying to block out the sweet agony of seeing the spectre before her. Rowan was dead, so she couldn't be looking at him. She'd been to his funeral, grieved with his mother, planted rosemary under the apple tree in her backyard in his memory. This was a cruel joke, it had to be. Or she was finally going crazy, her mind as cracked and broken as her heart.

Stiffening as she heard footsteps moving towards her, her breath caught, heart thumping like a wild thing in her chest. A hand came down on her shoulder, the warmth of its touch infusing her wet and shaking body with heat, drying her in an instant. Now it was fear, anticipation and the smallest and most reluctant sense of hope that was making her shiver.

She sensed someone sinking down on his knees in front of her, and felt a gentle hand lifting her chin to face him.

"Baby, I'm here." It was his voice, and suddenly the how and why of what was happening meant nothing. Opening her eyes, she gasped in surprise and joy and threw her arms around him as he lifted her to her feet, tears falling as she burrowed her face into his shoulder. She didn't care that she was making him wet as she cried. Or that there was no logical way he could actually be standing in the cottage with her.

The sweet agony as he gently stroked her hair nearly brought her to her knees again, but she stood firm. No force on earth could separate her from her beloved one second sooner than the inevitable end. Finally he broke the circle of his arms, but his hands were on her shoulders as he gazed at her, eyes sparkling with love. "Oh Carlie, my beloved, I've missed you so much," he said, a catch in his voice, which was even huskier than she remembered.

She smiled through her tears. "Me too," she whispered, voice a little shaky, but joy warming her through. Then all of a sudden she remembered. Her regret. Her guilt. Her fear. The emotions seared through her, alive and warring for dominance, her heart clenching with pain.

Swallowing down a sob, she tried to compose herself. "Oh Rowan, I'm so sorry that I left you thinking that I didn't want to be with you, or that I believed any of those terrible things Rhiannon said about you. It broke my heart all over again when they told me you were −" She stopped, horrified. *No, don't think about that right now. Don't break whatever spell this was.*

"Well, to imagine that you would think for even a moment that I didn't love you." Her voice faded away, and Rowan smiled at her, that heart-swelling, mood-lifting, love-filled smile that had always been just for her.

"Baby, don't worry about that," he whispered. "Of course I know how you felt, how you feel, how much you love me still. Even when you ran from me at the Yule retreat I knew it wasn't over between us. And I felt it, the moment that you changed your mind, the moment that you decided to be with me no matter what. And I loved you even more that you refused to choose between me and Rhiannon, that you chose us both − you're wiser than your years Carlie, and stronger than you know."

Breathlessly she stared at him, taking in every word, every expression, every crease and crinkle of his eyes as he gazed back at her, trying to capture it all and commit it to memory, to bury it deep within her heart where nothing could ever find it, and no power on earth would let it fade away. She reached her hand up to his face, wondering,

awestruck that he was standing there in front of her, solid as flesh and blood, his cheek warm under her fingers, seemingly so alive.

"It's not fair," she finally said, some of the anger returning even in this perfect moment, and her voice breaking, swollen with unshed tears. "Why did it happen?" she demanded fiercely.

Gently Rowan lifted a strand of her hair and tucked it back behind her ear as he used to, his touch electric. "Shhh, it doesn't matter now," he replied softly, soothingly.

"But it should have been me!" she cried. "You had so much to give the world still, so much to share."

"So do you Carlie," he insisted. "That's why I'm here. To remind you just how much you are loved, and valued. And to let you know that you'll be able to help so many people."

Shaking her head again, she buried her face in his shoulder, unable to trust her sight, but willing to believe the sensation of his arms around her, the strength that flowed from his body to hers. Eventually though he lifted her chin and dragged her down to the dusty floor, kneeling before her, eye to eye, and holding her hands still.

"You wanted to talk to me," he said, voice urgent, as he gazed into her eyes. "You had a question."

Her gaze drilled back into his, brain not wanting to think of anything except this single second in time, this precious, golden moment. "No, it doesn't matter. I just want to stay here with you and ignore the rest of the world, like that day at our special place by the stream," she said, desperation in her tone, in her expression, and her eyes and heart focused only on him. "I want to capture this, right here, right now, and hold on to it. Can't we just stay here, in this cottage in the mists? Together, forever, like we promised."

"My love, I don't have long," Rowan said, voice sad, and his eyes dark pools of despair. "But the answer you're seeking is in that book of your mother's, the one you were reading on the way to meet me on solstice eve."

She stared at him blankly.

"The curse, it's not real. It only has power because Mike believes it. But you know why it can't be true – and you need to remember, and let him know. He's suffered enough."

"I don't understand," she whispered, but she wasn't really paying attention to his words, she was just drinking him in, drifting between the real world and whichever magical dimension she was in now, some realm where he was still alive. She looked down at their joined hands resting on her knee, saw his beautiful tattoo of the phases of the moon, and traced over the outline with her finger. "Why can't you stay with me?" she begged.

A sudden clap of thunder exploded overhead, and Carlie jumped as the walls of the cottage shook, then screwed her eyes closed when a flash of lightning illuminated the dusty old cottage and made it seem, for just a moment, that the whole world was exploding around her. When the thunder had shaken the whole cottage, and the indistinct gloom of early evening had returned, she looked around wildly, but Rowan was gone.

The weight of the pain crushed her, and she collapsed onto the floor, tears spilling from her eyes. For a long time she sobbed, in great gasping and shuddering breaths, then for a while she seemed to sleep, suspended in some strange no man's land where things were hazy and mist-drenched, and she didn't have to think.

But finally she felt a paw on her face, and she woke up calling Luther's name. It wasn't him though, and this realisation felt like just another cruel blow in a series of devastatingly painful ones. As darkness closed in around her, she scrubbed at the tears stinging her cheeks, then slowly, unsteadily, dragged herself to her feet.

She couldn't give up yet, couldn't give in. More than anything she wanted to help Mike find peace, in honour of her mother who had cared for him so deeply, and in honour of him, for the love he had always shown to Violet and Rose. And she wanted to do it for Rhiannon's sake too, for the friend who had helped her so much. Slowly, sadly, she hobbled back home.

Chapter 26

Revealing Her Inner Heart

Dragging herself up the stairs to her room, Carlie pulled her mum's diary out of the bottom drawer where she'd hidden it and threw herself down on the bed. Before she could even open it though there was a knock on the front door. Sighing, she shoved it back under her pillow and limped downstairs, but when she saw that it was Rhiannon, she hugged her and welcomed her in.

"How did it go? Are you okay? Want a cup of tea?" she asked.

Her friend smiled. "It was fine, I'm okay, and I'd *kill* for a cup of tea," she replied, following her friend out to the kitchen.

As Carlie put on the kettle and grabbed tea leaves and the teapot from the cupboard, Rhiannon leaned against the bench, looking a little shaken as she watched her.

"So, we broke up," she finally revealed.

"I'm sorry," Carlie said automatically, and Rhiannon raised her eyebrows. "Well, even when it's for the best, I'm sure it's still difficult, and I know that you really liked him," she clarified.

Her friend nodded thoughtfully. "You're right, thank you. The whole way back I've been feeling really strange, wondering if I did the right thing, to-ing and fro-ing with my decision…"

Carlie handed her a mug of tea and led her to the table to sit down, then put some cookies on a plate and took them over.

"God, what a day," Rhiannon muttered. "I didn't sleep much last night, because I was still trying to figure it all out, so then of course I overslept and missed the first bus, which made me late as well as stressed, and that made me even *more* impatient with the whole thing. But I finally got there, and walked around to his place, and his mum was there, so we all had a cup of tea together, and she's so sweet. I'll miss her the most I think," she said, then rolled her eyes at herself. "Not exactly the best reason to stay with a guy, huh, liking hanging out with his mother?"

Carlie handed her another cookie. "It's understandable though, that you'd enjoy spending time with her, since, well..."

Rhiannon paled. "Oh god! I didn't even think of that. How predictable! The girl who lost her mother, dating someone because she likes having tea with his mum. Seems like I really did make the right decision," she said bleakly.

"Hey, don't be so hard on yourself. Just because you got on with his mum, it doesn't mean you thought she was going to replace yours or anything. I think it's nice that you liked talking to her. Rowan's mum was really lovely too," Carlie said, and although it hurt her heart to mention him so soon after seeing him, she didn't dissolve into tears as she'd expected. Rhiannon gazed at her closely, obviously a little concerned that she might break down and cry too, and pleasantly surprised when she didn't.

"Anyway, John and I went to this coffee shop we like, and chatted about our week – you know, school, annoying little brothers, the usual, then we sat in silence for a while. And it wasn't the comfortable kind either, I guess because I was still obsessing over what to do. So I was trying to remember how you'd put it the other night, you know, revealing my true self and being brave enough to risk my heart, but finally I just blurted it out – I asked him what he thought about witches and the goddess, and rituals to honour the cycle of the seasons."

"What did he say?" Carlie asked.

"He said it was superstitious nonsense that ancient peasants believed in because they didn't understand what made the sun rise and the earth turn, and that anyone who was interested in it was seriously lacking in intelligence."

"No!" Carlie cried. "He didn't!"

"He did."

"What did you say?"

"So, I guess you don't want to come to the Beltane fertility rite with me and leap over the fire hand in hand?" she recalled.

Carlie stared at her friend, not sure if she was being serious or sarcastic. "Really?"

"Really," she replied, brow furrowed. "And he stared at me like I'd grown an extra head, then finally he laughed, and decided that I must have been joking, and asked what I really meant."

"No way!"

Rhiannon laughed bitterly. "Way. My first instinct was to tell him where to go, but before I could, the waiter came over with our drinks, and John got up to get me some honey, which was sweet, so I took a deep breath and tried to figure out how I felt about it. Maybe he'd been caught off guard, and hadn't meant to be as rude as he was. Maybe he didn't understand what I was asking. And maybe it wouldn't really matter if he never came to a ritual with me – I mean, I'd rather do them with you anyway, so nothing would actually change. Anyway, I figured that I owed him the benefit of the doubt, so when he sat back down I asked if that was really how he felt about pagan spirituality."

Pausing for a moment, she took a sip of her tea while Carlie waited impatiently, then continued with her retelling. "He asked me what I meant by the term, because there are a couple of girls at his school who recently started dressing all gothic and wandering around holding crystals and muttering under their breath about putting curses on people, and he thought that anyone who could believe that curses had any power needed their head read," she said.

Carlie flinched. Admittedly she was on John's side there, although hers was as much wishful thinking that they had no power as believing that was true. Certainly she knew that Mike believed in them, and he was not a stupid or ignorant man.

"What did you say?" she asked her friend.

"I told him that no, I don't believe in curses, or casting spells on people without their knowledge, or even that gothic clothing makes a witch – that we have loads of beautiful, colourful velvet dresses for our rituals. And I tried to explain to him what I do believe, and how it feels to do a ritual with Rose, and the amazing energy that we raise together, but his face showed just what he thought of that – he looked disappointed, slightly disgusted and really horrified all at once."

Carlie's heart went out to her friend, who was trying to put on a brave face, but was obviously hurt by John's reaction to her courageous revelation of what she held so dear.

Rhiannon sighed, then she took a deep breath and bit into another cookie. "He did concede that he supposed we could get around my ill-informed views, and that we didn't have to agree on everything, but even the way he said that was really offensive. So then I suggested that maybe there was no point in us being together, if he was so dismissive of something that was so important to me, and he just kind of shrugged, and said fine, if that was what I wanted."

"Is it what you wanted?" Carlie asked.

"I don't know, but I wanted him to care! To be sad at the prospect of us breaking up," she replied, pouting.

"Rhi, that's not fair to him. You can't break up with him just to make a point. Or to blackmail him into changing his behaviour or subscribing to your view."

"I know," her friend sighed. "But, well, that made me kind of mad, so I stood up, said that it had been lovely spending time with him, and to give his mum my love, then I walked out and caught the bus home. Of course halfway back I realised that I hadn't given him any money for my coffee and cake, so I've written him a note, apologising for my oversight and enclosing a five pound note, and I'll post it on Monday."

The girls stared at each other in horrified silence for a moment, then burst out laughing.

"And are you sure this is what you want?" Carlie asked, when they'd finally managed to calm their giggles. "Does it really matter to you if he won't come to a ritual with you?"

Rhiannon smiled. "I am sure, which was a good realisation. I mean yes, we could have differences of opinion, no sweat. And if he'd not wanted to come to a sabbat festival or moon ritual with me but respected that I was going, that would have been fine too. But for him to be so scathing and judgemental, to say that anyone who enjoyed such a ceremony was stupid... well, why would I want to be with someone like that?" she asked.

"Rose is the cleverest person I know, as well as the kindest and most compassionate, and he was insulting her as well as me," she continued. "Plus it showed how closed-minded he is. I mean, we got together at the Yule Ball! We were part of the planning committee that made it solstice-themed. Surely he knew what I believed and how I felt about these things from the day we met, so he was either being deliberately cruel, or wilfully ignorant and uncaring, and none of those are desirable traits in a boyfriend."

Carlie smiled sadly. "I guess not."

"But the best thing?" Rhiannon ventured. "I'm actually relieved. I did think for a moment: 'Oh god, did I act too hastily? Should I have given him a chance to explain?' But I'm really not filled with regret, and I'm not wishing I hadn't said anything, or thinking I should go back tomorrow and tell him I've changed my mind."

She gazed into her empty cup, and Carlie jumped up to put the kettle on and make more tea.

"I'm glad Carlie, really I am," her friend continued. "Ever since you showed me Rowan's letters to you, I knew I wanted a love like that – a grand and beautiful romance, and a guy who loves me for who I really am. Someone who's passionate and caring, not indifferent, who knows what's in my heart, and shares the things that are important to me. He doesn't have to be a witch, or even have to come to rituals with me, but he can't think I'm stupid because *I* want to go. And of course it would be nice to have someone who shared that, and who was part of my magical life. Imagine going out with someone like Jake, who could be a part of it with you."

Carlie smiled. "Like Rowan was with me," she said, glossing over the Jake remark. "It's definitely a wonderful thing."

"Exactly! I'd rather be single than be ridiculed for what I hold dear, just to say that I have a boyfriend. I mean, I figured John wasn't pagan, but I was shocked that he would be so disparaging of those who are. And I guess we could have continued on for a while, but how could I be with someone like that for the long term? And how could he? And since I see no future with him, isn't it better to cut my losses now and free us both?" she asked.

The question hung in the air as Carlie made more tea, then brought the teapot over and settled back in her chair.

"I guess the answer to that is how do you feel now?" she replied. "Are you really relieved that it's over, or do you think you'll be regretting your decision in the morning? And be honest. Be brave enough to look within and discover what you're really feeling. It's no point of pride to say that you're over it if you're not, and not all relationships are the same."

Rhiannon stared at her friend. "When did you grow up and get all mature and kick-arse-advice-y?" she asked.

Carlie shrugged. "I guess I've just had more time to ponder the alternative. And someone has to play devil's advocate," she grinned. "I just remember how much you liked him at the Yule Ball, how happy you were when he kissed you, how ecstatic you were when you went to his place and decided you were dating. But I'm not trying to convince you to take him back, I promise," she added, as she saw Rhiannon's confused expression.

Her friend sat there for a moment, brow furrowed, thinking hard. Then she smiled. "He is really sweet, and we got on really well – but for me, I need to be with someone who I can express all of myself with. I don't want to diminish or hide what I hold dear, and I won't apologise for being who I am. You've taught me that. And surely if he was so totally unfazed by the prospect of it ending, he couldn't have been that into it anyway. But most importantly, if I really cared about him, if I *really* wanted to be with him, I wouldn't be feeling so relieved right now."

"And that's your answer then," Carlie said softly, and reached over to give her friend a hug. "You'll meet someone lovely, I'm sure of it. And it would be cool if they lived a bit closer too."

Rhiannon nodded. "It sure would. And hey, this means that we have more time together now – more time to study our magic and plan our future, and more time just to hang out and have fun, and there's nothing wrong with that!"

When Rose came in soon afterwards, the girls were sitting out the back, laughing hysterically as Rhiannon tried to pinpoint what traits would define her ideal boyfriend. Magical. Smart. Independent. Creative. Mature. Tattooed. Slightly wild. Witch.

Rose asked Rhiannon if she wanted to stay for dinner with them, but she reluctantly shook her head. She had to head home and pack, as they were going on a family holiday to Scotland for their week off from school, and her dad wanted to leave before dawn tomorrow to beat the traffic.

Carlie walked her out to the front door, hugged her goodbye, then headed back in for a simple meal with Rose. Then she conjured up an excuse about making a start on her homework and went up to her room. She wasn't ready to confide to her grandma that she'd seen Rowan that day, just as she hadn't been able to bring herself to share it with Rhiannon. For now she wanted to hold it close to her heart and keep it to herself, a treasured moment just for her.

Lighting the lemon-scented candle on her bedside table, she turned off the light and climbed into bed, then opened her Book of Shadows and started writing about her afternoon in the cottage. She wanted to capture every single detail, every word Rowan had said to her, every touch and caress. To commit it all to memory, and to paper, so it could sustain her through her saddest moments.

By the time she got to his cryptic comments about the curse she was yawning, so she scribbled them onto a scrap of paper that she placed under her pillow, in the hope that she would dream the answer into being, as well as into her book, which she slid under her bed. Then she blew out the candle and curled up under the covers, smiling as Luna leaped up onto the quilt next to her and snuggled her warm body into hers.

Chapter 27

Unlocking the Past

After passing the previous school holidays in a haze of oblivion following Rowan's death, Carlie was determined to make this one count. She got up early every day and climbed the tor, focusing on breathing in the energy of the spring mornings, and feeling happy as it gradually got easier to tackle the steep hill.

When she returned each morning she had a leisurely breakfast with her grandmother, rather than her usual grabbing-a-bite-on-the-run, on-her-way-to-school style, and learned more about the history of the healing centre, and how important it had become for Rose over the years. She'd been a nurse when she married Louis, then she'd taken time off when their daughter Violet was born, and her career had changed tack a little. Her best friend Elsie, who she'd been at college with, had started investigating alternative therapies, and the two women became intrigued.

Together they studied herbalism, naturopathy, nutrition, reiki, crystal healing and art therapy, and in an era where such things were far from mainstream, they worked to find a happy medium between their traditional medical training and the new information they were absorbing. Living in Summer Hill had no doubt helped – people in this village had always been a little more open to the metaphysical, and being many miles from the nearest major hospital, they were prepared to consult with Rose and Elsie, appreciating their nursing qualifications as well as the extra knowledge they added to them, and loving the passion with which they worked, growing their own herbs, constantly studying, and able to come to someone's aid at all hours of the day or night. Not to mention that their fees were barely enough to cover their costs, and if someone was struggling financially they would waive the charges altogether.

Later, when Rose embraced the goddess, apprenticed to become a priestess and began holding public rituals, the villagers simply saw it as an extension of what she was already doing for the community, and supported that too.

Carlie was glad the town accepted her grandmother and all that she stood for, and was touched that they also included her in their affections. There were more people wanting her to do reiki on them than she could fit in, and Rose was trusting her with more and more of the herbal remedy recipes every week.

So on her week off from school, she spent her mornings at home in the cottage studying herbalism texts, making potions and reading the books about grief counselling Rowan had ordered for her, then she went in to the shop in the afternoons to help out where she could – doing some energy healing work, answering queries, putting stock out, and relieving the staff when they needed breaks.

Rose even got her to accept some payment for her hours, after explaining that she'd have needed to employ someone else if Carlie wasn't there, and giving her a long lecture about valuing her own time and understanding her own worth.

The next step was to go in and open an account at the local bank, and organise for them to transfer the money from her Australian account into it. It was a strange feeling, to hold that deposit book in her hands and see her name and address typed out so clearly and officially. More and more roots were taking hold here, anchoring her to this village, and to Rose.

On Thursday Jake came in, and they went for coffee, catching up on their news and promising they'd get back to their assignment when school started the following week. He told her how much he was enjoying spending time with his grandfather, working with him in his huge vegie garden, and that he had finally managed to speak to his parents, who were loving their aid work in Africa, and relieved that he was content to be staying with Richard.

Most nights Carlie and Rose cooked together, sharing more stories from their lives, discussing plans for the garden, brainstorming upcoming courses – and spending more time than they probably should have crawling around on the floor with Luna, whose sweet nature and adorable antics were helping both their hearts to heal from Luther's loss.

And after Rose went to bed, Carlie lay awake in her big room, little Luna snuggled in her lap, and read through her mother's Book of Shadows, then her diary, feverishly searching for the answer Rowan had promised was there. The answer that the woman she'd met in the cafe insisted she already knew. But she didn't know what she was looking for, and there were times she almost cried in frustration as she went over and over her mother's distinctive curly writing.

On the Friday morning she woke up before dawn, just as the full moon was beginning to set, after a restless night of tossing and turning. She felt like the answer was on the tip of her tongue, or whatever the brain equivalent of that was, so close she could almost touch it. Picking up her own Book of Shadows, she flicked to the entry she'd written after she saw Rowan in the cottage, and went back over what he'd told her. The solution was in her mother's book, the one she'd been reading on her way to meet him at Yule. Clumsily she clattered out of bed and went to the chest of drawers to pull out her mum's diary, the one she'd tied up with metres of ribbon knotted to keep it closed, with a note to Carlie, written before she was born…

Dear Future Daughter,
I don't know whether you exist or ever will, but if you do, I want you to have this. I almost burned it, in a ritual of cleansing and closing of chapters, and who knows, perhaps I still might. But it is a cautionary tale of sorts for any young woman, and if you can take anything from this, it will have been worth me living through it…
Tomorrow I marry the man I love, and step from my past into my future. And so I am locking this book away, with a few other things

from my former life. I am grateful that it all led me here, but I no longer need the reminders of the things that I regret...

It hurt her every time she read this journal, to bear witness to the pain her mother had endured, the abuse that had led her to flee to the other side of the world with Oliver, the man who would one day become her husband and Carlie's dad.

There was beauty in it too. If she could get through the horror of her mum's relationship with the crazy shaman guy, and the awful things he'd said and done to her, things that had left her half-hoping he would kill her just so her pain would end, the final section of it read like a love letter to her dad, a prayer of gratitude that he had saved her, emotionally as well as physically and literally.

Wait. He'd managed to help her escape from Andre by borrowing a friend's identity for her – that's why she had become Fiona instead of Violet. It had never been about erasing her link to her beloved parents, it was only ever about finding a means to disappear from her violent boyfriend.

Quickly she skimmed through the pages, and then there it was, written out in faded blue pen, the reason the curse was not a curse, but just the empty threats of a vindictive and cruel man.

It sounded crazy, and wildly impossible, but he said a friend of his had an old passport in her maiden name, and no plans to travel for a few years, and we looked a little alike. So I became Fiona Scott, nineteen years old. I gained two years, and even got a new birthday. But I wasn't thinking about the future at all, by then I was just thinking day to day, how to survive one more day. If I thought about it at all, I guess I imagined that eventually I'd go back home and pick up my old life with Mum, become Violet Tyler again, and straighten out the ID issue. But that never happened.

Carlie read it over and over again, the words blurring before her eyes. Her mum had become Fiona Scott. She'd opened a bank account in that name, because the passport was the only ID she had. She'd gone back to school and graduated using that name, and studied at university and become a lawyer with that name too.

Eventually she'd married Oliver, her best friend and saviour, and had taken his last name, because Scott meant nothing to her. Well, it meant survival and strength, and escape from a situation that could really only have ended with her death, but it had no family connection for her. In the absence of her mother from her life, Oliver was all the family she had.

But that wasn't what was important right now. The crucial factor was that her mum had not died on the morning of her fortieth birthday, as she and Mike had believed. She'd gained two years with her ID switch, so she would have only been thirty-eight when the car crashed. And suddenly she remembered something from her mum's Book of Shadows as well – hadn't she left the morning after one of the sabbat rituals she'd performed with Rose?

Desperately she flicked through the heavy pages of her mum's Book of Shadows, smiling as she saw the words of magic her mother had written. Her heart broke for her as she realised how much she had given up to get away – she'd loved celebrating the festivals of the wheel of the year and performing rituals with Rose as much as, if not more than, Carlie did now.

There it was. Violet had run away from home a month after her seventeenth birthday, on the morning after the Mabon ritual at the healing centre, so her real birthday must have been in mid to late August. So she hadn't even turned thirty-eight when she died. How strange, that her mum had celebrated a fake birthday, on a fake day, with a fake age. And that the real Fiona had been born on June 21, the summer solstice in England, and the winter solstice in Australia – so her mum's pretend birthday fell on one of the sabbats she would have previously celebrated with Rose and their magical community.

Carlie's head was spinning. How had Rose not realised that something was amiss? Surely she would remember her own daughter's birthday? Then again, she wasn't sure her grandmother knew that the accident had happened on the eve of her mum's assumed birthday, or which birthday that allegedly was. And when Sandy had managed to track Rose down to tell her that Violet had died, she wouldn't have mentioned that it had happened on her birthday either. Should Mike not have realised? Possibly, but he probably wouldn't have known when she'd died either, just that she had, so when he'd asked her if Violet had died on the curse date, and she'd said yes, he'd believed her. After all, why would she lie about her mum's birthday?

Suddenly she couldn't wait to tell Mike, but he was in Scotland with Rhiannon and Brodie, and wouldn't be back until Sunday night. Three long days until she could tell him, and set his mind at ease.

"You look much cheerier today," Rose said, when Carlie finally ventured downstairs for breakfast, with Luna in her arms.

"A friend was really worried about something, but I just figured out why there was no need to be, and I can't wait to tell them!" she replied with a relieved grin.

Rose looked puzzled. "Rhiannon? But no, she's still away with her family isn't she? Jake?"

"It was Mike actually," Carlie blurted out, then grimaced.

"Is he okay?" Rose asked, voice panicked.

Damn, she'd decided that she wasn't going to tell Rose any of this, or get her involved. But how did she avoid it now? "He's fine," she said cautiously.

"Can I help?" her grandma asked.

Sighing, Carlie put Luna on the floor and sat down at the table, thinking fast. She didn't want to upset Rose by bringing up Violet's death, but if she didn't reveal what had happened, her gran was going to worry incessantly about Mike. "It's a long story," she began, voice hesitant. "And I don't even understand it all myself."

Then she smiled. Gazing up at her grandmother, at her wise face and compassion-filled eyes, she knew that if anyone would believe this crazy story, it was Rose. And if anyone would have words of wisdom and useful advice, it was this priestess of the goddess.

"Okay, where do I start? A few weeks ago Rhiannon mentioned to me that her dad had been thinking all these years that Mum hated him, and that he'd let her down, so I photocopied a few pages from her Book of Shadows and her diary —"

"You have her diary?" Rose breathed, as she handed her a mug of tea and sat down opposite her.

"Um, yeah, but... well, anyway," she stuttered, then quickly got back to the topic at hand. There was no way Rose should read all the awful things that had happened to her daughter – she wouldn't be able to endure it, tough though she was.

"I wanted Mike to know that Mum had always really cared about him, and that one of her biggest regrets in life was that she had hurt you and Mike, so he had to stop beating himself up. But he told me that he'd been to see Andre before Mum went away, to try to get him to leave her alone, because he didn't trust the guy, and he didn't think he was good for Mum – which he was right about, obviously," she said, sighing as she took a sip of tea.

"He confronted him, but the shaman guy didn't care. He just laughed, and threatened Mike, insisting that he'd turn Mum against him if he tried to break them up, and he would never see her again. And then he said that he would curse him, so that every woman he ever loved would die on her fortieth birthday."

"But there's no such thing as curses Sweetheart, and Mike knows that," Rose replied calmly. "The only way a so-called curse could have any power is if the person believed it did."

"And yet Beth died on her fortieth birthday," Carlie said quietly. "And so did Mum, or so I thought, and when I acknowledged that to Mike, he freaked out. He's been terrified that Rhiannon will die young ever since."

Rose looked confused. "But Violet was only thirty-seven."

"I know!" Carlie replied. "Well, I know now. That's what I finally discovered this morning."

"That makes no sense," her grandmother said. "You knew when her birthday was."

"Actually, it turns out that I didn't know," she admitted. "Mum always celebrated her birthday on June 21 – the winter solstice, as I've come to realise. And the accident happened on solstice eve, after we'd been out for dinner for her fortieth birthday, and she died the next morning."

"But..."

Carlie smiled sadly. "There was a good reason for why I thought that, and why she did that. When my dad helped her escape from the crazy shaman, she used the passport of a friend of his, Fiona, who was two years older than her. And since that was the only ID she had when she fled, she became Fiona Scott, and got a new date of birth too. That's why she changed her name Gran, it was nothing to do with rejecting you, or her life here."

Tears were sliding down Rose's cheeks, but she smiled through them. "That means a lot to me, to know that," she whispered, voice raw and cracked with pain. "Thank you Sweetheart."

Carlie stood up and went around the table to hug her, and she had a flash of memory, of the day she and Rose had been at this same table, her leaning in and holding her grandma while she'd sat frozen, staring at Violet's Book of Shadows and learning how much her daughter had adored her, and how desperately sad she had been to be leaving home, but that she was doing it because she thought her father would die if she stayed. Perhaps there were some parts of the diary that her grandma could read.

As if hearing the thought, Rose looked up at Carlie and asked if she would share it with her. She was torn. It would break her grandmother's heart to learn of the abuse her daughter had suffered, but there were also parts in there that would soothe it – from Violet's indecision and sadness about leaving home in the first place, to her constant missing of her parents and her beautiful relationship with the man she would later marry.

Finally she nodded, then went back upstairs and flicked quickly through the diary, tearing out the worst entries, the catalogue of her suffering, the awful violence, the pages that showed just how much the shaman guy had broken her brave mother, destroyed her to the point where she had prayed for death so her suffering would end.

Hiding the pain-filled pages in her bottom drawer, she took the censored diary downstairs and handed it to Rose, fear clutching at her heart. Was this the right thing to do? Should she be showing any of this to her? She didn't know, but if it could help soothe her heart to know that her daughter had missed her every day of her life, surely that could only be a good thing?

Rose smiled, her face calm and her hand steady as she reached out for the book. "It's not your responsibility Sweetheart, so please don't feel that way. I *want* to read it, and besides, I'm sure you took out the worst bits," she added, eyes twinkling.

Carlie blushed, but her grandmother just laughed. "I'll be fine, I promise. Now, would you mind going down and opening the healing centre for me? I'm going to stay here for a while, sit with this, sit with Violet. Do you feel able to do that for me? I promise I will be okay."

Reluctantly Carlie nodded, then she grabbed a banana from the fruit bowl and the keys from the bench, and walked into the village to open the shop and welcome the first customers. She was happy that she was capable of doing it, and proud that she could help her grandma in this way. Perhaps she could offer to open up on the weekends from now on, so Rose could have a bit more free time, and let go of a little bit of responsibility.

One of the massage therapists came in at midday and saw a few clients, but for the most part it was a fairly quiet day, and Carlie was able to accept a delivery of new books, and work out how to price them all, then put them out on the floor. She loved lifting each book out of its box, smelling that awesome new-book smell, then working out which shelf to position them on.

There were a few gems there, and she chose one that she'd buy when Rose came in. It was a thick text about healing grief, and she figured it would be good preparation to have read it before her uni course started. And who knew, it might even bring her some relief from her own sadness and regret.

Chapter 28

Return of the Curse

The sun shone all weekend and the sky remained blue, but Carlie struggled to enjoy it. She was anxious to tell Mike what she'd discovered, and to add Rose's assertion that curses had no power, just in case he still harboured any self-blame or doubt on the matter. And she was hoping that Rhiannon would now stop asking her what was wrong all the time, since her own preoccupation with the curse had come to an end.

But although the two friends had planned to catch up on Sunday night if Rhiannon and her family got back in time, Carlie didn't end up seeing her friend until school on Monday, and the poor girl couldn't stop yawning. A flat tyre on a dark and lonely road meant they didn't make it home from their Scottish adventure until the early hours of the morning, and Rhiannon and her little brother had collapsed into their beds, still fully clothed, the minute they got upstairs to their rooms.

Feeling increasingly apprehensive, and desperate to put Mike's mind at ease, Carlie decided she'd think up some excuse and go over and tell him that night – but she was thwarted in her plan when she got lumbered with revision for a surprise test the next morning. Rhiannon revealing that her dad would be at a work function that evening anyway didn't totally ease her frustration.

So it wasn't until their coven meeting on Tuesday night that she finally got the chance to tell Mike what she'd learned. Rhiannon hadn't finished setting up for their ritual, so Carlie offered to go downstairs and make them cups of tea.

Mike was washing the dishes when she walked into the kitchen, and they made small talk about his holiday in Scotland and her working in the shop for Rose while the kettle boiled, then she finally gathered her courage.

"Um, Mike, I wanted to let you know that, well, firstly Rose says there's no such thing as curses, and also, I was reading through Mum's diary again, and I realised that I was wrong – she didn't die on her fortieth birthday. So there is no curse, and there's nothing for you to blame yourself for."

He stared at her, bewildered by her words, and sank down onto one of the bar stools at the kitchen bench. "I don't understand," he whispered, voice faint, expression cautious, yet a spark of hope lighting up his eyes.

"Well, it's a long story, but for Mum to travel to Australia to get away from the violent shaman guy, she had to use someone else's passport, a friend of my dad's called Fiona, and she was two years older than Mum. So that means Mum was only thirty-seven when she died, not forty, and it wasn't on her real birthday anyway, it was two months earlier."

A range of emotions Carlie couldn't identify flitted across Mike's face, too fast for her to focus on any one of them. Then, unexpectedly, he laughed.

"You know, you'd think I would have realised there was something off about that. Violet and I were the same age after all. We were in the same classes all through school, went to each other's birthday parties every year. Why didn't I think of that?" he asked, frustration in his voice, but also relief.

"Well, you would expect that her daughter would know how old she was, and when her birthday was, so I guess you took my reply on faith. It's funny, I thought it was kind of cool, when I started learning about her life here, and how much she loved magic and ritual, that her birthday was on the winter solstice – well, the winter solstice in

Australia anyway, because up here it's the summer solstice in June. But that wasn't her birthday, that was just the day she died."

Suddenly her face went white, and she collapsed back against the kitchen bench. Mike rushed around to her, holding her up while she felt the whole world spin around her and collapse from under her.

"Carlie, what's wrong?" he asked urgently, worriedly. She stared at him, but couldn't focus on his face, couldn't focus on anything. She felt herself sinking down to the floor, and sensed Mike crouched next to her, trying to work out what was wrong, and what he could do to help her.

She stared up at him, eyes wild, haunted. "It's me that's cursed," she whispered with dawning horror. "Mum and Dad both died on the winter solstice. And Rowan died then too. Don't you see? It's me that's the link here, not you."

"No Carlie, that's not true. You know it's not true. It's like you told me, they were just tragic accidents," he insisted. "There are no curses – they have no power, remember? Rose promised us that." Quickly he grabbed a glass and filled it with water, then pushed it into her hands. "Drink a little bit, please, even if it's just a sip. You've had a bit of a shock. Now take a few deep breaths. Come on, in and out," he pressed. "In and out."

She did as she was told, closing her eyes and carefully inhaling and exhaling, and eventually the room stopped spinning, just as the kettle started to screech. Mike rushed over to turn it off, and Carlie slowly got to her feet, still feeling a little wobbly, but aware that the worst of the shock had subsided.

They were pouring boiling water into mugs when Rhiannon came into the room to announce that she was ready. Carlie shot Mike a pointed glance, begging him not to say anything to her friend about her strange moment. Smiling at her reassuringly, he shook his head almost imperceptibly, to let her know that he wouldn't tell, and her secret was safe with him, while not making Rhiannon suspicious that something was going on.

"Sorry, I overfilled the kettle and it took a while to boil. But the tea is coming right up," he assured his daughter. Yawning again as she shrugged her shoulders, Rhiannon didn't seem at all perturbed by the delay, but Mike saw his chance. "Darling, you look exhausted, and Carlie, you do too. How much homework are they giving you at school?" he asked.

"Too much," Rhiannon mumbled, yawning again.

"Girls, I hate to come over all parental on you, but it's already getting late, so I think you'd be very wise to skip tonight's magical working, and both try to get some sleep. What's the point of you getting a holiday if they just work you to the bone the moment you're back at school?" he continued.

Carlie looked over at Rhiannon, worried she would still want to do some magic, but her friend looked truly exhausted.

"I won't argue with you Dad, if that's okay with you Carlie?" she asked, trying to smother another yawn.

Smiling with relief, Carlie said that of course it was fine, and slowly made her way back to the cottage. She hadn't felt tired before, but now it was coming in waves, and all she wanted to do was crawl under the covers and close her eyes.

Rose was still awake when she came in though, and looked up in surprise when Carlie walked into the kitchen, where she'd just brewed a pot of her sweet-dreams, sleep-ease tea.

"Are you okay Sweetheart? How did it go with Mike?" she asked, as she poured out another cup and handed it to Carlie.

"Yeah, he was fine," she replied, then sighed. "As soon as I told him, he realised that of course Mum had been younger, because they were the same age. He was kind of mortified that he'd overlooked that fact. But sadly it seems that I'm the person who was cursed," she added, voice heavy with sorrow.

Settling into the chair opposite her, Rose stared at her granddaughter, trying to make sense of her words. "Sweetheart, there is no curse, I told you that. It's just a fictional construct, something to scare faerytale-reading kids into behaving," she said sternly.

Carlie shivered at her tone, at her words, but she smiled when Luna jumped up into her lap, and patted the kitten absentmindedly as she tried to collect her thoughts.

"My parents died on the winter solstice, long before I knew anything about the sabbats," she explained. "And Rowan died on the winter solstice too. I'm the only link there, so it's got to be my fault, something *I* did," she muttered.

Rose got up and hugged her, and told her to drink her tea. "Sweetheart, the only thing that links those two tragic events is that they were car accidents that occurred at midwinter, when the roads were slippery with ice and snow and rain. Of course there are more car accidents in the middle of winter, especially around here. Driving when it's snowing can be very dangerous, that's why there are warning signs everywhere, especially on that bend where Rowan went off the road," she said.

"And I have no doubt that once that drunk driver hit your car, it was going to be much harder to control the steering and come out of it in once piece because of the slipperiness of the cold, wet road."

Carlie gazed up at Rose, wanting so badly for that to be true, but scared that it was just a shoddy excuse to explain away her pain. But her grandmother reached across the table and took her hand. "It's the truth Sweetheart. I promise you there is no such thing as a curse, and that you had absolutely nothing to do with either of those tragic accidents."

Carlie smiled, a tiny, relieved smile, and Rose nodded. "Now, Luna looks exhausted, even though she appeared to have been napping all day, and so do you. So finish up that tea, because it will help you sleep, and then off to bed with you, okay? Things will look much rosier in the morning."

Obeying her grandmother, Carlie swigged back the rest of the herbal brew, lifted Luna into her arms, and made her way upstairs. Without even getting changed, she lay down on the bed and slept for ten hours straight, a dreamless, uninterrupted and healing sleep that was exactly what she needed.

Chapter 29

A New Love

Carlie and Rhiannon were sitting in the cafeteria on Friday, Rhiannon lamenting that she was single and Carlie trying to counsel patience – it had only been two weeks since she broke up with John after all – when Jake bounced over to them with his tray and slid in next to Carlie.

"Do you think we could get away with not working on our assignment this weekend?" he asked her hopefully. "It's just that my cousin is coming down from London to stay for a few days, and I haven't seen him for a couple of years. So I'd feel bad ditching him and leaving him all alone with Pop to go off and study."

"Of course, we'll be fine. And we can catch up Monday after school, yeah? Besides, we've got two more weeks and we're pretty much done, so no worries," Carlie said.

"Is he Australian too?" Rhiannon asked Jake.

"No, sadly he's English," he replied, face straight, then he laughed. "Just joking! He was born in London, and has spent most of his life there, although he did live with us for a year in Perth when I was, I don't know, ten maybe, and he was thirteen."

"And is he cute too?" Rhiannon pressed.

Carlie and Jake both stared at her, and she blushed a little. "What? Can't a girl ask these things? People need to know!"

Jake laughed. "I'm sorry, of course you can ask. But I'm not actually sure – I haven't seen him since he was sixteen, and that was only briefly, when I came to London with my parents for a family reunion. He seemed kinda gangly and goofy, but I probably wasn't the best judge. And he might have grown into himself now. I think he's been apprenticing at a tattoo studio the last couple of years, so for all I know he could be a long-haired biker with a huge beard and full sleeve art by now," he grinned. Then he looked thoughtful.

"Actually, would you guys want to have lunch with us tomorrow, or do something together? I'm not sure I'm going to be interesting enough for him, so I'm worried he'll be totally bored being stuck with just me and Pop all weekend."

Carlie was about to say no – the last thing she wanted to do was go on some weird kind of double date with a stranger, and a possible bikie no less. But Rhiannon was already making suggestions for what they could do and where they could go. Jake caught her eye and smiled at her, conveying in that single glance that he understood how she felt and was grateful to her for going along with Rhiannon's plan and helping him. She shrugged, then finally smiled too. She knew she wasn't going to be able to change Rhiannon's mind now that she'd decided to do this, so she may as well make the best of it.

In the end they'd decided to just meet for lunch then see what they all felt like doing after that, and Jake kept reminding them that they could both leave at any point if they weren't having a good time. But the moment Rhiannon laid eyes on Tom in the cafe she was transfixed, and all thoughts of their prearranged departure plan in case they got bored were instantly forgotten.

"This is Tom, although apparently he prefers to be called Raven now," Jake said, as he nervously introduced the girls to his cousin.

"Hi Carlie," he said, shaking her hand. "And you must be Rhiannon. Jake's been filling me in, but he didn't tell me how gorgeous you are."

Rhiannon giggled, a touch of shyness in her expression, but when Tom took her hand and held it to his lips, she shrugged off any hesitation and hugged him. "It's lovely to meet you. Any friend of

Jake's is a friend of ours!" she said, sliding into the booth so she was sitting next to him. Carlie and Jake smiled in amusement and sat opposite them, and were more than happy to let the outgoing pair carry the weight of the conversation.

"I hope this is okay for you Carlie," Jake whispered at one point. "I really appreciate you helping me out. I know you're not feeling particularly social at the moment."

Touched that he'd picked up on that, she smiled back at him. "You're very welcome. Although it looks like we won't need to make much effort – they seem to have it all under control."

A waitress came and took their orders, amused that they were all vegetarian in a place renowned for its beef burgers. Jake raised an eyebrow at his cousin. "I thought you only ate meat, the original paleo champion," he said. "I'm sorry if you're not any more, but that's why I chose this place."

Tom shrugged. "No problem. I guess it's been a while since we hung out – what were you, thirteen or something, last time you visited?" he asked, and Jake blushed, which made Carlie feel protective of him. "I've been plant-based for the last three years, ever since I got into paganism," Tom continued.

Rhiannon's ears pricked up. "Are you in a coven, or is it less structured for you? Have you been studying? Do you have a particular focus – witch, druid, shaman – or are you more eclectic?" she asked, then paused. "Sorry for the twenty questions, but I'm always excited to meet other magical folk."

He smiled at her, a flirty smile that she responded to in kind. "I've been attending public rituals with a group near where I live, and studying with a priest and priestess I met last Mabon. They were initiated into Wicca years ago, but are more broadly pagan now, so I guess I'd just say I'm a witch. I love the discipline of learning from them though, and I've been doing a lot of self-study too. Why, do you know much about magic?"

Rhiannon's eyes lit up. "I've been celebrating the wheel of the year and the phases of the moon since I was a kid. Carlie's grandma Rose is a priestess, and one of our teachers at school is part of her circle. So was my mum – it's all quite open here, attending rituals is just part of life," she said proudly, and only Carlie noticed that her voice had thickened with sorrow as she mentioned her mother.

"I consider myself a witch too," she continued. "We celebrate the sabbats and the new and full moons with Rose – and Jake and his grandad even came to the last one, at Imbolc. And Carlie and I formed a coven six months ago, and have been studying together and doing our own private rituals ever since."

Jake gazed at Carlie, curiosity burning in his eyes, while Tom was looking at Rhiannon with new respect, and even more interest. "Perhaps we could work some magic together," he said, tone suggestive.

Rhiannon batted her eyelashes at him. "I'd love to."

The waitress came over with their meals then, and they all paused for a moment as they sorted out sauces and dressings and ordered more juices. Carlie was lost in her own little world, wondering what she would call herself if she was asked. Rose considered herself a priestess of the goddess, a pagan and a witch. Rhiannon called herself a witch too, and Rowan had been described as both a shaman and a druid. Did she need a name? A descriptor?

As if reading her mind, Tom turned to Carlie and asked her how she saw herself. Blushing a little at the intensity of his gaze – he made her feel uneasy for some reason – she stammered out that she supposed she was a witch, although she didn't take the goddess as literally as Rhiannon or her grandmother did, so she wasn't sure if she could actually claim that word for herself.

"And her boyfriend was a druidic shaman, or a shamanic druid, and they worked a lot of magic together," Rhiannon added quickly. Tom stared at Carlie, then at Jake. "Where is he today?" he asked, and the judgement in his voice made Carlie feel uncomfortable again, as though he thought she was two-timing with Jake or something, while the mention of Rowan in Tom's sarcastic tone left her feeling as though she'd been punched in the stomach.

Regret crossed Rhiannon's face at bringing it up, and Jake put a comforting hand on her arm. "He died," he told Tom, simply, gently, but with no room for further questions. And there was a note of warning and challenge in his eyes as he glared at his cousin.

Rhiannon picked up on it and changed the subject, engaging Tom in a robust discussion about the pros and cons of working skyclad, especially at this time of year, when it was still a little chilly outside. And Carlie slowly composed herself, although she remained quiet and withdrawn while they ordered coffees and the conversation swirled, fuelled by Tom and Rhiannon, who were already as thick as thieves and planning activities independent of the group.

Finally the waitress came over and told them they were closing up to prep for dinner, and the four of them slouched out into the cold afternoon air, huddling in the doorway as they pondered what to do next. Rhiannon was telling Tom about another cafe they *had* to visit because they had the best chai lattes in town, but Carlie couldn't wait to escape. Surely she'd done her duty by now?

"I'm sorry, but I've got to get home, I promised Rose that I'd help her with the herbal blends this afternoon. But it was lovely to meet you Tom," she said, holding out her hand.

He smiled at her. "It was wonderful to meet you too, and I'm so sorry about –"

She shook her head, cutting him off. "It's fine, you didn't know," she replied stiffly. Hugging Rhiannon, she told her that she'd see her the next day, then turned to Jake to say goodbye.

"I'll walk you home," he offered, and held up his hands when she started to protest. "I have to see Rose about some herbs Pop needs, so we're going the same way." He turned to his cousin and their friend. "Are you guys okay if I leave you to it? Pop asked if I could bring the remedy home this afternoon, so…"

Looking delighted to be left on their own, Tom and Rhiannon both nodded. "I've got a key to get back in, so don't worry if I'm late home," Tom said to Jake with a wink, then turned and strode off down the street with an ecstatically happy Rhiannon, neither of them sparing the others a second glance.

Jake smiled ruefully at Carlie. "I'm so sorry about Tom, he's really full on," he began, but Carlie shook her head.

"Oh Jake, please, it's not your fault, and it's not his either. I guess it will eventually get easier for me to deal with, you know? It's just so raw still, and I was unprepared for the question, so I froze. Thank you for answering for me though, and for not over-explaining or making it into a big deal."

"I just wish I could do something to help you," he said, voice raw with longing.

"You do help me Jake, I promise, just by being so sweet, and so considerate. It means so much to me. And I really appreciate your friendship, and your understanding. I know it's not really fair to you, because I'm still so messed up, and I can't be what you want me to be. I wish I could," she said regretfully, looking away so he wouldn't see the pain on her face or the tears in her eyes.

But he could sense it, and although it broke his heart, he was determined to at least be her friend, and a real friend at that. He could pressure her – he knew that she liked him, and that he could have used the guilt she felt about his feelings for her to force something between them, but he didn't want to do that, he didn't want it to happen that way.

He wanted her to *choose* him, not to go out with him out of obligation or from feeling worn down by refusing him. Of course he hoped that wouldn't take too long, since he'd be going back to Perth at the end of the year, but he had resigned himself to trying to be patient. He really wished that she and Rowan had just broken up though, rather than him dying while they were still in love. It was so hard to compete with a dead guy, and one who seemed like some kind of magical hero no less.

"So how do you feel about your cousin?" Carlie asked him, bringing him abruptly back to the present. "Is he much like how you remembered him to be?"

"Was it that obvious?" he asked, laughing. "He is a lot more full on now, but I guess the difference between seeing him as a sixteen-year-old and meeting him again as a twenty-year-old was always going to be huge. He's a lot more outgoing than when I last saw him, a lot more confident. And he seems pretty wild. He is apprenticing with a tattooist – he did a year at a design school after he graduated, and I think he's still going, but he's also getting on-the-job training at the tattoo studio. He actually did the one of the raven on his wrist himself, which is amazing. I couldn't inflict pain on myself."

Carlie thought of Rhi's list. Tattooed. Check! Wild. Check! Witch. Check! She smiled at Jake. "Do you have any tattoos?" she asked.

He shook his head. "You?"

For a moment she pondered letting him believe that she did, but she couldn't say it with a straight face. "I was planning to get one," she finally said. "But I'm a bit cautious, because I don't know anyone here to get a recommendation from."

"What would you get?" he asked.

A dreamy expression crossed her face, and she looked up at the sky. "I'd like to get the symbol of the triple goddess, which represents the phases of the moon, and the phases of life, and would honour the magical workings I've been doing with Rose and the rituals I've been part of at her healing centre," she explained.

"How about you, have you ever thought of getting one?"

"I have considered it, although I'm not sure what I want to get," Jake replied. "Possibly a wave, to remind me of home and my connection to the ocean and my surfboard," he grinned. "Although after the Imbolc ritual, I feel as though I'd like to get something that honours my step into the magical realms too, and the impact Rose's amazing ceremony had on me and my grandfather, and the connection between the two of us. Maybe a candle flame, or even four symbols within a circle, to represent the four elements she drew on, sitting within the sacred circle I was part of."

"That sounds really beautiful," Carlie said. "So, do you think we should get one?" she asked, and she was only half joking. But they'd reached the cottage by then, so she quickly changed the subject as she led him inside and through to the kitchen.

Rose sat down with them for a cup of tea and a chat, then she bottled up the herbal remedy she'd made for Jake's grandfather, and he bade them both farewell, thanking Carlie again for helping him entertain his cousin. She shrugged and told him it was nothing – Rhiannon had done all the work after all, but she was always happy to help out a friend...

The next morning, Carlie was having an early breakfast with Rose, Luna curled up in her lap, when there was an impatient knock on the front door. Laughing, she stood up and put the kettle on, then turned to walk out of the kitchen.

"You expecting someone Sweetheart?" Rose asked, surprise in her voice at having a visitor so early on a Sunday.

"Just Rhiannon. I'm guessing she has some big news to share about a new guy," she replied, as she headed towards the front of the house. She missed the look of disappointment that crossed her grandmother's face as she went to greet her friend. It had been more than two months since Rowan had died, and Rose was hoping that her granddaughter would start finding some joy in life again soon. Jake obviously cared deeply for her, and she could tell Carlie liked him too, yet she seemed oblivious to him.

The impatient knocking came again, just as Carlie hauled open the door. Rhiannon stood on the front step, bouncing up and down with excitement. She threw her arms around Carlie, almost sending them both sprawling onto the hallway floor.

"Oh, sorry! I've just got so much to tell you!" she cried, cheeks flushed red with joy and anticipation as she followed Carlie back out to the kitchen.

"Hello sweet girl, it's lovely to see you," Rose said, amused and cheered by her high spirits. "Would you like a cup of tea?"

"I'd love one, thank you," she grinned. "Oh, isn't it a gorgeous day! I feel so alive!"

Rose smiled at her. "The joy of youth," she said, the faintest tinge of regret in her voice. "And love, if I had to guess," she continued, with a twinkle in her eye.

Rhiannon glanced at her friend. "I didn't say anything, I swear. I don't *know* anything," Carlie protested quickly.

"But you do look all excited and filled with the thrill of new love," she said, and busied herself making the tea so her friend couldn't see her sadness. It wasn't fair to bring her down, when she was so filled with happiness, but it did hurt her a bit to see her so lit up with passion and connection. Yet she was genuinely glad for her, she reminded herself. And Rhiannon finding love didn't make any difference to her or change her circumstances in any way – it didn't make her loss worse or narrow her chances of finding love one day. And her friend deserved happiness, and a guy who adored her.

And her support, she thought with a sigh, and made a conscious effort to adjust her attitude.

"Oh, he's just so lovely," Rhiannon blurted out, unable to keep it to herself. "And so magical, how awesome is that! He's been working in a coven, like us, and studying too, really experiencing it all, and he wants to share that with me," she said, then blushed. Carlie tried to hide her smile, and noticed that Rose was also trying not to reveal her mirth. So, it seemed Tom had been flirting with Rhiannon with suggestions that they do some kind of sex magic together.

Carlie took the mugs of tea over to the table and sat down opposite her friend as she tried to compose herself.

"After you and Jake left yesterday we went down to Kylie's Cafe and drank chai, and Tom was grilling me about the area, and the tor and its secrets, so I offered to take him up there. But he seemed to know it better than I do – he led me around the base of it, through the apple orchards, and each time we got to a stile, he told me it was a kissing gate, and I had to kiss him in order to get past."

Carlie's heart ached as she remembered Rowan doing the same thing, but she motioned for her friend to go on.

"Anyway, we finally got to the top, through this spiralling labyrinth path, like a maze, which was just, wow! There was so much energy coming up from the earth, I was vibrating from it! Although it might have been coming from him too – he's so powerful, and so spiritual. He talked about the ravens that were wheeling overhead, and about his raven tattoo, which is just gorgeous, and the shamanic journey he'd been on that had inspired it. And then the sun began to set, and it was just *so* magical," she enthused.

"And then he kissed me, properly kissed me! The world around us turned dark, but we kept kissing, and it was like we were the only two people on earth. Oh Carlie, if it was anything like this with Rowan then I totally understand now, how crushing it was for you to lose him. I feel alive in a way I never have before. It's like absolutely everything has changed – yet it's actually only me that has!"

Rhiannon beamed, her joy infectious, and Carlie willed her eyes to stay dry even as she felt the knife stab of pain in her heart.

"So, I'm meeting him at ten o'clock this morning for a chai, and hopefully lunch after that, and I wondered if you wanted to come with us? Jake will be there, so you won't feel left out if we, you know..." She looked so hopeful, so eager for acceptance and the sharing of her new adventure, but it felt like torture to Carlie, and as much as she wanted to be supportive, she just couldn't put herself through it for another day.

"I'm so sorry, but I promised Gran I'd help in the shop today," she said, looking over at her grandmother with a desperate plea in her eyes. But Rose refused to go along with it – she knew that it was time Carlie started living again, started opening her heart to new people, new experiences, new possibilities, and hiding away at home was not going to help her. Although it hurt her heart to do it, she knew her granddaughter needed a little push. And Jake was a good friend, a lovely boy with a sensitive nature, who would protect her from the worst of the pain.

"It's okay Sweetheart, Laurel is coming in today, so we'll be fine. You go and hang out with your friends."

"Awesome!" Rhiannon shrieked, as Carlie tried to mask her disappointment, and her annoyance with her grandmother. "Can you help me work out what to wear? I brought a few options," she grinned, holding up a huge bag.

Carlie felt as though she was dying inside, but she knew she had to be supportive of her friend, and she really wanted to be. It wasn't her fault that the thought of romance made her so sad. Giving her grandmother a withering stare that only made her shrug her shoulders in amusement, she finally led Rhiannon upstairs to her room, Luna bouncing around at their feet. They still had two hours before they had to meet the guys, and she was already feeling apprehensive.

"Oh Carlie, he's so wonderful," her friend said, flopping down on her bed with a melodramatic sigh. "And isn't he gorgeous? Just take-your-breath-away stunning! Oh my god, I totally know what you mean now, about the difference between Rowan and John. John was just a friend, almost a brother, compared to how I feel about Tom.

He's just so *amazing*. My tummy feels all fluttery when I think about him, and when he stares into my eyes, oh my god! It's so intense!"

Schooling her expression as carefully as possible, Carlie tried hard to ensure that only happy-for-you vibes flickered across her face. "So, you really hit it off, huh?" she commented, then smiled to herself. If nothing else, she was grateful that Rhiannon wanted to talk non-stop about her new obsession, and wouldn't even notice that she was remaining quiet.

"I know, wasn't it amazing!" her friend asked, voice full of excitement. "From the second he took my hand when Jake introduced us, I could feel it, this incredible energy between us, like fire. Like our Imbolc fire ritual. Maybe Aideen sent him to me!" she squealed, excitement colouring her voice.

"It was like we were connected, heart to heart. And just everything about him is perfect. He's magical, he's smart, he's independent, he loves music, he plays guitar, he has tattoos, he's wild – everything on my list! He's just so *cool*," she sighed, drifting off into a daydream for several moments. Carlie lifted Luna into her lap and stroked her soft head as she waited patiently for her friend to continue.

"Oh god, sorry, where was I?" Rhiannon finally asked, and Carlie laughed good-naturedly. "He's just so dreamy. And he wants to do a ritual with me, can you believe it? He's going to come down for the new moon next weekend, so we can do one up on the tor together. You'll cover for me, won't you?" she asked, glaring at Carlie as if she'd already refused. "You do owe me one you know," she insisted.

Carlie shrugged. "Okay."

"We were talking a lot about sex magic too," Rhiannon continued, enthusiasm bubbling over as she spoke. "But I'm sure he wouldn't mean to do that then, up on the tor, right? Not that I'd probably mind – every time he brushed against me I got all shivery inside, and we kissed for ages up there, and oh my god, it was so intense. Like I could have just melted into him, dissolved into him, merged into one being with him. Is that what it was like with Rowan?" she asked, but didn't wait for an answer. "My god, it was just mind-blowing."

Carlie stiffened, remembering the lectures she'd copped from Rhiannon about Rowan, the warnings that he only wanted one thing from her, that she'd better not have sex with him, because once she did he'd dump her for someone else. It seemed it was a different matter all together when it was herself getting all passionately involved with a guy.

But her friend had finally paused for breath, and she moved over closer to her and took her hand.

"I'm so sorry Carlie," she said, voice heartfelt and full of regret. "I realise I sound like the worst kind of hypocrite, and that I was out of line with you and Rowan, in so many ways. I just had no idea it could feel like this. And I know I just met Tom, and I hardly know him – and again, I can only apologise for not understanding that it could be so instant and so total – but already I feel the most amazing connection to him.

"It's like, this could be real love, you know what I mean?" Rhiannon continued. "What I had with John was just a childish friendship in comparison. There weren't any swept-off-my-feet, desperate-to-spend-every-second-with-him feelings there. But Tom makes me feel so alive, he lights me up inside in a way I've never felt before," she said, voice sober now.

"And I remember you trying to explain all of this to me when you were with Rowan, but I couldn't even begin to comprehend it then. So I'm just so deeply grateful to you for sharing your letters with me, and making me realise that being with John was nice, but would never be enough to bring me to life like this does. Because otherwise I would have been with John yesterday, and I never would have met Tom. And who knows, maybe *you* would be dating him instead of me, if you'd gone alone to lunch to help Jake."

Carlie seriously doubted that – Tom had seemed arrogant to her, too sure of himself by far, but clearly Rhiannon didn't share her view.

"And the weird thing is, even if I never see him again after this weekend, I'll feel blessed to have known him, to know this feeling, to know that this depth and passion is possible," she said. She took a deep breath, and squeezed Carlie's hand even tighter.

"I know this must be so hard for you to watch, and to listen to even, and I apologise. I just want you to know how much I appreciate your patience, and your support. I know the last thing you want to do is spend the day with us and watch us falling in love, and that you were annoyed with Rose for not giving you an excuse to avoid it."

Carlie blushed at being caught out, but Rhiannon just grinned and kept on talking. "It's okay, I understand that, I do, and it means the world to me that I know you have my back."

"I'm happy for you, I promise," Carlie said, and she smiled although the effort cost her. "It *is* hard for me, but this is not about me, or me and Rowan – it's about you, and I'll just have to work out a way to separate it so it doesn't hurt. Now, we should get you dressed. What did you bring? And what are we doing today? Just how glam versus practical do you have to be?"

Finally Rhiannon was happy with her outfit. Her indecision and panic had amused Carlie, since they'd both been wearing old jeans and plain t-shirts when they'd met Tom yesterday, and he'd seemed more than impressed with Rhiannon then.

Jake and Tom were at the cafe when they arrived, and both of their faces lit up when the girls came towards them and sat down, Rhiannon next to Tom on the two-seater couch, Carlie next to Jake in single armchairs opposite them. They both rolled their eyes when Tom and Rhiannon started kissing, but they were happy for them, and the new couple did draw apart for a moment when the waiter came to take their order.

"So, I was talking to Jake about the upcoming spring equinox," Tom began. "And we thought it would be awesome if you guys came up to London and joined us for our Ostara ritual. The Body Mind Spirit Festival is on during the day, then we'll be having a small gathering in the park that night..."

Rhiannon's face was transformed with joy, and she turned to Carlie, eyes sparkling. "Can we? Will you come with me? We can stay with my cousin again, like we did last time. Oh, please say yes!" she begged.

Carlie nodded, trying hard to mask her reluctance and dread. How could she not agree when it meant so much to her friend? But oh god, to go back to the place where she'd met Rowan? That would require some strength.

"Are you going too Jake?" she asked, turning to him in appeal.

"Do you want me to?" he replied softly.

"Please!" she said, and it was a heartfelt plea. Rhiannon and Tom were already kissing again. "You can't leave me with them, I beg of you!" she added, only half joking.

"Well, you did come along today *and* yesterday, for which I am eternally grateful," Jake said with a grin. "So yes, of course, I'll share your pain at the ritual too."

They both laughed, and spent the rest of the morning chatting together, since the other two were so caught up in each other.

"Do you miss Sydney?" Jake asked her, and she shrugged.

"Not as much any more," she said, voice slightly wistful. "When I got here I was determined that the minute I finished school I'd go straight back. But I feel a connection here that's hard to describe – to this village, to this land. And although I wanted to hate Gran when I arrived, thinking that she'd been a monster to my mum, once I realised that wasn't the case and gave myself a chance to get to know her, I realised how much I love her, and how much she loves me, and I don't think I could leave her. We both need each other – we're the only family each of us has now, which probably sounds a little melodramatic and sad, but it really isn't," she admitted.

"And there's Rhiannon. We've had some wild ups and downs, but she's my dearest friend, and we've decided to do the same uni course together, so I guess, as strange as it seems, I'm really settled here," she said, and surprised herself as she put her vague thoughts into words and comprehended the truth of them.

"Then there's the magic. I didn't know anything about it when I was in Sydney – Mum had closed down that side of herself, I guess because it made her too sad to remember what she'd lost. She'd denied its existence, and hidden all that she knew about it," she sighed, and Jake heard the pain in her voice.

"Sometimes I feel like I didn't even know her. So it's been such an incredible journey within, learning so much about myself, getting closer to Gran, seeing the world in a new way, becoming aware of all the potential that exists, within us, within nature, within and of the earth. Which of course would still be with me wherever I was, but for me it was all born of being in this place, working magic with the people I met here."

Her voice faltered as she thought of Rowan and all the things he'd taught her. "How about you?" she asked quickly, trying to deflect attention away from herself for a while.

Jake smiled, picking up on her not-so-subtle shift of topic, and going along with it. "I totally understand what you mean. It's been really lovely getting to know my grandfather so much better, now that I'm old enough to appreciate him, and it feels like he's opening up a little bit to me now too, after being so devastated, and shutting down, and shutting everyone out, after Nan died.

"And I know what you mean about the landscape here, I sense it as well," he added. "I feel so strangely comfortable in this place, like I've come home — which is weird, because I was born in Perth and have lived there my whole life," he mused.

"And thanks to you and your grandmother, I now feel my own magical self awakening too – I'm becoming more aware of things I had no idea of before. I'm really grateful to you for that, and to Rose for cheering my grandfather up."

Carlie stared at him, eyebrows raised in question.

"She's been so sweet to him, coming over to visit him a few afternoons every week, letting him really talk about Nan, and how he's feeling, how he's coping with his grief, in a way I'm not able to help him," Jake said. "She's an amazing woman. Just being around her is so calming, so healing."

A smile lit up Carlie's face. She hadn't known that Rose was visiting Richard, but she was glad. She knew what missing a loved one was like, and how much her grandmother had helped her cope, first with the loss of her parents, and more recently with her grief over Rowan. Not that she was over any of them by any means, but she really hoped that one day she would grow into half the woman Rose Tyler was. She really was the centre of the community here, the one who helped everyone, no matter what.

She didn't know what she – or indeed the whole village – would do when Rose was no longer with them, but she hoped that day was a long way off. Her grandma certainly looked as fit, and was as healthy, as a woman decades younger, and had such an incredible zest for life, that she was sure she'd be with them for many years to come.

Seeing Jake lift his cup to his mouth, Carlie snapped abruptly back to the present. "So what do you think you'll do after your year is up and you can meet your parents back home in Australia?" she asked, and was surprised to discover how curious she was about his answer. How strange. Yet now she saw that over the past few months she'd slowly become closer to Jake. So gradually that she hadn't even noticed, they'd developed a sweet friendship that she hadn't acknowledged to herself until today. Hadn't even recognised.

Jake had been sitting with her and Rhiannon at lunch for a while now, and they'd been working long hours on their assignment, which was going incredibly smoothly. She'd thought it was just the Aussie kids sticking together, but now it was dawning on her that she didn't really want him to leave at the end of the school year.

Right at that moment he smiled at her, and she blushed. *Please god don't let him be able to read my mind too!*

"I'm not sure any more," he finally said, and there was the hint of a question in his voice. "Like you, I assumed I'd go home as soon as school was done, go to uni in Perth, get a flat with a mate. But I'm really enjoying living here with Pop, and being in this village. I know it sounds odd, since I've spent half my life at the beach with a surfboard, but I really loved the snow of winter here, it was such a nice change from the sweltering heat back on the west coast. And, well, I hope this doesn't make you feel uncomfortable, but I really value your friendship, and I'll miss you and Rhiannon when I go home."

Carlie's cheeks reddened again in embarrassment, but she was surprised to realise that his words hadn't freaked her out, or made her want to flee, as they once would have. Instead she felt safe, and supported… and *happy*?

"I'll miss you too," she said shyly, and his face lit up with joy. Before she could panic about her admission, the waiter came over to ask if they wanted more drinks, and she was relieved when Rhiannon and Tom stopped kissing for a minute and they finally started talking as a group. She needed to ponder these new feelings when she was back in her room, away from Jake, and see what they could mean.

For now, she was relieved to discover that she liked Tom much better today – he seemed far less arrogant, and far more genuine, than he had yesterday. They discussed the upcoming spring equinox ritual they'd be doing together, and Carlie asked if they needed to bring anything – "just their good selves" – while Rhiannon was more concerned about what they should wear.

"I want to say skyclad, but I don't want to share you with anyone, gorgeous," Tom said to her with a wink. The intimacy of their shared look left Carlie feeling wistful and full of longing, which was at least an improvement on the bitterness she'd been feeling until now when she saw a happy couple. Maybe there was hope for her yet.

They all drank more tea then ordered lunch, talking all the while, then Tom announced that he had to leave to get home for work – he had a late shift at the tattoo studio that night.

"Walk me out?" he asked Rhiannon, who nodded happily and stood up as he dropped several twenty pound notes on the table and said farewell to Carlie and Jake, then walked outside to his motorbike. The two of them left inside tried not to watch, but their eyes kept being drawn back to the couple outside as they talked and kissed, talked and hugged, talked and kissed.

"He's okay isn't he?" Carlie asked suddenly, turning to Jake.

"What do you mean?"

"He's not just playing her is he? You know, string of women in London that he invites to skyclad rituals and to perform sex magic with him? Rhi just being one of many?"

Jake smiled. "He's really smitten with her," he said, voice reassuring. "He's not dating anyone else, and I think he genuinely likes her and wants to spend time with her. When he finally got home last night he talked about her non-stop, and he couldn't wait to get up this morning and come and meet her – apparently him getting up before midday for any reason is unheard of."

"Yeah, Rhiannon was the same," Carlie admitted, relief in her voice. "I'd just hate to see her get hurt, or feel used by some older city guy who was preying on her innocence, and her fascination with him because he's a witch too." Then she stopped short, suddenly paling.

"What's wrong?" Jake asked, instantly worried and protective.

She laughed, a short, mirthless laugh. "I was so angry at her, when she asked the same things about Rowan. I guess she really was just worried about me, but I thought she was just being jealous, trying to make me break up with him."

Jake touched her hand, the contact soothing. "Hey, it's great that you're worried – you should be. It's sweet, what friends should do. And he is older than us, so it's natural to wonder."

Carlie groaned. "Not as much older than her as Rowan was than me. I owe her an apology."

"Maybe now's not the best time," Jake said, and they both giggled as they watched Tom and Rhiannon locked in a passionate and very public display on the High Street.

"Or maybe it is," she interjected, as their embrace became raunchier. "I'm not sure she's going to want her dad to find out she's seeing a new guy – with long hair and tattoos no less – before she gets to tell him herself."

But as they stood up to pay so they could go and warn her, they saw Rhiannon pull the spare helmet onto her head, throw one leg over the back of the bike and wrap her arms around Tom's waist, before they roared off down the road.

Carlie sank back down in the armchair. "Okay, you win. I won't tell her now," she said with a grin. "Think you can handle another chai?" she asked, before they started reminiscing about their favourite Aussie surf breaks, artists and bands.

Half an hour later, Tom dropped Rhiannon back off in front of the cafe, kissed her briefly but passionately then sped off, and she floated back inside and flopped down on the couch, hair windswept and cheeks flushed, and a wide, joyous smile lighting up her face.

"Oh Jake, he's so lovely, thank you so much for introducing me to him. And Carlie, my god, now I get it!" she said, sighing loudly and dramatically.

"Get what?" Jake asked. Carlie looked uncomfortable, and tried desperately to send her friend "shut up" vibes, but Rhiannon was in love and oblivious to anyone else.

"Well, what she and Rowan had was amazing – it was totally real, true love, the whole let's-get-married-right-now-and-be-together-forever trip. He just adored her, and was cutting back on his work so that he could spend more time with her. And he put up with me being a total bitch to him because he loved her so much, and she loved him just as desperately," she raved.

"It was the most beautiful romance ever, cut tragically short. I didn't understand at the time though, I guess because I'd never felt anything like that. I was dating John, and he was nice, but there was no passion, not like they had. But now I get it!" she said, drifting off again with a dreamy smile on her face.

Jake was suddenly quiet, his posture rigid and cold, and Carlie was mortified. He really hadn't needed to hear that. She wished Rhiannon hadn't said anything, but it was too late – Jake was looking at her differently now, was withdrawn again, hurt, and the closeness she'd been feeling with him evaporated.

Rhiannon was blissfully unaware of the effect of her words though. "Oh, how will I survive the days until I see him?" she moaned. "I can't wait to be with him again. You'll both come to London with me for the equinox won't you? Dad will let me go if he knows I'm going with you Carlie. God, how will I get through the next week?" she wailed.

"I thought the equinox wasn't for another three weeks," Jake said stiffly, and Carlie smiled that he'd remembered the date.

"He's coming down next weekend so we can do our own ceremony on the tor, and go to Rose's new moon ritual at the healing centre together as well. You and your grandad should come too, they're really lovely evenings," she enthused.

"We probably will," Jake replied, his aloofness cooling as he remembered how magical Imbolc had been. "Pop said he really wanted to go to that one, and he'll be happy to see Tom again – not that he ended up seeing him much this weekend," he said, then laughed as Rhiannon blushed. "Just joking," he grinned, and Carlie was relieved that his good humour was returning.

Chapter 30

Big Doubts, Bad Excuses

Carlie's patience was severely tested on Monday at school though, when all Rhiannon could talk about was Tom. She tried to be good-humoured about it, and supportive and interested, and she mostly succeeded, but she had to admit that she was kind of relieved that she'd promised to catch up with Jake after school to work on their assignment, which was due in two short weeks.

It was only somewhat of a reprieve though, because Jake wanted to know what she thought of his cousin, and was having a dilemma himself, wondering if he was too boring or too bookish, not fun enough or outgoing enough, in comparison to Tom.

"Jake, of course you're not boring, and you *are* fun," she said with a touch of impatience. "What's gotten into you? And what has Tom unleashed? I'd much prefer to spend time with you than with him, you're way more interesting. And I'm glad you're not as outgoing and, well, full of yourself as he is. You're kind and considerate and sweet, and the three of us have awesome conversations at lunchtime, about all kinds of things, and do ritual together and weave magic. Why would you think you were boring?" she asked.

Cheeks turning pink with embarrassment, Jake shrugged and tried to look calm and unconcerned, but he seemed relieved by her words. "I don't know. It's just, well, Rhiannon was going on and on about how amazing Tom is, and how cool he is, and how adventurous and wild and rebellious and fascinating and magical and..."

"I know, I heard nothing else all day," she laughed. "But it's apples and oranges. You can't beat yourself up about it, and you shouldn't try to be more like him. There's no point. It wouldn't work, and it wouldn't be authentic, and worst of all, you wouldn't be happy. Please don't try to be something you're not, because what you are is really awesome. Just be yourself – I'd much rather hang out with you than Tom. Now come on, we need to get back to work, this assignment isn't going to write itself," she insisted, and Jake thanked her, a shy smile on his face, then opened his book again and got serious.

Rhiannon was still on the Tom bandwagon the next day at school, so when her friend knocked on the door that evening for their coven gathering, she realised she was feeling quite uncharitable, and hoped that they could speak of other things for a little while at least. But as it turned out, Rhiannon's next topic was just as bad.

"Jake really likes you," she blurted out, and Carlie looked up from the herbs she was blending and shook her head.

"Yes he does, I can see it in the way he looks at you. Plus Tom told me. And I hate to admit this, but I was really jealous when I realised this a few weeks ago, because it seemed like all the cool guys wanted you," she continued, a blush staining her cheeks.

"Oh Rhi, that's not true –"

"It's okay," Rhiannon interrupted. "I'm glad now that he didn't like me, because Tom is even *more* amazing – tattoos, a motorbike, a career, an artist, a witch! He's even better than I could have dreamed up with a love spell. And I know he's three years older than me, so I'm not sure when to break it to Dad, but I really appreciate you having my back on this, especially after what I did to you."

"About that..." Carlie began, and her friend looked up at her, worried that she wasn't going to keep her secret after all.

"Oh Rhi, of course I will," she insisted. "No, it's just, well, I think maybe I was a little unfair to you with the whole Rowan thing."

Rhiannon looked confused. "What do you mean? I was the one who was out of line."

"I was angry that you kept pointing out the age difference, and trying to convince me that he only wanted me for sex, and would cheat on me and all that," Carlie said.

Rhiannon grimaced. "I know, and you have every right to be angry. I'm really sorry about that."

"No, *I'm* sorry," Carlie continued. "I know now that you were just worried about me, and looking out for me, in your own unique way. I realised when you rode off on Tom's bike with him the other day – suddenly I was asking Jake all the same questions you challenged me with. 'Is he just playing her?' 'Is the making-magic-together, sky-clad-ritual promise a line he uses on lots of women?' 'Is he taking advantage of her innocence?'" she admitted reluctantly.

"All of which Jake rejected by the way – he told me that Tom is totally smitten with you. And I was only asking because I care about you and I was worried for you, but it made me realise that when you were asking me those questions, which made me so angry, it was coming from a place of love too."

Rhiannon smiled. "Well, thank you for caring about me – and for finding out the answers to those questions from Jake, because I've got to be honest, I've been wondering about them too. That's why I can't wait to see Tom again, to work out whether our feelings are real, or if I've just imagined it all."

"Oh Rhi, you didn't imagine it!" Carlie said, and finally she didn't mind talking about a relationship, since this was about how her friend was feeling, what she was worried about, not just endless babbling about how hot some guy was.

"Jake said Tom never gets up early, especially on a Sunday, yet he got up early just for you, and was so eager to see you that he beat us to the cafe. And he raved about you non-stop on Saturday night, after he finally got home to spend a few moments with his grandfather."

Rhiannon's face lit up, and she hugged Carlie tight. "Thank you for telling me that, it's a real relief. I wouldn't have blamed you if you'd wanted to smother me with a pillow rather than listen to one more thing about Tom, and I will try to talk about other things too, I promise!" she said.

And for a while they did. They finished blending their herbs while discussing the different properties and uses of them, then flicked through their own Book of Shadows and some of Rose's books to find a good recipe for new moon cookies. They'd be baking up several batches with Rose on Thursday night, for Friday evening's new moon ritual, and Carlie was also working on a healing ritual she wanted to do with Laura that night, for the community – if she managed to find the courage to put herself forward in that way.

Finally they took a break to go downstairs and make a fresh pot of tea, and Rhiannon returned to her second favourite subject. "I know you don't like Jake like that, and I'm not suggesting you date him – I've learned my lesson there – but he does really like you," she said. "What are you going to do about that?"

Carlie shrugged. "I don't know. I mean, there's not really anything I can do. What are you proposing that I should do? He asked me out during one of our study sessions, but –"

"You didn't tell me that!" Rhiannon exclaimed, looking a little hurt to have been left out.

"I just didn't want to make a big deal about it, or cause you to look at him any differently, because he's your friend too," Carlie explained gently.

"Fair enough. But what did you tell him?"

"I said that I couldn't, as nicely as possible. And that's when I told him about Rowan, and him dying so recently, so he knew it was nothing personal. I assured him that I had no plans to date anyone, that it wasn't just him."

"You *had* no plans?" Rhiannon asked cheekily.

"I had no plans and I still *have* no plans," Carlie retorted. "And I was very clear, I promise. I didn't want to lead him on, like some girls do, I wanted to be honest with him. And he took it really well, and said he was happy to be my friend, and I'm grateful for that. So we're all good," she insisted.

"But are you sure you don't want to date him? He's so lovely, and you both get on so well."

Carlie glared at her friend. "What happened to 'I'm not suggesting you date him'?" she asked, and Rhiannon had the decency to look a little sheepish. "I can't go out with someone just because he wants to, or because I feel guilty about saying no – that wouldn't last long anyway, because it would be for all the wrong reasons, and is surely not a sentiment anyone would support. And I value his friendship too much to do that to him anyway," she added.

Before the tension between them escalated any further, Rose arrived home, and Rhiannon mouthed "Sorry!" to Carlie before asking Rose how she was and getting the conversation back to more neutral ground. The three of them sat around the table drinking tea and chatting about lunar rites and recipes, and the spring equinox festival that was in less than three weeks. They discussed what kind of treats they would bake for that, and the herbs they could blend together for a sabbat incense, then Carlie broached the subject of going to London with Rhiannon to do a ritual with her cousin the night before their own, and the girls held their breath until Rose finally gave her permission.

The topic of Jake didn't come up again, and the two girls parted on good terms. But when Carlie curled up in bed later that night, with Luna nuzzling into her shoulder and purring gently, she pondered Rhiannon's words. Was Rowan the only reason she'd turned Jake down? When he'd asked her out six weeks ago, it had only been a month since Rowan had died, which was way too soon to even consider dating anyone.

She didn't feel any readier now, but a tiny voice in the back of her mind was asking whether she saw Jake as a potential future boyfriend, or if she didn't see him that way at all, and her dead boyfriend was just a good excuse to avoid hurting his feelings? As she patted the kitten's head, she thought about what she'd told him the night before as they'd studied together. It wasn't a lie, when she'd said that she would rather spend time with him than Tom, or when she'd admitted that he was fun and interesting and kind and considerate and sweet. But that didn't necessarily mean she wanted to be with him. He was more like a little brother to her. Wasn't he?

Chapter 31

Lilies For Love

Turning the key in the lock on Thursday afternoon, Carlie giggled when she heard Luna crying her squeaky little miaows from the other side of the door. As it creaked open, she crouched down and scooped the kitten up in her arms for a hug. Carrying her in one hand, she reached down and grabbed her school bag with the other and walked through to the kitchen.

"Hi Gran, I'm home," she called out, but there was no reply, and although she searched carefully, there was no note either. Which was strange, since Rose had said she wasn't working that afternoon and would be at home so they could start making the new moon cookies. Luna miaowed again, so she gently placed her on the ground and went to fill her bowl. She wondered if Rose would want her to start on dinner, or the baking, but she figured she may as well get some homework out of the way first.

By the time she finally heard the front door open, Carlie had finished everything that was due the next day and made a vegie chickpea curry, and night had long since fallen.

"Sorry I'm late Sweetheart," Rose said as she rustled into the kitchen with her arms filled with flowers and plant cuttings.

"Where were you?" Carlie asked, more sharply than she'd intended. "I was getting worried."

"I'm so sorry, I was just over at Richard's, and didn't realise how late it had become. He needed some help to plant out his herb garden, so I offered him a hand, and then he asked my advice about a recipe his wife used to make, so I showed him how to get it right, then we had a cup of tea, and all of a sudden it was dark. I'm sorry you were worried though."

Carlie smiled. "That's okay, it sounds like he really needed you today. And Jake will be glad he had a friend over to talk to."

"Well, it wasn't all one sided," Rose admitted, voice suddenly shy. "His garden is really amazing, and he gave me some great cuttings so I can grow them too, as well as these gorgeous lilies," she added, placing them on the bench then going to the pantry to find a vase. Her cheeks were pinker than usual when she started arranging the blooms, and Carlie stared at her, slightly suspicious thanks to her uncharacteristic behaviour. "Anyway, dinner smells really delicious, thank you so much for getting it sorted," Rose continued, voice striving for an innocent tone but not quite getting there.

Carlie looked more closely at her grandmother. "Are you blushing?" she asked her.

Rose laughed, although it sounded a little higher pitched than usual. "No Sweetheart, why would I be blushing?" she replied, although she ducked her head behind the flowers she was carefully placing in the vase. "Now, I'll just go and get washed up – do you need a hand first though?"

Carlie assured her that everything was under control and dinner would be ready to serve in five minutes, then started clearing up her books. By the time Rose returned she was composed again, and they spent dinnertime chatting about the new crystal therapist who'd started at the healing centre and Carlie's history assignment, which was due at the end of the following week.

Rose had just put the kettle on when Rhiannon knocked on the door, and she joined them in the warmth of the kitchen, Luna snoozing under the table as they baked cookies and chatted about their new moon wishes.

"I'm hoping that Tom will make it down in time to join us, if that's okay with you," Rhiannon asked, turning to Rose.

"Of course sweet girl," their priestess replied, eyes twinkling with joy and excitement. "So it sounds as though things are going well with this young man?" she added cheekily.

Carlie almost laughed as she watched Rhiannon blush and become tongue-tied. "Um, I hope so," she said shyly. "But I suppose I won't know until I see him tomorrow night. That's why I haven't told Dad about him yet – I wanted to wait until I knew a bit more before I mentioned it. Because who knows, Tom may just not turn up, or he might see me and change his mind, or... I don't know," she sighed.

"I'm just not confident enough that anything will come of it right now – part of me thinks that last weekend was just a wonderful dream, and he doesn't really exist. So if it's not putting you in too awkward of a position, could you not mention Tom to Dad just yet? I promise I'll tell him this weekend, if there's anything to tell," she begged. "And if there isn't, he will have been saved the trouble of needing to react."

Rose smiled at the nervous young woman in front of her. "Yes, I can keep your secret for a few days, until you've decided whether or not it's worth sharing. But don't leave it too long until you tell Mike. And I think you'll be surprised. He knows that you're growing up, and that there will be boys. All he wants from you is honesty, for you to earn the trust you already have. This goes for you too Carlie. We would rather know that you're dating someone, and have the chance to meet them, and know that you're safe," she insisted.

"I'm still really sorry that you felt you couldn't tell me about Rowan, Sweetheart, and Mike is the same. We just want you both to be happy, and not to feel that you have to keep any secrets from us in order to protect us. Because it really didn't end well when Violet tried to protect me by shutting me out," she said with a sigh, then trailed off into her own little world.

Rhiannon took that as her cue to leave, hugging both of them goodbye and walking out to the front door with Carlie.

"Oh god, I'm so nervous about tomorrow night," she confided to her friend. "What if Tom has forgotten, or he met someone more interesting than me this week, or he finally realises that I'm just a boring school student, and decides to avoid the village altogether – that would upset Jake and his grandfather no end!"

Carlie took her friend's hands and stared into her eyes. "Rhi, come on," she said firmly. "You know how much he likes you – hell, Jake and I know how much he likes you, going off your very public displays of affection all of last weekend," she said, unable to hide a giggle. "Now go home, get a good night of sleep, and you'll be hanging out with him in no time."

At school the next day, Jake asked Carlie to thank Rose for cheering his grandfather up, and she narrowed her eyes. "Is something going on with them?" she asked. "She was late home last night, because apparently 'time just got away from them'," she said.

"I've been wondering the same thing," Jake replied. "They seem to have been hanging out quite a lot, and Pop is always so much happier after she's been over. All they do is drink tea, but I think Rose has become really important to him. Is that okay?" he asked, suddenly panicked, and peering at her closely.

Grinning, she nodded enthusiastically. "It's more than okay. I'm so glad they both have someone great to talk to – I'm sure your grandfather has far more wisdom than I do to share."

Rhiannon bounced over to them then, so talk turned back to Tom. The new couple planned to attend Rose's new moon ceremony with everyone else, then head up the tor to celebrate alone together. How Carlie missed having someone to be alone together with, but she smiled at her friend. "Take something warm," she warned good-naturedly. "It's going to be cold up there tonight, so I'll be snuggled up at home in bed with Luna."

When Carlie arrived at the healing centre that night with Rose, and as many containers of the moon cookies they'd baked as they could carry, she was swept up in the magic of the occasion. She helped Rose and Laura set up, gathering all the colourful cushions from the storeroom and placing them in a large circle around the room. Then as the first people started to arrive, she skipped over to the doorway to welcome them, handing each one a green pen and a few small white cards, along with a beeswax candle. Richard gave her a hug as he walked in, while Jake smiled at her and thanked her, and Rhiannon, holding hands with Tom, beamed at her with such joy that it made even her feel happy just to see it, and bask in the reflected good vibes. Rose came over to shake Tom's hand and hug Richard and Jake, and Jake and Carlie exchanged knowing glances that they quickly tried to hide from their priestess.

Finally Rose instructed everyone to gather in a circle and make themselves comfortable on a cushion, then she stepped up to the altar in the centre to begin. She smiled as everyone linked hands. "Welcome everyone. Tonight you have created the sacred circle yourselves, and have imbued it with just as much magic and protection as I ever could," she announced with a smile.

"It's wonderful to see a few new faces. Thank you for bringing your energy and intent to our gathering," she said, smiling over at Tom, then letting her eyes linger on Richard for a long moment. "I just want to outline tonight's ritual for those unfamiliar with how we work, and if anyone has any questions, please feel free to ask, at any point. There's no standing on ceremony here," she said.

Glancing around the room, Carlie saw that every person had all their attention focused on Rose, their eyes lit up already with the power of her presence and the magic of the night.

"In a moment Miri, Laura, Paulette and Belinda will call the directions and invoke the elements, then I'll welcome the god and the goddess to be with us during our rite," Rose continued. "Since it's the new moon, it's the perfect time to set our intentions for the month to come, which is why Carlie greeted you all with pen and paper. I'll facilitate a meditation, where we can each ponder on the weeks just gone, and the ones to come, and decide what intention we want to set, which area requires a new beginning, what we hope to manifest into our life. It can be a physical thing, a new commitment to an old resolution, a character trait you wish to develop, a wish for healing

for yourself or another – whatever your heart yearns for, we will sow the seeds tonight, fuelled by our combined energy and woven with the power of this beautiful moon phase," she said.

"Once it has become strong and clear for you, write it out. It can be a single word, or as many sentences as you require – all it requires is that it be meaningful to you. Then you can burn the paper in the cauldron fire on the altar, and watch your intention being carried up and out into the universe with the smoke, or you can take it home with you and sleep with it under your pillow."

Turning to her left, Carlie smiled as she watched Richard's face, concentrating so hard on Rose's words, and lit up with a fierce intelligence mixed with wonder at his surroundings.

"After that, Carlie and Laura will send some reiki healing energy around the circle, then help us all do some distance healing. And then we'll farewell the deities and directions and close the circle, and ground ourselves with tea and lunar cookies," Rose continued.

"And the candle is for you to take home, to light each evening for the next month, as you focus on the intention you set tonight, staring into the flame as you concentrate on what you want. Then you can blow it out, sending the energy of your wish out into the universe. Making a wish as you blow out the candles on your birthday cake is a piece of candle magic that has survived from pagan times, and is a potent way to manifest your dreams, whatever day it is. So, are we ready to begin?" Rose asked, and an excited murmur reached her from the circle she stood within.

Later, as they drank tea and ate cookies, Richard thanked Carlie for inviting him and Jake into the magical fold, and told her how much he appreciated Rose's wisdom. "She's a wonderful woman, and I'm so grateful to her for spending some of her precious time with me, comforting me and helping me heal."

"She sees it as an honour, not an imposition," she replied. "Don't ever feel that helping you is a burden to her, or that she doesn't appreciate the gift that your presence gives her."

He smiled at her and took her hand. "I hope you realise that goes double for you," he said cheekily, and she winced, remembering how often she'd thought that exact thing, that she was nothing but a

hardship to Rose, an encumbrance she would rather not have had to suffer. "And I hope she's been able to help you heal too Carlie. I know how much you have lost, and how hard it can be to find meaning in life after a loved one has left us."

Before she was reduced to a sobbing mess, Rhiannon and Tom came over, hands full of cookies, and joined the conversation. "These are the yummiest ones we've ever made," Rhiannon grinned, and Richard laughed as he agreed, while Tom planted a kiss on her forehead before turning serious.

"It was lovely to do a ritual with you Pop," Tom said, as he leaned in and hugged his grandfather. "I'm looking forward to spending more time with you, and doing more of them together."

Jake walked over and joined them at that moment, and rolled his eyes as he heard what his cousin was saying. "And I suppose that would have nothing to do with wanting to spend time with Rhiannon?" he asked, but his tone was friendly.

"Hey, there's nothing wrong with having two reasons to get out of the city now is there?" Tom grinned. "Or three I suppose, if I was to count hanging out with you, Cuz," he teased.

By the time Rose joined them they were all laughing, and as Carlie took in the circle of friends and family around her, she felt a rush of gratitude for what she did have. When her parents had died last year, she'd thought that she would never feel happy again. And while she still missed them terribly, every day – and despaired so deeply at having lost Rowan too – she was starting to become more aware of the blessings in her life as well as the tragedies.

As she said farewell to Rhiannon and Tom and watched them set off for their tor adventure hand in hand, hugged Jake and Richard goodbye, and helped Rose lock up before walking home with her through the cool night air, she sent her wish out to the universe. For the people she had grown to care about to be happy and healthy, and for loss to leave them alone for a long while.

Chapter 32

Tattoos and Memories

The next two weeks passed by in a blur – their history assignments were due on the first Friday, so Jake and Carlie had a few late-night study sessions to get it all done, and Rhiannon reluctantly trekked out to Dave's place with him after school to finish theirs, cursing the fact that she had to tell Tom not to visit her that week. And there was no respite once they'd handed them in – the whole class now had print-outs of all the papers, on all the different British colonies, so they spent their lunchtimes and after school grilling each other on the facts they were learning. Carlie and Jake were doing a little better than Rhiannon at committing all the information to memory, because she was still preoccupied by the thrill of new love.

But finally the weekend of Ostara, the spring equinox, rolled around, and Carlie, Rhiannon and Jake were lounging around on the Saturday morning train to London, finally relaxing, for a day at least. They'd caught the earliest train possible so they could spend the day at the Body Mind Spirit Festival with Tom, before they would go out for dinner – a double date of sorts, Rhi had said gleefully – then meet up with Tom's coven for their sabbat ritual.

As they stood at the entrance, Carlie felt just as overwhelmed as she had the first time she'd attended this festival, by the noise and the colour and the crush of the crowd, and tears pricked her eyes.

It was six months to the day since she'd met Rowan here, and fallen in love for the first time in her life.

"You okay?" Rhiannon asked her softly, as she put an arm around her shoulder and held her close as they walked in. "Thank you so much for coming with me. I know this isn't easy for you, but I really appreciate it."

"I'm okay," Carlie responded, trying to reassure herself as much as her friend. It helped that Rhiannon had acknowledged what this was costing her. Besides, if she wanted to move forward with her life, she had to face these things…

Rhiannon's arm slipped from her shoulder though when she saw Tom walking towards them. They both ran to each other, and he scooped her up and swung her around before kissing her long and hard and passionately. Carlie averted her eyes. She was happy for them, but she didn't need to see their joy in being reunited.

Anticipating her reaction, Jake took her elbow and steered her into the next aisle. "Could you help me find a present for Rose today?" he asked. "Pop wanted me to buy something for him to give to her, as a thank-you gesture for her kindness."

Carlie almost threw her arms around him, so grateful was she for his consideration and empathy, for always knowing what she was feeling and how to fix it. But she managed to restrain herself, not wanting to lead him on. "Thank you," she said instead. "You really are the best friend a girl could have."

An expression she couldn't identify flitted across his face, then was gone before she could work it out. Anger, frustration, disappointment? But he smiled at her, and she tried to let her worry go. "Happy to help," he finally conceded, and they started their lap of the hall so they could check everything out.

They spent the morning going from stall to stall together, chatting and looking at all the products, some so weird they couldn't even work out what they were, others beautiful or powerful or potentially healing enough to go on their list of gift possibilities. Carlie was surprised when she had to admit that she was actually having fun. It definitely helped that Jake was just as curious-slash-sceptical-slash-amused-slash-impressed as her by the event.

When they reached the stand that Rowan had been at during the previous festival, being manned today by another shamanic healer, she froze for a moment, before quickly leading Jake to the stall opposite, where they looked at incense and herbal blends as well as cloaks in a myriad of colours and styles, Carlie carefully keeping her back to the shaman guy.

They stopped for a cup of tea, to rest their feet and unclutter their brains for a moment, then continued on with their mission, amazed at just how many different stands there were, and the wide variety of wares. When they turned into the last aisle, Carlie was overjoyed to see Jasmine in one of the booths. Her stand was called Blessed Bee, and the table was filled with gorgeously scented beeswax candles and honey-infused lotions, bath crystals, shampoos and conditioners, as well as jars of honey in different herb and flower flavours. "Oh, Gran would love these," Carlie told Jake as she approached the stand.

"Carlie, my love, I'm so glad to see you," Jasmine cried. "And I'm so sorry for your loss," she continued, ignoring the man who was browsing her products and coming out into the aisle to hug Carlie. "You poor thing, I was so desperately sad for you when I heard. How are you coping?

"It's been rough, but I'm… I'm okay," she said, and realised she was. "Rose has been amazing, and I have two dear friends who have helped me through it. This is one of them – Jake, this is Jasmine, a friend of my mum's from a long time ago. Jasmine, Jake. Another Aussie," she giggled. "But how have you been? And congratulations on the stall, it's gorgeous," she babbled.

Jasmine took her hands and smiled at her. "I'm doing really well. I got in touch with Rowan's mother when I heard the news, and we've been spending time together, which has been very healing for both of us. She's doing okay too."

Guilt washed over Carlie. She hadn't seen Rowan's mum since the funeral, and she felt bad. "Louisa is not your responsibility – and she doesn't expect you to visit her. She knows how painful that would be for you," Jasmine said, and Carlie smiled with gratitude. "Now, did you say Rose would like some of these? I can make her up a gift basket, my treat," she suggested.

"That's really kind of you, but I need to buy something for her, as a gift from my grandfather, and he would want to pay you. But maybe Carlie would appreciate something – I'm sure the relaxing bath salt mix would do her the world of good," said Jake, who'd been studiously examining the products while they talked, trying not to look like he was listening.

Jasmine smiled at him. "You're a wise young man, knowing the importance of an energy exchange," she said. "How about you have a look, see what you'd like to get, and I'll give you a discount. So you're still paying, just getting a better deal. And Carlie, if you come back here, you can decide what you'd like," she said, leading her behind the counter.

Reaching under the table, Jasmine pulled out a tray of body lotions, and leaned forward to hug her again. "He's lovely Carlie," she whispered. "And he really cares about you."

"He's just a friend," Carlie insisted, horrified that someone who knew Rowan's mum would think she'd moved on so quickly.

"I know, I can tell, but you should really think about opening your heart to this one. He has a beautiful soul, and he cares about you even more than you realise," Jasmine advised.

Carlie smiled sadly. "I know," she said, voice raw. "But I can't."

"You should think about it," Jasmine pressed. "He knows what you've lost, and won't seek to replace Rowan or make you forget him. Don't push him away just because you feel guilty."

Feeling Jake's eyes on her, Carlie blushed and looked away. Jasmine laughed, and turned her attention back to the young man she already liked, who was thoughtfully reading the labels on the jars of herb-infused honey. "Rose would love all of these, I'm sure," he said. "And the honey body lotion too."

Pulling out his wallet, he pointed at several items, and Jasmine reached under the table for a pretty straw basket. After filling it up with a sweet-scented collection of jars and bottles, she wrapped it carefully in vivid green silk and tied it with ribbons in several shades of the same hue. Then she handed it to Jake, asking for only a fraction of the value in return. As he gave her the money and she looked for change, Rhiannon swooped down and grabbed Carlie then dragged her down the aisle, calling out to Jake that she just needed to show her friend something.

Jasmine smiled at Jake. "Thank you for caring so much about Carlie," she said. "She's been through so much, and not many people are strong enough to be able to support someone through that, to put their own needs second."

"We're just friends," Jake replied quickly. "Please don't get the wrong idea. I'm not trying to take advantage of her grief or anything," he blurted out, looking incredibly uncomfortable.

"Oh Sweetie, no one thinks that. I'm just grateful that Carlie has someone to talk to, someone who cares about her. Thank you."

Relaxing a little, Jake finally managed to smile. "I just hope she'll be able to find some joy again," he said softly.

"She'll be ready to open her heart soon Jake, and I can tell she already cares about you deeply. Don't be too shy, when the time comes, to tell her how you feel."

"But I don't want to scare her," he replied. "It would break my heart to push her too soon or hurt her in any way."

Jasmine took his hand. "You don't have a scary bone in your body," she said, trying not to laugh. Then she sobered. "Jake, right now being her friend is the best thing you can do for her, the thing she needs most in the world. She needs to know she can trust you, and she needs to get to the point where she won't feel guilty taking things further. But she'll get there, and I can't imagine a sweeter person to be there for her when she does."

The girls came back then, giggling together, Carlie holding a bag and Rhiannon holding Tom's hand. When Jasmine and Tom saw each other, they both started laughing.

"These are the friends that you're bringing to the ritual tonight?" Jasmine asked, eyes dancing with humour, and Tom raised his eyebrows, clearly confused.

"You know Rhiannon?" he asked her.

"Actually no – hi Rhiannon," she smiled. "Carlie has told me so much about you. I'm Jasmine."

"Right, from the Yule retreat," Rhiannon said, then winced that she'd brought it up. "Carlie's mum's friend," she finished softly, as they leaned over the table and hugged.

Jasmine turned back to Tom. "I knew Carlie's mum years ago, and I spent some time with Carlie at winter solstice. And I've just been getting to know Jake," she explained. Carlie wondered why he was blushing, but decided she could ask about that later.

"Small world," Tom grinned. "Jake is my cousin, that's how I met Rhiannon and Carlie, they're all school friends."

"So you'll be at the ritual tonight too?" Carlie asked Jasmine, and was relieved when the older woman nodded. "Is it okay if we all come? We don't want to intrude if it's a closed sabbat."

"Of course you're welcome, the more the merrier. I was actually planning to ask you if you and your friends could come, but I guess I don't need to now," Jasmine replied.

Tom dragged Jake off to show him something, leaving the girls to catch up on their afternoon. Rhiannon could barely speak straight for her excitement, bubbling over with so much joy and enthusiasm about her boyfriend and how wonderful he was.

"He's so beautiful Carlie, isn't he!" she exclaimed, not stopping for an answer. "I'm trying not to rave about him endlessly, because I imagine you're not quite as excited about him as I am, but I can't even think about anything else," she grinned. "How could you hide how you felt about Rowan the way you did? I want to shout from the rooftops that I love Tom."

Carlie tried to keep her tone light. "Well, I wasn't ready to share it with Gran, and my best friend wasn't his biggest fan, so I kept it inside. Although poor Luther had to put up with my stories," she added. She still felt so sad about Luther's loss – but she was happily surprised to realise that she didn't feel any resentment towards Rhiannon any more. She really had let that go.

Her friend still felt guilty though. "I'm really sorry," she said again, but Carlie shook her head.

"I know you're sorry, and I appreciate it, but it's in the past now, and there's no point dwelling on it. Besides, I remember a wise person once told me to stop saying sorry all the time. That woman I met in the cafe recently reminded me of that. I'm not sure who she was, or how she knew about our conversation, but she reminded me of you. Anyway, I honestly don't feel any bitterness now, so let's put it behind us as we vowed to do at our Imbolc ritual."

Nodding gratefully, Rhiannon hugged her friend, then led her over to a table of beautiful jewellery. "Aren't these gorgeous," she said, pointing at the beautiful coloured crystals designed into intricate silverwork settings. "Which one's your favourite?"

Carlie smiled as she took them all in, then finally pointed to a large round moonstone with a silver crescent moon on either side of it, representing the triple goddess and the lunar phases. "It's just like Rowan's tattoo, and the crystal is so beautiful – it feels really strong yet also gentle, if that makes sense."

Rhiannon called the stall holder over, picking up the necklace and opening her wallet to pull some money out.

"What are you doing?" Carlie asked, panic in her voice.

Her friend smiled at her as she handed over the pound notes. "I'm buying you a present – an Ostara gift of love and new beginnings. And no, you don't have any say in it," she insisted, as Carlie tried to protest. "You honour the giver by receiving it graciously. Now put it on and show me, because it's so totally you."

Blushing with embarrassment at the unexpected gift, Carlie thanked her friend, then placed the necklace around her neck and lifted up her long dark hair so Rhiannon could do up the clasp. The pendant rested against her heart, and she felt a warm, soothing energy radiating from it into her body. She smiled. It was the first time she'd felt the joy of beautiful memories when she thought of Rowan, rather than the usual crushing sadness.

Today was the spring equinox, three months to the day since he'd died, and while she wasn't over him, she finally felt the possibility of her heart healing. Maybe it was the energy of spring, or the healing power of time, or the love and support she felt from Rose and Rhiannon, and the women of their ritual circle. She supposed it didn't really matter what it was, the important thing was the sensation of hope she was feeling. Rowan would always be a part of her, but she had to make the most of her life, for him as much as for herself. *Was this what acceptance felt like?*

"Are you okay?" Rhiannon asked, bringing her back to earth.

Carlie smiled. "You know, I think I will be," she replied, and felt her heart lift a little as she spoke the words. Well, words did have power. Words were spells, after all. Yes, she was going to be okay.

They were engulfed in a wave of energy as Tom returned and scooped Rhiannon up to kiss her. "Jake's just grabbing us coffee, but I missed you too much gorgeous girl," he said. He smiled when he saw Carlie's necklace. "I did a tattoo like that a while ago, with the yin and yang symbol within the orb of the full moon, and crescent moons either side. It was really beautiful."

Carlie stared at him. "That's the tattoo I want to get. Would you be able to do it for me?" she asked quickly, before she chickened out.

"Sure. We can do it now if you want to, I live close by. I was going to suggest that we go out for dinner before the ritual, but we can hang out at my place and order pizza while I tattoo you."

Joy lit up Carlie's face. "That would be amazing, thank you!"

He laughed. "The pleasure's all mine. I love tattooing people, especially when it means something to them. The tattoo I told you about was for a druid guy, what was his name? Hawthorn? Willow? No, different tree. I think it was Rowan," he finally said.

Rhiannon stared at Carlie. "No way!" she exclaimed.

Carlie smiled. "Even more perfect. Maybe destiny and fate do exist," she mused, then she quickly sobered. No. If that was the case, she wouldn't need Rowan's tattoo, she'd have him instead because he'd still be here. But Tom's voice broke into her thoughts before they became too melancholy.

"Is that cool babe?" he was asking Rhiannon. "Going back to my place instead of going out?" She nodded happily, although if she was honest with herself, she'd have to admit that she would have been content to follow him anywhere. Wow, she really did like him.

When Jake returned, they said goodbye to Jasmine before heading off through a park and down into the underground rail system. Tom's flat was only three stops away then a short walk, and they were soon climbing the stairs and walking through his door.

Suddenly Carlie felt nervous. Was she really going to do this? Get her first tattoo? Was it going to hurt? Would Rose be angry? What would it look like on her skin? Which wrist should she get it on? How had one off-the-cuff comment led to her agreeing to this? Ah, who was she kidding – she'd sought it out. But did she really want a tattoo? It was a forever kind of commitment, and her history with forever wasn't exactly stellar.

Tom led them into the small apartment and out to a sunroom furnished with a fold-out table, two chairs and a compact set of drawers on wheels, which appeared to hold all his tattooing equipment. He threw the phone to Jake and asked him to order the pizza, then let the girls thumb through his design folio as he set up.

His work was stunning, and there were so many beautiful designs, but Carlie had been wanting to get the triple moon tattoo even before Rowan had died, and finding the man who had created his seemed to be some kind of fate, sceptical though she was of that concept.

When Tom told Rhiannon and Jake to head out to the lounge room and read or watch TV, leaving them alone, Carlie was relieved. She needed to psyche herself up for this, and she didn't want to be their entertainment, especially if she wimped out. Nervously she watched as Tom traced the pattern she wanted onto greaseproof paper, consulting with her on size and shape, then transferring it onto her skin. Then he turned to her, tattoo gun in hand, and she smiled bravely and pulled up her sleeve to expose her inner wrist.

"Try to relax," he said. "I know that's easier said than done, but it will help. It stings a bit, but the bursts are really short, and you can breathe in between."

Carlie shrugged, trying to remain cool and calm. She didn't think a bit of pain would upset her – she felt as though she'd become immune to it over the past year. It was the memories it would unleash, and whether she could keep it together in front of her friends, that worried her more. Curiously she watched as Tom drew the ink into the tattoo machine, then her heart rate rose as he held her wrist with one hand and directed the needle onto her skin.

When it broke through she felt a burst of euphoria. It didn't really hurt, it was just a little uncomfortable, but it made her feel close to

Rowan somehow. Closing her eyes, she let her mind wander back to the night she'd met him – six months ago today – and how she'd felt as he spoke to her. So strong and grown-up, so whole, so *seen*. He'd recognised parts of her she hadn't even been aware of, seen her potential and somehow helped her to see it too. She'd always be grateful to him for that. It had truly been a gift.

As the tattoo gun kept sweeping its lines into her skin, Carlie felt one part of her mind following the drilling sound, while another part flew free. She heard Rowan's voice, whispering in her ear, words of love, of encouragement, of strength. Idly she wondered if he would always appear to her when her body was anchored in pain and her mind was soaring above her, but he shook his head at that.

"My love, I'll always be with you, but it's time for you to let me go," he said softly. "You are still alive with potential and possibility, so don't cut yourself off from the world, or from those who love you. You're surrounded by love, and the potential for love, so don't take it for granted. It's right in front of you Carlie. Don't wait so long that you lose your chance."

Suddenly the buzzing sound of the machine stopped, and she opened her eyes. Tom smiled at her. "You looked like you were a million miles away, in a happy place. That's how I feel when I'm getting inked too," he said quietly.

Shy again with this man she barely knew, she nodded, then glanced down at her wrist. The black outline was flawless, the yin and yang perfectly balanced, the crescent moons gently rounded.

"I've finished the outline, but if there's anything else you'd like to incorporate, now is the time to tell me," he offered.

Curiously she looked at him. "How did you know?"

Smiling broadly, he tapped his chest, over his heart. "I could see it in your face, and you went into the same kind of trance state that I do while I work, so I could feel some of it."

Carlie gasped and blushed ruby red, but he shook his head.

"Don't be alarmed, please, I don't eavesdrop, and I didn't get any of the specifics, but my tattooing is part of my spirituality, it's the way I express my witchyness, so I seem to be able to tune in when people are getting one as a way to express their inner heart.

I'm sensing that this is the past," he said, indicating the lunar symbol on her wrist. "And while it will be an anchor for you always, you're at a threshold – poised between where you were and moving forward to where you're scared to go. So I'm guessing ivy leaves, for this sabbat, and for this feeling," he said.

"I don't know how you did that, but yes, I was thinking about ivy leaves," she replied, voice incredulous.

"I'd suggest one here and one here," he said, voice almost shy, and very respectful. She'd underestimated him. As he caught that thought, he grinned, back to cheeky, and told her that most people felt the same way when they first met him – it took a little while for his charm to slip through his outward confidence, the aloof facade he presented on first meeting to protect himself from those he found annoying and not worthy of his time.

She giggled at that, then nodded yes to the placement of the leaves, still shocked that he'd known what was in her heart. Picking up the gun, he tattooed the ivy pattern directly onto her skin, without bothering about the stencilling, and they were beautiful, ornate and delicately drawn, and perfectly balanced with each other and with the full and crescent moon symbols.

"What colours were you thinking?" he asked.

She laughed. "I'm guessing you know that too."

He was already pulling out coloured inks. "I thought yellow and red for the full moon, with the opposite colour for the dots within the yin and yang symbol, blues and purples for the crescent moons, and green for the ivy."

Carlie nodded happily and watched him as he began colouring it in, wanting to stay present with it now, breathing through the heat in her skin as though it was a ritual.

"It is, I think," Tom said to her as he worked. "A ritual, I mean. Most ancient cultures have used tattooing as part of their rituals, to denote graduation from one stage of life to another, or the achievement of a new rank or role. And although some people today get them as a fashion statement, for most it's still a form of ritual, and represents something important to them – surviving something, in your case, or celebrating an accomplishment or a new state of awareness. For many their tattoos are a diary of their life, symbols of transformation, and reminders of the beautiful moments of their life."

Carlie thought suddenly that she'd misjudged him, that first time they'd met, had missed his depth and the layers of his soul. But he shook his head.

"Nah, you were spot on that day," he said, and she couldn't help but laugh at his honesty, although she was dying of embarrassment on the inside. "I was feeling all superior, and a bit resentful that I had to hang out with my young cousin and his young friends. So I was being silly, trying to impress Rhiannon as a game, just to amuse myself and fill in time – until I realised how much I actually liked her. And how grown up Jake had become. Don't tell them that though, please," he implored her, and Carlie smiled. "Cross my heart."

"Thank you," he said, switching colours. It was almost finished, and it was so much more beautiful than she'd imagined. "I misjudged you too, and I'm sorry for that," he continued.

"Well, we're even then," she said, then changed the subject quickly, not wanting to know what he'd thought of her. "I was suspicious of your motives with Rhiannon, and I apologise for that."

He put the tattoo gun down for a moment and took her hand, gazing into her eyes. "No, you were right, and I can't tell you how grateful I am that Rhiannon has such a protective and caring friend. That first day, when I met her, I had no intention of ever seeing her again. But then after we said goodbye that night she was all I could think about, and by the next morning I knew that I liked her far more than I'd imagined. So from that moment on my intentions have been honourable, I promise."

Carlie smiled. "I can see that now," she said. "And thank you for being honest with me."

"She values your friendship more than anything Carlie, and I will always respect that," Tom said, picking up the gun to complete the work of art on her wrist. He worked in silence for several minutes, until he finally spread the completed tattoo with bepanthen cream and plastic wrap and taped it on.

"How does it feel?" he asked, just as the buzzer rang for the pizza.

Carlie's face lit up. "I love it, thank you! Now how much do I owe you?" she asked, reaching for her bag.

Tom shook his head. "No charge, I'm just really happy that I could do your first tattoo for you, and honoured that it means so much to you," he said, glancing up at Rhiannon as she walked into the room to let them know the pizza had arrived. She blushed.

"I don't mind that you told him," Carlie said to her friend, realising that she must have filled Tom in on her reasons for wanting Rowan's tattoo. Then she turned back to Tom. "But surely I can give you something for your time, or for the inks and equipment at least?"

Shaking his head again, he took her hand – the non-tattooed one – and stared into her eyes, serious for a moment. "I feel like we didn't get off on the right foot," he said softly, and it was her turn to blush. "You're very important to Rhi, so I hope we will become friends. Besides, you honour the giver by receiving with grace," he added, echoing Rhiannon's words from the festival. "And I'm honoured that I could help you," he said firmly.

"Thank you," she replied, simply yet heartfelt, and he smiled at her. "It means the world to me, really. I love it so much."

"I'm glad," he replied. "Now, we'd better get in there and eat some pizza before it's all gone, and then get ready to go."

They all sat down on the floor of the lounge room, laughing and joking as they ate pizza from the boxes, Jake entertaining their English friends with Aussie slang and traditions. Then Carlie grabbed her backpack and headed into the bathroom to change into her ritual dress, while Tom led Rhi into his bedroom.

"There's no time for that guys," Jake called out, joking, as he sat on the couch and flicked through a magazine. Carlie soon joined him, and he smiled as she sat down next to him.

"You look beautiful," he said, and she felt her cheeks grow hot. "So how's your tattoo feeling?" he asked, steering the conversation back to neutral territory. "Did it hurt?"

Grateful that he'd changed the subject, she gazed down at her wrist and wrinkled her nose. It looked weird under the plastic.

"Not really. It felt like a hot, sharp lead pencil being scraped across my skin, but every time it felt like it was about to be too much to bear, it would stop for a second, then start up somewhere else. It was kind of meditative," she said, then laughed. "Okay, it's a bit uncomfortable, but it's worth it. Are you going to get one?"

Before he could reply, Rhiannon burst out of Tom's room, long dress rustling around her legs, face transformed by joy and excitement, and her low-cut top highlighting a stunning piece of jewellery. "Look Carlie, isn't it beautiful!" she cried, pointing at the elaborate crystal setting nestled around her neck. "Tom gave it to me, an Ostara gift," she said, smiling widely.

"It's gorgeous," Carlie said. It was huge too, very different to her friend's usual taste in delicate jewellery, but the large rose quartz heart at the centre of the explosion of multi-coloured crystals definitely reinforced that his intentions were honourable, which made Carlie happy. This was certainly not the kind of gift you gave a girl you didn't care about.

When Tom emerged a few minutes later he had a deep green velvet cloak on, an intricate silver headpiece woven through his long hair, and a bag containing his ritual tools.

"You look so magical," Rhiannon breathed as she gazed at him admiringly. "I'm so excited that we can share this ritual."

"It's a shame it's not Beltane," he replied, winking at Rhiannon and wiggling his eyebrows suggestively.

She grinned back. "Don't worry my love, it's not far off."

Carlie and Jake rolled their eyes at each other, but before they could get too concerned, Tom ushered them out of the apartment and led them to a nearby park, where several people in pagan finery had already gathered. Carlie was surprised – in a good way – that there were just as many men as women there, since she was so used to working in a predominantly female circle. Glancing at Jake, she saw that he'd also noticed this, and his face was alight with possibility.

"Have you asked Tom about his coven?" she asked him. "Maybe you could study with them. You'd probably only have to be physically present for their eight sabbats."

He nodded, excitement on his face and in his stance. "Yes, we were talking about it earlier, and he said I could come up for all their celebrations, and for his monthly study circle too if I wanted to, or

I could do that part online if it was too difficult to attend in person. And he said he'll be in our neck of the woods quite a bit – although I'm guessing he'll want to spend most of that time with Rhiannon," he grinned, as they watched their friend kiss Tom, then walk back over to their side, her face aflame with happiness, while Tom joined Jasmine and a few other witches for the final preparations.

"Thank you so much for coming with me, both of you," Rhiannon said, her eyes shining. "It's going to be such a magical night, and I'm so glad that the three of us are sharing it with each other."

Soon Jasmine called for everyone's attention, and they all gathered in a large circle around the central altar. Tom was one of the direction callers, and while he didn't skip a beat or miss a single word of the invocation, he and Rhiannon couldn't keep their eyes off each other, both totally focused on the other to the exclusion of everything else, and both glowing from within as they responded to one another.

"It's beautiful isn't it," Jake whispered to Carlie, indicating the couple, and she nodded. And suddenly became aware that it had stopped hurting her to see her friend loving and being loved the way she had been with Rowan. Relief coursed through her, before she turned her attention back to Jasmine as she invoked the god and the goddess, and began to feel the magic of the ritual take hold as she dropped into the light trance state she'd come to love so much.

Happiness surged through her. She'd been apprehensive about being at someone else's ritual, at revealing her ignorance if they did things she was unfamiliar with, but it was not so dissimilar to one of Rose's sabbats. The wording was a little different, a bit more traditional, but a wave of relief swept over her, that she wasn't out of her depth as she'd feared. And finally she relaxed and let Jasmine's voice, and the magic of the night, wash over her. Healing, revealing, inspiring.

Rebirth and renewal were the themes of the spring equinox, and the words of the ritual affected Carlie deeply, making her realise that she was a million miles from the person she'd been a year ago. She'd had no idea then about the magic of ritual, the power of words, this connection she now had with nature and the earth.

It saddened her that her mother had left all this behind when she'd fled to Australia, but perhaps it hurt her too much to have been cut off from Rose and her circle, and maybe trying to recreate it in a new country, with new people, would have just exacerbated the pain.

Letting her mind drift, she tried to reimagine her business-suit-wearing mother in a long velvet gown with flowers in her hair. And a flash of memory emerged, of her mum in a pretty floral dress, bare feet in the earth as she planted herbs in their back garden in Sydney. Another, of waking up one night when they'd been camping on a beach up north, the full moon shining into her tent, and peeking out of the opening to see her parents dancing on the sand, the lunar glow shining down on them and casting their shadows out into the water.

And one more, from a rainy middle-of-winter night, when the house smelled of cinnamon and cloves, and her mother had followed their dinner of herb-sprinkled roasted vegies and spicy nut loaf with a fancy dessert she'd created which she called a Yule log.

Maybe the magic and the sense of connection had still been there in her mum, just hidden from public view. Maybe at her core she had still been her mother's daughter. That thought made Carlie happy, and she made a mental note to tell Rose when she got home the next day.

After the formal part of the ritual was completed, and Jasmine had farewelled the god and the goddess and closed the circle, they all wandered over to a nearby cafe, which had an upstairs room reserved for them. Rhiannon and Tom huddled together in a tiny corner booth, only coming up for air to order pots of tea that they didn't end up drinking, so absorbed in each other had they become. Carlie and Jake looked around nervously, feeling a little lost, but Jasmine called them over to her small candlelit table, introduced them to her girlfriend Samantha, and gestured for them to take a seat.

"Carlie, I thought you might like to speak with Sam, because she's a pantheist," Jasmine said. Carlie stared at the two women quizzically, puzzled by the unfamiliar word, but was intrigued as soon as Jasmine elaborated. The priestess said that while she was a goddess-worshipping witch who believed in the deities as literal beings, the way that Rose did, her partner was an environmental activist and scientist who held nature and the natural world as sacred, like all witches, but didn't believe in supernatural beings or powers.

It was the first time Carlie had heard the term, or the explanation, or felt such a zing of connection. Chills ran up her spine, her breath caught, and her heart felt suddenly lighter, and so much freer. It had been bothering her, she had to admit, that she couldn't make herself believe literally in gods and goddesses, as Rose and Rhiannon did. She'd wondered if it made her a fraud, to attend all the rituals and feel the magic, but accept it on a far more symbolic level than everyone else seemed to do. But as Samantha discussed her beliefs, or the lack there-of, Carlie felt more and more at peace.

She'd always admired and respected Rose's love of the goddess, and her belief in her, but she hadn't been able to make herself feel the same way, no matter how hard she tried. But perhaps there was a place for her after all, a philosophy she could embrace, people she could talk with and learn from and be inspired by. So while Jasmine continued her conversation with Jake, Carlie listened wide-eyed and rapt as Samantha shared her take on spirituality with her.

"Pantheism is a philosophy and a way of life, and a valid form of spirituality – it's just not a literal form," she explained, smiling at Carlie as she saw relief flow across her face. "There are similarities in outlook with witches and druids and other earth-based spiritualities, because we all care about the planet and our connection with the earth, but we see the goddess as a personification of nature, not as a woman or a being existing in some other realm or dimension who we can pray to or communicate with," Samantha explained.

"We have great reverence for the universe – it inspires awe in us, and an almost religious-seeming appreciation, but when we are moved by the incredible beauty of a sunset or the power of a thunder storm, it inspires a search for a deeper understanding of nature within us, rather than assuming that the goddess of the dawn had painted it for us to enjoy, or that the thunder god was angry at his brother and hurling lightning bolts at him."

Carlie laughed, but her head was spinning. It was everything she'd been thinking and feeling since she'd arrived in Summer Hill and started doing ritual with Rose, but she hadn't had the words to express it with. As Samantha spoke, it was like a weight lifted from her heart – and then she remembered Rose telling her that a few of the women in her ritual circle were atheists, and were the kindest, sweetest and most caring people she knew, more caring and "moral" than many of the religious people she'd met.

When a waiter brought them fresh pots of tea, along with platters of scones, bite-sized cupcakes and luscious fresh fruit, Carlie took a deep breath and tried to still her spinning mind, but once their mugs were full again, she turned her attention back to Samantha.

"For me, my spirituality is expressed through my work to protect the earth and its creatures, and to oppose businesses that threaten endangered animals or negatively impact on nature," Sam told her.

"I have a friend with a similar outlook who works with herbs and healing, who calls herself an atheist witch, and another who describes himself as a humanist," she continued. "But the labels don't really matter, other than to help you find like-minded people and realise that you're not alone, and that what is deep within your heart is shared and experienced by others."

"Yes!" Carlie said breathlessly. "Thank you so much for sharing all of this with me. It's such a relief to me that you've given voice to what I've been feeling so deeply within me, but haven't been able to articulate, even to myself. The beauty of nature in the village where I live now fills me with such awe, and climbing the sacred hill to watch the sun set or the full moon rise feels so magical, so mysterious and awe-inspiring, in a way I can't really explain. But it being the work of a supernatural being never rang true to me," she admitted, still finding it difficult to express what she was feeling.

Samantha smiled at her. "It's funny, people assume that not believing in a literal god or goddess means we miss out on all the wonder and beauty of the world, but I think it's the opposite. We hold nature itself as sacred and worthy of reverence, almost of worship, and we definitely feel that magic exists, it's just that rather than needing to be explained away as a supernatural being, or a supernatural force, we see it as simply unexplained science. And we hope that one day we might be able to comprehend its vast scope."

As Samantha poured more tea, Jake and Jasmine drew them back into their conversation, along with a few of the other ritual participants, and Carlie became quiet and slightly awestruck, thrilled to listen to everyone and just soak it all in. She marvelled at the gracious way people spoke to each other, and also their ability and willingness to really pay attention to what others said. It was like talking to Rose – people here believed many different things, but they all respected each other's views, and had wonderful discussions, fiery at times, but always polite, and she had the sense that they were all open to expanding or even changing their beliefs if they experienced something that made more sense to them.

When the last pot of tea had been drunk and the final platter of food had been emptied, and the owner had come upstairs to tell them they were closing, Carlie was surprised to realise how much she'd enjoyed the night. She had only come as a favour to Rhiannon, yet she'd had an unexpectedly wonderful time. Jake grinned at her, his eyes sparkling with just as much fire and intent as hers.

"Thank you for letting me be part of all this," he said, glancing around the room as they stood up and prepared to leave. "I feel so at home here because of you, and so inspired."

"Thank *you*," she smiled. "And it's *our* thing, not just mine, and you're always welcome to be part of it. Besides, if I hadn't known Jasmine, I would have felt like I was *your* guest."

"Or we're just Rhiannon and Tom's tag-alongs," Jake added, but he was laughing. "Do you think we'll be able to pry them apart?"

Carlie was dubious, and dreaded having to tell her friend it was time for them to go back to her cousin's place and get some sleep. They'd promised they would be home by midnight – how faery godmother of them – and they didn't have much time left.

"Guess we need to try," she sighed, but when they headed over to the corner booth, Rhiannon stood up without them having to ask, took Tom's hand and followed them downstairs.

As they all stood together out on the deserted street, stars twinkling and the almost-full moon sailing overhead, Carlie hugged Jasmine and Samantha, and thanked them for the wonderful night and all the intriguing, inspiring conversations.

Then she turned to Tom to express her gratitude and appreciation for the beautiful tattoo he'd done for her.

"It was my pleasure," he replied, taking her hands and staring deep into her eyes. Images flooded her mind, of Tom holding Rhiannon close, protecting her from hurt and treating her with love and respect. A weight lifted from Carlie's shoulders as she understood the message he was sending her, and she nodded in acknowledgement.

Smiling, Tom dropped her hands and took Rhiannon's. "Now let me hail a cab, and we'll drop you girls off on our way home," he said.

Jake and Carlie raised their eyebrows at each other in surprise, having expected a real battle to separate the love birds, but they were too tired and relieved to question it. They'd both started yawning, and were just happy to know that they'd soon be in bed.

There was one awkward moment when Carlie got out of the cab, then had to wait while Rhiannon and Tom kissed goodbye, a seemingly never-ending and increasingly passionate kiss. But finally her friend emerged, eyes shining, and they crept into her cousin's apartment and tiptoed down the hall to the spare room.

It was still dark when Rhiannon's alarm went off what felt like just a few hours later, and Carlie groggily rolled over, groaned, and asked what time it was.

"Sorry," Rhiannon whispered. "It's only half past five, but Tom's taking me out for breakfast before we have to go home. You're welcome to come with us though," she added, somewhat reluctantly, but Carlie mumbled "no" and pulled the pillow over her head.

"I'll be back by eleven, I promise, so we'll have plenty of time to get to the station. Is that okay? Will you be all right here on your own?" Rhiannon asked nervously.

Carlie let out a muffled: "Fine," then drifted back off to sleep, while Rhiannon pulled on her clothes in the dark then tiptoed down the hall and outside into the chilly morning air, breathing in the beauty of the about-to-rise sun and the joy of her first real love.

Chapter 33

Heart of Darkness

When the girls met up with Jake at the station later, he proudly showed off his new tattoo, which Tom had done for him in the early hours of the morning, after they got home from the ritual and before he met Rhiannon for breakfast. It was gorgeous, a delicate circle of ivy, with four quarters marked out within it, each one holding a symbol for fire, earth, air or water – a golden candle flame, a purple crystal, a black feather and a blue ocean wave.

"It's perfect," Carlie said, deeply impressed. "It's really beautiful, and it symbolises everything, even your surfing," she added, and was surprised that she felt sad at the thought of him leaving England to go home to his Aussie beach life. She would miss him.

"Thanks," Jake said proudly. "It also reminds me of you, and our friendship, and the magic that you've shared with me. The candle flame was to represent my first ritual, at Imbolc, and the crystal was from our wander through the festival yesterday and all the amazing things we saw. And the feather is to remind me of a little black bird I encountered at the base of the tor when I walked home after our first study session at your place," he said shyly.

"He was like you, so fragile, yet strong too, and wanting to fly, but too scared to spread his wings and try. I've seen him since, or one like him, flitting around the lower slopes, daring to go higher, and singing with joyful abandon. He's really come into his own, just like you have," he said softly, then blushed. "I'm sorry, I hope that doesn't offend you, he was just such a sweet little thing, and it's been amazing to see him slowly become stronger and more confident over the last few months, which you have too."

Panic clutched at Carlie's heart for a moment, at the strangely intimate way Jake was speaking, but she was saved from answering when the train pulled into the station. Rhiannon kissed Tom one last time, then the three of them climbed on board and found some seats together. But while they'd promised themselves they would study on the way home, they didn't even pull their books out and pretend to try, instead talking excitedly about their ritual the night before, how different tonight's ceremony at the healing centre would be, and tattoo designs that Rhiannon might like to get.

Carlie and Jake groaned when Rhi kept bring the conversation back to Tom, but soon they all started dozing off. Rhiannon curled up across one long bench seat and fell asleep, and although Carlie tried to stay awake, she eventually succumbed to slumber too, her head falling onto Jake's shoulder. The last thing she remembered thinking before her eyes closed was how comfortable she now felt being close to him.

Feeling somewhat refreshed when the train finally let them off in their village, they went their separate ways, to unpack and then get ready to celebrate the spring equinox all over again.

It was an evening filled with magic and power, heightened even further by the full moon, and Carlie felt it filling her up, energising her and reminding her how precious life was, no matter what you had lost. Gazing across the circle at Rhiannon made her smile, as she thought of their plans to go to uni together to study grief counselling, and continue their magical explorations as well. They'd be just like Rose and Elsie, mixing modern medical methods with traditional healing, alternative therapies and the power of ritual, and the thought of growing into a woman like her grandmother made her smile.

A few nights later, Carlie and Rose were grinding herbs together, when her grandmother brought up the topic of Jake again.

"Sweetheart, I know how much you loved Rowan, and how much you want to be faithful to his memory, but there can be room in a lifetime for more than one great love. Look at your mum, she had three. She adored Mike with all her heart, and was adored by him in turn, and for better or worse it seems she loved Andre, which he reciprocated, for a while at least, and she definitely loved your dad. You deserve to love and be loved again too, and I really hope you won't close off your heart forever out of some misguided attempt at remaining true to Rowan. He'll always be part of you, but –"

"I know, but I don't want to be like that woman at his funeral, who dated him briefly then forgot all about him, until she turned up at the church – married and pregnant no less – pretending he had always been so important to her. I don't want to minimise how much he meant to me by dating the next person I meet."

"Carlie, you are nothing like her," Rose said sternly. "Of course he was important to you, and you to him. He will always have a place within your heart, and he'll live on in the way he helped you heal your grief over your parents and develop along your magical path. A lot of people remember their first love with great fondness, but go on to have other great loves throughout their life too."

Carlie tried to interject, but her grandmother held up her hand to stop her. "I know it's different, and that if he was still here you would be with him now. But loving someone else, either now or in the future, doesn't mean you didn't love Rowan. It doesn't diminish your feelings for him, or his for you, in any way. But you honour that love by living a full life, not by shutting out the world."

"It's still so soon though," she whispered. "I'm not ready to give my heart away again, to risk all that pain."

Her grandma smiled at her, eyes filled with so much love and compassion. "Darling girl, the risk is always worth it. Love is the driving force of the universe – it can bring so much joy, and transform any pain, and truly make life worth living."

"I'm sure it can, but isn't your advice a little hypocritical?" Carlie asked her, her voice cautious but firm.

Rose stared at her, aghast. "What do you mean?" she stuttered.

"After Grandpa died, did you open your heart to anyone else? Did you let yourself love and be loved again, or did you close yourself off and deny yourself the chance to meet someone else – for more than twenty years no less?"

"That's different Sweetheart, I had to stay here in case your mum came back," she said, although her voice sounded a little uncertain.

"But you could have dated someone, right?" Carlie pressed. "Yet as far as I can tell, you've been alone ever since Grandpa died. Is that right? Did you even try? Did you go out with *anyone* after him? Or did you just give up on yourself, and think you had to punish yourself for the rest of your life?"

"Well, I suppose I didn't try very hard..." Rose reluctantly admitted, then trailed off.

Carlie's eyes flashed. "Very?"

"Okay, I didn't try at all. But I was just so busy trying to keep the shop going, trying to keep up with the healing circles and rituals, trying to help as many people as I could."

"Now you're blaming the *community*?" Carlie asked, tone pitched somewhere between outrage and disbelief. "How do you think they'd feel about that?" Rose winced, but Carlie continued her tirade.

"And there were chances, weren't there?" she insisted. "Men who showed interest, who wanted to get to know you, who wanted to love you – until you sent them packing."

Rose blushed and looked increasingly uncomfortable. "Sweetheart, it wasn't like that, I just didn't have time, and I –" She broke off, then her shoulders slumped, and she sighed. "Okay, maybe I discouraged them," she finally conceded. "But not on purpose!"

"And what about Richard?" Carlie demanded.

Cheeks flushing even redder, Rose tried but failed to look innocent. "What do you mean?" she stuttered. It was the first time Carlie had seen her lost for words in a long time.

She rolled her eyes. "You obviously enjoy each other's company. He's always asking about you, and popping over with silly excuses in an attempt to see you, and spend time with you. And apparently you spend a lot of time over there too."

"What would you have me do?" Rose challenged, trying to shift the focus off herself and avoid admitting to anything.

Shrugging, Carlie turned the tables back on her grandmother. "What do you want to do? And more importantly, what are you scared of? What's stopping you this time? It can't be Grandpa, all these years later, and sadly it can no longer be Mum, because she's not coming home to either of us."

The deep truth and the raw pain of her words echoed around the kitchen, and Rose busied herself pulling pretty glass jars out of the cupboard for them to put their concoctions in. When she finally spoke, she'd managed to compose herself – and to seize on some of Carlie's words in an attempt to change the subject.

"I want to be here for you Carlie, in a way I couldn't be for your mum. It's your final year of school, and you're still getting over the death of your parents, and of your boyfriend. You're in a new country, at a new school. I'm not going to go gallivanting around the countryside on wild nights out with someone just for my pleasure. I have a responsibility to you."

Carlie stared at Rose, shock and surprise battling for supremacy in her expression, before she finally laughed. "Seriously? That's insane. You can't blame me for this, or use me as the reason to lock away your heart and turn down the chance for love – especially when you're telling me to be brave and let someone in!" she exclaimed.

"You can do whatever it is you feel you have to do for me, which you're more than doing by the way, and still have time for yourself," she continued. "Please don't use me as an excuse to deny yourself happiness – that's not fair to me or to you. You've been amazing, and you *are* helping me through my grief, and helping me to forge a new life, but it's not a twenty-four/seven occupation. You can go out and enjoy yourself too."

Rose filled the kettle and put it on to boil, then gazed at her granddaughter with narrowed eyes. "When did you become so mature?" she asked.

Carlie smiled. "I have a good teacher," she said. "You, in case you missed that. But I always spend Tuesday nights with Rhiannon, either at her place or up in my room, and any other night I'm fine to be on my own too. There are plenty of nights you stay out late teaching and I survive, so why would it be any different to stay out late for fun? That's just a terrible excuse for avoiding taking any kind of risk, and giving yourself any kind of chance for happiness," she huffed.

Reaching up to pull down a teapot and a jar of tea leaves, Rose looked thoughtful. "Even if I could do that, what do you propose should happen afterwards? We're too old for dating, or weddings and honeymoons. And what about you and Jake?" she asked, voice veering between hope and terror.

"I'm just suggesting you go out for dinner with the guy, you don't have to get married next week," Carlie retorted. "Although I do find it interesting that you used the word propose."

She giggled as Rose looked at her sternly. "Joking! But seriously, if it did go that far, you'd just figure things out then. He'd move in here, or you'd move in there, whatever you'd prefer. Rhiannon and I are going to university later this year, so we could get a place together, and Jake will be going home to Perth. There's always a way to find a solution Gran – *if you want one*," she said.

Carefully Rose poured out two mugs of tea and took them over to the table, sitting down and waiting until her granddaughter had taken the seat opposite her. "How did this even become about me?" she asked defensively.

Carlie took a sip of her tea and gazed levelly at her grandmother. "Because you're telling me to open my heart, yet you've spent more than twenty years locked away from the world, guarding yourself from real joy, with a fortress up around your *own* heart. For all your priestess wisdom and the love and admiration so many people have for you, somehow you don't feel that you deserve to love or be loved."

Suddenly worried that she'd gone too far, Carlie watched in astonishment as her grandmother's face crumpled in on itself and tears fell from her eyes. Eyes that usually held joy and compassion now looked scared and defeated.

Shock radiated from Carlie, before a crashing sense of acknowledgement washed over her. "Oh my god," she exclaimed, as understanding dawned on her. She walked around to Rose and hugged her tight. "That's it, isn't it? You've blamed yourself for Mum running away, and Grandpa taking his life, so you don't think you deserve to have love, to be loved. You've been torturing yourself all these years, thinking that you have to pay some kind of penance by being alone for the rest of your life."

Rose's body shook as she cried harder, and Carlie held her tight, fragile bones echoing the fragility of her emotions, and her very soul. She cried until the tea had gone cold, her granddaughter patting her shoulder as soothingly as she could. But finally she began to mentally gather herself, her sobs growing quieter and further apart, and her body slowly becoming still.

"I'm sorry," Carlie whispered.

"Whatever for, darling girl?" her grandma asked, wiping her eyes and taking a few deep breaths, her priestess cloak of composure settling around her as she became herself again.

"I didn't mean to upset you."

Rose smiled. "You've just given me the key to transform my life Sweetheart. I was crying because it's true. All these years I've thought I was happy, that I was so spiritually aware and emotionally secure. People came to me for advice, for wisdom, for truth. And I couldn't see the biggest fault of my own life."

"It's not a *fault…*" Carlie offered, but Rose interrupted her.

"Yes it is, and continuing in this way now that I'm aware of it would be compounding it many times over. The time for denial of my past and my actions is done," she said, squaring her shoulders and smiling at her granddaughter.

"Are you okay?" Carlie asked. "Can I get you anything?"

"Maybe a new pot of tea?" her grandmother suggested. "I'm sorry, I've let this one go cold."

So Carlie busied herself with the kettle and new tea leaves, and Rose started to think about Richard in a brand new way.

Chapter 34

Blessings of Solitude

Time sped up and blurred over the next two weeks. Carlie worked hard on her assignments and cramming for the pre-holiday exams that were looming, and still managed to fit in some reiki at the healing centre on the weekends. For a few nights she helped Rose blend herbal potions for the shop, and she dedicated an afternoon to writing letters to Sandy and her friend Emily back in Australia. She barely saw Rhiannon outside of school though, because Tom was visiting a few times a week and monopolising all her free time.

Ostensibly he was coming down from London to stay with Jake and their grandfather, but Jake revealed that he'd barely seen him, as Tom slipped in long after midnight, and was still asleep when he got up and headed off to school the next day. But he did spend the mornings with Richard before heading back home, and Jake said their grandfather really appreciated these visits, so neither of them could begrudge the lovebirds the time they were spending together.

Rhiannon also missed both of their coven meetings, since Tuesdays were good nights for Tom to travel to their village. But despite a flash of annoyance at her hypocrisy, since Rhiannon had been so angry at her when she'd missed a single coven night to be with Rowan, Carlie didn't mind too much. She studied on her own, adding new research to her Book of Shadows, and was genuinely happy for her friend.

She was also glad when Rhiannon confessed between classes that she'd organised a dinner the previous night with her dad, Jake and Richard, both of whom Mike liked, so she could introduce him to Tom and let him know they were dating. Richard vouched for his grandson's character, but Tom had charmed her father so much that she could have done it without the extra back-up. Either way, she was relieved that she no longer had to sneak around or hide her relationship from her dad, and Carlie understood that, while feeling a little hurt that she hadn't been invited too.

Then, after the stress of their exams came and went, and the relief that they'd all done well subsided, they had two weeks of freedom from school. Rhiannon went to Brittany for the duration though, for a family holiday they'd booked the previous year. She sent postcards to Carlie almost every day, and promised she was taking lots of photos, and writing lots of notes, at all the sacred sites they visited.

She also wrote her a long letter, revealing that Tom had managed to get a few days off work to drive over to France and stay nearby, which had made it the "best holiday ever!". He'd taken her to the standing stones of Carnac and the magical Broceliande Forest, which was home to many Arthurian legends – the tomb of Merlin the Magician, where ribbons, flowers and baby booties were left in the hope he would grant people's wishes, Vivianne's Fountain of Eternal Youth, said to bestow immortality on those who drank from it, and the dramatic Valley of No Return, bewitched by the priestess Morgaine to imprison any knights who came by, in revenge for her broken heart.

A pang of longing shot through Carlie. It all sounded so beautiful, and so romantic, and she was overwhelmed by the desire to be able to share the things that meant so much to her with someone else again too, though she fought hard to conquer her jealousy.

It wasn't just Rhiannon who was falling in love either. Rose had finally summoned up the courage to invite Richard out for dinner, so they'd enjoyed several evenings together, watching movies, cooking for each other, and one night driving over to Smithfield to see a theatre production. And Jake was spending a lot of time studying with Tom in London, falling in love with magic, and with the ancient city, so she barely saw him either.

But while she'd thought she might feel lonely, Carlie was enjoying the solitude and space, and realising how desperately her heart and soul needed it. Each morning she got up before the sun to walk through the countryside, which was so beautiful as spring flourished and tiny hints of the approaching summer emerged, the wild hedgerows ablaze with pretty blossoms, ripening blackberries and the sound of bees. Now the sun was rising earlier, she loved being outside, soaking up the fresh air and sunshine, drinking in the scent of flowers and cool breezes, and feeling her body attuning itself to the energy of the land.

It suited her mood to be on her own too, to not have to talk to anyone, or explain herself, to try to come to terms with her pain and her loss and her sense of injustice in her own time and in her own way. When she was home, Luna barely left her side, and she loved the kitten's uncomplicated company, the sweet sound of her purring as she curled up in her lap while she read or slept on her pillow right next to her at night, soothing the ache inside her.

And while she wasn't ready to admit it to anyone, she'd stopped sensing Rowan around her all the time, which was making her sad. Although she'd tried many times to find the cottage again, to find him again, she hadn't been able to. The last time she'd heard him speak to her had been when she was getting tattooed, and he'd told her she had to let him go. So, slowly, reluctantly, she was starting to accept that it was almost time to look forward. There was guilt in that thought, and regret for what might have been, but also gratitude for the time they'd had together.

Looking down at her wrist, she marvelled again at the intricate tattoo design. She really loved it, and Rose had too, which had been a relief. And while the triple goddess moon symbol made her smile and remember Rowan, the ivy leaves made her think of their spring equinox ritual, and Tom and Rhiannon, and Jake. When she thought of him she thought of summer sunshine, sparkling waves, his sweet smile and his gentle nature. He was so kind to her, so patient, so respectful. It was such a shame she couldn't picture him as anything more than a friend.

Chapter 35

Ghosts of the Heart

By the time school resumed and life had returned almost to normal, Carlie was feeling much stronger. So when Rhiannon and Jake expressed their guilt at having abandoned her over the holidays, she shrugged it off and insisted it had been a good thing. She'd needed the time alone to come to her own conclusions about moving forward – if Rhiannon had been pressuring her again to get over Rowan, she probably would have dug in her heels and stayed where she was. Stuck. Stubborn. Her journey to acceptance was one she'd had to take on her own, and on her own terms.

Now there were less than two weeks until Beltane, so both girls were relieved that they could resume their Tuesday night coven meetings, after missing the last four. "I'm so sorry I put seeing Tom before our rituals, especially as I was so mean to you when you missed one," Rhiannon said, tone conciliatory, as she ushered her friend inside and led the way upstairs to her bedroom. "It was especially bad timing coming just before our France trip," she admitted. "But oh, it was so magical."

Carlie smiled as she slipped off her shoes and gazed around the room. Rhiannon had done a declutter when she got home, and there were new photos on her corkboard. "It's fine, life happens," she replied, as she walked over to look at the pictures.

"That's me and Brodie at Merlin's tomb," Rhiannon said. "And me and Tom at Carnac…"

Carlie froze when she saw the bottom image.

"And that's Mum, from when we went to Brittany four years ago. This trip was kind of a remembrance, one we did in her honour, retracing the steps of the holiday we took with her. I don't know, it probably sounds silly –"

"That's your mum?" Carlie broke in.

"Yes, haven't I shown you pictures of her before?" Rhiannon asked, surprised.

"I've only seen the ones from that dress-up party, when she was wearing a masquerade mask, and a few from towards the end of… well, from when she was really sick and had lost a lot of weight," Carlie replied.

"And lost her hair," Rhiannon acknowledged. "But this is what she looked like before she got sick. She was really so beautiful." Sighing, she walked over to look at the photo with her friend, before realising that something was upsetting her.

"What's wrong?" she asked, puzzled by her response.

"That's the woman I was talking to in the cafe that night, the one who reminded me a little of you," Carlie whispered.

Rhiannon stared at her blankly. "What woman?"

"Remember when I told you I'd met a woman who I didn't know, but who seemed to know me, and I tried to describe her, but she sounded like she could have been any of the women in Rose's circle? Well, it was her," she said, pointing to the photo.

"But she's –"

"I know," Carlie replied, wonder in her voice. "But she was wearing that exact same outfit too. And looked just as beautiful."

Rhiannon had sunk to the floor in a heap, her face frozen with fear and longing, and her eyes lit up with hope. "What did she say?" she implored.

Part of Carlie's mind registered the fact that her friend didn't doubt for a second that she had seen the ghost of her dead mother, and didn't find it at all strange – she just wanted to know everything she had said, any tiny clue as to how she was. And the rest of her mind was desperately working to try to remember every word the woman had said to her, so she could offer this small gift to her friend.

"The first thing she said was how much she loved the hot chocolate in that cafe," she recalled. "She was holding a mug of it, inhaling the scent, but I realised after she left that she didn't drink even a sip of it, which did seem weird."

Rhiannon smiled. "That was her favourite treat. When we'd ask for pizza or chips or whatever, all she wanted was a mug of hot chocolate from Kylie's Cafe," she said, eyes misting over with memories. "Even when she was too sick to leave the house, she'd send me or Brodie out to get her a takeaway cup of it. But what else did she say?" she begged.

"I asked her how she knew so much about me, and she said we hadn't met before, so I could stop thinking I was rude to have forgotten her. 'You could say I'm a friend of Rhiannon's,' she added, then told me that she knew I was worried about you, and she was glad we'd reconnected, and were such good friends, and that you would never knowingly hurt me," Carlie said, then stopped, slightly panicked. She'd never mentioned the curse to Rhi, or that she was worried about her, but her friend hadn't noticed her slip of the tongue. Instead she was staring at her, spellbound. "What else?"

"She said she could sense I was worried about Mike – it was after you'd told me he thought my mum hated him, and he'd let her down, so I'd copied some pages from her diary for him, to reassure him that she'd always considered him a dear friend, and her only regret had been hurting him and Gran," Carlie replied.

"Wow, I didn't know you'd done that. Thank you so much for sharing that with him," Rhiannon said softly.

Carlie smiled at her. "It was the least I could do."

Rhiannon was holding the photo, tracing the outline of her mother's face. Then she glanced up at her friend, eyes begging for anything more she could offer her, but Carlie was hesitant.

"What aren't you telling me?" she asked.

"Um, well, she said that I was kind like my mother, so of course I wanted to know if she'd known Mum, and she told me that she had, and that everyone in the village had loved her, and felt her loss when she left. Then she said she knew that Mike had never stopped loving her. Which made me mad, so I told her that wasn't true – that he had married an amazing woman who he adored, who he adores still, and whose children miss her terribly."

Tears pricked Rhiannon's eyes, just as they'd seemed to prick Beth's that night in the cafe. "Then what?" she asked, voice a desperate whisper. "And thank you for telling her that."

"She said: 'I'm sure she misses them more than anything too,'" Carlie replied, then threw her arms around her friend.

Rhiannon smiled at her through her tears. "Thank you."

"What for?" she asked, mystified. "I feel even worse now that it was your mum who said Mike always loved mine."

"Oh Carlie, of course he did, and that's okay. It didn't diminish his love for Mum in any way, and it just made her like him even more, to know that he would always care about someone even when they were gone," Rhiannon explained.

"It sounds like she got confirmation from you that he still loves her, and I'm so grateful to you for that. I remember just before she died, when it was getting really difficult and she was so sick, I heard her telling Dad that she wanted him to find love again after she was gone. He told her that there was no way, but she insisted – she said she knew it wouldn't ever lessen the love he had for her, he would just find some more room in his heart for a new person."

She sniffed a little, and wiped her eyes, trying to compose herself, so Carlie headed downstairs to make tea and give her friend a minute alone. When she returned soon after with two mugs, she handed one to Rhiannon, who was still holding the photo of her mother, but looking far happier now than she had before. "What's wrong," she asked as she sipped the tea. "You look a little worried."

Carlie smiled. "Am I really that obvious?" she replied. "I'm just… well, I don't know… Do you think I'm going crazy, to be seeing things that aren't really there, to be having conversations with… um, what would you call them? Ghosts?" she asked.

"I don't know. I've never seen one, but obviously I very much want to believe that you *did* speak to my mother," Rhiannon said with a half smile. "Has it ever happened to you before?"

Carlie hesitated. What if this really did mean that she was crazy, like lock-you-up crazy? "Your mum was the first one, but a few days after that I found the cottage again, the one in the mists, and Rowan was there," she admitted, voice soft, and bruised sounding.

Her friend gasped. "You never said anything about that!"

"To be honest, I thought you'd think I was going mad," Carlie admitted. "And it was the day you'd gone to see John, to break up with him. I knew you were hurt by his reaction, after you'd finally gathered the courage to reveal yourself to him, so I didn't want to start rambling on about ghosts and mists and things that were there but not there, if that makes sense. I didn't want to twist the conversation around to being all about me – I wanted to be there for you."

Rhiannon smiled. "I appreciate that. But what did he say?"

"Just that he loved me, and he knew that I loved him too, and that he'd felt it, that moment when I changed my mind and decided that I was going to choose both of you," she whispered.

"And he wanted me to stop wishing it had been me that died instead of him – I'd said it wasn't fair because he had so much still to do, so much to give, so many people to help, but he insisted that I was going to do amazing things too, and he wanted me to know how much I am loved, and valued, and that I will help lots of people."

"That's beautiful," Rhiannon said.

"I guess," Carlie replied sadly, and her friend raised her eyebrows at her. "I mean, yes, it was beautiful, but I'd pretty much convinced myself I was just dreaming it, or imagining it, that it was some kind of wishful thinking, confirming to myself that he died knowing I loved him, because that's what I've been torturing myself over. Now that I know I saw your mum though, it makes it seem more real, in a weird way. But then I wonder why I haven't seen him again? Why has he left me?" she asked, voice anxious, imploring.

"He'll never leave you," Rhiannon said emphatically.

Sighing, Carlie shook her head. "But I can't find him any more, and I no longer hear his voice either. The last time he spoke to me was a month ago, at Ostara, when Tom was tattooing me. But he hasn't spoken to me since then."

Rhiannon's eyes were wide. "But that's amazing that he did speak to you. What else did he say?" she pressed.

Carlie blushed, then reluctantly pulled out her Book of Shadows and flicked through it to a section up the back. "My love, I'll always be with you, but it's time for you to let me go," she read out, voice soft. "You are still alive with potential and possibility, so don't cut yourself off from the world, or from those who love you…"

Then abruptly she stopped. She couldn't tell Rhiannon that he'd also insisted that she was surrounded by love, and the potential for love – that it was right in front of her and she should grab it with both hands before it was too late. She knew her friend would agree with him, would push her towards Jake, and she wasn't ready to argue about that again.

"I don't want to let him go," she said instead, and it was Rhiannon's turn to lean across and hug her friend.

"Maybe my mum's words are for you too – that you can eventually love someone else, and it won't mean that you love Rowan any less, just that you've made room in your heart for another person too. Like your mum did, and my dad did – they still loved each other, even when they married someone else. And I know that if Dad does meet someone, even remarry, it won't diminish his love for Mum, or for Violet, or for the new person. His heart will just grow even bigger."

Suddenly they heard the front door open then bang shut, and Rhiannon looked over at the clock by her bed. "Oh my god, how did it get to ten o'clock?" she asked, slightly panicked. "We haven't organised a single thing for Beltane!"

Carlie tried to smother a yawn. "We'll have to do it next week, but we'll be fine, I'm sure. Maybe we can coordinate with Gran and share some of her wisdom while we help her prepare for the ritual? Not that she's been home much lately – she and Jake's grandfather have been seeing each other, so to speak, and I think it's getting serious," she revealed, and there was joy in her voice.

"Really? When did this start?" Rhiannon asked excitedly.

"Oh yeah, I guess we've barely seen each other in the last month, what with exams and boyfriends and holidays," Carlie teased, and Rhiannon rolled her eyes, pretending to be hurt.

"They'd been spending a bit of time together, gardening and stuff, and I know at first Gran was just helping him with his grief, helping him move forward. But after Ostara we were grinding herbs one night, and she brought up Jake, and suggested that there could be room in my life for more than one great love. And for some reason I called her on it – I said it was a bit hypocritical of her to tell me to move on and open my heart, when she'd denied herself love for more than twenty years."

"You didn't!" Rhiannon gasped.

"I'm afraid I did," Carlie said. "It was a long conversation, and I was as gentle as I could be, although there were definitely some tears. But in the end she thanked me – because when she really opened up and looked within, she was shocked to realise that she had denied herself love, had walled up her heart, ever since Grandpa died. And despite healing so many other people, helping them become brave enough to risk everything for love, she'd never done it herself. She didn't think she deserved it."

"Wow," Rhiannon breathed.

A knock on the door brought their conversation to a halt, and Mike opened it and poked his head in.

"Sorry Dad, we didn't realise how late it was, we were just finishing up," Rhiannon said. "I'll be in bed soon."

Mike laughed. "I'm pretty sure you're both old enough to work out what time you need to get to sleep. I just wanted to say hi, and wish you a good night, because I know *I* have to get to bed."

Carlie smiled hello to Mike, said goodbye to Rhiannon, then made her way home through the crisp darkness. It was time for her to snuggle up with Luna and get some sleep too.

Chapter 36

Another Sad Farewell

As the days grew a little longer and got a little warmer, Carlie continued to get up before dawn and go walking. It was so peaceful, so gentle, so soul soothing, to watch the world wake up and see the sky slowly colour pink-gold-lavender-blue. It calmed her, being out in nature, wandering down winding country laneways, marvelling at the simple beauty of honeysuckle blossoms, smiling at the birds she saw and wondering if one of them was Jake's friend. Sometimes she'd climb the tor, when her legs were willing, and one Saturday morning she found herself down by the stream at the place she still thought of as hers and Rowan's.

Sitting with her back against the willow tree, now so much more green and lush than when she'd been there last, in the harsh chill of winter, she laughed as she watched the ducklings dipping down into the water, little bottoms wiggling as they tried to right themselves. Then sadness engulfed her as she realised that Rowan was no longer with her, not even here, in their special place.

Yet she also felt a sense of peace and acceptance as she realised that he was in her heart, not outside of her. As long as she remembered him he would live on, and be part of her. Casting one last look around her, she slowly got to her feet, took a deep breath, then released the bunch of wildflowers she'd picked into the water.

She stood watching them until they disappeared around a bend in the stream, then began the lonely wander back home.

As she walked, she started thinking about Rowan's mother, and feeling guilty that she hadn't gone to visit her as she'd vowed that she would. But when she turned in at her gate, she was shocked to find his mum sitting on the front steps of the cottage, as though she'd conjured her into being with the power of her imagining.

"Mrs Dunbar! Hello. I was just thinking about you," she stammered. "Are you okay?"

The elegantly dressed woman stood up and hugged Carlie. "Please, it's Louisa," she said. "And I've been thinking of you too. How are you going?"

As she sat back down on the step, Carlie sank down next to her and smiled bravely, conscious of how much harder Rowan's loss must be for his mum. "I'm all right," she said softly. "I miss him constantly, but Rose has been wonderful, and so patient, and I'm getting through the days." She wondered that she'd listed patience as a major virtue, but dismissed the thought and focused on Rowan's mum.

"I'm doing okay too," Louisa said with a sad smile. "One day at a time, right?"

Carlie nodded, her heart breaking for the grieving mum.

"I wanted to come over and see you though, because I'm moving up to Scotland next week to live with my sister for a while – her daughter has just moved out, so she's feeling lonely too. So I wanted to say goodbye to you, and thank you for loving Rowan so much, and making him so happy. And, well, I was packing up his apartment, and I thought you might like a few of his things," she said, indicating a wonderful old wooden trunk she must have hauled onto the verandah earlier, which Luna was pacing around suspiciously.

"Oh my gosh, thank you!" Carlie replied, truly touched. "But are you sure? Maybe you should keep them?"

Louisa smiled, sadness and defeat warring with strength in her expression, and her posture. "No, I have lots of things to remember him by. And these might be useful to you – there are lots of his magical books, and some of his ritual tools too."

Carlie hugged her tight, tears welling in her eyes. "Thank you so much. I really appreciate it, and I would be honoured to be their keeper," she replied.

His mother smiled a little. There wasn't much joy in it though, it was like the echo of a smile from long ago, a ghost of something that no longer existed. "I know this sounds kind of weird, but Rowan mentioned to me not long before he died that if anything happened to him, he wanted you to have these," Louisa said, her voice a sigh.

Carlie recoiled in horror at her words. "You mean he knew that he was going to die?" she asked.

"I don't know," his mum admitted. "I'm not sure if it was a premonition, or if he just loved you so deeply, and was telling me this to make sure that I knew how much. But… oh, and this will sound strange, but I saw him a few times, after he died," she said.

"Once when I was walking through the park near his place, another time in a small bookstore in Smithfield that he liked, and then in his apartment, a few weeks ago, while I was sorting through his things. And you'll probably think I'm crazy when I tell you this, but the last time I saw him he spoke to me, and it was like he was there with me, talking to me, holding me while I cried. It was he who suggested that I move back to Scotland to spend some time with my sister. And he reassured me that he would still be with me no matter where I lived, but that I had to start picking up the pieces and moving forward with my life."

Taking a deep breath, she tried to hold her emotions in check before continuing. "But that was the last time I saw him, or heard him, and I hate that he's gone. It probably sounds selfish, because I'm sure he has somewhere better to be now, and I have to learn to go on without him, but I miss that, even if it wasn't real."

Carlie smiled sadly. "I saw him too," she whispered. "In a cottage that doesn't really exist. And he held me as I cried, and told me I had to be strong because I would help a lot of people. I'd already decided that I want to be a grief counsellor, but now I'm even more driven.

"And he was with me when I was getting my tattoo," she added, glancing down at her wrist. "Speaking to me, telling me he still loved me. But I don't sense him around me any more either – I haven't seen him or heard him for a few weeks, which makes me really sad. He said I had to let him go and start moving forward too," she admitted. "But I don't want to. How can it be selfish for us to want him to stick around?"

Louisa leaned across and hugged her, and for a moment they sat like that, tears mingling, sharing their grief and finding some solace in being able to talk about the man they'd both loved so much. "Maybe he feels that it's selfish of him to stick around, and keep us from living our lives," she said gently. "Especially you Carlie, you have your whole life ahead of you, and I hope it will be a life filled with love and joy."

Carlie shook her head, not wanting to think of that. "I'll never forget him," she said fiercely. "He changed me, in so many positive ways. I'm a better person now for having known him."

His mother smiled through her tears. "Thank you for telling me that. It helps me, to know that he did so much good while he was here. That he may not have been with us for a long time, but that he made a difference, however small."

They sat in silence for a long time, lost in their memories, bound by their grief yet both feeling terribly alone. Finally Louisa said she should go, just as Carlie asked her if she'd like a cup of tea. Rowan's mum smiled at her, so like her son, but shook her head.

"Thank you, but I should be getting back, I've still got lots of packing to do. I'd like to give you my new address though, if that's okay, in case you ever want to talk to me?" Her voice trailed off anxiously, and Carlie's heart broke all over again as she saw the pain etched deep into every line of her face, in the way she sat and even the way she held herself.

"I'd like that, thank you," she whispered, and reached out to take the piece of paper with the black ink scrawled across it.

Awkwardly the grieving mother clambered to her feet, and started to walk down the front path to the street. But just before she reached it, she turned back to the young girl, who'd sunk down onto the top step again, weighed down by her own pain. "And Carlie, please, don't put your life on hold," Louisa said. "You're young, and you deserve to find love again. Please don't feel guilty to live your life."

Carlie shrugged, and gazed down at her hands, clasped so tightly together in her lap to stop her reaching out for his mother. As she heard the gate open though, she called out. "Wait."

Louisa turned back to her. "I've been meaning to tell you..." Carlie began, then paused. Would this be a good thing to share with her, or would it just compound her pain?

"Please don't feel bad about my mum," she finally said, voice cracked with pain. "Rowan told me you were worried his dad had hurt her, or worse. And he did, but she survived. She got away, and found her beloved, and had a wonderful life. She wouldn't have met Dad if she didn't go through everything she did. So please, don't feel responsible in any way, or bad for her. You did nothing wrong."

Louisa's face collapsed in on itself, and as tears spilled down her face, she stumbled back along the pathway and pulled Carlie close to her, squeezing her until she could barely breathe.

"Oh Carlie, thank you," she whispered, her voice croaky, and seemingly ripped from somewhere deep and broken within her. "You can't imagine how heavily that has weighed on me."

Taking a deep breath, she slowly let go of her, and a fleeting sense of peace flickered across Louisa's face before the sadness returned. "You have no idea what a gift you have given me. Two gifts now, because I'll always be so grateful that Rowan met you."

Wiping her eyes, she backed slowly away down the path to the street. "Be well Carlie," she called out. "And let yourself be loved, please." Then she hurried into her car and drove away.

When Rose came home later that day, Carlie was still sitting on the front step, frozen there, Luna curled up in her lap. Her grandmother sank down next to her and put an arm around her shoulder. "Are you okay Sweetheart?" she asked tentatively.

"I will be," Carlie finally said. Rose nodded, then her gaze alighted on the trunk, and she stared at it, a question in her eyes.

A small smile flitted across Carlie's face. "Rowan's mum came over to say goodbye, because she's moving up to Scotland to live with her sister, and she wanted to leave me some of Rowan's books." Suddenly determined, she stood up and dragged the chest inside, then slowly and clumsily lugged it up the stairs to her room.

Chapter 37

Hanging On, Letting Go

Carlie spent the rest of the day sitting cross-legged on the floor, Luna nestled against her, slowly looking through the old trunk at all its treasures. There were beautiful books on spirituality and magic – some shamanic, some druidic, some from a witchcraft perspective – and others on different forms of divination and healing, including an amazing herbal encyclopaedia. Some seemed almost new, while others had been thumbed through many times, and it was these ones that she sat with for the longest time, flipping through the pages and reading random passages, tracing over Rowan's handwritten notes in the margins, running her hand over the precious pages that had meant so much to him. She could picture him sitting in his old apartment, poring over these books, reading by candlelight, dreaming up magic and rituals, and absorbing the information and adding it to his own personal experiences and hard-won knowledge. The world had lost a remarkable wisdom keeper when he died.

Excited by this amazing beginning to her magical library, Carlie finally hauled all of the books over to her mother's old bookshelf and arranged them by subject, spending a lot of time holding each book and considering where to put it, wanting to keep these gems that had been Rowan's physically close to her heart before she placed them in their new position.

Hearing Luna miaow as she balanced on the side of the trunk, Carlie walked back over and peered inside. Underneath where the books had been stored was a smaller chest, which she gently lifted out. Inside were several velvet-wrapped packages, which she carefully opened to reveal a host of beautiful ritual tools. There was an elaborate silver chalice, a shallow scrying bowl, a wand made from willow and tipped with a moonstone, and an athame that brought tears to her eyes as she lifted it, because it flooded her with memories of the new moon ritual she'd done with Rowan.

There was also a white-handled boline for inscribing candles and cutting herbs, gorgeous silver and gold statues of gods and goddesses, a pretty brass incense censer, and two smaller wands. And when she finally lifted the last of the tools out, she found the most precious and intimate thing of all – Rowan's personal Book of Shadows. It was even thicker than the herbal encyclopaedia, the cover crafted from weathered timber carved with Celtic knotwork and intricate spirals, and bound together with silver metalwork. The pages within were parchment-thick and covered in his beautiful handwriting, interspersed with his delicate illustrations of herbs and flowers, some of which he'd included in his herbal oracle deck.

A shiver ran down her spine when she saw the tansy plant, which was on the card she'd received in his seminar at the Body Mind Spirit Festival. Magically tansy was associated with the dead, and used in rites of death and rebirth, and she felt the same chill now that she'd felt that day. Rhiannon had told her that the plant symbolised rebirth of the self, but she shuddered as she gazed at the image. She didn't want any more rebirth, any more change, any more loss, any more grieving. Surely enough was enough.

She smiled though as she remembered that day when she'd first met Rowan. Rhiannon had insisted she get a spirit guide painting done by him, and she'd somehow ended up spilling out her story of losing her parents to him while he painted. And he'd held her as she cried, then told her to be patient with herself and allow as much time as she needed to heal and start to move forward. To not feel any pressure to stop grieving, or to keep grieving either.

Clutching his Book of Shadows to her chest, she closed her eyes and allowed herself to wallow in her memories, and to recall every moment of that magical day. The protection charm Rowan had cast so that no one at the festival even saw them as he painted her, the comfort she'd felt when he held her as she cried, when normally she would have been terrified that a stranger was touching her. His sweet insistence that they'd shared many past lives together, including one as King Arthur and the priestess Morgaine, lovers throughout time – which admittedly she'd rolled her eyes at, and was still unconvinced by, lovely though the thought was.

And then the party that night, which Rhiannon had insisted they go to no matter how hard she'd tried to say no, where Rowan had stayed by her side all evening, talking to her, making her laugh, and ignoring all the other people there who she'd been sure were far more interesting than her.

At seven o'clock Rose knocked on her bedroom door to tell her that dinner was ready, and they ate chilli bean tacos together and caught up on their days. Carlie's mind was upstairs for much of it though, floating around in the old trunk, reliving the memories held in Rowan's drawings and his words. But she snapped back to the present when her grandmother nervously told her that she'd spent the afternoon with Richard, and she finally noticed her shining eyes and the smile that was lighting up her face.

"I just wanted to thank you Sweetheart, for forcing me to face my fears and finally realise that I'd been sabotaging my chances for love. All those wasted years," Rose sighed. Then she brightened. "I can't quite believe how happy I've been since Richard and I started... well, spending time together," she said, then laughed.

"The concept of dating just sounds too bizarre at our age. And I wouldn't know how to do it anyway – the last time I went out on a date was more than forty years ago. Your grandfather was the first man I ever went out with, and I was married to him for more than two decades. And since then... well, I've barely spoken to a man, besides Mike," she admitted. "How strange that I didn't even notice."

Carlie beamed at her. "I'm so glad," she said, and she meant it. Mostly for her grandma's sake, since she absolutely deserved to love and be loved, but also because it had terrified her when she'd realised that after Rose's husband had died, she'd pushed any chance of a relationship away, had denied herself any possibility of love. It was what she'd felt like doing when Rowan died too, but when she'd pictured her life playing out like her grandmother's, it had seemed too lonely and bleak to contemplate.

"Thank you Sweetheart. It means so much to both of us to have your blessing, and Jake's too," Rose replied, face filled with love and joy. "Richard is telling him tonight as well."

Carlie peered at her, puzzled. "Telling him what?"

Her grandmother blushed. "Well, we're both too old for the dating scene, and for the casual entanglements people seem to have these days. So we've decided that we want to make it official in some way, and we thought we'd let people know next weekend at Beltane. Tom will be down from London for the ritual..."

"And Beltane is the time for making commitments, and leaping the fires with your beloved!" Carlie finished for her, excitement in her voice. "What are you going to do?"

"Well, we thought maybe Elsie could come down and do a little handfasting ceremony as part of the ritual," Rose said, her voice trembling with nerves. "But we wanted to tell you and Jake first, and see if you were okay with it before we asked her."

Jumping up, Carlie went around the table to hug her grandmother. "Of course we're okay with it! We've been wondering for a little while now, when you were going to tell us. Jake will be as overjoyed as I am. We couldn't think of two better people to find each other, or who deserve happiness more. Ooh, I'm so thrilled for you Gran!"

"You already knew?" Rose asked, half relieved, half anxious.

"Well, not for sure, but we've had our suspicions for a while," she replied, giggling. "Shall we have tea to toast the good news?"

"Actually, I baked a honey cake this afternoon, and picked up some sparkling apple juice, just in case we wanted to celebrate a bit," Rose said, sounding uncharacteristically shy again.

Hurrying over to the pantry, Carlie found the freshly-baked cake sitting covered on a shelf, still warm from the oven, so she grabbed some plates and a knife and took it over to the table, then found two pretty wine glasses at the back of the cupboard and brought over the pitcher of juice from the fridge.

Pouring out two glasses as Rose cut the cake, Carlie handed one to her grandmother then raised hers in the air. "To you Gran," she said, eyes alight with joy. "I'm so happy that you've found love, and I wish you both many years of precious moments together."

"Thank you Sweetheart. It wouldn't have happened without you," she responded, handing her a piece of the warm honey cake. "And it was the same for Richard, with Jake. He was feeling guilty about spending time with me, but Jake let him know that he deserved a chance to be happy, and even pushed him a little in my direction. He's a wonderful boy," Rose said.

"Yeah, he is," Carlie agreed, then turned the subject back to Richard and what he was like, and what the happy couple was hoping for the future. Hours later, when Rose had gone to bed and she figured she probably should too, Carlie was running her hand over Rowan's ritual tools, which she'd placed back in the small leather chest. Suddenly she had a memory of another box, another time.

Carefully she lifted Luna from her lap and lay her on the bed, where the kitten squeaked out a tiny miaow then drifted back to sleep, then she opened her bedroom door and tiptoed down the stairs to the little room she used to sleep in. Switching on the light, she walked the few steps to the wardrobe and reached carefully inside, to the back of the top shelf. When her fingers hit something, wedged right in the corner, she clumsily drew it towards her.

It was the package her mum's friend Sandy had sent her last year, which had contained the diary that had taught Carlie so much about both of her parents, and about herself as well. At the time she had been so distracted by the journal that she'd forgotten to look at the other items.

Creeping quietly back up to her room, she sat cross-legged on her bed and opened the parcel. There was a bundle of what looked like clothes, which she unfolded carefully – then she smiled when she saw the small, faded white teddy bear in the middle, with a blue ribbon around his neck. Cuddling him for a moment, she tried to imagine her mother holding him. Had it been Violet's, or was it her own, from when she was a kid? She couldn't recollect a teddy bear though, and she remembered other stuffed toys – a sweet giraffe, a fuzzy lion, an adorable elephant, a cute little monkey. The bear must have been her mother's, which made it all the more precious to her. Gently she placed it on her pillow, next to Luna, and the little kitten snuggled up against it, without even opening her eyes.

Lifting up a bright red dress next, she held it against herself, amazed at the style. She couldn't recall her mum ever wearing it, but it was beautiful, soft and warm and brightly coloured, so unlike the rest of Violet's Sydney wardrobe of lawyerly suits in neutral tones.

Next she ran her hands over a deep purple velvet gown, like something her grandmother would sell in her shop, and wear at a ritual. She couldn't remember her mum wearing that one either, but maybe she'd bought it to remind herself of the beauty of her life with her parents, and the magic she'd woven with Rose.

As she unfolded the dress to better see its pretty jagged hem and lacy edges, a small box fell out of a pocket, and she picked it up and opened it. Inside were four rings. The first two were her mum's wedding and engagement rings, two pretty, delicate, rose-gold rings, the wedding band studded with tiny diamonds and etched with swirls, while the other featured three coloured stones – a ruby in the centre, flanked on each side by teardrop sapphires, one green and one blue.

Her dad's rose gold wedding band was there too, engraved with ivy leaves on the outside, and with the words *Lives entwined, souls in harmony, hearts as one* inscribed on the inside. Just like on the ring Rowan had given her. She couldn't quite get her head around that coincidence, so she picked up the fourth ring instead, deeply curious.

It was beautiful, with a large heart-shaped rose quartz set in a raised strip of silver entwined with ivy leaves, hearts and butterflies. Carlie had never seen her mum wear it, and there was no note to say whose it was or why she'd had it. But it looked like the wedding ring you'd choose if you were being handfasted in a Beltane rite. It would be so perfect for Rose, and she wondered if she should offer it to Richard for the ceremony.

Then she gasped, as she picked up a pretty pale green dress, the skirt full with layers of tulle, lace and satin, and embroidered with ivy leaves. It was her mum's wedding dress, but she'd only ever seen it in black and white photos, so she'd assumed it was white, and somehow the ivy leaves hadn't been captured on film. It was really beautiful. And so magical. So witchy. So her-mum's-life-in-Summer-Hill-not-Sydney. So Beltane. Again she felt sad, as though she hadn't known her mother at all, or she'd only known one small side of her, while the rest had been totally hidden. As she turned the dress over, a little note unfurled from within it and landed on the bed.

Dear Mum,
I don't know if I'll ever see you again, and that thought breaks my heart. But you were with me in spirit as I sewed together my wedding dress (oh how I wish I'd had your help with it – you were always so much better than me at this!). And you were with me too while I dreamed it up, adding ivy leaves to represent our rituals, and making it green for Beltane, which is when I married my beloved.
You are with me always, and I hope you know that I have always loved you, and always will.
Your loving daughter, Violet xx

A Beltane dress for a Beltane bride. And a week from today, Rose would have her handfasting and be a Beltane bride too. The wheel of the year turning, the wheel of life turning. Sadness and joy. Love and grief. Hope and despair. The many shades of a life. The thought inspired Carlie as much as it depressed her, and she finally switched out the light and climbed into bed beside Luna and the teddy bear, drifting off into a dream where the scent of flowers drenched everything, and all she could recall of it the next day was jasmine blooms and ivy leaves.

Chapter 38

Blossoming Into Love

On Monday morning, Jake came running up to the girls as soon as they climbed the front steps at school, eyes sparkling with excitement. "Oh my god, can you believe it? Isn't it amazing!" he cried, then stared at Rhiannon in panic. "Oh, um, can we talk about it yet?" he asked quietly, turning to Carlie.

Relief washed over him as Carlie giggled, then nodded. "It's okay, Gran said we can share the news with Rhi. I was just waiting for you so we could be together when we spilled the beans," she said with a grin. "I think Gran knew it would torture us to have to try to keep it a secret from her."

"Guys, I'm right here! What is it?" Rhiannon begged, impatience and curiosity burning in her.

Jake smiled at Carlie. "Do you want to –"

"Oh god, someone tell me," Rhiannon shrieked.

Carlie laughed. "Sorry, it's just... well, you know how Beltane is all about –"

"Carlie, get to the point! Jake, what is it?" Rhiannon demanded.

"Rose and Pop are having a handfasting ceremony next weekend, at the Beltane ritual," he blurted out.

Rhiannon squealed and grabbed Carlie's hands. "Oh my god, that's so beautiful! How long have you known?"

"They told us both on Saturday night, but you were off with Tom yesterday and we couldn't find you to share the news," Jake replied. "Carlie wanted to tell you straight away, don't worry. But isn't it sweet? They're so cute together."

The bell for class rang, interrupting their excited recounting of the news, and Jake rushed off to his with a cheerful wave.

"And they want us to help during the ritual, if you want to," Carlie said, as the two girls walked down the hall together. "And Tom too, obviously. It's like we'll all be related in some way!"

"Oh Carlie, I'd be honoured," Rhiannon grinned. "How beautiful, after so much sadness. And Rose has given so much to everyone here, since way before I was born, so the whole village will be really thrilled that she's found some happiness."

"I hope so," Carlie said. "She is definitely due some joy."

The following night Rhiannon skipped over to Carlie's for dinner and their magical meeting. Their coven time was spent learning more about Beltane, the sabbat that marks the beginning of summer, from their wise priestess. Then they excitedly helped Rose plan her handfasting ritual, everything from the flowers they'd use in the ceremony to the food they'd prepare for the feast afterwards.

On Saturday morning, Beltane Eve, Carlie and Rhiannon got up early to gather pretty white blossoms from the sacred hawthorn tree, which was associated with the sabbat and used for love spells and in marriage rituals, as well as for protection and healing. And that evening they wove them together with jasmine flowers, white rose buds, violets and meadowsweet, making a handfasting wreath for Rose's hair. They spoke the words of a spell as they worked, infusing it with love and blessings.

Quickly they wove their own smaller floral wreaths too, then started on the food. A beautiful passionfruit cake in the shape of a heart, topped with cream cheese icing and crystallised violets. Rose petal biscuits, strawberry and dandelion salad, stuffed zucchini flowers, honey joys, scones with lavender jam, and mead infused with woodruff and other summery herbs.

Chapter 39

A New Beginning

Just before dawn on Beltane morning, Carlie woke to the sound of Luna's contented purring as the kitten snuggled up against her on her pillow. This afternoon she'd be helping Rose get ready for her handfasting ceremony with Richard, and her heart flooded with joy at the thought. If anyone deserved happiness after a life of tragedy interspersed with unconditional and constant giving, it was her grandmother. While most people only saw the strong and capable priestess, Carlie knew how fragile Rose could be — although she hid it well, even from herself — and how deeply sad and lonely she'd been for much of the last two decades. Her life had had purpose and meaning, and she'd created a circle of dear goddess-loving friends, but she'd walled up her heart and denied herself any chance of love.

Patting Luna, Carlie smiled at the adorable kitten. She still missed Luther dreadfully, but she was so grateful that he'd brought Luna to her and Rose. Slowly she sat up, took a few deep breaths, then dragged herself out of bed. Getting up in the dark hadn't become any easier, but the pay-off was always worth it. Slipping into her long green velvet dress, she laced up her mother's warm boots, because dawn up on the tor was still chilly, even on the first day of summer.

Tiptoeing downstairs, she grabbed an apple and slipped out the back door, stifling a laugh as Luna sat indignantly on the kitchen step and watched her creep out the back gate. Unlike Luther, the fuzzy little kitten was no fan of wet grass or early morning wanderings.

The tiniest wash of light was starting to fan out along the horizon as she began to climb the hill. It was still a while before the sun would rise, but the world was slowly awakening. Mist danced around the summit as well as the lower slopes, and Carlie felt it reaching out cool fingers, like ice-cold kisses, to touch her face, and swirling around her legs. Then, as she reached the top, her breath caught.

Someone, or some thing, was emerging from the mists. Clad in a gold robe, she seemed more real, more flesh and blood, than the other beings she'd encountered, her whole demeanour sweet and light in comparison to Aideen's strength and power, Brianna's occasional surliness and Brauna's heavy comfort.

Staring at her, mesmerised, Carlie wondered how to react. What were you supposed to do with these Otherworldly beings? Should she wait for the woman to address her, or greet her first?

The gold-clad figure smiled at her. "There are no rules beloved, and no need to stand on ceremony with me."

Relief flooded her, even as one part of her brain noticed that the woman was speaking to her without moving her lips. "It's just that Aideen and Brianna were a bit annoyed with me at times," she admitted. "I'd hate to unknowingly offend you."

Suddenly she was wrapped in the being's arms, warmth and comfort coursing through her. It was unnerving though, like a vampire standing at a distance, then in a split second enfolding you in a loving yet lethal embrace. The woman laughed, a sweet, tinkling laugh, and Carlie blushed. *Another freakin' mind reader.*

"Have no fear, you have not offended any of us. We are all so very proud of you, and impressed with how you have handled all the loss you have had to endure, and how much you have grown. As a granddaughter, as a friend, as a student. As a witch."

Shock left Carlie speechless for a moment. A witch? Was she? And more importantly, did she even want to be?

The woman of mist smiled at her. "It is nothing to be scared of Carlie. You have worked hard, you have read widely, you have practised. You have spent time in nature, and attuned yourself to the energy of the moon and sun and seasons, to the magic of the earth. You have suffered much, yet you chose to become more compassionate, where others choose the path of bitterness and revenge."

Carlie gazed into her eyes, shy all of a sudden, and feeling inadequate. A fraud. "But I'm not like Gran. I'm not sure I believe in the goddess the way she does," she whispered.

"But you are on a journey to discover what is true to *you* Carlie. You are on a quest both within and without, seeking knowledge and understanding, learning rituals and forging the confidence to change them to suit you. And you have opened your heart and your mind to experiences that would have made some people unravel, applying logic as well as intuition, and managing to marry the two without conflict," she explained.

"Most importantly, you hold nature as sacred and want to work in the healing arts, to aid people physically and emotionally. You spoke to Samantha – what could be more magical, more witchy, than protecting the earth and helping people to heal?"

Carlie smiled. Wasn't that what everyone wanted to do? Were there actually people who actively *didn't* want to protect the environment or help others?

"You would be surprised," her companion said sadly, then flinched as from somewhere far away a dog barked, and the sky lightened imperceptibly in the east. The gold-clad woman pulled her robes more tightly around herself. "I have something for you for Rose," she said, and handed over a gold-velvet-wrapped parcel. "But my gift for you is less tangible. Do you know who I am?" she asked.

"I'm guessing that you're the woman in yellow, or maybe gold. And friend to Brauna, Brianna and Aideen, which would make you the symbol of air?" she replied softly, nervously, questioningly.

"Very good," the figure of mist said, and although her words could have sounded patronising coming from someone else, somehow they didn't when they were delivered in her sweet and gentle manner. "My name is Liana. And what does air bring?"

Carlie smiled wryly. "Is this a test?"

Shrugging delicately, the woman in gold returned her smile. "There is no pass or fail, if that is what you are alluding to."

As she laughed, Carlie felt the first rays of the sun spilling over the horizon, illuminating her face and piercing through the mantle of mist of the being before her. Slowly she sank down onto the wet grass, overwhelmed, and Liana sank with her.

"Air represents thought, intellect, communication, clarity and truth," Carlie offered, voice barely a whisper as she rattled off the traits she'd learned through her studies. "It's about the dawning of a new day – moving forward, letting go of regrets and starting again, free of preconceptions and limitations. It heralds fresh starts and new beginnings, and the world and your life born anew."

The woman smiled proudly as she nodded. "Now listen carefully," she said, her voice urgent now. "Your gift is a new beginning, the opportunity for new love, but you have to open your heart and allow it in – it is not something we can hand to you in a gift-wrapped box. You have to decide whether you will take the risk or not. You have to choose to dive in, or not, and sink or swim from there."

Tears welled in Carlie's eyes, but didn't fall. "You mean Jake?"

"I mean anyone who will make you happy," Liana replied softly. "Jake cares about you, and he is patient and kind and compassionate. But you will have to let him know if you want to be more than friends, because he vowed to give you space, and he will honour that. He respects you too much to push you, which could work against him. However, if you are not ready now, if you lack the courage, I am sure there will be other opportunities for love in your future."

Surprising herself, Carlie realised that the thought of waiting into the undetermined future was making her feel a little panicky. She didn't want to wait, like her grandmother had, and end up resentful and lonely. She didn't want to miss the chance that she had.

"It is up to you now," the mist-shrouded being continued softly. "You can use Rowan as an excuse to cut yourself off from everyone, or not. Today you stand on the precipice of a new beginning, but you have to decide whether to grasp it yourself, or end up like your grandmother and spend a lifetime denying yourself joy. You have already recognised the futility of her sacrifice – and helped her to see it too, as evidenced by her happy occasion today – so I am hoping that you will not turn your back on the chance of happiness that stands before *you*," she said with a warm smile.

"Your life is yours, and it will be the sum total of all the choices you make, or do not make. Never think that avoiding something delays your decision. Not choosing one path because you are scared means you have chosen the other path by default. Inaction is an action, it is a choice, it is simply a lazy one."

"I just don't want to hurt Jake, I care about him too much," Carlie whispered, voice tortured. "And what if I say yes, then change my mind? Or he realises that he doesn't actually like me like that after all? I couldn't bear to disappoint him."

"Then you will deal with it then. You are not responsible for Jake's happiness, or anyone else's. But not giving him the chance – not giving yourself the chance – just in case it does not work, is not fair to him or to you. Refusing to open your heart in case you hurt someone just ensures pain. Did that work out for Rose?" Liana demanded.

"No," Carlie reluctantly conceded.

"Do you wish that you had never met Rowan, so that you could have avoided experiencing the agony of his loss?"

"Of course not!" she snapped.

"Well then," the woman in gold said with a triumphant smile, and Carlie almost laughed at the expression on her face. "Besides, it is not up to you to decide for Jake. He has free will, and he has the right to choose for himself. He is stronger than you give him credit for."

"I know," Carlie mused. She thought of all the time they'd spent together. How kind he was, how patient with her, how selfless he'd been to lock away his feelings for her so she wouldn't feel pressured. And slowly it dawned on her, that it was joy she was feeling as she thought of him, and a warmth and comfort she really liked.

And was that an undercurrent of *excitement* she felt as she opened her mind to the idea of being with Jake? Her friend Jake. Her strong Aussie mate, who let her cry on his shoulder, and who understood her sense of humour, her culture and her past. Who let her talk about Rowan even when it hurt him, and was there for her while Rhiannon was neglecting her as she fell in love with Tom.

Sweet, dependable Jake, who she obviously cared for far more than she'd admitted to herself. It wasn't the wild and dramatic passion she'd experienced with Rowan, but she was starting to realise that she didn't want that right now. She wanted slow and sweet. Companionship and sensitivity. Compassion rather than drama. Simple, uncomplicated joy. And just being, rather than becoming.

As the sun rose above the horizon, she closed her eyes against the glare, and when she opened them again she felt as though she was seeing everything in a totally new way, the whole world washed clean and born anew. Her heart born anew.

Eyes dazzled by the rising sun, she turned to tell all of this to Liana, but wasn't especially surprised to discover that the gold-clad woman had slipped away as the swirling mists dispersed. She was alone on the hill now, alone with her thoughts, and her decision.

Her decision of whether or not to take this precious opportunity for love. To treasure it, and to be brave enough to put her heart on the line for the chance. Of course Jake might have gotten over her by now, might have found someone else – Rhiannon had mentioned recently that he'd been spending a bit of time with Abby, who was in the school play with him. But she owed it to herself, and to him, to let him know how she felt.

As she wandered dreamily back down the hill, she started to laugh. She was realising that her liking Jake wasn't new, wasn't really a shock, and she wondered when her feelings for him had changed from school friend to something more. When he'd smiled across the room at her at the Imbolc ritual, his aura all lit up and golden? When he'd spent so much time helping her prepare for their presentation, because the thought of speaking in front of the class terrified her? Or was it when he'd been so kind and attentive to her at the London festival, as she'd battled the ghosts? Or at the ritual that night, after Rhiannon had ditched her for Tom?

Her pace increased, and within minutes she was knocking furiously on Rhiannon's door. Her friend ushered her inside, listening impatiently as she tried to explain what she was suddenly feeling, as she tried herself to understand what had happened to her, and when.

Smiling her knowing smile, Rhiannon led her upstairs to her bedroom. "It's about time," she grinned. "I'm not sure how much longer he would have waited."

Carlie felt suddenly panicked. "Am I too late?"

Rhiannon shook her head. "I don't think so, he doesn't seem the fickle type, but I wouldn't risk leaving it too much longer."

"But do I really like him? And can I do this? And should I? I mean, what if I hurt him? I'd never forgive myself," she sighed.

"Oh Carlie, you're hurting him by not giving him a chance. No one knows what will happen – hell, Tom and I could break up next week – but you can't live like that, you can't tiptoe through life in the shadows, too afraid to try anything just in case it won't work out, just in case it will hurt. You taught me that," Rhiannon insisted.

"Life is pain, yet it's also incredible joy. But you need to move out of your comfort zone, you need to take a risk sometimes, stop protecting your heart out of fear, in order to feel the joy."

Carlie laughed. That's what she'd told Rose too. "But is it too soon?" she asked. "What will people think? Does this make me fickle?"

"Oh hon, it's not too soon, I promise. You've been holding on to Rowan for a long time, longer even than you were with him. And besides, letting Jake in doesn't mean that you're turning your back on Rowan. He'll always be part of you. He'll always be your first relationship, your first love, that will never change. And he helped you grow and blossom and become who you are today – someone who can open her heart to love," Rhiannon said gently.

"But he's not here any more, and you can't spend the rest of your life wishing that he was. You deserve to be happy, more than anyone I know you deserve to be happy. And so does Jake."

Carlie smiled, a genuine, joy-filled smile. "Thank you Rhi. I'm sorry I'm such hard work."

Her friend hugged her. "You're not hard work at all, silly. But what made you finally realise how you felt about Jake?" she asked. Then she laughed. "No, don't tell me – you met the yellow-clad woman. There's gotta be four of them, am I right? Is that from her?"

she grinned, looking down at the gold-velvet-wrapped parcel Carlie still clutched in her hand.

Smiling, Carlie nodded. "Yes, I met Liana, the woman in gold, the being of light and air and new beginnings," she admitted. "But this is for Rose, not me. My gift, she said, was the gift of new beginnings, but she told me that I have to go out and make it happen myself, I have to take the risk... I'm not sure that I can though," she added, suddenly terrified all over again.

Rhiannon took her hands. "This is Jake we're talking about, your friend Jake, your study buddy, your thank-god-you're-here-too, I'll-throw-up-if-I-have-to-watch-Rhiannon-and-Tom-kiss-each-other-again partner-in-crime. There's no reason to feel nervous about talking to him," she assured her.

"I guess you're right," Carlie sighed. "But that reminds me, has Tom arrived yet? And do you think he brought his equipment?"

Rhiannon gazed at her quizzically. "Yep, he got here this morning, although he's been round at Jake's, seeing his grandad. And I imagine he brought his stuff – he never goes anywhere without it. But you can ask him yourself, he'll be here any minute."

The sound of knocking interrupted them, and they rushed downstairs to open the door. Tom stood there, a bag over his shoulder, a bemused expression on his face. "What's going on?" he asked, as he embraced his girlfriend then peered curiously at Carlie.

"Come in, come in," Rhiannon said, dragging him inside. "I think Carlie wants another tattoo. And to kiss your cousin," she added cheekily, then raced up the stairs, the other two in hot pursuit.

Chapter 40

Into the Light

Two hours later, after a brief stop at Richard's, Carlie was back at home and pulling her mum's pale green wedding dress over her head. It seemed fitting that she'd wear it to her grandmother's handfasting, so that Violet could be there, in spirit at least. "Oh Mum, I really wish you were here," she sighed. "Today would be even more magical if you and Dad could take part too."

Hearing a sound at the door, she spun around guiltily, and blushed when she saw that it was Rose.

"You look beautiful Sweetheart," said her grandma, who was smiling even as a tear trickled down her cheek.

"So do you Gran. You're glowing, and the dress is divine." It was soft and floaty, with layers of fine lace and tulle, and crafted from the palest gold material, which made Carlie think of Liana. "You look like an angel, or a sunshine faery," she said, wonder in her voice.

Spinning in a circle, the hem held up in one hand, Rose laughed, enjoying the feel of the fabric swirling around her. "I kind of feel like a faery," she grinned. "Now I'll just grab some flowers from the garden for my hair and I'll be ready," she said, turning to walk back down the stairs.

"Wait!" Carlie called out, and Rose halted.

"What is it?" she asked, concern in her voice.

"Nothing's wrong, but Rhi and I already did the flowers – we made you a wreath of hawthorn blossoms, jasmine, violets and roses for your hair, and did your bouquet too, and ours to match. They're all in the kitchen. But I have something for you," she added, and handed over the gold-velvet-wrapped parcel.

The priestess's eyes widened. "You met Liana," she breathed.

"You know her?" Carlie asked, surprised.

Rose nodded. "I met her on the eve of my wedding to Louis," she explained. "It was my first experience of magic, so it took me a while to understand how special the encounter was." She sank onto Carlie's bed, holding the package carefully.

"I'd gone for a walk around the base of the tor, the night before the ceremony. I needed to escape my house, and escape my family. My parents were deeply religious, and my mother had been lecturing me all day on the duties of a bride and a wife, and I needed a moment to myself, a moment of peace, to be sure that this marriage was what *I* wanted, and not just *her* plan."

Laughing as she saw the shock on Carlie's face, she quickly continued. "It *was* what I wanted, don't worry, but it took me finding that moment of stillness to really appreciate Louis, and what our life could be. After walking for a while, I sat down under a tree and closed my eyes to look within – and when I opened them she was perched right next to me, this mist-shrouded figure, so still, so mysterious. I panicked, of course, but she took my hand, and I felt this incredible peace and comfort, and I forgot to be scared of her," Rose revealed.

"And as she gazed into my eyes she showed me how beautiful our life would be. I saw Violet, and an image of me and Louis, older but still so happy, and the absence of the stress of my parents. And she was right, thank goddess. My father was offered an overseas post the next day, and they moved to America soon after, which was wonderful. My mother was cruel, a real monster, which made it even harder for me, that you thought *I* was a monster."

"I'm so sorry," Carlie said, voice dripping with pain and regret.

"Oh Sweetheart, you didn't know. And we got through it. But Liana gave me a necklace to wear at the wedding, to keep me calm and remind me how much I was loved. It was beautiful – a huge, gorgeous rose quartz heart perched in a delicate silver setting, with ivy leaves, hearts and butterflies surrounding the crystal."

Carlie stared at her. "Was there a ring too?"

"Well, I bought one for Violet for her seventeenth birthday that perfectly matched it. Why?" Rose questioned her, but Carlie's mind was whirring with relief. She had done the right thing, offering the ring to Richard – it would be like Rose's daughter was at the ceremony, in spirit at least, and would prove that Violet had still loved her mother, and treasured the things she had given her, even though they'd been parted for so long.

"Do you still have the necklace?" Carlie asked her grandma.

"You're right, I should definitely wear it today! Thank you Sweetheart," she grinned, then bustled out of the room. Carlie called out to her to come back again, because she'd forgotten Liana's parcel. Smiling apologetically, the soon-to-be bride walked over to pick it up, but froze when they heard a loud knock on the door.

"It's okay Gran, it's just Rhiannon," Carlie reassured her. "We still have a bit of time. Go find your necklace and open your gift, and we'll grab the flowers. Then we can walk over together when you're ready. All the food we made last night is already at the healing centre, and Laura and Miri have been there all morning, getting the ritual room ready, so everything is under control."

Rose hugged her granddaughter, then headed downstairs to finish preparing. As she flung open the door, Carlie was already babbling to her friend, their floral wreaths in her hand. But she stopped mid-sentence when she saw it was Mike in the doorway, not Rhiannon.

"Hi Carlie," he said, bemused by her confusion. "I was wondering if you'd mind if I accompany Rose today? Since our lives have been so intertwined all these years and all? And you and Rhi can follow us, carrying her bouquet, checking the dress is okay and all that?"

Carlie stared at him, surprised by the question, but was distracted by the sight of her friend racing up the steps, flustered and out of breath, and full of stammered apologies for being late.

"It's fine," she shrugged, then turned back to Mike. "Of course you can," she replied. "And Gran's almost ready, so we can be off in a moment. Come in."

She handed Rhiannon one of the smaller flower bands they'd woven for themselves, then pulled the hair clip out of her messy bun, letting her long dark curls tumble down her back, and placing the other wreath on her head. The scent of jasmine, roses and violets surrounded her, and she breathed it in. They were all flowers of love, and their heady aroma filled her with joy.

As Rose came out of her room to join them, Carlie glanced at Mike, about to say something, and was shocked to see his eyes fill with pain. Confused, she turned to her grandmother, and saw its echo in her own expression.

"Oh Sweetheart, you look so beautiful, and so much like your mum," she whispered. But while there were sad tears in Rose's eyes, she looked ecstatically happy as well. "Thank you so much for coming here Carlie, for being part of my life. You have no idea just how deeply you've changed me, how much better you've made me, and my life. Not just because you encouraged me to find love again, but because *you* have loved me, and healed me."

Carlie leaned in and hugged her, the words a healing balm for her own pain, her own soul. "Thank you Gran," she said, voice thick with emotion. "I love you so much, and Mum did too, every day of her life, in ways I'm only just coming to realise."

She felt a gentle hand on her back, and turned to see Mike, face more composed now. "I want to thank you too," he told her. "For helping Rhiannon to heal, and for bringing me peace. You're very much loved and appreciated here."

"Don't make me cry," Carlie warned, voice stern, but she was smiling. "Now we really should get our act together and go. We have a ritual to create, and some love and magic to weave."

Mike took Rose's arm, while Carlie picked up their pretty bouquets and Rhiannon lifted the hem of Rose's dress and the gold velvet cloak she wore over it, her gift from Liana. Today she looked even more like a priestess, like a goddess even, radiant with love and joy, exuding strength and power in her regal bearing, while also revealing a hint of her fragility and vulnerability, which softened her in a beautiful way.

As the four of them approached the meadow at the base of the tor, Carlie smiled at the hum of conversation and the sight of so many colourfully dressed people, all friends of Rose's, and all so happy that she was finally allowing love into her own heart, after giving so much to all of them for so long.

Richard was there, with Jake and Tom on either side of him, looking excited yet calm. Carlie's heart lifted as she saw the look he gave Rose, so filled with love and respect. Tom winked at her when she caught his eye, then motioned to Jake with a tilt of his head. Blushing a little, she glanced over at her school friend, and breathed a sigh of relief when she saw the expression in his eyes as he gazed back at her. Hopefully she wasn't too late.

"Welcome," cried a tall, imposing stranger wreathed in mist and sunshine, and wearing a long purple gown that looked as though it had been woven from a summer sunset sky. Carlie's head turned sharply towards the unfamiliar voice, confused. Rose's best friend Elsie was officiating the handfasting, wasn't she?

Her jaw dropped when she saw Liana standing behind the purple-clad woman, at the easterly point of the circle, and her head spun as she noticed Aideen in the south, representing fire, Brianna in the north, for earth, and Brauna in the west, for water. Yet no one else seemed perturbed by their presence, or even curious. Not even Rhiannon, who'd met two of them before.

Liana stared back at her, one eyebrow raised in amusement, then in an instant she was at her side, that weird vampire trick they all seemed to share. "You look beautiful Carlie, and so much more at peace than you did this morning. Nice tattoo, by the way," she grinned. "I see that you are ready to leap off the edge and test your wings, or your heart at least."

"Yes, but what... I don't understand... Where's Elsie? Why isn't anyone here freaking out at seeing four people who aren't really people? Wait, five. Who is that?" she asked, words spilling out all over each other, tripping her up as she tried to frame a coherent thought, and work out which question was most pressing.

Liana reached up her hand and cupped Carlie's cheek, and she felt the familiar sense of peace and contentment flow into her. "Beloved, calm down. Elsie is not well, so I told her that I would officiate in her place. Well, Ailia will," she said, turning to look at the purple-robed woman in the centre of the circle.

"Ailia?" Carlie asked. "I thought there were only four elements, four directions? Who is she?"

"Ailia means light, and she is here because it is time for you and your grandmother to finally walk out of the darkness and into the light," Liana replied softly. Carlie felt the truth of the sentiment viscerally, felt herself open up to the possibility of some joy diluting the sorrow that seemed to be her life.

"Do not worry, for as far as anyone here knows, Elsie is officiating. That is who they are seeing, and we are just her friends, helping so Rose's circle can relax and enjoy the ritual."

"And what do they see when they look at me?" Carlie demanded. "Am I the mad woman talking to herself, holding up her grandmother's handfasting with her delusions?"

Liana laughed, a sweet, tinkling laugh that held no malice. "Beloved, you have never been mad. But no, this moment is a pause, a breath between breaths. Time has not really stopped, we have just stepped outside of it for a beat."

Gazing at the woman in purple, who was watching them carefully, a stern expression on her face, Liana smiled at Carlie, then spoke one last time. "Afterwards, at the party tonight, tell your grandmother that Elsie is fine, that there is no need to worry. And thank her for all of us, for being such a light in the world."

Rose had turned to look at them too, and her eyes were widening in recognition. "Tell her yourself," Carlie said, slightly grumpy, as she handed the bouquet of flowers to her grandma.

Liana's laugh washed over her, and time seemed to slow down even further, leaving her in a bubble of silence. Then suddenly the gold-clad woman was back in her place, winking at Carlie, Rose was standing stoically at her side, but with a twinkle in her eye, and Ailia was calling for everyone's attention. Sound rushed back at Carlie, and she heard the gentle hum of the bees, the call of a small black bird overhead, and Laura's voice as she formally welcomed Elsie, or the purple-robed woman, to their ritual.

Focusing on the circle again, Carlie looked over at Jake and Tom, standing on either side of their grandfather, arms linked with his as he walked slowly towards Rose, who was holding Carlie's hand on one side of her, and Mike's on the other, as she moved forward to meet Richard in the middle. When they reached the central altar, the four attendants released their charges and melted back into the circle of friends and family surrounding them.

Tom found his place next to Rhiannon, and Carlie felt their joy ripple over her physically as they linked hands. Mike headed back to where Brodie stood, holding on to Laura, and she saw peace on his face, and the lifting of a weight that he'd carried for far too long.

Suddenly she realised just how much she'd come to care for everyone here, and marvelled at their acceptance of her, a virtual stranger. Then, slowly becoming aware that Jake was waiting for her, she turned towards him and offered her hand. When he saw the new tattoo on her wrist, with its circle of ivy leaves holding within it a candle flame, a rose quartz, a feather and a wave, he stared up at her, a question in his eyes.

A rush of emotion washed over her as she sensed the cautious hope rising within him, and she felt a pang of regret that she'd made him wait so long. But there was no point dwelling in the past – it was time to move forward, into the now, into the light.

"Yes," she whispered, and felt his energy expand outwards to hold her close, even as they turned to the centre of the circle and concentrated on the ceremony.

No one but Rose and Carlie knew that the women conducting the ritual were figments of light and mist, although she sensed that Laura and Miri could feel their magic, and were responding to it on some level. For a moment she thought Tom was aware of it too, as he gazed over at her quizzically, but when he saw her holding hands with Jake he just smiled and turned back to the purple-clad priestess in their midst and held the energy for her.

The handfasting was beautiful, although Carlie was so conscious of her hand in Jake's, even when the rest of the circle let go, that the details flowed over her, leaving her with a sensation of love and magic but no grasp of the specifics. But she knew Rhiannon would fill her in later. All that mattered now was that Rose and Richard were happy, and the golden shimmer around them as they spoke their vows let her know that they were.

Her focus snapped back to the ceremony when Richard offered Rose the rose quartz ring she'd entrusted to him earlier that day. The same one that Rose had given to her daughter all those years ago, and which Violet had kept, close to her heart, all that time, wrapping it up with her most precious belongings. Rose gasped, then turned and gazed at Carlie with such love and gratitude, and in that moment she knew her grandmother understood its significance, and that another piece of her heart was healing because of it.

Later, as Ailia closed the circle and people started meandering down to the healing centre to continue the celebrations, her hand was still in Jake's. He turned to her, smiling, but there was fear in his eyes too, and something else she couldn't quite figure out. She felt a shiver of apprehension, and almost chickened out, but she knew that she had to make the first move. "Are you okay?" she asked gently.

He gazed down at their hands, still entwined, and seemed to gain strength from their matching tattoos. "Does this mean…" he began, then paused. "I just… I don't want to push you… Or jump to any conclusions either, just because you're holding my hand?"

Her heart clenched at the pain and fear in his voice. "Oh Jake, I'm so sorry I took so long to be ready. You've been more patient than I deserve," she whispered. "But I, well, I really like you. I want to… well, you know." Her eyes drifted ahead of them, to where Rhiannon and Tom were kissing while they waited to cross the road, oblivious to the fact that there were no more cars in either direction.

"Really?" Jake asked, and the uncertainty that was still in his voice stabbed at Carlie, even while the hope in his eyes cheered her.

"Really," she replied, smiling up at him. He blushed, and his eyes broke contact with hers. "What's wrong?" she asked, and panicked all over again. Had she waited too long?

But finally he gathered his courage and stared back into her eyes. He was braver than she was.

"I'm not a shaman or a druid Carlie, I'm not very spiritual. I haven't studied plant medicine or crystal healing or psychic divination, or any of that stuff. I love taking part in the rituals with you and Rose, and I want to learn more, but I just… well, I'm not magical enough for you, or old enough, or special enough," he finally blurted out. "You deserve someone better, someone more… well, someone more like Rowan."

His words stung her, and she felt tears well in her eyes, but this wasn't about her hurt, it was about his, so she buried hers away to dwell on later. "I'm sorry I've made you feel like that," she said softly, and reached up her hand to cup his cheek, the way Liana had done with her to offer comfort and security. He closed his eyes and leaned in to her touch, and a little of the tightness in his expression relaxed.

Steeling herself, she took a deep breath. "I don't know what will happen with us, but I know that I want to try. And I know that I care about you deeply, in a way I never have before," she added, and was relieved when he opened his eyes and looked back into hers, hope alive again. "I know that I want to risk my heart with you Jake, and that I'm *ready* to risk my heart with you. For you."

Finally he smiled, and her lips curved up in response. "If you think I'm enough…" he said, but it was a question.

"I *know* that you are," she whispered, voice sure and strong. And she felt it, the moment his heart opened to her.

"I don't expect you to never talk about him, or what you learned from him, or to throw out all the books and ritual tools he gave you," he said then, voice low and cautious. "He's part of your magical journey, and I know that he and Rose were your teachers, the same way that Tom is for me. So he'll always be part of you, and I'm okay with that, because it's *you* that I've been falling for since that moment in Pop's kitchen all those months ago. The you that grew from being with him, and losing him. I'm not going to try to compete with someone who is no longer here, and I promise I won't be angry if you want to talk about him. I know I'm not him, and I'll never try to be."

Tears shimmered on her lashes as she circled her arms around him and held him close. "Oh Jake, I don't want you to be him. I don't want you to be anyone else, just you. Because it's you that I've been falling for, without even being aware of it," she said, marvelling at the truth of those words as she spoke them.

For a moment she wondered how long she'd been feeling this way, but she supposed it really didn't matter. She knew now.

As people started to catch up to them, Carlie let Jake go, but she took his hand again as they walked towards the village. Then as they climbed the stairs to the ritual room, Rhiannon linked her arm through Carlie's free one. "I'm so happy for you," she beamed, voice low. "And so is Tom." Carlie blushed, but didn't shush her. She was too happy to worry about her friend teasing her, or the reaction of anyone else to their new and constant need to hold hands.

They jostled inside, and Laura welcomed everyone to the celebration. Then a hush fell over the candlelit room as Rose and Richard walked in. Carlie rushed over and hugged her grandma, while Jake approached Richard and embraced him too. Then they stepped back and gave their guardians some space so everyone else in the village could congratulate them too.

Throughout the afternoon there were speeches, some funny, and some moving everyone to tears. Mike's was especially heartfelt, summing up the immense love the community had for Rose, and their joy at welcoming Richard to their ranks. Then Laura brought out the largest ritual cauldron and lit the sweetly scented apple wood within it, so the happy couple could leap over the Beltane fire hand in hand, to wild cheers, closely followed by Tom and Rhiannon.

As the excitement died down, Miri and Laura served the Beltane feast, then as night fell and moonlight shone in the window, people took to the makeshift dancefloor and the celebrations began in earnest.

When Jake asked her to dance, Carlie let him lead her to the centre of the room. As he put his hand on her shoulder and drew her close, she felt calm, and safe, and filled with warmth. She looked into his kind blue eyes and felt herself diving into his sweetness, his patience, his heart. He wasn't Rowan, no one ever would be, but that was perfectly okay. This was Jake, the guy who was prepared to be her friend if that was all she could handle, who was willing to wait for her to finally realise her feelings, and who showed her every day that consideration existed, and love was kindness.

If Rowan had been her Oliver, then maybe Jake was her Mike – the kind and considerate boy-next-door, the best friend who might, in a parallel universe, have made her mother as happy as Ollie had. Or maybe he was just himself – Jake, enough just the way he was, with no need to be anyone else, no need to sweep her off her feet with grand gestures and wild magics.

Slowly, heart in her throat, she rested her head on his shoulder. He froze for a moment, and she could picture him trying to figure out if what she'd said on the walk into the village was real. But it was only for a second, and then his hand rested on her head, and stroked her hair, and she let go of a breath she felt she'd been holding forever and relaxed into his arms. She didn't know what would happen between them, or even whether he would stay here in England or go home to Perth. But that wasn't important right now. It was only this moment that mattered.

Glancing over Jake's shoulder, she saw Rose smile at her from the circle of Richard's arms, and watched the joy on Rhiannon and Tom's faces as they danced together, and the love in Mike's eyes as he stood with Brodie. As Jake took her hand and spun her around, she tipped back her head and looked up into the twinkling faery lights on the ceiling. She felt her mother there with her as the layers of the pale green wedding dress swirled around her, and her dad's presence too as his wedding ring nestled against her heart on a delicate golden chain. She was where she belonged.

"Are you okay Carlie?" Jake asked her softly, tenderly, and her soul exhaled as she heard the love in his voice.

"I am," she whispered. "I finally am." And she smiled up at him, a smile that reached her eyes this time, and transformed her face with joy. Then she slowly leaned in to kiss him.

"Don't you know yet?
It is your light that lights the world."

Rumi, Persian poet and mystic

Thank You!

Thank you so much for reading this book,
and sharing the magic of Carlie, Rose and Violet's stories.
As an indie author, I rely on word of mouth and reader reviews
to get the word out. If you enjoyed *Into the Light*, I would be
so grateful if you could take a moment to leave a review on
any book site. Reviews help improve sales and ranking,
and are of immense help to all indie writers.

If you'd like to stay in touch and receive free exclusive content,
be the first to hear about book news and events info, giveaways
and more, you can sign up for my newsletter at

www.sereneconneeley.com/subscribe.

(And don't worry, you can unsubscribe at any time...)

With love and gratitude,
Serene xx

Carlie's adventures began in...

Into the Mists

Enter the swirling mists of an enchanted land, and open your heart to the mystery...

Carlie has the perfect life. A wonderful family and a best friend she adores. A house by the beach so she can go surfing after school. A clever, rational mind and big dreams of becoming a lawyer. A future she's excited about and can't wait to begin.

But in a split second her perfect life shatters, and she is sent to the other side of the world to live with a stranger. In this mystical, mist-drenched new land, she is faced with a mystery that will make her question everything she's ever known about her parents, her life and her very self. A dark secret that made her mother run away from home as a teenager. An old family friend who is not what he seems. A woman in blue who she's not convinced is real. A shadowy black cat that she'd swear is reading her mind. A deserted old cottage she can't always find. And a circle of wild-haired witches who want her to join their ranks.

Will she have the courage to journey into the mists, and into her own heart, to discover the truth? And can she somehow weave together a life that she'll want to live – or will she give up and allow despair to sweep her away from the world forever?

"I can't put this book down. It's so compelling and beautifully realised – there's so much magic. Absolutely recommended!"
Lucy Cavendish, author of Spellbound and White Magic

"*Into the Mists* is Amazing with a capital A. It's comforting, healing, empowering, inspiring and, like all the author's work, truly magical. While I was reading it I felt like the little kid in *The NeverEnding Story*, tucked into my own little world with Carlie and Rose. I absolutely loved it – it's one of my favourite novels ever. It has opened my heart and inspired the magic within me. "
Sarah Byrne, teacher

Into the Dark

**A best friend. A forever love. A promise.
A betrayal. An ultimatum. A choice...**

Carlie coped with moving from her home in Sydney, Australia to a small village in England to live with a stranger. She battled her way through the mists she thought would drown her, and emerged transformed. She was even starting to think she'd survive the death of her parents. But now an old diary, which promises to reveal the mystery of her mother, threatens to tear her world apart. How will the words she reads affect her? Will she wish the truth had died with her mum? And what is the connection to her own life hidden within the pages?

In the second book of the gripping Into the Mists Trilogy, a new relationship with her grandmother is opening Carlie's soul to the energy and power of the earth. A new friend is opening her mind to the magic and potential within her. And a new love is opening her heart to the sweetest enchantment of all. Yet betrayal hovers, and she will face an ultimatum, a sacrifice and a cruel choice that might just break her.

Will Carlie find the courage to go into the darkness of her own heart and seek the wisdom and strength she needs to survive, or will the tragedies and the pain of her life break her into a million little pieces?

"A compelling novel that haunted my dreams while I was reading it, and lingered in my mind long after I'd finished. It's very powerful writing, and very real – and very haunting, the mark of a good novel."
Felicity Pulman, author of I, Morgana and The Janna Chronicles

"Serene Conneeley's magical and very intoxicating new novel *Into the Dark* has me under its spell – I relish every shiver Carlie's descent into darkness is giving me. *Into the Mists* was wonderful, but this is another level, a huge leap. I LOVED this book – it ended way too soon!"
Lucy Cavendish, author of Spellbound and White Magic

Into the Mists, Into the Dark and *Into the Light*
are also available as audiobooks, narrated by
British voice actor Gabrielle Baker, from
Audible, iTunes and Amazon.

Also in the Into the Mists Series...

Into the Mists – A Journal

Awaken your inner voice and unlock the power and strength within you...

Keeping a journal is a powerful way to make sense of the world, and of your inner universe, whether you're recording the events of your life or journeying within to discover your own truths. It is a valuable tool of self-knowledge and self-discovery, a sacred place to reveal your inner being, and a mirror to reflect back your shadows and light, showing you who you truly are, and the beauty of all that you are becoming.

Including words of wisdom from priestess Rose, the Otherworldly women Carlie encounters and more beloved characters, this will inspire you to look within and express the feelings at the core of your being, encouraging you to let go of past pain, forgive yourself and others, and move forward with joy and confidence so you can achieve all that you dream of. Whether you use it as a daily diary, a gratitude book, a travel record or a place to write your novel, *Into the Mists: A Journal* will help awaken your inner voice, unlock the power and strength within you and allow you to start seeing the magic in every moment.

"This is *divine!* The lovely quotes throughout are very inspiring, and the feel of the journal is heart-warming and comforting to me. It sits on my bedside table for writing in during the quiet times of reflection, to hold my thoughts and personal inspirations. Just beautiful."

Cheralyn Darcey, eco artist and author of Flowerpaedia

The Into the Mists Trilogy – Hardcover Omnibus

The three books of the Into the Mists Trilogy are available in a beautiful hardcover omnibus edition.

"I couldn't put it down. This series is healing, empowering, inspiring and magical. I loved it. I haven't enjoyed a story so much since *Heart's Blood* by Juliet Marillier."

Julia Burdock, healer

Two Sides to Every Story...

A companion to the Into the Mists Trilogy, *Into the Storm*
is Rhiannon's story, beginning before she meets Carlie.
It can be read after the Mists books or as a standalone.

Into the Storm

**A spell to weave. A life to save.
A heart to break. A storm to brave.**

When Rhiannon's mother dies, her whole world
falls apart, and she withdraws from her family, her
friends and her life. As grief and anger rage within
her, she connects with the wildness of the winter storms – until she's
consumed by the powers they unleash. A priestess tries to help her, a
woman from the mists seeks to comfort her and her little brother
attempts to reach her, but she doesn't know how to find her way back.

Entwined throughout is the story of her mother, which reveals a
haunting mystery. Why did her parents keep such a dark secret? How
will a spell she casts in the woods one full moon night unravel her?
Who is the woman in red she encounters atop the sacred hill? And
what chaos will be wrought by a girl from the other side of the world
with a strange link to her father?

As the darkness of her shadow self is revealed, Rhiannon must
find the courage to go into the storm and face her greatest fears. But
if she does, will she be transformed by its terrible power, or broken
and lost in the wreckage?

"*Into the Storm* takes you on such an emotional journey, and makes
you believe in real magic. I loved it."

Selina Fenech, author of *The Memory's Wake Trilogy*

Coming soon...
New Into the Mists Chronicles, featuring other
beloved characters, including *Into the Fire*
and *Out of the Shadows*.

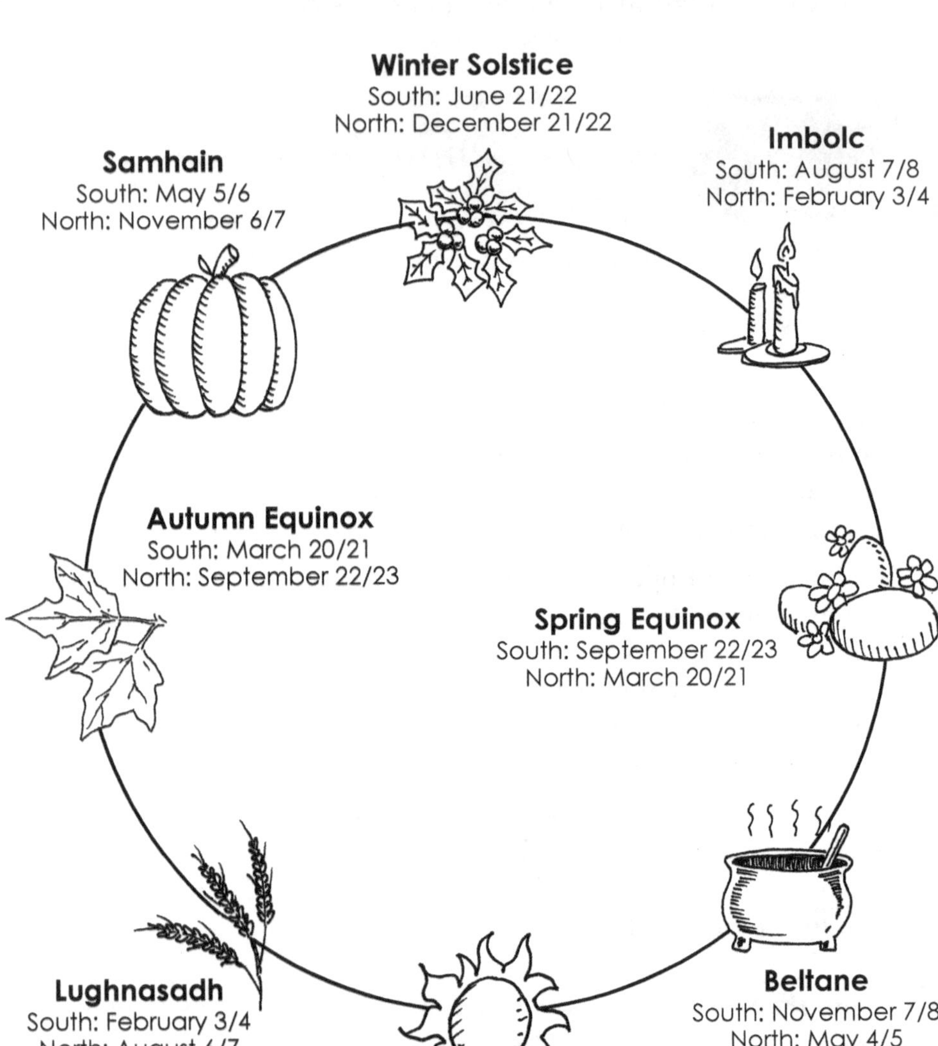
Winter Solstice
South: June 21/22
North: December 21/22

Samhain
South: May 5/6
North: November 6/7

Imbolc
South: August 7/8
North: February 3/4

Autumn Equinox
South: March 20/21
North: September 22/23

Spring Equinox
South: September 22/23
North: March 20/21

Lughnasadh
South: February 3/4
North: August 6/7

Beltane
South: November 7/8
North: May 4/5

Summer Solstice
South: December 21/22
North: June 20/21

The Wheel of the Year

Rose and her witchy friends celebrate the eight sacred sabbats, or festivals, of the Wheel of the Year, as the ancient priestesses did, and modern pagans still do. In *Into the Mists*, Carlie took part in her first ritual, the harvest festival of Lughnasadh, where she met Rose's circle of magical, supportive women friends and saw her grandmother as a powerful, loving priestess for the first time.

In *Into the Dark*, she celebrated Mabon, the autumn equinox, with Rhiannon at London's Body Mind Spirit festival, where she met Rowan, then with Rose's circle back in Summer Hill the next night. She honoured her lost loved ones at the Samhain feast of the dead at Mike's house, then did a deeper ritual with Rhiannon in the ruins of an old temple. And tragedy visited her again at the winter solstice.

And in *Into the Light*, Rose invited Jake and his grandfather Richard to her circle's Imbolc celebration, then Carlie, Rhiannon and Jake travelled to London to share the spring equinox Ostara festival with Tom and Jasmine. And at the cross-quarter day of Beltane, which marks the beginning of summer and embodies love and commitment, Rose was part of a very special ritual...

> "The festivals of the Wheel of the Year are defined by the cycle
> of nature, by the dance of the weather gods and spirits of place.
> They require us to look not to the heavens but to the earth.
> They are set within our soul, watching the leaves on the trees,
> feeling the shifting temperature and the changing light,
> within and around."
>
> *Emma Restall Orr, British druid priestess, ritualist and author*

A powerful way to become more aware of your inner world is to harness the natural magic of the cycles of the seasons. The shifting energies of the earth's turning have been celebrated and utilised for thousands of years, and even today, when we are so far removed from nature, you can still tangibly feel the introspection of winter, the crisp change of autumn, the potent energy of summer and the vibrant power of spring.

Attuning yourself to the vibrations of the eight sacred festivals that make up the enchanted Wheel of the Year will fill you with strength, magic and a sense of grand possibility and potential. You'll become more in sync with your inner self and your intuition, and start to connect with your own emotional tides as you connect with the earth's.

These special days, determined by the position of the earth in relation to the sun, mark the beginning, midpoint and end of each season, and are measured today by astronomers and scientists. In the past they were calculated by druids, the philosophers and scientists of their age, and recorded in stone circles and cairns. They have been honoured for thousands of years in cultures throughout the world, so the imprint of their energy can be tapped in to and absorbed.

Long ago, when life revolved around agriculture, and the sun and moon were considered deities to be worshipped, the Celtic peoples of Europe, and many others around the globe, were in tune with nature. They had to know when each season began and how long it would last so they could plant and harvest crops, hunt migratory prey and prepare for the harsh winters. They divided their year by seasons, not months, and honoured each change, celebrating eight festivals that marked the turning of these seasons and the cycles of the earth.

There are four astronomical and four agricultural festivals. The astronomical celebrations are determined by the position of the earth in relation to the sun. These include the spring and autumn equinoxes (Latin for "equal night"), which occur when the sun is directly above the equator and the length of day and night is equal, and the summer and winter solstices (Latin for "sun stand still"), which occur when the sun is at its northern or southernmost extreme, the furthest it ever gets from the equator. These four events are the midpoint of each season – thus the summer solstice being referred to as Midsummer's Day and the winter solstice as Midwinter.

The agricultural celebrations are known as cross-quarter days, because they fall midway between the astronomical festivals. Traditionally they were tied to agricultural events such as the sowing and harvesting of crops, and they mark the beginning of each season.

Even today, when we no longer live in harmony with the earth's rhythms or agricultural cycles, people celebrate the Wheel of the Year as an honouring of nature and an acknowledgement of the continuing cycle of life, death and rebirth, both literally and symbolically.

Literally this refers to the changing seasons – the fertility and vibrant life force of summer, the harvest energy of autumn, the introspection and endings (death) of winter, and the rebirth of spring. Mythologically it was tied to the story of the god and goddess. At the spring equinox they meet and court, before consummating their love during the rites of Beltane. At the summer solstice the goddess blooms into the mother, pregnant with new life, and the sun god reaches his energetic peak. From then he weakens through the harvest time of Lughnasadh and the autumn equinox, before going to the underworld at Samhain to learn new wisdom, then being reborn at the winter solstice when the goddess gives birth to the infant sun god and the Wheel turns again, playing out the cycle on and on through time.

Once this creation story was accepted as fact. Today some still think of it as a literal retelling of a historical truth, while others feel it's simply a parable that humanises nature. Either way, it's now the symbolic meaning that's most relevant to our lives – planting the seeds of our dreams in the metaphorical spring, watching them grow and manifest in the world before we give thanks for our literal harvest, allow the things that no longer serve us to die off or be released, then start all over again with new dreams as we celebrate our own rebirth.

Becoming aware of the seasonal shifts and the patterns of nature wherever you live, and celebrating these ancient but still relevant festivals, is a simple way to tap in to the magic of the earth and start to connect with nature and your inner self.

Channelling this energy and creating meaningful rituals in your life doesn't conflict with any religion or require a belief system, as it's a celebration of the science of nature and the cycles of the planet. Many pagans, like Rose and her friends, do call on gods and goddesses, and have a personal concept of the divine as a universal creative force, but others don't believe in any form of deity, simply revering nature as sacred and as the source of life, and believing that divinity is an inner not an outer power, an energy within themselves and every other person alive.

Lughnasadh : First Day of Autumn : Gratitude

Lughnasadh, also known as Lammas, is celebrated in the first week of August in the northern hemisphere and the first week of February in the southern hemisphere, and marks the end of summer and the beginning of autumn. It's the first harvest festival, traditionally a time of feasting and of thanksgiving for the life-giving properties of the grain and nature's bounty, as well as a recognition of the cycle of sowing and reaping of the crops.

It is also the time to honour the things you have grown and created in your life, a day to harvest the fruits of your labours and acknowledge your successes and what you've achieved in the past year. Celebrate the goals you've reached and have your own festival of gratitude, in whatever form that takes. Toast your success, throw a party or do something special to mark the occasion – maybe reward yourself for your hard work with a gift you've long wanted, or some precious time off to rest and chill out. Make a list of all the things you've gained over the past year – the gifts you've been given, the new talents you've developed, the friends you've made, the experiences you've had, the healings you've received – and give thanks for it all.

Then, out of gratitude and in the spirit of the ancestors who shared the bounty of their harvest with those less well off, pay your good fortune forward. Donate to a local charity or collect food for the homeless, as Rose and her friends do, lend to a business in the developing world, or give your time to help someone, ensuring the energy of abundance continues and is strengthened. Give joyfully, with no expectation of receiving anything in return. And work out small ways in which you can make a difference to the people around you all year long as well.

As the energy begins to subtly slow, this is also a time to be patient and to trust that everything is as it should be, because there are still harvests to come. Not everything has to be achieved right now – some things take longer to manifest. The lesson of the Wheel of the Year is that everything continues, everything happens when it should, and everything is eternal.

Mabon : Autumn Equinox : Harvest

The autumn equinox, known as Mabon and celebrated on September 22/23 in the northern hemisphere and March 20/21 in the southern, is characterised by the length of day and night being equal as the sun travels back across the equator to the other hemisphere. From this point on, the days will become shorter and cooler, but this is a moment of balance in nature and within – a point of harmony and calm.

Vibrationally Mabon is a season of withdrawal, of being alone to meditate, recharge, reassess and ponder where you're at in life. The energy of the earth retreats and goes within, as does your personal power, but from this cycle you will emerge with immense strength and wisdom. It's a time to honour your achievements, experiences and growth, and to ensure balance by integrating all parts of your self. Acknowledge and celebrate what you've reaped in your own life. Feel fulfilment from each goal reached, releasing what no longer serves you in order to move forward. In the wild, old growth is cleared. In your life, cut out anything that's holding you back or preventing new life and love from flourishing, whether it's work, people, a belief system, regret or the past.

On this day, when all is balanced, witches traditionally renewed their magical commitments, and you can renew any vows you've made or pledge a new one, be it to do with magic, love, friendship, career or anything else. As the shadows lengthen, it's also a good time to scry for insight into your future. If you can, light a fire and stare into the flames, allowing your mind to go blank and your vision to blur a little, or go outside and watch the clouds scuttling across the sky, analysing the shapes and symbols you see within flame and cloud. Without over-thinking it, write down what they mean to you.

Pyromancy (fire reading) and nephomancy (cloud reading) are forms of divination that have been used for millennia. You should develop your own dictionary of symbols, as you know better than anyone what any shape or image means to you, but you can begin with standard readings, such as a heart indicating romance, a cat referring to a need to trust your intuition, a tree meaning you will make new friends and a plane foreshadowing travel.

Samhain : First Day of Winter : Death

Samhain, which is celebrated in early November in the northern hemisphere and early May in the southern, is a cross-quarter day marking the end of autumn and the beginning of the cold and dark of winter. Symbolically it is about rest and renewal, of preparing for what's ahead and withdrawing a little to conserve your energy, and releasing the things you've been holding on to in order to ready yourself for new challenges and experiences. It's also the night when the veil between the worlds is said to be at its thinnest, when people honour their ancestors and try to commune with the dead. Some set a place at the dinner table for any loved ones passed over, as Rhiannon's dad Mike did at their Feast of the Dead ritual, while others cast spells to bring their spirit back, or perform mediumship rituals to converse. This magical time and its purpose has been conserved in modern-day Halloween, which celebrates ghosts, witches and restless spirits.

The beginning of winter is a period of reflection, so spend time in contemplation. If you've lost someone close to you, light a candle and remember them. Look at photos or letters and feel their presence with you. This shouldn't be morbid – you're celebrating their life and all they meant to you. Also honour those who are here now. Call your mum and dad, visit your grandparents, or write to someone who meant a lot to you when you were growing up and thank them.

Long ago, Samhain was the end of one year and the start of the next, so it's also a powerful time to let go of the energy of the old year and old memories so you can move forward with lightness and strength. Light another candle, and by its flickering illumination, write out all the worries, frustrations, regrets and seeming failures you've held on to over the previous twelve months. See the candle flame burning them away and leaving you purified and refreshed, and breathe in this positive new energy. Then burn the list in the flame, releasing your attachment to those emotions and their power over you.

This is the time to prepare yourself for the rebirth you'll experience at Yule, but for that to happen there must be death – the death of fears and doubts, and anything holding you back.

Yule : Winter Solstice : Rebirth

The winter solstice, known to pagans as Yule and Midwinter, falls around December 21/22 in the northern hemisphere and June 21/22 in the southern, and marks the middle of winter. It's the shortest day and the longest night of the year, and marks the transition between dark and light, both emotionally and physically. It's the lowest point of the Wheel in terms of daylight and energy, with the sun rising later and night falling earlier. The land is barren and cold, there is less light, and energetically people feel tired and unmotivated.

Winter is a time to rest and reflect, to acknowledge sadness and loss – of dreams, of friendships, of parts of your self – and conserve your energy. But the solstice is the turning point in this time of darkness, introspection and dreaming. Considered the dark night of the soul, it also marks the period when the dark half of the year relinquishes its hold to the light half. From this time forward, the days will start to lengthen, the sun will become stronger, and the energy within and without will start to increase and build.

In pagan times an evergreen tree was brought inside as a symbol of the hope of spring's return, and Yule was a time of feasting, celebration and gift-giving in honour of the birth of the sun god – traditions that live on today in the Christmas tree we decorate, the presents we put under it, the huge family meal we cook, and the celebration of the birth of the son of God.

To attune yourself to this festival of rebirth, light a candle on solstice eve to symbolise the sun and its activating energy, and list your dreams for the coming year. Traditionally people stayed up all night to await the return of the light, but if you can't do that, get up for the sunrise to toast the dawn and give thanks for this energetic reawakening. Open yourself to the promise of new growth and achievement, and the rebirth of your own self and your creativity, as the sun is also reborn. Symbolically and energetically it's a time to honour your inner wisdom, consider the lessons you learned during winter's introspection, and integrate them into your life so you can start to initiate change and prepare for the rush of growth of the coming springtime.

Imbolc : First Day of Spring : Purification

Imbolc, which is celebrated in the first week of February in the northern hemisphere and the first week of August in the southern, is a cross-quarter day marking the end of winter and the start of spring. It celebrates the return of light to the land, and to our own hearts, and is a time of hope, renewal and fresh starts after winter's sluggishness.

Energetically it's a time of awakening, rebirth and re-emergence. Nature fills with life force and begins to quiver with the energy to grow again, and we start to emerge from the chill of winter, shaking off our lack of motivation and re-engaging with the world, making it a great day to sow the seeds of what you want to achieve in the coming year.

Imbolc is dedicated to Bridie, the goddess of inspiration, creativity and fire, who was later supplanted by Saint Bridget, whose festival is also celebrated at this time. Talk to Bridie – or Bridget, or the higher-self aspect of yourself – or write her a letter, and tell her what you want to create in the next twelve months. Meditate on your goals and what you hope to achieve. Don't worry about how to do it, as that will be revealed later in flashes of inspiration, guidance or outside help.

Physically it's a time of purification and cleansing after the long dark of winter, so clean your house and clear your space, sweeping out old energy and thoughts so the new can thrive. It's a good time to write about your beliefs and examine how you feel about your spiritual path too, exploring the reasons you think the way you do and perhaps questioning if there are other viewpoints you might also embrace. It's also about new beginnings, and in some magical traditions it is the day chosen for initiations and rededications, so if you want to make a pledge to a new path or a new goal, or a personal vow of any kind, you will be supported by the energy of the season.

You may like to ignite a candle to represent the coming back of the light and do some candle magic. Stare into the flame as you concentrate on what you want, then blow it out, sending your desire out to the universe. Making a wish as you blow out the candles on your birthday cake is a magic that has survived from pagan times, and is a potent way to manifest your wishes into reality, whatever day it is.

Ostara : Spring Equinox : Blossoming

The spring or vernal equinox, known to pagans as Ostara, is celebrated around March 20/21 in the northern hemisphere and September 22/23 in the southern. It's one of only two times in the year when the length of day and night is equal, as the sun sits directly above the equator on its journey north or south, creating equal light and dark in both hemispheres.

This equinox is about growth, passion and the unfurling and release of the immense potential you have within you. On both a universal and a personal level, it's a time of balance and harmony, of union between the physical and the spiritual, and the integration of your heart and soul. This can be harnessed to anchor your dreams in reality and enhance your own inner harmony as the balance of universal outer energies is reflected within. Relationships are harmonious now too, making it a good time for weddings and for healing rifts.

It's a time of growth and fertility, when new crops are sown, new shoots break through the earth, buds on the trees open, birds build nests and lay eggs, and new life is celebrated. Thanks was traditionally given to the fertility goddess Ostara, whose symbols were an egg and a hare, and who is still honoured around the world today, albeit unknowingly, in the form of chocolate eggs and the Easter bunny.

Energetically it's also a very fertile time, as the seeds you sowed of your goals at Imbolc begin to sprout and gain momentum. Paint some hard-boiled eggs with symbols that represent your desires, or buy or make the chocolate version, meditating on your own metaphorical fertility and your ability to manifest dreams into reality. Choose an affirmation relating to your desired outcome, write it down and pin it up where you'll be able to see it every day.

Go outside during the day and breathe in the fresh spring air, filling your heart with new energy and inspiration as you fill your lungs with oxygen. In many ancient cultures, including the Roman one whose calendar we have based ours upon, the spring equinox was the first day of the year, and the sense of new hope and optimism reflected in this time remains today. It's a celebration of new life, hope, passion, growth and energy.

Beltane : First Day of Summer : Growth

Beltane, celebrated in early May in the northern hemisphere and early November in the southern, is a cross-quarter day marking the end of spring and the start of the heat and energy of summer. Evidence of new life is everywhere, in abundant blossoms, the hatching of birds and bees pollinating flowers, showing that time is moving forward and life is progressing. Women bathed their faces in the dew gathered from their garden on Beltane morning to harness the energy of youth, and flowers were brought inside to symbolise fresh beginnings and the power of nature.

Beltane was the major fertility festival. Handfasting rituals were conducted, and lovers leaped over bonfires then came together in sacred union in the fields to bless the crops with fertility. Maypole dancing, representing the union of the god (the pole) and the goddess (the ribbons), was performed to join the forces of masculine and feminine, and May Day remains a popular day to wed in the northern hemisphere.

It's a time of lovers and spells to attract love, and celebrating the fertility of life, not just physically, but also of your dreams and ambitions. Symbolically this day marks the igniting of the fires of creativity and passion, of the fertility of your dreams being made manifest, and is the time to take steps to achieve what you want. Check in on the projects you started at Ostara, and write about their progress and the ways in which they've sprouted into reality. If you need to fine tune anything, learn a new skill or let go of one aspect so it can germinate further on its own, the energy of this day will support you. Make a commitment to yourself – start a new project, apply for a new job or take up a new hobby, knowing the universe is bursting with raw energy and power that you can tap in to.

It's also a powerful time to repledge your love to your partner. You don't have to build a bonfire and leap over it, although you can! Simply lighting a red or gold candle as you stare into each other's eyes and speak your love and commitment will invoke the power and passion of the element of fire. If you're single, make a commitment of some kind to yourself, nurture a friendship, or if you seek love, sing your intention and wanting of a romantic partner to the universe.

Litha : Summer Solstice : Fruition

The summer solstice, known to pagans as Litha, is celebrated around June 20/21 in the northern hemisphere and December 21/22 in the southern. It's the longest day and the shortest night of the year, and marks the peak of energy and solar power for the year. On this day the sun reaches its northern or southernmost latitude before it turns and heads back towards the equator, so near the poles daylight lasts for twenty-four hours – the sun just doesn't set for weeks at a time. In nature, everything is ripe and abundant, and life is blooming.

It's a time of high, hot and active energy. Creativity and expression is at a peak, so stand in your power and express your needs, saying what you want rather than assuming that people know. Whereas the winter solstice is slow and introspective, its opposite is fast and effective. Make use of the active energy – this is a time to do, to get out there and harness the energising earth power and make things happen.

Follow your passion, take a chance, say yes to new opportunities and express your creativity and your inner self. This is not the time to be withdrawn or shy, it's for getting out amongst it and making your dreams come true. It's also a time when relationships – and you – will mature, and you'll apply new wisdom and forethought to your passion, so give thanks for the lessons you've learned, and allow the person you are maturing into to unfold.

It's a time of celebration too, of acknowledging how far you've come and what you've achieved. Enjoy the happiness and abundance of this season and soak up the sunshine and festive atmosphere. Traditionally people stayed up all night on solstice eve, partying around bonfires or within sacred circles of stone, then watched the sun rise the next morning, feeling it bathe them in warmth and light.

At dawn, stand with your arms outstretched and breathe in the sun's life-giving power. Let it wash over you with its healing energy and burn away anything you no longer need. Take note of how your dreams and goals are manifesting into the world, and meditate on anything that could be blocking your progress. Be open to letting go of whatever isn't working so you can move forward in a new direction.

The Magic of the Moon

Rose works with the phases of the moon in her spellcasting and her healings, and performs rituals at the new moon, dark moon and the full. Carlie and Rhiannon planned their coven dedication for a full moon, to take advantage of the energy of this phase, and witches, druids and shamans have long harnessed its power too.

The moon is a thing of mystery, enchantment and wonder, linked to intuition, inner power and imagination. To the Celts, its phases reflected the phases of a human life – birth, adolescence, adulthood, death and rebirth – and were associated with the Triple Goddess who included the aspects of maiden, mother and crone, represented by Rhiannon, maiden goddess of inspiration and the waxing moon, Arianrhod, mother goddess of fertility and the full moon, and Ceridwen, crone goddess of death, rebirth and the waning moon. In countless other cultures the moon was also seen as a goddess, who not only marked the passing of time, but increased fertility, deepened psychic powers and improved wellbeing.

Harnessing the energy of the phases of the moon can help bring a goal to fruition. These phases are determined by the moon's position in relation to the earth and the sun, as it orbits our planet every 29.5 days. The moon has no light of its own – it's illuminated by the light of the sun reflecting off its surface, and its phases are created by the amount of the illuminated side we can see from earth.

You can picture these phases by imagining a clock. The earth sits in the centre of the clock face, with the sun above twelve o'clock. The moon is at the end of the minute hand, circling around the clock face, and the earth, in an anticlockwise direction. It begins its cycle at twelve, directly between the sun and the earth, which makes the moon invisible to us because the side that's reflecting the light of the sun is facing away from the earth, towards the sun. This is the dark moon.

A day later, as the moon moves towards eleven o'clock, a tiny sliver of the illuminated side can be seen, which appears as a thin crescent. This is the new moon. In the southern hemisphere it looks like a C, while in the northern hemisphere it's reversed, appearing as a backward C, and at the equator it's horizontal rather than vertical.

The crescent continues to grow as the moon moves from between the earth and the sun, and the angle between them allows us to see more of the moon's reflected light. By the time it gets to nine o'clock, which takes about a week, it's at right angles to the earth in relation to the sun, and we see a half circle. This is the first quarter moon.

When the moon gets to six o'clock, it's on the other side of the earth from the sun, with the earth in between. The whole of the side that is visible to us is reflecting back sunlight, so we see a round moon in all its shining, golden full moon glory. The size of the moon hasn't changed, it's just that we're seeing the fully illuminated side.

After that it appears to decrease again it progresses back to the dark moon. When it gets to three o'clock we again see a half moon, but this time it's facing in the other direction. This is the third or last quarter moon. From there it continues back to twelve, with the crescent getting smaller each night, until it returns to the beginning, where it's invisible again, and the cycle starts over.

Lunar phases are printed in newspapers, moon diaries and websites like www.sunrisesunset.com, and you can also determine the phase of the moon by its shape, as well as by the time it rises, which occurs about fifty minutes later each day. It can be remembered by the old adage: "The new moon rises at sunrise, and the first quarter at noon. The full moon rises at sunset, and the last quarter at midnight."

As the moon progresses from dark to full it's the waxing or growing period, a time of new beginnings and increasing energy. As it goes from full back to dark it's the waning period, a time of lowering energy and introspection. Magical practitioners use the cycles of the moon to increase the power of spellworking, harnessing the energies inherent in each phase. So do fishermen, who understand the incredible pull the moon has on the tides of the ocean and its creatures.

Gardening also operates to the rhythms of the moon, as the lunar phase can enhance or hinder plant growth. To boost it, sow crops that produce above the ground between new moon and full, as the light and energy increases, and crops that produce below ground, such as root vegetables and bulbs, between full moon and dark.

Surfers understand its power too. The full moon magnifies weather patterns, so a winter full moon will bring stormier swells and bigger waves. The tides are more extreme at both the full moon and the dark moon – high tides are higher, and low tides lower. These two phases have an intense influence on the ocean, heightening conditions and drawing huge swells – or, if the ocean is flat, making it even flatter. Surfers going to Indonesia for a wave-riding safari book around a full moon, so they'll have optimum conditions and even bigger waves.

Hair growth is also influenced by the moon. If you want your hair to grow faster, trim the ends between the new moon and the first quarter. If you want it to grow thicker and fuller, trim it during the full moon phase. And if you really like the style and want to maintain it, have it cut around the third quarter, so it grows out more slowly.

The moon affects tides, plants, animals and the behaviour of people. Some can't sleep during the full moon, others feel more emotional or have strange dreams. It's common to feel more energetic during the waxing phase, and more tired when it's waning. There are also many tales of accidents and psychic breakdown increasing at the full moon. Today the moon's journey across the sky is obscured by buildings, and even women's cycles, which used to be connected to the moon, are often controlled by chemicals. But it still impacts our energy and emotions, and can be used to influence the outcome and power of rituals, and empower any project you want to complete.

Phases of the Moon

One lunar cycle runs for 29.5 days, beginning with the tiny crescent of the new moon, building in energy through the waxing phase to the full moon, then decreasing and withdrawing through the waning period to the dark moon, before starting a new cycle. Here are some ways to take advantage of the phases of the moon to set your goal or intention, then watch it grow to beautiful, abundant completion.

New Moon: Day 1

The new moon rises just after dawn and is up all day, often unnoticed in contrast to the sun and the bright sky, and sets just after sunset. From the moment the tiny new crescent moon is first sighted, and for a day or two afterwards, is a time of heightened energy and new beginnings. It's a good time to start new projects, make resolutions and vows you want to stick to, go in a new direction, invite something new into your life or look for a different job. Chinese New Year always falls on a new moon, as it brings energy and vitality to the coming year.

This is the time to plant seeds, both literally and metaphorically, be it in the garden or in your life, sowing the seeds of new ideas, dreams and hopes. Magical workings are most powerful during the day, when the moon is visible; during this phase there is no moon at night.

A simple yet powerful new moon ritual is to sit outside as dawn breaks, watching the sun rise and feeling the energy of the new moon as it peeks above the horizon, and write down your wish for the coming month. Work out an affirmation to support it, and keep it somewhere you'll see it often. You can also invoke maiden lunar goddesses such as Rhiannon, Bridie and Persephone to add sweet, innocent yet powerful energy to your intent.

Waxing Moon: Days 1 to 14

During the two weeks from new moon to full, the energy is strong and positive, so concentrate on attracting and drawing things to you. It's the optimal time for magical workings to manifest love, abundance and new career opportunities, and for learning new things, expanding your outlook, increasing spirituality and boosting fertility. In the waxing period the lunar energy continues to build, so whatever seeds you planted at the new moon will sprout rapidly. It's an energy of gathering, growing, strengthening and increase, so if you need to release something while the moon is waxing, reverse the intent of the spell so it fits with the energies. Rather than giving up smoking by releasing your addiction, create a ceremony to attract willpower.

If you're doing healings, draw good health to you when it's waxing, and release illness when it's waning. Maiden goddesses can also be invoked, such as Bridie, Artemis, Athena, Aphrodite and Aine.

Waxing crescent moon: Days 1 to 6

In the week following the new moon, it rises a little later each day, through the morning, and sets after sunset. This is the sprouting phase, when you nurture the seeds you planted at the new moon. It's the time to set things in motion, and brings energy and new growth to projects, helping you manifest them into reality and flooding you with strength and the energy of growth. The sliver of light represents your growing consciousness and the dawning of your potential.

Waxing half moon – the first quarter: Days 7 to 8

At the end of the first week is the first quarter moon, which rises at noon and sets at midnight (this is why you can see it in the evening but not in the morning, as it's appearing to the other side of the world then). It's halfway between new and full, and looks like a half moon. This is the growth phase, where you build upon what you've already begun, although the energy can be challenging at times, pushing you towards achieving your goals and urging you to work hard to get the projects you've planned completed. Issues can come to a head, which can be uncomfortable, but it's all part of the process of growth.

Waxing gibbous moon: Days 9 to 14

In the second week of the lunar cycle, as the moon moves towards full, it rises in the afternoon and sets in the early hours of the morning. This phase is conducive to expressing yourself, getting in touch with your feelings and taking action. It requires some patience, as things are almost, but not quite, at the peak of their potential and energy.

Full Moon: Days 14 to 16

The full moon rises as the sun sets, which is why it's so obvious and clearly seen, because it sails across the sky all night, contrasting with the velvety blackness, before setting around dawn, just as the sun is rising. The three days of the full moon – the day of, day before and day after – can be used to boost any intention or project. It represents achievement, culmination and abundance. The world is filled with energy and potential, so it's a great time for healing and manifestation.

Midnight is the most powerful time for magical work, as the moon is directly overhead. Stand beneath the golden orb and give thanks for what you've achieved so far, and breathe in the energy and power so you can harness it for self-expression and strength. Perform a Drawing Down the Moon ritual, bringing the energy of the moon, and the moon goddess, into your heart and soul. This is also a great time to charge crystals and amulets with the moon's energy, and cleanse your own physical and etheric bodies. And psychic abilities are thought to be at their strongest, so practise any divination methods you are drawn to, looking within to find answers to your questions and clues to your future.

The full moon is the high tide of power in a lunar cycle, so cast spells for completion, things you want to achieve, and anything requiring a boost of intensity, such as healing work, job hunting or love. You can also invoke mother goddesses Arianrhod, Isis, Selene, Diana, Lakshmi, Quan Yin, Demeter, Ishtar and Mama Quilla, who embody the full moon, motherhood, fertility, the earth and creation.

Waning Moon: Days 16 to 29

During the two weeks from full moon to dark, the energy is slowing, so it's a time for banishing and release work. Do a ritual to let go of anything that no longer serves you, such as a past relationship, a bad habit, a trait like procrastination, or any material objects or issues weighing you down and blocking your progress. If you need to attract something while the moon is waning, reverse the intent. Rather than doing a spell to draw love to you, which works against the energy of this phase, cast one to banish loneliness. This is a time of retreat and withdrawal, when you can invoke darker crone energy goddesses such as Ceridwen, the Morrigan and Grandmother Spiderwoman, who hold the wisdom and power of transformation, endings and rebirth.

Waning gibbous moon: Days 16 to 21

In the week following the full moon, it rises a little later each day, between dusk and midnight, and sets in the morning. This is a phase of introspection and self-assessment. In the garden this energy promotes root development; in life it's a time to stand strong and find your inner power, delving within for the answers imparted by the full moon. Magical workings are most effective from midnight to dawn, particularly releasement rituals to banish things, people or situations from your life.

Waning half moon – third quarter: Days 22 to 23

At the end of the third week is the third quarter moon, which rises around midnight and sets at midday, so if you see a half moon in the morning it's this waning one, but if you see it in the afternoon it's the waxing first quarter moon. It brings a reflective energy, and is a great time to assimilate what you've learned and achieved, and determine what you still need to do. If an issue requires resolution, work your magic and put your intent out to the universe. The energy is waning, but you can draw it inside for later use. Work on banishing illness, addictions, negativity and bad habits, releasing anything that will slow the fruition of your earlier spellworking.

Waning crescent moon: Days 24 to 29

In the fourth week, as the moon moves towards dark, it rises in the early hours of the morning and sets in the afternoon. This is the letting go phase, a time to release and banish anything you don't need so you can prepare again for the fresh beginnings of the new moon. It's the closing of the cycle, the time to reap what you sowed at the start of the month and integrate the lessons you've learned. You've done the inner work, and now you must release the outcome to the universe.

Dark Moon: Day 29

The dark moon rises at dawn, with the sun, and sets at sunset. It is between the earth and the sun the whole time, making it invisible to us. While some people take the dark moon as a day off from magic, others use it to go within, using the introspective energies to examine their feelings and thoughts and delve deep within their psyche.

While the moon is hidden it's also a powerful time to scry and perform any kind of divination that will uncover your hidden truths, and for getting in touch with your inner wisdom and approaching the Mysteries. This energy helps you explore the darkest recesses of your mind and your heart, and acknowledge your passions, your fears and your anger so you can release them to the approaching light.

This is a time to rest and renew your strength, and also to evaluate your life and your progress. The powerful, deep and transforming energy of the dark moon is an internalised vibration, so be aware of your thoughts, avoiding focusing on negativity or self-loathing in case you manifest the fears you're supposed to banish. The dark moon celebrates the crone, so invoke the energies of Ceridwen, Kali, the Cailleach, Hekate, Baba Yaga or Nephthys to help you descend to your metaphorical underworld and examine the layers of your subconscious.

Eclipses of the Moon and Sun

Lunar and solar eclipses, while fairly rare, also affect the energies of the universe, and our emotions. An eclipse occurs when one celestial body obscures another, either partially or fully. Because of the angle of their orbits, the sun, moon and earth rarely align precisely, which is the condition required for an eclipse. But when the moon is directly between the other two, which can only happen at the dark moon, it blocks the sun's light from reaching the earth, creating a solar eclipse that makes the sun seem either totally or partially invisible. And when the earth is directly between the sun and the moon, which can only happen at the full moon, the earth blocks the sun's light from reaching the moon, producing a lunar eclipse that dims or even totally obscures the moon for a brief time.

Energetically, eclipses create opportunities for change. They can sometimes push you a bit further than you wanted to go, forcing you to move forward and continue along your path. To some they are a wake-up call, nudging you on and making sure you don't lose sight of your dream. A solar eclipse, when the moon blocks the sun, is considered a peak of feminine power, and gets you in touch with your intuition. It is the perfect time to take stock of where you're at and examine your inner self. The energy of a lunar eclipse, when the earth blocks the sun and plunges the moon into darkness, gives you the strength to be honest, to yourself and others, about who you are, and to move forward without fear of judgement.

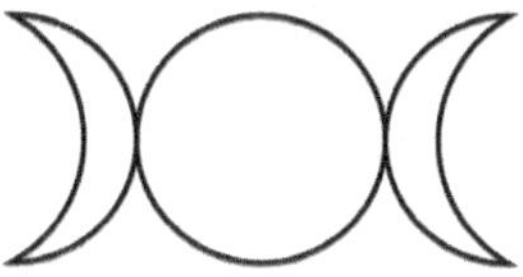

About the Author

Serene Conneeley is an Australian writer with a fascination for history, travel, ritual and the myth and magic of ancient places and cultures. She's written for magazines about news, travel, health, spirituality, entertainment and social and environmental issues, been editor of several preschool magazines, and contributed to international books on history, witchcraft, psychic development and personal transformation.

She is the author of the Into the Mists Trilogy – *Into the Mists, Into the Dark* and *Into the Light* – and is finishing a new series in that world that includes *Into the Storm* and *Into the Fire*. She also wrote the non-fiction books *Seven Sacred Sites, A Magical Journey, Witchy Magic, Mermaid Magic* and *Faery Magic*, and created the meditation CD *Sacred Journey*.

Serene is a reconnective healing practitioner, and has studied magical and medicinal herbalism, bereavement counselling, reiki and many other healing modalities, plus politics and journalism. She loves reading, rainbows, drinking tea with her friends, and celebrating the energy of the moon and the magic of the earth. Her pagan heart blossomed as she climbed mountains, sat in stone circles, wandered through ancient cathedrals and stood in the shadow of the pyramids on her travels, and she's also learned the magic of finding true happiness and peace at home.

www.SereneConneeley.com

With Thanks...

I am so grateful to my sweet husband, for his love, encouragement, support, inspiration and belief in me. For making me countless cups of tea as I wrote. For being patient when I hated the story, and hated writing, and wanted to quit. For not complaining when I'd banish myself to my little purple office and write for days. And for being the first person to read each of these books, and loving them so much...

I'm indebted to amazingly talented, kind and generous artist (and magical writer too!) Selina Fenech, for the stunning cover images for the Into the Mists Trilogy – it would not be as beautiful and as inviting without them – and to my sweet hubby and my faery friend Daniella Spinetti for the illustrations throughout.

Love and gratitude to book editor, writer and lovely friend Kylie Matthews, for sitting with Rose and Carlie in their cosy kitchen and drinking endless cups of tea with them, and reassuring me that their stories are filled with magic and worthy of being told.

Love and blessings to my wonderful writer friends, including Felicity Pulman, Lucy Cavendish, Selina Fenech, Cheralyn Darcey, Elisabeth Knowles and Nigel Bartlett, for sharing the book launches and festivals, the discussions of characters and plot, the trials and triumphs, challenges and successes, and all the craziness and wonder of our writing adventures.

Love and thanks to my inspiring workout buddies Claire, Janine and our fun fit group friends – I love sharing our progress, our challenges and our No Excuses motto for life. Working out every day keeps me sane amongst the book deadlines and work stress, and there's nothing like punching my way through a Combat session or upping my weights in Pump to gain a new perspective on a plot dilemma.

And I'm proud of, and grateful to, my NaNoWriMo buddies – Laura, Miri, Karen, Kylie, Penny, Annalie, Hannah, Jasmin, Katie, Ally, Brooke, Pea, Belinda, Carla, Cynthia, Laneth and Sharne.

With much love, Serene xx

NaNoWriMo...

Into the Mists began as a fun challenge with a few friends – to write 50,000 words in thirty days for the 2012 National Novel Writing Month (nanowrimo.org). I'd planned to spend all of October plotting out my story, but I finished work on my previous book, *Witchy Magic*, on October 31, so on November 1st I had to just dive in and start writing. And somehow I managed to flesh out my one paragraph idea – about a girl who loses her parents, gets sent to a relative in England she didn't know she had, and finds a cottage in the mists that may or may not exist – into a novel. While I spent several months afterwards rewriting and revising, Carlie's story was born in that single NaNoWriMo month, and the first draft wasn't dramatically different to the final one.

I decided to do it again in 2013 – and figured that travelling through Scotland with my hubby for the whole of November was no reason to back out. So I spent my days dancing in stone circles, crawling into ancient burial chambers, climbing snow-capped mountains and sailing across the ocean to Orkney and the Outer Hebrides, and my nights scribbling in a notebook or tapping away on a crappy little laptop. I did pass 50,000 words before November 30, but this time only half of them ended up in the finished book, *Into the Dark*, and I spent several months afterwards writing new chapters, changing a major plot line, introducing a new character, and generally messing with poor Carlie's head...

And in 2014 I signed up for NaNoWriMo again, determined to finish the trilogy. It was tough – my day job at the magazines gets even busier in November, and day one was spent with three sweet friends working out with Jillian Michaels, going to her show then meeting her – luckily she's so inspiring that I got home at midnight and started writing! Like the previous two NaNos, I'd thought I would spend October planning out the story, but also like them, I ended up starting on November 1st with a blank page... Turns out that I'm a pantser not a plotter ☺

I won't lie, it's not easy to write 1667 words a day, every day. Many days I've wanted to throw my notebook across the room and give up. Sometimes I'd rather collapse on the couch and watch *Star Wars* with my hubby than banish myself to my little purple office and painstakingly write another few pages. There are nights I get home from twelve hours at the magazines and would much prefer to crawl into bed than force myself to stay awake and type in the words I hastily scrawled on the bus to work, then write some new ones as well. *Most* days I'd much rather curl up and read a book than torture myself trying to write one.

I also spend most of the NaNoWriMo month thinking that my story is boring, there's no point, it's too much effort, no one cares anyway, and why am I bothering… According to my hubby though, I wrestle with these particular demons with every book, and my doubts seem to increase, rather than diminish, the more books I write.

But, I do it anyway. I tell the "it's boring" and "you're useless" voices in my head to shut up, and force myself to get at least 1200 words a day done – while aiming for 2000 to average out the less productive days. If at the end of the month I decide it's all terrible, I can delete the file and move on, or rewrite it until I'm happy with it.

Because it's only thirty days. Thirty days is nothing. It's one moon cycle. Half of one of my workout programs. Four episodes of *Arrow*. You can do anything for thirty days. And at the end of each November I have 50,000 words of a novel written, and no matter how boring or bad or whatever I think this first draft is, it's *way* easier to work with and improve than a blank page is.

Life is short. I want to live it with no regrets, and no excuses. Five years from now will I wish I'd spent more time on the couch watching superhero shows in November, or getting to bed a bit earlier, or will I be happy that I knuckled down and hit my word count targets and got the first draft of my next book finished? Like most things that are worth doing, it's not easy, but it is possible, and it *is* worth it…

My point in sharing this is that there is no secret to writing a book – you just have to sit down and write it. It's that easy, and that hard. And I've discovered that the more I write, the more I want to write, and the more the story unfolds. So don't wait for an idea to find you or inspiration to grab you – if you want to write a book (or do anything really), sit down and do it now. And don't worry, no one ever has time – you just have to *make* time…

Will I do it again? Absolutely! For NaNoWriMo 2015, I started writing about Rose and her magical life. In 2016 and 2017 I worked on Rhiannon's story – and discovered that her mother Beth also had a tale to tell, so a new series emerged. And in 2018 I'll be wrapping up Rose's epic journey – then hopefully starting a whole new world!

Also by Serene Conneeley

Seven Sacred Sites: Magical Journeys That Will Change Your Life is part spiritual adventure story, part history, part travel guide. Discover what makes these places sacred, when to go and how to get there, the fascinating histories, the rituals that were performed there, the cultural and magical significance of each sacred site, both now and in the past, and the many ways in which they still inspire, touch and initiate growth and learning in all who visit.

"By far the best travel book this year. Her style evokes the great travel writers like James A Michener, who weave cultural anthropology into an entertaining traveller's tale – a recipe for pure reading pleasure. And it's absolute gold for those interested in the spiritual traditions that shape our world."

Joanne Lock, Spheres magazine

A Magical Journey: Your Diary of Inspiration, Adventure and Transformation combines a diary where you write the story of your life with a guidebook that includes the physical, mental and spiritual health benefits of journalling, and tools to release emotional blockages and unleash your authentic self. Make a wish come true using the cycles of the moon, celebrate worldwide festivals, and create magic in your life by harnessing the ancient, sacred energy of the seasonal turning points of the year.

"This helped me connect to self, and venture forth with boldness and compassion. I am so much more aware, and I thank the author from the depths of my heart and soul for the opportunity to grow."

Marissa Clarkson, bereavement counsellor

Sacred Journey: A Meditation to Connect You to the Magic of the Earth is a CD of seven guided meditations set over beautiful music. Each runs for around seven minutes, and can be done on its own, or all together as a fifty-minute meditation journey. Attune yourself with the sacred elements and energies of the earth to soothe your soul, uplift your spirit and heal your heart.

"A gem to treasure. Serene is a gentle, loving, wise teacher of wisdoms we can all benefit from. This takes us on a sacred journey into the earthly and heavenly elements and realms, and into history, spirituality and self-love too."

Lucy Cavendish, creator of As Above, So Below CD

Sacred Sites: The Pocket Guides to Your Magical Journey are seven mini books that are perfect for travelling, or collecting. They include each of the places in *Seven Sacred Sites*, with extra practical information and websites added, plus pages for your notes, the better to plan your magical adventure.

Witchy Magic (with Lucy Cavendish) is an enchanting adventure into the Craft of the Wise, with clear guidance on how you can access this ancient knowledge to create the life you dream of. It is an earth-honouring spiritual path and an empowering, beautiful way to be at one with the universe, taking responsibility for your life and transforming every word and action into an alchemical tool of change. Step into the world between the worlds and the wisdom of your inner witch to create an inspiring, magical life.

"This is a definitive reference for the would-be witch, and entertaining and enlightening for the witch-curious... For the history buff, ritualist and nature lover to the magician, pagan or spiritualist – and well beyond."

Kylie Matthews, freelance book reviewer

Mermaid Magic: Connecting With the Energy of the Ocean and the Healing Power of Water (with Lucy Cavendish) is brimming with sea magic, inner journeys, marine conservation and rich research, and will help you develop a deep connection with the element of water. Work with the ocean and its creatures, learn about tides and lunar phases, divine your future with sea oracles, absorb the healing energies of sacred wells and springs, become an eco warrior, and discover the beauty of mermaid lore and love.

"This is a wonderfully inspiring read. It really made me want to shed my twenty-first century shackles and dive into the ocean to embrace its wonderful healing powers. Thanks magical ladies for the journey!"

Sabina Collins, freelance writer

The Book of Faery Magic (with Lucy Cavendish) is rich in tradition, history, research and lore, and is filled with whimsical interactions with the fae, grounded guidance on how to work with them, and beautiful ideas for reconnection with nature and the magical realms. Whether you believe that faeries are truth or fantasy, *Faery Magic* is your portal to a state of being where fun and healing energy will help you fulfil your dreams, transform your life, and improve your relationship with the earth, your self and others.

"The ultimate guide to all things faery – entertaining, informative and enthralling. Whether you believe in faeries or are just curious, there is much to learn in this book, from their history and legends, their magical gifts and nature sites, to the unique beings from around the world."

Larissa Chapman, Good Reads

www.BlessedBeeBooks.com

www.ingramcontent.com/pod-product-compliance
Lightning Source LLC
Chambersburg PA
CBHW030655120726
47905CB00001B/217